New World Order

James A. Clayton

New World Order

Published by:

Betoi Publishing
5804 W Vista #355
Glendale AZ 85301

©1999 James A. Clayton

All rights Reserved.
Printed in the United States of America.

Cover Art by Marilyn Timmerman

ISBN 0-9670687-0-3
$19.95

Acknowledgments

Although this is, technically-speaking, a work of fiction, no one lives in a vacuum. There is a Red Willow County, Nebraska; and McCook is the county seat. In this I have tried to stay faithful, insofar as is possible, to the city and the county; although I hasten to add that there is no "patriot militia" activity there. McCook was selected, rather, because it is about as "middle-America" as you can get, and filled with about as many nice people as you can find. Among these are: Virginia McClure and her staff at McCook Townhouses, Ivan Schmidt of McCook Main Street, Doris at the Senator George Norris Home unit of the Nebraska Historical Society, The Sehnert family of Sehnert's Dutch Oven Bakery & Coffee Shoppe .... There are many others in McCook, Marion, Danbury, Indianola, et cetera, who, due to limitations of space and time, cannot be mentioned herein. I also owe a debt of gratitude to other individuals in other locations, people who helped because I swore not to reveal their name or location. It is appalling that the United States government can induce such widespread paranoia among those it claims as citizens. But thank you for your help ... and for your trust. ....

J.A.C.; Glendale, Arizona; 1999

James A. Clayton

Prologue

It was a time of innocence, a time when the pristine white beaches of Virginia were warmed by soft breezes and gentle swells of a clean and clear Atlantic Ocean. Just beyond the darkness of the empty beach the light of a singular lantern flickered warmly through the window of the summer cottage occupied by a distinguished and elderly United States' Senator.

It was early in 1913. The Sixteenth Amendment, authorizing income taxes, had been ratified on February Third. On March Fourth, Thomas Woodrow Wilson had been sworn in as the twenty-eighth President of the United States. One month later, on April Eighth, the Seventeenth Amendment had been ratified, establishing direct popular elections of U.S. Senators. And the distinguished and elderly Senator read the handwriting on the wall and knew his time at the top was limited.

And then, not quite by accident, he had met the brilliant European, a man named Warburg who understood his dilemma and his worries, his fears and his concerns. After the usual prefatory and bland comments, Warburg had gone straight from the problem to the solution: let professional bankers handle the banking problems of America through a centralized banking system.

"Your present banking system, such as it is, has fallen into disrepute," Warburg continued, judiciously selecting his phrases. "No one trusts these financial institutions, regardless of their sincerity or their integrity. You need an organization to watch over them."

"Quite true. Quite true." the Senator spoke softly, weighing each word. "I do not, however, understand this ... proposal. And I have my doubts about Senator Aldrich."

The European smiled with the perfidious innocence of pure deceit. "Quite so. It has been almost three years now, but I do recall speaking with him during a banking symposium held on Jekyl Island

New World Order

in the state of Georgia. I am able, therefore, to understand your doubts. I would not, however, permit my personal feelings cloud my judgment."

"Of course not!"

Warburg's deceitful smile was not wasted on the Senator's abiding gullibility. "Senator Aldrich's bill will ultimately bring the necessary controls to the banking industry without too much damage. He will, however, need your support."

"Under the circumstances, a reasonable request," the Senator said.

It sounded reasonable. Let the bankers determine the value of money and of debt; and let Congress concentrate on the more important policy matters.

The Senator had unwittingly made a deal with the devil — a devil disguised as a Eurpean banker. He had sold his soul, and the future of the United States of America, to secure and insure the financial well-being of his children and grandchildren — his heirs and relatives. He had convinced himself that this new concept in international banking would benefit everyone.

He was wrong.

Late at night just a week before Christmas, with many Congressmen heading home for the holidays, but with just enough members available to constitute a quorum, a distinguished and elderly Senator's careful preparations violated the Constitution of the United States of America with impunity.

It has been said that five percent make things happen, fifteen percent watch things happen, and eighty percent wonder what happened. But on that day of infamy, an obscure United States' Senator skewered the percentages even further, and introduced a private corporation known as the Federal Reserve Banking System.

It was the end of 1913. It was the beginning of a nightmare.

New tools must be tested. Thus on a given day, upon the orders of certain controlling financial interests, the Federal Reserve Banking System withdrew some eight billion dollars from circulation. The stock market crashed and prosperity died in agony, plunging the entire world into a deep, dark, Great Depression.

Their test exceeded expectations. Uncooperative banks died and vanished, while the Federal Reserve drove the Federal National

James A. Clayton

Debt through the ceiling. Selected banks and financial institutions grew to predominance, over-shadowing even the governmental organizations which allegedly controlled them.

In Europe in 1934, Paul von Beneckendorff und Von Hindenburg died, allowing a 45-year-old upstart named Adolph Hitler and his National Socialist Party to seize power and institute totalitarianism in Germany.

In America in 1938, a select group of judges and lawyers were brought together and told that their country was now bankrupt, that the Constitution of the United States was no longer valid, and that all courts would now be administered under the British Admiralty Laws.

(They were also told that, in order to avoid a public backlash, the British Admiralty Laws would be incorporated into individual state law and would be referred to henceforth as the "Uniform Commercial Code.")

In America in 1962, the implementation of the so-called RICO laws openly and effectively nullified the Fourth, Fifth, and Sixth Amendments to the Constitution of the United States.

And that was just the beginning.

Welcome to the New World Order.

* * *

Chapter One

The Chairman spoke:

"Gentlemen, in nineteen-thirteen our forefathers set into motion a plan to gain control of the world's financial institutions, and to thereby take control of the various governments throughout the world, to unite them under one banner, one flag. Thus, due to their foresight, we now also control all of the media and most of the major religions. We make the laws, gentlemen, and they serve us.

There is only one problem. An element within the United States of America — a so-called patriot militia — has refused to surrender their weapons. And their federal government cannot, or will not, secure complete and total control over their own people.

"We must, therefore, take action.

Since an appropriate budget dispute already exists, I would propose that in sixty days we publicly declare the United States to be bankrupt. Their President will be forced to declare a State of Emergency, followed by Martial Law. Our friends in FEMA — their Federal Emergency Management Agency — can then take control. .... And we can, 'eh, pull their strings, as they say.

"Any questions, gentlemen?"

Special Agent in Charge Edward Eugene Robinson of the Bureau of Alcohol, Tobacco, and Firearms (BATF) studied the patterns of water trickling down the outside of his office window, but found no inspiration in the random rivulets that distorted his view of the rain-soaked Washington, D.C., skyline. His pallid face and graying hair, occasionally reflected from the rain-washed window, revealed the tired old man hidden within the bureaucratic maze.

He reluctantly directed his attention back to the stacks of memos threatening to bury his desk. The Director was asking for yet another report on paramilitary activities in the Midwest—including

James A. Clayton

Michigan, Montana, and Arizona. Arizona? — Montana? — The Director had a rather unusual geographical view of the Midwest.

A second memo referred to a query by United Parcel Service about weapons being delivered to something called the Branch Davidians at Mount Carmel near Waco, Texas. Robinson scrawled a jurisdictional directive across the bottom, sending the memo to Oklahoma City.

It took him another hour to dig his way down through Denver, Kansas City, and Omaha. He issued an expletive-deleted comment and asked his secretary to bring him a cup of coffee. Then he began searching his office for a bottle of aspirin tablets.

He never found the aspirins, but the coffee took the edge off his depression. It returned as he re-read the Denver memo.

A man with the dubious name of Ben Franklyn was allegedly operating a paramilitary "patriot" group in southwestern Nebraska, and had (according to Denver) enough guns to start World War Three.

Robinson shook his head and took another sip of coffee. Franklyn was a hopeless dead end. The old man had a shotgun and a rifle, both purchased legally. Denver was investigating rumors, but they did not want to get involved. They wanted Chicago to dispatch an undercover operative. But even Edward Robinson knew that no operative dispatched from anywhere would ever find any cover in rural southwestern Nebraska.

Robinson finished his coffee, punched-up Franklyn's file on his computer screen, and called Kansas City. Within three minutes he wanted to shoot the telephone — and strangle the agent in Kansas City.

"Yes, Ed, I have the file right here," the agent began. ".... Benjamin Ellsworth Franklyn, born March 3, 1939, the third son of Hiram and Elsie Franklyn. He grew up on a farm in southwestern Nebraska with four brothers and three sisters. The eldest brother was killed in Korea in April of 1952.

"Hmmm, graduated from high school in 1957 and immediately enlisted in the army, served three tours, rose to the rank of sergeant. Volunteered for Vietnam, received two Purple Hearts and several commendations. On the other hand, his superiors expressed some concern about the, quote 'hostile savagery' unquote, displayed in some of his actions."

New World Order

Robinson smiled as his secretary brought him a second cup of coffee. At least she understood his misery.

He turned back to the computer monitor. "Go on."

"Let's see. .... Returned to Nebraska in '69, but neighbors say he was different, withdrawn and distrustful, bordering on paranoia. Treated at Veterans' Hospital in Denver for Post-Traumatic Stress Syndrome. Results disputed.

"By then his three sisters had married and moved away, and his parents had died. His younger brother was killed in a Marine training exercise at Quantico. And he started collecting 'patriot' and survivalist literature.

"His elder brother, Roger Franklyn, had apparently been traveling around the world, but now returned home to help Benjamin run the farm. Reports from an undercover agent state that Roger ran the farm, but that Benjamin earned unreported income by conducting clandestine training classes in survivalist techniques and underground militia tactics. He's also alleged to be connected to other survivalist and militia groups through an underground communications grid. Or net. Or web. Or whatever."

"Weapons?" Robinson asked, departing from the computerized report.

"No proof," Kansas City said, "but we think he's heavily armed by unknown sources. That's still under investigation."

"By Denver?"

"By us!" the agent snapped. "Denver couldn't investigate a hamburger at McDonald's!"

"What about your undercover agent?"

"He disappeared. Probably hiding out down in Mexico by now."

(Robinson had already concluded that their "undercover agent" was probably a compromised criminal.)

But Robinson remained unsatisfied. "Opinion?"

"I suspect," Kansas City said, "that the local sheriff, a guy named Dobbins, has been conspiring with Mr. Franklyn. After our undercover agent went A.W.O.L., we raided Franklyn's farm. Dobbins insisted that one of his deputies go along. Bastard watched us like a hawk. Anyway, Franklyn's place was clean. Very clean. — Too clean, in my opinion."

"So next time don't tell the sheriff," Robinson laughed, hanging up the telephone. ".... Asshole."

Sheriff Louis Dobbins enjoyed his work. While others might seek "a good bust," Dobbins preferred a less painful solution. He preferred counseling parents, children, and alcoholics. He preferred crisis intervention to prison. And he preferred a friendly discussion to an angry confrontation. As he often told his deputies, "There's no such thing as a good arrest."

At times, however, he wondered if federal agents might be an exception to the rule. They were remote and isolated individuals who hated everyone and respected nothing. They could not ask a simple question without adding an ugly threat. They were overbearing, rude, and boastful. They twisted facts to support their own conclusions. They were suppose to represent the law of the land, yet they often violated that law with glib humor and crass arrogance. They would lie, cheat, steal, intimidate, and coerce with impunity. There were even rumors that they had committed murder under the color of law.

The telephone rang four times before Dobbins answered its summons. He was in no mood for polite chitchat.

"Dobbins."

"This is Hank in Wichita," the voice said. "A.T.F. out of K.C. is headed your way on the Q.T. They're after someone named Benjamin Franklyn."

"They usually are," Dobbins muttered, stroking his graying mustache. "Thanks, Hank. I owe you."

He pressed the phone button twice. "Lawrence, tell Bartlett and Hudson to get over to Ben Franklyn's place. Lights and sirens all the way."

"Yes, sir."

He checked his Rolodex and dialed a number. "Stan, better tell Ben that he's about to have federal company from Kansas City. I've got Bartlett and Hudson on the way now."

"Well, that should ruin a perfectly good afternoon," Stan Gorman said before breaking the connection.

Dobbins again tapped the phone button twice. "Lawrence."

"They're on their way. Lights and sirens."

"I want all cars at Ben Franklyn's, Lawrence. I'll be there too. You'll have to hold the fort alone."

"And what if I'm surrounded by Indians?"
"Then raise a white flag, son. .... Raise a white flag."

Special Agent Avery Lucas of the Bureau of Alcohol, Tobacco, and Firearms in Kansas City swallowed an antacid tablet, repositioned his bluish sunglasses, and leaned forward as they turned into Ben Franklyn's farmyard.

Trees and underbrush concealed most of the property. Only the second story of the farmhouse and the top of the barn were partially visible from the road.

"Well, if we can't see them, they can't see us."

But Special Agent Avery Lucas was wrong. Someone in the barn had already sighted their militarily-precise procession driving along the graveled road. And when the BATF turned into Ben Franklyn's farmyard, they found themselves facing all three shifts of the Red Willow County Sheriff's Office.

Avery Lucas took a moment to collect himself before stepping from the car. His foot hit the ground and nine deputies pumped their riot shotguns in unison.

"Special Agent Avery Lucas, Bureau of Alcohol, Tobacco, and Firearms."

"Kansas City," Dobbins amended.

"We were obviously expected."

"Obviously."

"But we're on the same side."

"Are we?" Dobbins asked. "Your Denver office comes out here at least once a year. Last year, when they couldn't find anything, we caught them trying to plant evidence from the trunk of their car."

For one long moment, Lucas remained thoughtfully silent.

"Okay, so maybe they got carried away by all the frustration," the BATF man protested. "So what? We both know that this slimebag's guilty."

"Bullshit."

Special Agent Avery Lucas studied the old sheriff's pallid, weather-beaten face and took a deep breath. "I have a warrant to search this property. Do you intend to resist?"

"I intend to examine the warrant," Sheriff Dobbins said. "Do you intend to kill us?"

Lucas took another deep breath and handed the warrant to Dobbins. Over a dozen neatly-coiffured federal agents in almost-matching business-suit-and-tie uniforms emerged from hiding within the four BATF cars. Nine riot shotguns rose in protest.

"Tell 'em to stay in the cars," Dobbins said without looking up. "I haven't had a chance to look this over ... and I damn well won't tolerate another riot by you people!"

"A riot?"

"What else would you call it when they come running in here, screaming and shouting and breaking up furniture? Damn near destroyed the house and the barn. And when they couldn't find any weapons, they tried to plant some on him!"

For another long moment, Lucas remained silent. Denver had obviously made a very bad impression on this old hick sheriff and his easygoing ways.

"Take a look around you," the government man whispered. "Those bales of hay stacked over there. And that pile of lumber over there. And that whatever-it-is —"

"It's called a *combine*," Dobbins said. "It's a very common farm implement ... in these parts."

"Don't you understand? We could be caught in a deadly crossfire!"

"Never been shot by a bale of hay before," Dobbins said, returning the warrant.

"So can we search the place?"

"Seven of your men may search. Each one will be accompanied by one of my deputies. You will not cut open any cushions or mattresses. You will not bust open any hay bales. And you will not break anything. Understood?"

Lucas understood. He clearly did not like it. He did not like Dobbins treating him like a naive child. He did not like the five-foot, ten-inch-tall, elderly man staring down at his receding hairline. He did not like the stubborn determination etched in the sheriff's jawline. He did not like Dobbins' calm maturity. But he understood.

"Oh, one other thing," Dobbins added. "Please, no shouting or screaming. My ears might get offended."

Mumbling quietly to himself, Lucas selected seven of his best agents.

Dobbins paired agents to deputies and followed Lucas to the

farmhouse.

"You want to break it open?" Lucas sneered, pointing to the solid-looking wood of the front door.

Reaching up to the projecting ledge of the lintel, Dobbins' fingers found the key. "Try this."

"You're a close friend of this Ben Franklyn, aren't you?"

"Not close." Dobbins turned the handle, and the door creaked open. "After he came back from 'Nam, he suffered a mental breakdown. It was years ago, and I was just a rookie then ... but I remember driving him to Denver."

"Uh-huh." But Lucas' mind was obviously elsewhere as he wandered through the house, opening cupboards and closet doors.

"Living room, dining room, kitchen, downstair's bathroom, and den," Dobbins said. "But no illegal weapons."

"Looks innocent. Too fuckin' innocent!"

"Want me to show you where he keeps his silverware?" Dobbins asked, opening a kitchen drawer.

"Damn!" Lucas blurted, marching into the den. "This motherfucker has a computer!"

"Most farmers do," said Dobbins, avoiding a yawn. "It's just as important as a tractor or a combine."

"I'm taking this in for examination," Lucas snapped, reaching for the electric plugs.

"No, you're not," Dobbins said firmly. "It's not on your warrant."

"The warrant says, 'related items' ... and this is a related item."

"The only thing his computer is 'related-to' is farming," Dobbins growled. "You touch it and I'll arrest you for attempted theft under color of law."

"You would, wouldn't you?"

"Yes, I would."

There was no joy in watching Special Agent Avery Lucas and his band of felonious subordinates drive away. Dobbins had watched them leave, but he felt no relief in their leaving. He had stepped on some bureaucratic toes, and these double-think contortionists would never forgive nor forget.

"What the hell was that all about?"

"Damned if I know, Bob. ....Something has changed within

the federal government. Something I don't recognize."

"Maybe it's all this talk about terrorists and 'Patriot' militia and such," Bob Lowell said. "Suddenly ordinary people are criminals. — It's just not right."

"It's something more than that," Dobbins said slowly, examining his young protege's too-neat uniform. "Maybe I'm going crazy, but at times those Washington bureaucrats seem to be trying to create ... an incident."

"Not so crazy. At times it seems as if the United States' government is trying to overthrow the people."

"Now that's a chilling thought." But it made Sheriff Louis Dobbins think.

"So do you want a permanent guard out here?"

"That is neither practical nor possible," Dobbins said.

"You take Myers, Schmidt, and Robbins back into town. I'm sending Turner, Hanson, and young Mahon home on stand-by."

"But you already put Bartlett and Hudson back on patrol?"

Dobbins nodded. "Yup."

"You're gonna stay out here and guard his place alone?"

"Only until he gets back."

"Where is he, anyway?"

"Damned if I know," Dobbins chuckled. "Somebody probably called Stan Gorman. And if I know Stan, he probably called Ben and told him to take cover."

"You've always been close to Ben, haven't you?"

Had it been anyone else, Sheriff Louis Dobbins probably would have ignored the question. But he had always had a special relationship, an almost father-and-son relationship, with Deputy Sheriff Robert Lowell.

"No, not really," Dobbins sighed. "Ben was four or five grades ahead of me in school. And something happened to him in Vietnam. .... But this is his home. He's one of us."

Bob Lowell nodded glumly. Dobbins represented the only father-figure in his life, a relationship that had created a rare honesty between them.

"Later?"

"Yeah," Dobbins agreed. "Later."

Sheriff Louis Dobbins stood alone beside his patrol car in the middle of Ben Franklyn's farmyard, watching his deputies depart.

New World Order

Now isolated in his own grim and terrifying thoughts, each minute seemed like an eternity. He had given up cigarettes over three years before, but now he wished ....

He flipped open the glove compartment. Buried behind the road maps and reference manuals, he found an ancient and dusty pack of Doral Full-Flavor 100s. For a moment he wondered how long they'd lain there, but then he was too busy ripping open the pack.

The first few puffs made him choke and gasp, and that first cigarette made him dizzy. But it was a distraction he needed, a self-contained defense mechanism against a plethora of dark and demented daydreams.

He usually did not mind waiting alone, but today something was different. Today something was wrong. And even this short wait was straining his patience.

"Ben."

"Lou."

Stuffed into the ancient and battered black Chevy pickup, the grizzled old farmer in bib overalls did not seem to be such an imposing figure.

"You had visitors."

"Federal?"

"Of course."

"Sorry to disappoint them," Ben Franklyn said. "Had to go to Cambridge. — Electric bill."

"Clever. So what was this all about?"

"Officially? — They were looking for guns."

Only a few individuals in Red Willow County knew that Ben Franklyn maintained a large arsenal of weapons and ammunition. Dobbins knew, of course, but he also knew that Ben's stockpile was not a threat to anyone. It had, in fact, occasionally aided his own underfunded department in various investigations.

"And unofficially?" Dobbins asked.

"Unofficially ... these government types would like to disarm every person in this country. They would like to put everyone in a cubicle and have them take public transportation to and from a nine-to-five assembly-line job."

"Ben!"

"Funny thing is, those government types are actually the unwitting agents of a foreign power intent on the conquest and subjugation not only of this country, but of the entire world."

"Ben, if I didn't know you better, I'd have you committed."

"Yes, and they would like to do it with or without your permission. No one likes to admit that they're being played for a sucker. And somebody in Europe has been playing these guys like a violin."

"Somebody in Europe?"

"Through the United Nations."

"Sounds complicated."

"It is complicated. Very complicated."

"But if I took that to Judge Carter, you'd say it was just a joke on me."

"Only in court, Lou. Only in court."

"Ben, I think you're trying to drive me crazy!"

"Heck, Lou, I ain't tryin' at all!"

Sheriff Louis Dobbins started his patrol car and drove away, half lost in unpleasant and convoluted thoughts. All the speeches and political rhetoric about gun-control and crime-control always, and invariably, sounded glib and hollow. But why would somebody in Europe be concerned about Ben Franklyn's arsenal?

* * *

Chapter Two

Ruby Ridge had been a minor embarrassment. The World Trade Center bombing had been humiliating. But the government-sponsored murder and arson at the Mount Carmel Retreat near Waco, Texas, became a national disgrace.

Within a few short days agents of the federal government managed to violate and destroy the Bill of Rights, and rape the rest of the Constitution, all in the righteous name of law and order.

It started with BATF agents trying to serve a dubious warrant before its expiration date. It grew violent as one agent accidentally shot himself in the foot. It intensified as they smashed their way into the building, only to be shot by their fellow agents.

Then the FBI took over ... and immediately violated the *posse comitus* act, attacking the compound with tanks and helicopters and heavy weapons. They tried to hide their actions through heavy-handed censorship, and by creating a perimeter three miles wide around Mount Carmel. (That could not, however, hide the cold-blooded murder of three unarmed civilians trying to enter the compound. A thousand-meter camera lense offered graphic and dramatic video scenes of the body of a man left dangling from a high wire fence, and of another victim left to die on a water tower.) And after killing all the men, women, and children in the compound; the FBI burnt the buildings down and blew the place up, making certain that no usable evidence of their crimes would be left for anyone to discover.

Few spoke out against the atrocity. Few dared oppose the all-powerful tyranny and harsh brutality of the Federal Bureau of Investigation. Even the United States' Senate was cowered into white-washing the bloody massacre with a carefully-orchestrated subcommittee hearing.

But for over two years no government-types paid any attention to Benjamin Franklyn's farm.

Deputy Bob Lowell hit the lights and siren, and followed the speeder into the Hinky-Dinky parking lot. The driver looked frantic. "It's my wife! She's expecting! Now!"

One look inside the car told Bob Lowell that the woman was very pregnant. Her moans told him that her time was very short.

"Steinmetz, isn't it? Indianola?"

"Yeah. Did I pass the hospital?"

"By over a mile," Lowell said. "Follow me."

Bob Lowell hit his lights and siren again, and led Steinmetz through a red light across "B" Street. They ran two more red lights, but caught the green past Norris and the Highway 83 turn-off at "B" and East Sixth Street.

'This is what police work is really all about,' Lowell thought as he turned left off "B" at East Eleventh. 'Helping, not hurting.'

The Chairman stared out at the passing scenery with a mixture of disdain and boredom. Travel no longer appealed to him. The Black Forest was beautiful, but he had seen it a hundred times before. And although most of Europe and Great Britain were sufficiently secure, The Chairman did not want to go any further afield than Baden-Baden in Germany or Burgenstock in Switzerland. Let the rest of the world go to hell or wherever, as long as it did not disturb his own peace and tranquility.

He had been in "the game" for a long, long time. After his initial five-year apprenticeship, it had taken another three years of intricate craftsmanship to carry out his first set of instructions. Through a series of adroit maneuvers, he managed to assassinate the President of the United States and plunge that country into a prolonged and disastrous war in a faraway land. The assassination and the war produced the desired effect, however, destroying the soul and the spirit of that country.

By the end of the war he had become The Chairman. And he could do no wrong. The Bank followed his orders implicitly and prospered. The terrorists within the Islamic fundamentalist movement unwittingly carried out his plans within the darkness of their own paranoia. The Soviet Union cracked and disintegrated at the end of a prolonged economic assault. And the American Federal Bureau of Investigation soon became his personal plaything.

New World Order

The United Nations, once hated and reviled, had been penetrated with ease many years before through its more-powerful member nations. Its carefully controlled military might, and its influential control of NATO, made it The Bank's weapon of choice against the more belligerent opponents of the New World Order.

Years before, The Chairman's predecessor had, for personal reasons, established a small communications center within an excavation tunnel under *"The Sacred Blood of Jesus" Roman Catholic Church* (locally known colloquially around Brussels, Belgium, as *"The Blood Church"*). In assuming the mantle of chairmanship, he had vowed to carry his predecessor's plans forward with conservative extravagance. And with unique foresight he kept that vow, expanding the little communications center into a large and complicated, computerized, command-and-control complex overloaded with technological marvels enough to run the world — and provide him with a communications buffer against the "common people" of the United Nations.

The car phone rang and The Chairman cursed. Everyone knew better than to use an open line for communications. Even the use of a "scrambled" phone on a "secure" line was dangerous.

"Yes?"

"Hatchet is go."

"Understood."

The Chairman frowned and hung up. The conversation had been too short and too cryptic for analysis. And the violation of security could be easily defended. But The Chairman frowned upon the carelessness of the call. It just wasn't that urgent.

The Chairman flipped open the file folder and studied the captioned photograph of the *"Alfred P. Murrah Federal Building in Oklahoma City, Oklahoma."* 'Wherever that is,' The Chairman thought, closing the file folder.

No convoluted plot here; Boardman Six thought more like an American than a European. Two suitable scapegoats would be maneuvered around the countryside. A select Special Agent of the FBI with a private grudge against Oklahoma and certain occupants of the Murrah Building would push the button and blow up the building. The two scapegoats would be arrested and convicted with carefully planted evidence. And with that psychological shock, the Americans would demand more *"security."* They would willingly abandon their precious *"freedom"* along with many other *"rights"* in their search for personal safety.

A disaster in mid-America involving a local "terrorist" would be the ultimate psychological and socioeconomic shock, according to Boardman Six. It was reasoning The Chairman could understand. The American ideals of *"freedom"* and *"civil rights"* only created confusion and disorder, a kind of fatalistic and self-destructive anarchy that endorsed crime and violence. Yet the Americans seemed to think that they were somehow entitled to their rights and their freedom.

But The Chairman knew that rights and freedom are gifts from the national government, a reward for good citizenship. Even the righteous elite had earned their rights and their freedom through their service and/or their hereditary birthright. But that was something the Americans would have to learn. It was something he would have to teach them.

―――

On the morning of April 19, 1995, the *Alfred P. Murrah Federal Building* in downtown Oklahoma City was ripped asunder by a powerful explosion. Within minutes federal disaster-relief forces across the United States were mobilized. Within hours one man was in jail and federal agents had several warrants for several others. Within a day or two they had composite sketches of three men. It was almost as if they anticipated trouble.

Two men were arrested, isolated, and convicted before their trial. The third man simply disappeared into history. And everyone speculated rather noisily about the date of the bombing and its tie-in with the Waco fiasco.

Sheriff Louis Dobbins did not speculate, but he did ask Ben Franklyn several pointed and overheated questions. To his credit, Ben Franklyn's answers were equally to the point.

"I don't know."

Dobbins growled, but carefully measured his response.

"Ben, you know me," Dobbins said. "We went to school together. Okay, so you graduated a few years before I did. Still ...."

"If I don't answer these questions from you, I'll have to answer to the feds? .... That is your next line, isn't it?"

"Ben! ...."

"I've already told you, Lou. This guy was not patriot militia.

New World Order

And as far as I know, he was not in contact with anyone I know."

"You also told me that he was probably innocent."

"No, Lou. I said that in my opinion he probably was not guilty. I also mentioned that it was only my opinion, and that I was speculating on the basis of probability. .... Frankly, it was all just a bit too neat, and just a bit too fast, to satisfy my intellectual curiosity. .... Or whatever."

"Oh, come on, Ben! Some kind of giant conspiracy between the F.B.I., the B.A.T.F., the Justice Department, and who-knows-what-else?"

Ben Franklyn shook his head, stroked his chin, and smiled. "They're sheep, Lou. They're sheep, and you know it. They follow the herd-mentality ... blindly and brainlessly. The bankers tell the politicians to jump, and the politicians shout, 'How high?' .... If you want to talk about a conspiracy, you'll have to include the entire government. Only trouble is, most of them don't know about it. —They're just following the herd."

"And you really believe that?"

"You can fool some of the people all of the time, and all of the people some of the time. What more do you need?"

"Rather cynical."

"Goes with the territory," Ben Franklyn said. "Goes with the territory."

"And you think they're not guilty?"

"Just too much coincidence, Lou. — Oh, they'll be found guilty, all right. But whether they are guilty ...."

Sheriff Louis Dobbins found doubts creeping into his thoughts. It was no longer just a question of the guilt or innocence of two men. The government itself was on trial. Everything the government did, or had done, was now questionable. And that made the State of Nebraska, Red Willow County, and Sheriff Louis Dobbins co-conspirators, along with the agents of the federal government.

"Not today," Dobbins muttered as he drove away from Ben Franklyn's farm. "Not today."

―――

As Ben Franklyn predicted, the government amassed a bunch of circumstantial evidence and convicted the two men with a good deal of alacrity and a great deal of coercion. Lacking the money for a good defense, their conviction was practically inevitable.

James A. Clayton

After the noise and hysteria of the Murrah Building's destruction, the government terrorists were more cautious. Too many rumors and too many photos of the Waco nightmare made the bureaucrats nervous. Unanswerable questions about the Oklahoma City bombing created political embarrassment. And orders from the top to reduce the bloodshed were, for a change, obeyed.

But the fear and the terror remained, reinforced by a series of mass arrests and the inevitable convictions carried out under the direction of a coerced and controlled Department of Justice, which found new applications for the laws ... and new ways of creating and interpreting pseudo-evidence.

Like so many others, few judges or lawyers had any knowledge of the forces which controlled and guided them into violating the very laws they were sworn to uphold. Like many others, they found themselves manipulated with such skill that if they ever realized it, they did not object. They were, they thought, just bending the rules a bit in the name of "law and order."

It was raining in Baden-Baden, Germany. The Chairman, of course, did not notice the rain. Neither the weather nor the landscape were important to him.

The Chairman had neither family nor friends. He was The Chairman of *The Bank* — and nothing else mattered. As The Chairman, he had achieved a quiet and comfortable life with all of the amenities due the Chief Executive Officer of any major corporation. But, as he often reminded the other members of the board, he only followed orders.

Officially this board did not exist. They did not bother with the routine, day-to-day operations of their respective banks. Originally created to handle long-range planning, the organization now controlled not only their own respective banks, but also everything controlled by their own respective banks.

A directive from the organization could hire or fire anyone. They had absolute control over their banks, and over the governments that allegedly controlled those banks. If necessary, they could reach down to the media and the ministers, the cop on the beat and the housewife in the kitchen. Directly or indirectly, their control was almost always absolute. But officially they did not exist.

The elderly Chairman turned from the rain-streaked window

New World Order

to face the boardmembers and their chrome-and-plastic conference table — their monument to frugality. Like The Chairman, they were nameless. First Boardman on his left, Second Boardman on his right, Third Boardman on his left, Fourth Boardman on his right, Fifth Boardman on his left, Sixth Boardman on his right, Seventh Boardman on his left: eight men dedicated to greed, corruption, and control.

The boardmen did not ask, but The Chairman knew that three young men were waiting in an adjacent "ready-room" to transmit any instruction or directive the board might give them. Each of the three was connected by blood to at least one major European banking family. None of them, however, would ever sit at this table. Each had a higher calling. They would benefit from the decisions made at this table.

'Like hell they will,' The Chairman thought. 'Once we take control — total control — they will be weeded out with the rest of the flotsam and jetsam of humanity.'

But he did not say that.

"Gentlemen, our friends in the Internal Revenue Service of the United States of America have been withholding rather sizeable sums from us; credit money which would assure our control of that country ... and the United States as a whole. Boardman Six, report."

"To date we believe they have withheld one-point-eight trillion U.S. dollars," the Sixth Boardman began, "transferring the funds past our Federal Reserve Corporation into various non-aligned banks and organizations in South America and the Iberian Peninsula. This betrayal was, and is, a major conspiracy involving one hundred and twenty high officials of the Internal Revenue over a period of three years.

"It is my recommendation that we should advise the American Justice Department of this embezzlement and let them resolve the situation. I would also suggest that the subsequent turmoil could be used to our advantage."

The Chairman nodded. It may have been a minor case, but it provided a wealth of training for the youthful Sixth Boardman. "Opinions?"

"How did it happen?" Boardman Two asked.

"Frighteningly simple," the Sixth Boardman said. "Simple check-routing and numbered accounts."

"And the Federal Reserve did not know?" the First Boardman

demanded.
"They first alerted us to the possibility," Boardman Six replied. "They also assisted in my investigation."
"Was it really that simple?" asked Boardman Seven.
"By virtue of their position," Boardman Six said, "they could act with impunity."
Boardman Three had to say it. "And you're sure? ...."
"We're sure," The Chairman said. "Boardman Six requested that I re-check his findings, just to be certain."
The other six boardmen nodded, but not in unison. Each one had to carefully consider the problem ... and reach his own conclusion.
"Do you have the instructions?" The Chairman asked.
Boardman Six handed a single sheet of paper to The Chairman without comment. After reading it, The Chairman touched a button on his pager. A rear door opened and another young man entered the room. The Chairman handed him the single sheet of paper.
"Immediately."
"Yes, sir." And the young man was gone.
"Now," The Chairman said, "about Project Americana ...."

* * *

Chapter Three

The President of the United States smiled. Through the gut-wrenching walk from the helicopter to the doors of the White House, he smiled and he waved with confident assurance. His smile and his stance did not change until he was well within the glass doors of 1600 Pennsylvania Avenue, and beyond the prying eyes of the television cameras. Then, however, his smile collapsed into a grimace of anguish and disgust.

"They lied," he said, but he was speaking as much to himself as to his wife. "They lied, and they made sure I knew it. Oh, I can keep my membership in the Bilderberg Group ... if I raise enough taxes to cover our twenty percent of their international superfund for underdeveloped countries."

"Can you?" she asked.

"No," the President said, shaking his head. "Even if I wanted to, I don't have nearly enough votes in Congress to push it through. .... But that, of course, is not what they want."

"Okay, I'll bite. What do they want?"

The President grimaced again. "The bastards want me to declare that ... our country — The United States of America — is bankrupt."

"Bankrupt? .... Are they serious?"

Her husband nodded. "They want me to declare a State of Emergency, followed by Martial Law."

"As if Waco, Oklahoma City, Whitewater, Ken Starr, and the Millennium Crunch weren't bad enough," the First Lady growled.

"It's enough to make me take up smoking," the President said. But the humor was lost almost before he said it.

"I wouldn't blame you," his wife murmured. "The computer fiasco, the battle over the budget, the government shut down, and now this."

"At least the public hasn't blamed me for the computer crash or the shut down. .... At least, not yet."

"Batten down the hatches, men. Little Willie's back again.'"

"Don't blame him for —"

"I'm not," she said. "I was quoting an old poem."

"Wonder what Charlie wants?"

Charlie, the President's Appointments Secretary, looked rather frazzled and disheveled lumbering down the hallway towards them.

"Advice on diet and exercise?" The First Lady offered.

"The end of the world?" The President asked.

"Sir, Camp David is on the line."

The President glanced first at his Appointments Secretary, then at his wife. "Camp David?"

"The Vice-President," she reminded him. "The Cuban thing."

"Oh, yes. — I'll take it in The Office." He turned back to Charlie. "And where-the-hell is my Chief of Staff?"

"In his office, sir."

"Well, tell him to get his ass into the Oval Office P.D.Q.," the President growled, taking off down the hallway fast enough to make the Secret Service agents nervous.

The man had three guns: a shotgun, a rifle, and a semi-automatic pistol. Agents of the BATF confirmed the weapons. Agents if the FBI conducted the raid. Unfortunately the man tried to fight back against the warrantless raid by six agents who refused to identify themselves.

According to his neighbors, the man had been dragged from his home, hit repeatedly over the head and neck with anodized batons, and thrown into the back seat of an unmarked car. The hospital listed his cause of death as: "severe cranial trauma."

It was a nice way of saying he had been beaten to death.

Under the guidance and direction of three domineering Internal Revenue Service agents, the local police used a hand-held battering ram to smash open the front door of the recently-widowed housewife's Cape Cod house in Mesa, Arizona. Dazed and distraught, she listened without comprehension as they read and re-read her rights until they had enough of a response — more of a moan of anguish than an actual answer. Handcuffed and shackled with leg-irons, she

New World Order

was led to a squad car and driven to the local jail for booking and confinement. The police and the IRS agents, meanwhile, seized her Cape Cod home, her five-figure bank account, her old Lincoln Town Car, her new DVD color television, her laptop computer, and her jewelry under provisions of the RICO statutes.

Without money for a decent and competent attorney, she was fed to a "public defender," who promptly plea bargained her into a felony conviction and five years in a federal penitentiary for a crime she could not comprehend.

About six-months before her husband unexpectedly passed away, she had withdrawn three thousand eight hundred dollars from their bank account to send a money order to her son, who was then in college, for a used car. And that was her crime. Prior to January, 1998, banks would file the required Currency Transaction Report — IRS Form 4789 — on amounts over three thousand dollars. Under a new set of Draconian laws, however, the banks not only were not required to file this little one-page form, but were also handsomely rewarded for reporting individuals who failed to file the required form.

And again, Big Brother was watching.

The frail and elderly, gray-haired lady carried a double-barreled, two-shot, .22-caliber Derringer pistol around the house as compensation for an inordinate fear of burglars and rapists. It provided no protection, however, against the sudden invasion of screaming and shouting FBI and BATF agents who broke through her front door with a sledgehammer and knocked her onto the couch with a rough backhand that cracked her cheek bone and broke three ribs. The cause of death was listed as: "coronary thrombosis" — a heart attack. And according to the report, they had the wrong address.

The President of the United States delivered the eulogy with grace and dignity in precisely measured phrases reflecting his own personal sorrow. The Vice-President had become a close and valued friend through two campaigns and three stormy years of trials and tribulations, a man the President could rely upon in times of crisis, and someone he could trust when discretion was essential. He was — he had been — a man too good for his job, a man who rose above petty party politics to personal greatness.

James A. Clayton

Even the cynical media now acknowledged both the worth of the man and the sincerity of his eulogist. Any lingering doubts were dispelled within a few moments as the President eloquently exposed a deep and personal but private friendship for a man who had casually been called "his running mate." This relationship, the press later admitted, had been unique.

The drive back to the White House from Arlington seemed longer, and filled with painful and troubling thoughts. Protective Services had already declared, privately, that the Vice-President's auto accident was no accident. All three brake systems had been tampered with, and the ignition and transmission had been damaged by person or persons unknown.

According to Protective Services, the Vice-President's regular car had been in the shop for routine maintenance, and the back-up vehicle had been thoroughly checked. But somewhere, somehow, security had failed. The Vice-President and his wife apparently left Camp David in a third vehicle.

With a sadness born of cold harsh reality, the President knew that even if they could identify the culprit, he would never be brought to justice. By now he had been spirited from the United States to one of a dozen or more countries that would not acknowledge his presence.

The President swore. The President cursed. The President lit a Marlboro cigarette. And everyone in the limosine realized the depth of his anguish. But only the President understood that it had been far more than a political assassination. The auto accident was a personal message, aimed directly at the President of the United States ... and at the heart of America.

And for the President, it marked the point of no return.

―――

"But who could ever dream of such a sick plot?" the DCI demanded. "The Arabs? Qaddafi?"

"No," the President said thoughtfully, "there is a distinctive European flavor to this brutality."

"You mean, keeping it a secret within the government?"

"Yes," the President sighed. "That and the method they used. .... This twisted, covert, technological terrorism."

The Director of Central Intelligence followed the President's logic with deadly precision. "Red Brigade? The Russian Mafia?

New World Order

Neo-Nazis?"

The President shook his head. "These people must be overtly connected to our government."

"Mr. President!" It was an idea the young DCI did not want to entertain.

"I want your people to dig into the Bilderberg Group."

"That bunch of fuddy-duddy old bankers?"

"That's right," the President grimly acknowledged. "They control several European governments, and have connections with all the rest. Hell, half my administration either works for them or is influenced by them. And I'm fairly certain that they have at least partial control of the Federal Reserve."

"But, sir, such an implication ...."

"Frightening, isn't it? Even now I find it hard to believe that I was once a part of it."

"Sir?"

"Sorry, but yes, like my predecessor, I was an unwitting part of Bilderberg. I thought that they had the answers, that we could somehow create enough wealth so that everyone would be rich. Instead, we have economic warfare on a global scale. One world government. The New World Order."

The President pulled an ashtray from his desk drawer and slid it in front of his DCI.

"Excuse me, Mr. President." The DCI took a Marlboro from a packet in his pocket.

"Don't apologize," the President said, lighting the DCI's cigarette. "After this, I wouldn't trust the F.D.A. or the A.M.A. Within a few days, we might all be dead."

The DCI nodded grimly, acknowledging reality. As an afterthought, he placed the packet of Marlboro Gold on the President's desk.

"One other thing," the President added. "It's strictly against the law, but .... "

"Name it."

"I don't trust the F.B.I. I suspect some of them have connections with Bilderberg. I want you to open an operation here in the United States, and see if you can sort out who's working for whom."

"Tricky," the DCI said, adjusting his bifocals, "but if we've already been subverted ...."

James A. Clayton

The President bummed a Marlboro from the packet on his desk and lit it with a flourish, then searched for words within the clouds of smoke.

"I'm losing control, Jack. Everyone's going their own way, following laws that don't exist. Waco and Oklahoma City were just the beginning. And the death of the Vice-President was the end. If I don't do what they want, they'll eliminate me and get someone else. But make no mistake, their target is the United States of America."

"The Bilderberg Group?"

"Perhaps," the President said. "Or perhaps they too are being manipulated behind the scenes by some sort of executive council. Either way, once I've declared bankruptcy, I will become ... expendable."

"We'll straighten it out, Mr. President."

The President crushed out his cigarette and offered an awkward smile. "Just tell me who I can trust ... and who I should fire."

Jacob (Jack) Andrew Kent, the new Director of Central Intelligence, was a history buff who distrusted history books. There was, he noted, a tendency to gloss-over the facts in deference to a "politically-correct" viewpoint of society. He preferred to keep the facts as straight as possible, if possible.

But now he found himself facing a nightmare in red, white, and blue. In 1913 a distinguished United States' Senator had sold out his country in the name of financial security, persuading others to join him in passing Senator Aldrich's "Federal Reserve Act."

No one seemed to notice that the Federal Reserve Act was blatantly unconstitutional. The Constitution clearly stated that only "Congress shall have the power ... to coin money, (and) regulate the value thereof." Yet Congress had casually created an untouchable private corporation owned by certain banks and operated solely for their own personal profit.

Their profit, however, stunned DCI Jack Kent.

If Congress needed a billion dollars, and they usually needed a good deal more than that, the Federal Reserve would willingly deliver that one billion dollars in money or credit in exchange for the government's agreement to pay it back — with interest. Congress would then authorize the Treasury Department to print one billion dollars in United States' bonds, and deliver them to the Federal Reserve Bank.

The Federal Reserve magnanimously paid the cost of printing that one billion dollars, which amounted to about a thousand dollars, and then made the actual exchange.

The government's bills were paid, and the United States' government had now indebted the people of the United States to the private Federal Reserve bankers for another one billion dollars ... plus interest. But that, as the DCI discovered, was only the beginning.

The one billion dollars in bonds were now part of the bank's assets. But since U.S. banking laws require only a ten percent reserve, the bankers can lend up to ten times the amount of the bonds they have on hand. In other words, the Federal Reserve bankers can now loan out ten billion dollars to commercial banks, and charge interest on that loan. Then the commercial banks can lend up to ten times the amount of their share, which must eventually be paid back with compounded interest by some businessman or homeowner, who must also pay taxes to cover the original loan. And all for an original cost of about one thousand dollars.

That and a few other gimmicks made the Federal Reserve the wealthiest and most powerful corporation in the world. It also crushed their seventeen-man board of directors between the United States' government and the owners of the private corporation.

But who owned the Federal Reserve?

It had taken almost one full week for Jack Kent's analysts to compile the data confirming that eight major banks owned the Federal Reserve Banking Corporation. What should have been public information, available to all, had been classified as top secret and carefully hidden from prying eyes. Even his own analysts, with all their "top secret" clearances, encountered multiple layers of resistance and red tape, all for a list of just eight rich banks.

"Rothschild Banks of London and Berlin;
Lazard Brothers Bank of Paris;
Israel Moses Seif Banks of Italy;
Warburg Bank of Hamburg and Amsterdam;
Lehman Brothers Bank of New York; Kuhn,
Loeb Bank of New York;
[*—from: THE FACT FINDER; December 15, 1991]

James A. Clayton

Chase Manhattan Bank of New York;
Goldman, Sachs Bank of New York." *

DCI Jack Kent stroked his four o'clock shadow and read the list again. Twice. With over half of the controlling stocks of the Federal Reserve Corporation being held by European banking families, the entire country was being systematically looted; and the government was falling under the domination of the foreign bankers.

For a moment the DCI wondered if the President knew. But he then realized that the President also needed a confirmation. One does not declare war, economic or otherwise, on a mere whim.

Jack Kent picked up his telephone and punched angrily at the buttons. Now was not the time for social niceties.

"General? — Jack Kent. This comes from 'The Man' ... and its ultra-hush. I need Echo-Three, and I need it right now. And nothing on paper."

―――

Once it had been started, it could not be stopped. The move to Echo-Three was actually a built-in series of command-and-control orders dating back to the so-called "Cold War," where it had existed within a plethora of code names. But it was now, in effect, a series of evacuation and relocation directives for all of the strategic implements of modern warfare — especially the computers, communications, and satellite surveillance systems — to several highly classified sites.

A second built-in Presidential Directive locked-down all the remaining nuclear missiles buried under the prairies of the western United States. Someone suggested re-programming those weapons of massive destruction, but the war was against a few bankers, not all of Europe.

Not bombing Europe might be very noble, but DCI Jacob Andrew Kent had traveled throughout Europe and the Middle East, first as a CIA field agent and later as the head of European Ops. He knew that Europeans could often be less than trustworthy. They had elevated back-stabbing to a sophisticated art, and nothing could be accepted at face value.

In European society, the people did not question the government. In the United States, the people demanded answers.

In Europe, one was generally guilty until proven innocent. In the United States, one was generally innocent until proven guilty.

New World Order

In Europe, the people obeyed the wishes of the government. In the United States, the government obeyed the wishes of the people.

Founded and mired within the belief that *"The King Can Do No Wrong,"* the Europeans had become slaves to the dictatorial hypocrisy of governmental domination. And now those same self-righteous Europeans were exporting their hypocrisy, their legalized tyranny, across the Atlantic Ocean.

DCI Jack Kent uttered an expletive epistle about the European appreciation of oral sex, and turned on CNN, before trying to resume work on his computerized "flow-chart" of world history. He tried to concentrate on the parametric impact of the global elite, and upon setting up another meeting with the President, only to find his thoughts suddenly interrupted when the news quietly erupted from his television set.

".... And in Washington, D.C., the Justice Department today announced the indictment of an additional thirty-two officers and agents of the Internal Revenue Service on charges of fraud and embezzlement."

Now what the hell did that mean? He grabbed the telephone and began punching buttons.

* * *

Chapter Four

People who live in Beverly Hills, California, might regard the south side of McCook, Nebraska, to be decrepit. On the other hand, the people who live on the south side of McCook, Nebraska, might regard Beverly Hills, California, to be ostentatious. But for the people in the gray four-door sedans driving west on "B" Street, the whole world was one gigantic slum ... and everyone else was a criminal.

There were four such sedans. Two had the letters "A.T.F." painted on their roofs. Two had the letters "F.B.I." painted on their roofs. And the four gray sedans were followed by a large blue van with the letters "S.I.S." boldly emblazoned on its side.

All five vehicles moved at a slow and almost majestic pace through the little Midwestern town, seemingly oblivious to the town and its people. They turned left off "B" onto West Tenth, and into a more decrepit part of McCook.

The two BATF cars took the lead, squealing their tires as they accelerated towards the old two-story house with the white picket fence. The first car ripped out a section of that picket fencing as it slid to a turf-tearing halt at the front door. The second car smashed the remainder of the white picket fence, knocked aside two trash cans, and bulldozed three bushes into compost mulch before stopping.

The two FBI cars and the SIS van stopped in the street just in time to see the BATF agents bash open the front door with a sledgehammer. From that point on, it was utter confusion and chaos.

Eight heavily-armed federal agents rushed into the house, screaming and shouting, as a series of rapid-fire shots thundered through the building. A thunderous explosion blasted the body of an unidentified woman through a front, ground-floor window. The bloody body fell onto the porch and rolled off into the mud, leaving a trail of reddish gore to mark its passage. Then another small but powerful blast shattered the windows on the other side of the first floor, firing dagger-like shards of glass across the lawn and across the street.

More shots rang out. Another powerful explosion drowned the gunfire, the shouting, the screaming, and the other cacophonous noises echoing throughout the monstrous old house.

More FBI and BATF agents ran through the front door or climbed through a shattered window into total pandemonium. Inside, federal agents were running madly about, screaming and yelling. A BATF man yanked open a closet door and was promptly blown to pieces by a shotgun. Four agents fired wildly into the closet but hit nothing. The booby trap had done its job.

Upstairs, a partially-clad young man was shot five times before they realized he was unarmed. By then, of course, he was also dead.

Downstairs, caught up in the madness of the moment, an FBI agent spun about and fired his riot shotgun out a living room window, wounding a disoriented federal agent standing on the front porch. The wounded agent returned fire, but by then the FBI man was on the floor and crawling towards the kitchen.

"Run, Kathy, run!"

The FBI agent crawled into the kitchen as the woman screamed. Crashing noises, breaking glass, a dull clanging sound, and thundering pain all hit him at once. Through blurred and blood-smeared vision he saw two of his fellow agents rush into the kitchen with submachine guns blazing.

The middle-aged housewife holding the dented sauce pan performed a macabre dance of death across her kitchen as submachine gun bullets ripped her dress and her body to bloody shreds. Expended shell casings clattered across the linoleum floor. Window glass, ceramic figurines, and porcelain plates shattered and crashed around the room, while the submachine guns bounced the housewife against the refrigerator and the sink and the kitchen table. Then they stopped shooting, and her remains dropped to the linoleum tile, blasted beyond recognition.

The submachine guns roared again, and a small ten-year-old boy flew out the back door, only to choke and gurgle to death on his own blood.

Somebody murmured, "Oh, shit!"

The FBI agent's friends grabbed his arms and dragged his semi-conscious form from the house. Moments later he was in the back seat of an FBI sedan with a dull ringing sound in his ears and flashing white lights all around him.

"It's a bad bump," someone said, "but you'll live."

For a moment he thought he saw the girl Kathy darting among the bushes and trees in back. And at about the same time, the entire town started spinning.

They came out of the house in groups of two or three, carrying their dead and wounded with them. A couple stopped to throw the body of the dead female back into the house. A few stopped to check their weapons and equipment. Others just ran around and tried to look busy.

"How do we justify this mess?"

A BATF pulled two submachine guns from the trunk of his car and held them up for display. "Don't you know, boy? We just busted an illegal arms dealer! You have any problems and I'll help you write up the report."

Two minutes later only one BATF car remained in front of the two-story house, waiting for one lone passenger. And a few seconds later that one lone passenger ran from the house and jumped into the waiting car.

"Fire in the hole!" the BATF agent said.

His partner nodded, and within a few more seconds the two-story house and their wreckage were left far behind.

A McCook Police Department patrol car arrived at the scene just in time to see the first of four firebombs explode, just in time to see the old two-story house disappear within a roaring conflagration.

By the time the McCook Fire Department arrived, some four minutes later, the single torch of flame and fury had totally engulfed the building. Within minutes only a few hot bricks and smoldering ashes remained to mark the location of someone's home.

Robert L. Jenkins, the Director of the Federal Bureau of Investigation, re-read the report and the letter twice before selecting a button on the intercom.

"Paul, could you come in here for a minute or two?"

"On my way."

The Director brushed his hand over the shiny dome of his prematurely-bald scalp and pushed another button. "Millie, have my car brought around to the front. And tell Jerry it will be a long trip. A very long trip."

"Yes, sir."

The side door opened and Special Agent Paul Bernard Latimer, Assistant Director for Internal Affairs, slipped into the Director's office. One look at the Director's face told him that this would not be an easy chitchat interview.

"Something's wrong."

"Very. Sit down."

Special Agent Paul Latimer sat down, but he was not comfortable. "What's it all about?"

"Remember Waco?"

"Of course. Bloody disaster, from all sides."

"And have you seen this?" the Director asked, holding up the report. "Kansas City. Last month."

"Oh, yeah. .... A bit excessive, but technically within the limits."

"Yes. Technically," the Director said. "But we used that excuse just before Waco — and we were almost embarrassed by a few agents who crossed the line. We don't want any more charges of excessive violence, Paul."

"You want me to check into Kansas City?"

"And Denver. And Lincoln. And Des Moines. .... Something is going on out in the Midwest, Paul. I'm not sure what, but it frightens me."

"You don't think the report is ... accurate?"

"They've hedged before. Hell, the B.A.T.F. lied out their ass about Waco. And our minimal response was tanks and flamethrowers!"

"Excessive, yes. But based on the information we had —"

"Spare me the bullshit! Murder, arson, and beating confessions out of prisoners are not in the manual!" Jenkins exploded. "Understand?"

"Are you kidding? — That's half my caseload right there!"

"Uh-huh. Well, check on Kansas City, Denver, Lincoln, and Des Moines, anyway. I don't want some agent getting excited and having the whole thing blow up in our face."

"Of course not," Latimer said. "I'll check into it."

"Thank you."

With a brief nod of acknowledgment, Special Agent Paul Bernard Latimer slipped through the side door and headed back to his smaller office, stopping only long enough to order a cup of coffee and three headache tablets from his secretary.

Once inside his office, he turned on the air-filtering unit, pulled an ashtray from the bottom drawer, and lit an English Oval cigarette. Seeing the cigarette, his secretary quietly deposited the headache tablets and his cup of coffee on his desk, then silently left his office. She knew he needed time to think, even if she didn't know what he was thinking about.

But the dark and devious thoughts of the Assistant Director for Internal Affairs could not be resolved by a cup of coffee, two cigarettes, and three headache tablets. The Director had asked about Waco, knowing that Paul Latimer had been watching the fiasco from the sidelines. Did the Director suspect?

Without his knowledge, Latimer had been recruited shortly after his graduation from the academy. From the start he had been told repeatedly that they, whoever they were, were not interested in "secret" information. They wanted only his valued friendship and an occasional tip on policy, areas the Bureau considered to be worthy of special attention. (For several years he actually thought "they" were CIA agents!) Did the Director know about that?

After Waco he had been transferred to New York City and promoted. After Oklahoma City he had been transferred to Washington, D.C., and promoted. And after he had covered-up some of the "mistakes" made at the FBI laboratory, he was again promoted. Then the previous Director had resigned, and Special Agent Paul Bernard Latimer became the new Assistant Director for Internal Affairs. Did the Director ever wonder about his rapid promotions?

Finally, in desperation, he reluctantly telephoned an associate in an office a few blocks away.

"I have a problem," he began. "The Director has questioned some of the reports ... especially those from the Midwest."

"Understood," the associate said. "This is not, however, a problem for you."

"Explain."

"Your boss is going to Piney Point," the associate said. "In

an hour or so he will suffer a fatal auto accident. And within five hours or less you will again be promoted ... Mister Director."
"Oh, my God." But it was not a prayer.

Jerry Longstreet had enjoyed twenty-three productive years with the Bureau, including ten months as personal chauffeur for the Director. At forty-seven he knew he was pushing it, but the Bureau looked after its own. Thus Jerry Longstreet stood beside the limosine's open passenger door as his boss, the Director of the Federal Bureau of Investigation, emerged from the main entrance.

"Sorry, but I want to be conspicuous today."

"Yes, sir!" Jerry snapped.

"Be sure to tell the dispatcher you're taking me to Piney Point."

"Yes, sir?"

"Then drop me off at the Skyline Inn, and continue on to Piney Point. But don't tell the dispatcher."

"Yes, sir." And Jerry closed the door.

The idea of the married Director being involved in some sort of sleazy assignation bothered him for the first half of the trip. Then Jerry realized, quite suddenly, that the Skyline was only about five blocks from Capitol Hill. The day seemed a bit brighter.

"Drop me off in front and never mind the door. Just keep going on to Piney Point, and don't tell anybody anything. — Got it?"

"Yes, sir."

Jerry Longstreet did not really stop at the Skyline Inn. The Director was out and away before he could bring the big metal monster to a complete stop. And Jerry Longstreet was on his way to Piney Point almost before he realized it.

The Director of the Federal Bureau of Investigation and the Director of the Central Intelligence Agency met over a steak-and-mashed-potatoes dinner in the center of a conference room of the Skyline Inn. Although the large room had been "swept for bugs" and was assiduously guarded by CIA personnel, both men spoke in muted tones.

"This meeting is authorized and approved," the DCI said, "by the President of the United States."

"Recorded?"

"Of course not."

"Formal?"

"No."

"Then why the formal announcement? Eyes only?"

The DCI nodded. "It was imperative that we confirm your repudiation of certain actions and activities which your subordinates are incorporating into their agenda."

The Director of the FBI nodded slowly as he finished off the last bites of his *filet mignon*. "In other words, whether I approve or disapprove of my field agents turning a prisoner into a punching bag?"

The DCI nodded again. With his lined and leathery face, bald scalp, and dark skin; Jenkins did not look like an FBI agent, and even less like the Director of that collection of bilateral pedants. But the DCI was careful to conceal his own thoughts and opinions.

"For the record," the FBI man continued, "I find such actions reprehensible. I've personally ordered the dismissal of about thirty agents for various breaches of discipline."

"We know," the DCI said. "We also suspect that your Mr. Latimer's reports have been less-than-factual. None of those agents were dismissed. Or even reprimanded."

"He lied to me?"

"And that's just the beginning. He also set into motion a plan to have you assassinated," the DCI checked his watch, "in about ten minutes."

"Oh, hell. .... What about Jerry, my driver?"

"Hopefully he will be out of harm's way. We can't risk radio communications, but the plan is to have him pulled over by a couple of Maryland State Troopers and replaced by one of my field agents. We may lose the car, of course, but —"

"Cars can be replaced. Men like Jerry Longstreet cannot."

"Jerry should be at Andrews Air Force Base in about fifteen to twenty minutes," Jack Kent said, checking his watch again. "If things go badly, you'll be joining him there for a night flight to Echo-Three."

"It's that bad?"

"Your wife and about forty selected F.B.I. agents will join you there."

They waited while a waiter, whose last assignment had been Istanbul, brought pie and coffee.

"It's that bad?" Jenkins repeated.

"Yes. It involves several congressmen. Among others."

"And the Bureau has been ... compromised?"

DCI Jack Kent nodded.

"Shit! How — how did you find out about Latimer?"

The DCI shrugged. "He kept showing up here and there. Places he shouldn't have been. So we checked his travel vouchers and tapped his telephone. And we hit pay dirt almost immediately."

"So you bugged his office, his home, his car, et cetera."

"Sorry, but your Assistant Director Paul Bernard Latimer is dirty. Very dirty."

"I'll have to rebuild the whole department, won't I?"

"When you can," the DCI said. "If you can."

"What the hell is going on, Jack?"

"Backgrounders," the DCI said, handing Jenkins a slim file folder. "You may find them ... difficult to believe. But then, after this is all over with, they'll have to rewrite the history books. .... Again."

———

The building was an overgrown mausoleum in white marble, lost in a saddle between the green hills above Burgenstock, Switzerland, and lost between Greco-Roman and Modern architectural styles. White columns outlined a covered driveway in front of the funeral-parlor building, but green trees and shrubbery hid the edifice from the prying eyes of the villagers below.

The white marble walls concealed, among other things, a rather small conference room decorated in tubular chrome and plastic. It was not designed for beauty or efficiency. Its furnishings would not distract the occupants from their laptop computers, and their computers would not distract them from listening to The Chairman speak.

Today, however, the occupants were listening to a tinny-sounding tape recorder.

"Gentlemen, in nineteen-thirteen our forefathers set into motion a plan to gain control of the world's financial institutions, and to thereby take control of the various governments throughout the world, to unite them under one banner, one flag. Thus, due to their foresight, we now also control all of the media and most of the major religions. .... We make the laws, gentlemen, and they serve us."

The Chairman switched the tape recorder off.

"Gentlemen," he said, "the following report will not be recorded, although you may wish to take notes. Please feel free to do so.

"As you may know, we have found one minor flaw in our security in the person of one Paul Bernard Latimer. We would normally terminate such a person in the most efficient manner available. In this case, however, we feel it would be more expedient to allow the Americans to handle the ... wet work.*

"Mr. Latimer is careless and cowardly, but he does not have any information which would endanger the project. And in his current position, he provides an excellent distraction for our other ... representatives."

In a towering display of confidence, The Chairman stood up and helped himself to the newly-installed tea service on the table under the window behind him. Teacup in hand, The Chairman returned to the chrome-and-plastic conference table. But now, for a brief instant, he actually offered his fellow associates a weak but encouraging half-smile.

"With the United Nations and NATO now alerted to the problems that the United States of America might face, most of our work is finished."

"What problems?" the Third Boardman asked.

The Chairman took a sip of his tasteless tea and studied their expressionless faces. "Certain acts of violence. An erosion of their sociopolitical infrastructure.. The apparent disintegration of their criminal justice system. .... The usual things."

"When?" the Fifth Boardman demanded.

The Chairman took another sip of his tasteless tea.

"We've already begun."

"That I know," the Fifth Boardman snapped.

"Oh!" Embarrassingly caught off-guard by a rare moment of human error, The Chairman swiftly recovered the professionally-aloof self-assurance that was his trademark.

"We are ready. Either their President declares bankruptcy, or ...."

The Fifth Boardman reluctantly nodded acknowledgment. The Chairman's silence spoke to each of them. Only no one wanted

[— an old espionage euphemism for assassination]*

to contemplate the alternative bloodbath.

"But we are still quite premature in our activities," the Sixth Boardman protested. "We must expect resistance."

"We have considered all of the possible alternatives," The Chairman said. "Whether this resistance could ever achieve the level of insurrection you anticipate is a matter of conjecture. In this case, however, it is better to err on the side of caution. NATO has already agreed to the application of sufficient force, should things become unpleasant during the occupation."

"But what about their President?" the Second Boardman asked.

"He does not represent any threat to our plans," The Chairman said. "I doubt if he is even capable of understanding such an affair. Regardless of that, after the impeachment of his predecessor, his power and authority were completely and totally destroyed. He is now utterly incapable of offering any form of opposition to our efforts. Poor sod probably can't even go to the toilet without permission."

Dismissing them with a nod; he rose, turned, and stared with sullenly-blank eyes through the double-glazed bulletproof windows. The jagged alpine peaks were, however, too familiar to his ancient eyes.

"It is lonely at the top," he sighed.

* * *

Chapter Five

"You're expected," the White House guard said, opening the door to the State Dining Room.

"I know," Jack Kent countered, leaving the guard to close the door.

The State Dining Room could, in theory, host 140 guests at a time. The President, however, found such overcrowding — with ten-to-twelve persons at each table — unpalatable; insisting that no more than five persons should be seated at one table. It made the gold-and-white State Dining Room seem even larger, and allowed the President to hide under the portrait of Lincoln which hung over the fireplace mantel.

DCI Jacob Andrew Kent lit a Marlboro and studied the twilight of floodlamps in the darkness beyond the windows. The President bummed a cigarette from his DCI and pushed the elegant glass ashtray to the center of the table.

"So what have you learned about the Justice Department and the I.R.S.?"

"Those guys at Justice wouldn't go to the bathroom without permission from Europe," the President said bitterly. "My guess is that someone over there wanted to eliminate some of their less reliable people over here. Hell, I.R.S. accounting has been sloppy for years! Maybe somebody took it personally."

"And the Bureau?" the DCI asked, poring himself a cup of coffee.

The President took a sip of coffee before lighting the cigarette and blowing the smoke towards the ceiling.

"Jenkins ... is dead," the President said with finality. "Their plane crashed into the ocean shortly after takeoff, about an hour ago."

"Damn!" Jack Kent took a long drag off his Marlboro and exhaled. "That means command-and-control has been compromised."

New World Order

"With Latimer strutting around like a bantam rooster, thinking he's pulled the coup of the century," the President said, blowing another cloud of smoke upward.

"Remember the federal building in Oklahoma City that was blown up back in ninety-five?"

"The Murrah Building? Yes, I remember."

"Well, we now know that Paul Latimer didn't like some of the people in the building. And although the technicians can't prove it, we've always wondered about planted evidence."

"Son-of-a-bitch!" The President crushed out the cigarette. "Well, I guess it wouldn't be the first time we've put innocent men into a federal penitentiary. .... And why not? Everything else is going to hell in a handbag! Yesterday the Speaker of the House suggested we install video cameras and sound equipment in the White House ... to avoid rumors of impropriety, as he called it."

"Sweep for 'bugs'?"

The President nodded. "Found three. Probably F.B.I."

"I'll send some of my people over at ten, tomorrow morning."

"Thank you. .... I need the reassurance."

DCI Jack Kent shrugged with simple eloquence. It was his job. In protecting the Presidency, he was protecting the United States.

"No Continuing Resolution?" the DCI finally asked.

"No," the President sighed. "They're trying to squeeze me, to crush me. I've vetoed over three dozen different bills, including one to create a national police force with almost unlimited powers, and one to eliminate the minimum wage."

"Don't forget the one to do away with federal housing and wipe out the E.P.A."

"But why?"

"Money," the DCI said flatly. "At least two hundred and seventeen Congressmen and thirty-four Senators are 'on-the-take' for legal and semi-legal bribes and payoffs from assorted lobbyists and influence-peddlers. Most of it is under-the-table, but far too many simply don't care. Not after you vetoed their salary hike."

"Surely common sense alone would tell them —"

"Common sense? In Washington, D.C.? This is a city of laws. — Hell, we're mired in their laws."

"I tried talking to them," the President said. "I tried, but they don't want to listen. And they won't even consider a compromise."

"It's only a matter of time." The DCI crushed out his cigarette and adjusted his bifocals. "The federal government has been shut down for too long as it is. Too many government employees are now standing in unemployment lines."

"That's the way they planned it, isn't it?"

"In a way, yes." Jack Kent lit another Marlboro to cover his hesitation. "But something is wrong. They're rushing it. .... And I don't know why."

"A mistake?"

"Maybe. Or maybe they're afraid of the upcoming elections. After all, they have a lot of money invested in this government."

"If I refused payment and cancelled the national debt, Congress and the United Nations would tear me into a thousand little pieces," the President said, thinking aloud. "And if I do declare bankruptcy, the citizens of this country will string me up from the nearest lamppost."

DCI Jacob Andrew Kent again hesitated as he considered the President's present predicament.

"Maybe there's another alternative ...."

They met in a cone of light in the middle of a black darkness; in an isolated, unearthly, non-location within an empty airplane hangar on a European airbase. The Senator had just flown in from the United States. The General was a U.S. Army liaisons officer attached to NATO. They shook hands and sat down on wooden chairs. They silently studied each other across a wooden table. Some things would never be listed in briefings and backgrounders: the set of a jawline, a facial expression, a message in body language.

"General Wilder."

"Senator."

"Sorry about the accommodations, General, but absolute secrecy is absolutely essential."

"I hate this cloak-and-dagger stuff," Wilder growled.

"Cloak, yes. But no dagger. This is something else." Senator hesitated, studying the gray-haired liaisons officer's dour expression. "The World Bank and the Federal Reserve are about to tell the President of the United States that our country is bankrupt."

Wilder studied the Senator's ill-matched hair dye job and

raised a questioning eyebrow. "So I'm not going to get paid?"

"Once they've declared bankruptcy, the President will be forced to declare a State of Emergency ... followed by Martial Law."

"Hmmm," Wilder mused, "so that's how he makes friends and influences people."

"Yes, well, the President thinks that Martial Law will give him more power," the Senator lied. "We've been trying to tell him, but he just won't listen."

"Trying to tell him what, Senator?"

"Trying to tell him that the Federal Reserve and a major faction of the United Nations intend to usurp Presidential authority and take over the country."

"Oh, my God!" Wilder was speechless. "So what do you want me to do about it, Senator?" "We've managed to get the Air Force to ground its aircraft and missiles. The Navy has set sail under sealed orders for *Diego Garcia*. And the Army has agreed to restrict the movement of tanks and artillery."

"Senator, I cannot stop NATO. It's all Command Staff. I'm only liaisons for the European Directorate."

"I am not ignorant, General. I know we have a large military contingent tied-up in Bosnia, and an even larger deployment in Saudi Arabia."

"Yes. And what's left is a bunch of paper-pushers and bureaucrats scattered across half of Europe. *That* is my command, Senator."

"I understand, General. Just do what you can .... even if it's just for yourself."

General Donald Thornton Wilder's eyes dissected the Senator, for this was not the political animal Wilder remembered. Except for the incredible message, the Senator sounded like DCI Jack Kent.

"A warning?" Wilder asked. "From Jack Kent?"

"From both of us," the Senator said. "And not just because I owe him a favor, either."

"Thank you," Wilder said, shaking the Senator's hand.

"Dark days are coming, my friend. This New World Order wishes only to protect us ... from too much freedom." The Senator hesitated again, adding a cold smile to complete the private message. "Perhaps you should take a vacation."

"Perhaps I should — right after my press conference this afternoon."

The Senator nodded once, and then evaporated into the darkness. 'Just like Jack Kent,' the General thought as he turned off the single light switch.

The Military Command Headquarters of the North Atlantic Treaty Organization (NATO) near Brussels, Belgium, is hidden within a decidedly unmilitary and almost-Doric facade of gray-white stone. Its collegiate look, decorative pillars, and ornate lobby offer an impressive impression of luxurious understatement. But beyond the ornate lobby, it is simply cheap.

That might explain why the doorknob to General Donald Wilder's inner office was so loose, and why he had to share a desk with Air Commodore Sir George Wesley Harmon of the British Royal Air Force. Perhaps that cheap attitude also contributed to the argumentative friendship which had developed between the two military men.

Wilder did not mention where he had been, nor why he had been there. And after one dry joke about "sleeping-in," Harmon decided it was not a matter Wilder wished to discuss — with anyone.

Just before noon they left the outer office together, followed by nine NATO aides and assistants. Both officers suffered a distaste for the aides and assistants NATO had foisted upon them, but they kept their own counsel.

"I fail to see why you are so upset," Harmon was saying as they emerged into the central corridor. "Surely you realize the value of these training exercises."

"It seems to me as if we're being trained to invade the United States of America," Wilder snorted. "And I'll be damned if I'm going to declare war on my own country!"

"Nonsense, my boy! It's just in case things get out of hand. With your government completely shut down for three months now, it's only natural that we should be concerned. .... Why, your President and your Congress won't even speak to each other."

"There are times, Commodore, when my wife will not speak to me — but that doesn't mean we're getting a divorce."

"Really?" Harmon said. "I did not know your President and your Congress were married to each other."

Wilder grinned broadly, trying hard not to laugh aloud, as

they marched into the ornate lobby. His humor died a swift death, however, when the two sergeants wearing blue United Nations' helmets interrupted his advance.

"Excuse me, General Wilder, but I have orders to escort you to Major Hoffman's office."

"The hell you will," Wilder snapped. "I have a press conference in fifteen minutes and —"

"I'm sorry, sir," the other sergeant interrupted. "Your press conference has been cancelled."

"On whose authority?"

"On the orders of Major Hoffman, sir."

"Major Hoffman does not have the authority to cancel my press conference, Sergeant! And you do not have any authority to detain me!"

But that did not impress the two sergeants. They grabbed General Wilder's arms and started to drag him down the hallway.

"I say there, this is really quite outrageous!" Harmon objected loudly, stepping forward to block the retreating sergeants.

Then a U.S. Marine security guard, a Lieutenant Victor McVey, stepped out of the crowd to join the British Air Commodore in defending General Wilder.

The first sergeant backhanded Harmon, knocking the older man down. The second sergeant released Wilder to defend against Lt. McVey's left jab. Freed from the sergeant's grasp, Wilder spun around and slug the first sergeant. Behind him, the second sergeant crumpled to the floor.

With the second sergeant down and the first sergeant headed to the floor, the nine aides and assistants recklessly charged into the melee. Harmon staggered to his feet and stumbled into the brawl as McVey lashed out with karate kicks, punches, and chops that scattered four attacking assistants. Wilder punched out a fifth aide and leaped on a sixth, while Air Commodore Harmon created a stumbling blockade for two others.

But then the first UN sergeant scrambled to his feet and clobbered McVey from behind, while the second knocked General Wilder down the hallway. Confusion and chaos finally won the day, sending the Air Commodore crashing to the floor. The last thing Harmon saw, the two United Nations' sergeants were dragging an unconscious General Donald T. Wilder down the corridor and into oblivion, followed closely by nine aides and assistants.

"Damn motherfuckin' yellow-bellied bastards!" Lieutenant Victor McVey was in no shape for anything except verbal assaults.

"Calmly, son. Calmly. No point in fighting a battle you cannot win." Harmon stopped for a moment to catch his breath and to think. But he had been in difficult situations before. "We'd best find another domicile for you, and quickly. I have some friends in town ...."

For some inexplicable reason, the ornate lobby was now empty. Even the usual guards at the security checkpoints were gone, allowing Air Commodore Harmon and Lieutenant McVey to stagger from the almost-Doric facade of the gray-white building virtually unobserved.

The monolithic gray granite tomb of the Federal Reserve Corporate Headquarters in Washington, D.C., is an imposing monument to mankind's avarice and greed. Few, if any, refer to it as a "Corporate Headquarters." Few, if any, are willing to admit that it is a private corporation. And few, if any, are willing to admit that the greed and avarice of the Federal Reserve Corporation controls and dominates the government of the United States of America.

Founded by an Act of Congress in late December of 1913, the Federal Reserve Corporation openly violates Article One of the Constitution of the United States of America, in that only Congress "shall have the power to coin money, and establish the value thereof."

This, of course, means little to the boardmembers and stockholders of the Federal Reserve, many of whom are not even Americans. Although it is a zealously-guarded secret, the major stockholders of the Federal Reserve are, in fact, the Rothschild Banks of London and Berlin, the Lazard Brothers Bank of Paris, the Israel Moses Seif Banks of Italy, the Warburg Banks of Hamburg and Amsterdam, Lehman Brothers Bank of New York, Kuhn Loeb Bank of New York, Chase Manhattan Bank of New York, and Coldman Sachs Bank of New York. And they don't give a damn.

Except for employees, very few people are ever granted access to the inner workings of the Federal Reserve Headquarters. Very few have seen the luxuriously-paneled walls which surround the polished dark-wood conference table. Very few have seen the elegantly-

New World Order

tailored and neatly-coiffured gentlemen who sit in paranoid silence around that dark conference table. And very few are even acquainted with the two female secretaries sitting at small tables at either end of the room, taking copious notes in a rarely-used version of shorthand.

No cameras or recording devices of any kind are allowed within these hallowed walls. Telephones, FAX machines, and other communication devices are restricted. All mail is examined and censored before leaving the building. And the security system would make the CIA jealous — if they knew about it.

Of course the Federal Reserve Chairman knew about it. And the Federal Reserve Boardmen knew about it. It was there for them, protecting their privacy, providing their security. But nothing could protect them from their own fears and their own paranoia.

Five years earlier the Fed Chairman and two of his closest deputies had liquidated their assets — stocks, bonds, and real estate holdings — and hid the cash in numbered offshore bank accounts, fueling their rampant paranoia. Then Von Hagen and his associates had been brought in, adding new dimensions to their fears and their doubts. And now ....

Von Hagen stroked his Van Dyke beard half-a-dozen times with his thumb and index finger, adding to the tension. Then he asked the inevitable question. "Would you explain to us, Mr. Chairman, why you have so vociferously objected to the Bilderberg Group's proposal for reorganization?"

This was the question the Fed Chairman dreaded beyond all others. He could not bring himself to participate in the Bilderberg Group's design for the destruction of America. On the other hand, he could not stop them, either.

Turning abruptly back to Von Hagen, he again wondered if the Bilderberg man came from Germany, Switzerland, the Netherlands, or Austria. His suit, vest, and tie were Saville Row; his shoes were Via Venito; but his conduct was pure Reeperbahn. He was, the Fed Chairman concluded, a well-dressed alley cat; trying to cover his amorality with sumptuous clothing. But Von Hagen's had to be answered. Formally and precisely answered.

"Certainly, sir," the Fed Chairman finally said, taking a deep breath. "As you know, government indebtedness has declined both in real money and vis-a-vis the Gross National Product. Their financial stability is now stronger than ever. And their balance-of-payments has been favorable for the past two fiscal quarters.

"Thus, I can find no reason — no justification — for the authorization of a Declaration of Bankruptcy. .... Do you understand?"

Von Hagen smiled. "I understand perfectly, Mr. Chairman."

If the Federal Reserve Chairman expected something more, he was due for a disappointment. There was no sharp retort nor understated threat. There was no reference to the disastrously declining stock market nor the invisible bond market. Von Hagen simply smiled and nodded, filling the conference room with fear and loathing.

Then a Page entered the dark conference room, handed the Fed Chairman a piece-of-scratch-paper note, and left without saying a word.

With his perplexity expressed in a frown, the Federal Reserve Chairman read the note twice, closed the file folder in front of him, and noisily cleared his throat.

"If you will excuse me, gentlemen, I have been summoned ... elsewhere."

The Federal Reserve Chairman rose, pocketed the note, and left the room in stunned silence.

"I understand you perfectly, Mr. Chairman," Von Hagen repeated in a voice that was almost inaudible. "I understand, but the World Bank will not. In fact, I doubt they even give a damn. And Burgenstock has their own plans for you, I'm afraid."

Von Hagen cleared his throat and raised his voice. "Now, if there are no further objections ...."

"Should we not adjourn until the Chairman returns?"

"I seriously doubt that he will," Von Hagen said without inflection. "Now, where were we?"

His car was waiting when the Fed Chairman emerged from the gray monolith. Ron was illegally parked in a "No Parking Zone" again, but this time the Fed Chairman did not object. The call from the White House took precedence.

Only Ron did not open the limosine's rear door. The dress uniform was correct to the last button, but the gaunt and pockmarked face bothered the Fed Chairman's sense of propriety.

"Sorry, sir, but Ron caught a touch of the flu, or something," the driver said, opening the door and tipping his cap.

The Fed Chairman nodded, grunted, and sat down.

Then the driver shot the Chairman three times — once in each eye and once through the forehead — with a silenced semi-automatic pistol. He tossed the gun into the front seat, closed the rear door, climbed behind the wheel, and drove away. But in the middle of a hot and humid day, on a wide and busy street in the middle of Washington, D.C.; no one noticed.

* * *

Chapter Six

Special Agent Avery Lucas of the Bureau of Alcohol, Tobacco, and Firearms slammed his fist against the front door of the aged house three times before pulling his nine-millimeter Luger. With all the cutbacks and downsizing, they were spread thin across the Midwest. And with only one backup man, Lucas was nervous. But this one, according to the report, was suppose to be easy.

McCook, Nebraska. The name bothered BATF agent Lucas....something he could not remember; something from the distant past.

He glanced at Larson, his partner, and slammed his fist against the door three more times. Then he stepped back, preparing to kick the door open

But the door swung inward without his assistance.

"Yes?"

The barefooted, blurry-eyed, muscular young man in his mid-thirties wore a vested tee-shirt and blue jeans. "Wha'ja want?"

"Wake up, Lazy!" Lucas threw his entire weight against the front door, shoving the young man back and onto the floor. "You're under arrest, Punk!"

Larson, the backup man, muttered a frustrating, "Oh, hell," as Lucas forced his way into the house.

"You got a warrant?" the young man gasped, staggering to his feet. "— I wanna see the warrant."

But Lucas was in no mood for trivialities. He backhanded the young man with his pistol, sending the kid spinning into the living room and onto the carpet.

"Fuck you, asshole!" Lucas growled. "There's your fuckin' warrant!"

Lucas kicked the blond-haired youth a couple of times, just to be sure. Then the kid groaned, so Lucas hit him again with the pistol. Just to be sure.

"You finished?" Larson asked as he set a revolver and two automatics on the coffee table.

Lucas kicked the semi-conscious kid again, and was rewarded with an agonizing moan. "I think so."

Larson reappeared with an M-5 automatic rifle, two riot shotguns, and a hunting rifle. "Looks like he was preparing for World War Three."

"Jeez!" Lucas muttered. "Looks like a dealer."

"Let's find out." Larson half-pulled, half-lifted the young man off the floor.

"Oops! He's dead."

"Stupid motherfucker!" Lucas snapped. "Who the hell was he, anyway?"

"His name was Bartlett," Larson said, reading the dead man's identification card. "He was a deputy sheriff."

A sickly feeling started welling-up from the pit of Lucas' stomach. "Oh, shit!"

"You said a mouthful."

Lucas looked up into the barrel of a very big gun. Behind it were two badges and two uniformed officers. And they looked very mean.

"Who the hell are you?" Larson demanded.

"Louis Dobbins, Red Willow County Sheriff. My deputy, Bob Lowell. And you are under arrest."

"Not today, I'm afraid," Larson countered, handing his identification to Deputy Lowell. "We're federal agents."

"Bureau of Alcohol, Tobacco, and Firearms," Lowell read.

"Oh, yeah," Dobbins said. "I ran you people outa here ten years ago, after you started harassing all those farmers."

"We remember," Lucas said. "You were wrong then ... and you're wrong now."

"Last time I ran you out of the county," Dobbins growled. "This time you're going to jail. Now up against the wall, motherfuckers!"

One does not argue with two loaded guns. Lucas and Larson leaned against the wall and contemplated their revenge.

———

Her name was Lisa. Just Lisa. She would not admit to a

middle name or a last name. Her age was also a mystery, hidden between twelve and twenty-two, between childlike adolescence and sexual promiscuity. She sported a short, masculine haircut, blue jeans, and a ragged tee-shirt; but she could not hide her body's voluptuous femininity.

She had arrived at Ben Franklyn's farm several years before, a hungry waif (she claimed) looking for work. Ben gave her food, cigarettes, and a place to sleep. She helped with his computer (which he had not fully mastered) and put him on the Internet. And after a few weeks she decided to stay with him.

But while she did not acknowledge her past, she was grimly aware of the immediate future. Standing next to Stan Gorman within a grove of elm trees near a simplistic and forlorn farmhouse just off an unmarked graveled road; she scrutinized the old man's wrinkled and dour face, and studied his icy-blue eyes; searching for reassurance.

She'd spent most of the predawn hours moving the Groff family elsewhere, and wondered now if all the effort had been worth it. Then she saw two gray FBI cars and two gray BATF cars race into the farmyard, followed by a dark-brown and cumbersome SIS van.

She glanced up at the overcast sky. "They're late."

"Uh-huh."

Half-a-dozen federal agents silently formed a perimeter around the farmhouse, while a dozen more surrounded the front door. One agent, armed with a sledgehammer battering ram, opened the door ... and the others rushed in, screaming and cursing and shouting and waving their guns.

From inside the house a muffled voice shouted, "What the fuck?"

Then the farmhouse exploded in a hellish fireball of death and destruction, flinging flaming bodies and burning wood across the lawn and across the yard. Nearby trees and shrubs burst into flames. The SIS van, slammed by fiery debris, flipped on its side. A BATF car, parked too close to the fireball, ignited and was blown apart.

A federal agent, burning like an evergreen tree, staggered around the corner of the flaming farmhouse and fell to the ground. Another human torch made it to the driveway. The flames went out, but the smoldering nightmare remained.

"They use to enforce the law. Now they break it," Stan Gorman sighed, watching the flames consume the wreckage. ".... I guess that Ben was right. But like so many others, I refused to listen. After all, it could never happen here, could it?"

"Ruby Ridge. Waco. Oklahoma City. Jordan, Montana. Kingman, Arizona. Alpine, Texas. Fuck! They control the press, the courts, the judges!" Lisa snapped. "You either goose-step to their tyranny or you die."

"So whatever happened to the land of the free and the home of the brave?"

"I think somebody sold it for thirty pieces of silver."

The sign on the highly-polished rosewood door read:

Judge William Jennings Carter, P.C.
19th Judicial District
State of Nebraska

And like the sign, the room was a glistening reflection of luxurious sterility. The floor-to-ceiling shelves of neatly-aligned law books left little space for the memorabilia collected by the occupant during his many years on the bench. Plaques and certificates surrounded the two darkened windows that stared covetously over Norris Avenue. A large and ancient globe sat silently on its massive pedestal, ignoring everything including the soft, plush carpet supporting its weight. And a singular executive desk dominated this superfluous luxury.

Only the man hiding behind the executive desk and brass nameplate looked out-of-place. It was not really Judge Carter's room, although he had occupied it for over two and a half decades. For the homespun Judge Carter, the room was little more than a collection of bric-a-brac and demented lithography; for he was part of a vanishing breed who felt that "the Law" should come compassionately from the heart and the head, rather than from an intimidating set of voluminous tomes.

Judge William Carter knew those voluminous tomes, and he was not intimidated by them. At times like these, however, he did find them irritating. At times like these they seemed to ignore common sense.

James A. Clayton

"Bill, they were way out of line and way out of their jurisdiction. They murdered my deputy. And now you're telling me that I have to release them?"

Judge William Jennings Carter studied the green felt of his desk blotter and sighed heavily. "Sorry, Lou. The Feds insist. They're claiming jurisdiction."

"That's bullshit!"

"I know," Carter said, "but there's nothing I can do about it. Federal enforcement agents have killed hundreds, perhaps even thousands, of people — good, bad, or otherwise. But not one has ever been arrested or indicted while he was — on the job."

"Really? What about those two I've got locked up down in the jail?" "Officially — they're not under arrest."

"*That* stinks to high heaven. Hell, Bill, we've had run-ins with the Feds before."

"I know, but ... something's changed. Actually I've seen this coming for some time now." Carter took a file folder from his desk drawer and handed it to Sheriff Dobbins as if it were a poisonous snake. "Tell me, Lou, have you ever heard of the S.I.S.?"

"S.I.S.?" He opened the file folder, but his mind was elsewhere. "Special Investigative Services, the enforcement unit of a C.I.R.G., or Critical Incident Response Group."

Carter nodded in agreement while Dobbins continued to think aloud. "They're an elite F.B.I. unit, sort of a super-SWAT team for hostage situations, terrorist groups, and so forth."

"That was the original idea," Carter said. "Just a few units scattered around the country, an administrative response to the standoff at Waco. But like everything else that Washington creates, it grew far beyond their stated intent and took on a life of its own. Now they've even assigned a group to Western Nebraska."

"You're kidding!"

"I wish I was," Carter said, pointing at the file folder, "but that file is their hit list for the next three months. Everyone around here who owns a rifle, shotgun, B.B. gun, or cap pistol. They might as well have used a telephone book."

Judge Carter pulled a cigarette lighter, an ash tray, and a pack of Doral Full-Flavor 100s from his desk drawer. "I was going to give these up," he said as he lit up.

"I'm on the list. You're on the list. Your deputies are on the list. The mayor and the city council are on the list." Carter sighed and shook his head. "In fact, most of McCook is on their list."

"What should I do about it, Bill?"

"I really don't know what you can do about these guys," Carter admitted with another sigh. "They're Feds, so you can't arrest them. But ...."

"But?"

"Well, I'll leave that up to you." Dobbins thought about it for a long time. He studied the globe and read the titles on the law books. He gazed into the darkness at the church across the street and read the plaques positioned around the windows. He even smoked one of Carter's cigarettes ... and almost choked on it.

"Okay. First things first. I want Turner to stay with you tonight. And preferably some place out of town. If I have to turn those two lose ...."

"A point well taken," Carter agreed. "What about you?"

"Oh, I'll be at an all-night poker game with some of my deputies," Dobbins said. "And tomorrow you and I will make a phone call to Washington, D.C. Hell, there must be some sort of civilization left in this country!"

―――

They met after midnight in the shadows of the Lincoln Memorial with their hearts in their throats and the weight of the world on their shoulders. The DCI waited, however, for the three Secret Service agents to move away before he spoke. "The Chairman of the Federal Reserve was your man?"

"Yes," the President acknowledged. "Did you find him?"

"Yes," the DCI said. "We found him in the back seat of his car in a Pentagon parking lot."

"Audacious."

"Professional hitman. Three shots at close range."

"And the chauffeur?"

"We found him floating face down in the Potomac."

The President stoically acknowledged the loss with a single, curt nod. "You've seen my Secret Service contingent. People are leaving left and right. Some leave letters of resignation. Others just leave. .... Hell! The White House is practically empty."

"On the other hand, Echo-Three is relatively secure, and the Satellite Surveillance Systems have been shut down. You've grounded all the planes and missiles, locked-up most of the tanks and heavy artillery, and sank the Navy."

The President of the United States bummed a cigarette and a light from his DCI while shaking his head. "What about Wilder?"

"Unknown." Jack Kent lit a Marlboro and pocketed his lighter. "An Air Commodore Harmon and a Lieutenant McVey are also reported missing."

"Any connection?"

"Harmon and Wilder shared a desk at NATO. I've talked to Wilder several times. And Harmon was an asset over there on more than one occasion."

"Damn!"

The President took a long drag and blew the smoke skyward. "I got a call earlier today from the Secretary-General of the United Nations. Both the World Bank and the International Monetary Fund are worried about our balance-of-payments."

"Then it's started?"

"They've got six out of ten military district commanders in their hip pocket," the President sighed. "Either I declare bankruptcy or they'll declare civil war — and move in anyway. To keep the peace and maintain order, of course."

"So day-after-tomorrow you declare that this country is bankrupt and vanish off the face of the Earth?"

"In Wainwright, Alaska."

"Everything's ready for the switch in Denver."

"Good. What about Latimer?"

"He's moving people around, but they're stretched pretty thin. And he's losing agents left and right. We screened an additional two hundred more and sent them on to Echo-Three."

"Take care of that son-of-a-bitch, Jack. Whatever else you do, take care of him."

DCI Jack Kent stepped on the President's discarded cigarette butt and nodded.

———

Stan Gorman's convenience store on "B" Street after baseball practice. Deputy Sheriff Lou Dobbins and his foster son, Bob Lowell, had stopped in for Cokes and cream puffs, as usual. Three kids from a car with out-of-state plates had also stopped in ... to rob the place. The oldest and most nervous kid spotted the badge, swung around, and fired. The gun went off like a cannon, ripping his shoulder apart. He dropped to the floor, writhing in fiery pain, while his own gun went flying elsewhere. Then the young punk was standing over him, preparing to shoot him at point-blank range. Only another gun exploded. And Bob Lowell kept firing his foster-father's revolver until it was empty ... and the young punk was dead.

Sheriff Louis Dobbins awoke screaming. Deputy Tod Lawrence arrived first, shaking Dobbins awake.

"Bad dreams?"

"The worst."

"The shooting at Stan Gorman's convenience store?"

"Of course," Dobbins nodded, sitting up and trying to shake the sleep from his eyes.

"But that was years ago."

"It comes back now and then," Dobbins muttered. "Not very often any more, but ..."

"Bob was still in high school then, wasn't he?"

"Uh-huh. And I'd just gotten married at the ripe old age of forty-one."

"Yeah, well, maybe we should play some poker," Lawrence offered, "just to keep it honest."

"Yeah. Who's on guard?"

"Ed. And before you ask, it's eleven p.m."

"Great," Dobbins muttered, reaching for his telephone. "Now's a great time for checking on Dora and the kids."

Judge William Jennings Carter parked the ancient but serviceable pickup behind the decrepit farmhouse, checking to make certain it could not be seen from the road. Deputy Charles Turner, in full uniform and sparse mustache, climbed out and studied the dark landscape with a practiced eye. But Judge Carter was not impressed.

"Look, I know Lou means well, but let's face it, one deputy out here won't even slow 'em down."

Turner pulled his riot shotgun from behind the seat, slammed the passenger door shut, and shook his head. "You think this lonely little place out in the country, out in the middle of nowhere, will stop them?"

"No," Carter chuckled, "but at least they'll have a hard time finding me."

James A. Clayton

"Hell, I don't even know where I'm at," Turner complained.

"Sure you do. The middle of nowhere." Carter opened the back door and Turner followed him in.

From the ancient and musty smell, Turner concluded that Judge Carter did not really spend a lot of time here in the middle of nowhere.

"Now where's that damn switch?" Carter flipped on the lights, revealing a kitchen recently cleaned — several weeks earlier. "A friend of mine lets me use this place from time to time, so I can be alone."

"Well, you're alone all right," Turner agreed, examining the coffee pot. "Far away from everything."

"There are times when I prefer solitude," Carter said, sitting down at the barren kitchen table.

"Like when you're forced to release a couple of killers simply because they worked for the federal government?"

Yes," Carter sighed, watching Turner measure teaspoonfuls of coffee into the electric percolator. "We use to have a government of the people, for the people, and by the people. Now it seems to be a government of the bureaucrats, for the politicians, by the federal goon squads."

"Yeah, well, this whole thing sounds crazy to me," Turner said, turning on the percolator. "I guess I'm too young to remember the good old days — whatever they were."

Carter smiled. "There's a lot of your father in you."

"So I've been told — repeatedly."

Carter lit a cigarette and Turner found an ash tray in the kitchen sink. "It's in the history books, if you read between the lines. The people use to run the government. Now the government runs the people."

"And you're beginning to sound like my father," Charlie Turner said. "Of course! Hell! Ned knew. The government has used crime and terrorism as an excuse to grab and hold power. Rather ironic, since they are the criminals and the terrorists."

Turner pored two cups of steaming coffee and stuck the pot back under the coffeemaker. "That is frightening."

"Not to mention illegal," Carter mused, sipping his coffee. "Maybe it's time for me to retire."

He might have said more, but six FBI agents smashed down

the door and rushed into the kitchen. Four agents literally came through the back door, screaming and shouting and waving their pistols. Two more broke in through the front, cursing and stumbling over the dining room chairs en route.

"Hands!" one agent screamed hysterically. "Let's see your hands!"

"This is an illegal assembly!" another agent shouted. "You're all under arrest!"

"Down on the floor! Face down! Now!" yelled a third. "Down, you mothers! Down!"

But neither the old man nor the young man could react fast enough to satisfy these terrorists. Amidst much shouting, cursing, and screaming; the FBI knocked Judge Carter and Deputy Turner from their chairs and onto the floor. They kicked Turner in the stomach a couple of times before jerking him to his feet. Then they clubbed him on his head while another agent snatched his pistol from its holster to reinforce a backhand swipe at a tottering Judge Carter.

Two agents flipped the kitchen table, splashing hot coffee against the walls and breaking both cups. One smashed a wooden chair over a battered and bloodied Deputy Turner, smearing him across the kitchen's linoleum floor. The other just smashed the two remaining chairs.

With nothing better to do, the remaining agents smashed cups, plates, dishes, the coffeemaker, the coffee pot, the window panes, vases, bric-a-brac, and anything else that could be broken or smashed. They ripped the doors off the cupboards and dumped the contents of each kitchen drawer onto the scarred linoleum floor. Then a couple of them took time-off to kick Judge Carter and Deputy Turner a few more times — just for the fun of it.

Special Agent in Charge Matthew Sullivan entered the kitchen through the smashed back door, abruptly ending their wanton destruction and silencing their loud obscenities. Without a word he crossed the kitchen and set his briefcase down by the doorway into the dining room. Then he turned to face his men, and in his best Clint Eastwood imitation whispered, "Bravo. Bravo."

His eyes swept the room, icily recording the damage and the two battered bodies. The judge and one of the deputies — hardly worth all this effort, he concluded.

The youngest agent had more bravery than brains. "Is this

legal?" he asked. "There's just two of 'em."

"They're part of a much bigger gang of terrorists!"

"Yes, it's legal," Sullivan said, sensing trouble. "But a little too rough. Let's talk outside, gentlemen."

He hesitated at the back door, then turned to the youthful agent. "Josh, keep an eye on 'em. But for heaven's sake, don't hurt 'em."

"Yes, sir!"

"Christ, looks like they've been through a meat grinder!"

Sullivan and the other FBI agents left; leaving their smiling young protege in charge of Judge Carter, Deputy Turner, a vandalized farmhouse, and an official-looking briefcase. They walked around the pickup, past the bales of hay, and beyond the line of trees to where their cars were hidden. No one spoke until they'd reached their destination.

Then Sullivan said, "I guess that kid will never learn that you can't always do things by the book, especially not with these criminals. .... Sorry, kid."

He produced a small remote-control device, flipped open the cover, and pushed the red button.

Behind them, in the darkness, the decrepit farmhouse blew apart in a tremendous blast that shook the countryside, scattered flaming wood splinters and debris across the lawn, and engulfed the remaining ruins in a hellish fireball that was visible for miles.

"Let's go home," Sullivan sighed.

* * *

Chapter Seven

There is a sign painted on the second window east of the double glass doors on the south side of the gray-white granite fortress of the Red Willow County Courthouse. The sign reads:

"Sheriff Louis Dobbins
McCook, Nebraska"

Being the county sheriff is an elected position in Nebraska, and Dobbins never took the elections for granted, even when his opponents voted for him. He ran fast and hard just to stay in the same position. But he was not a political animal.

Today, however, he felt something less than human. He had read the SIS hit list several times, always with a sinking sensation. Each name in the long and depressing alphabetical listing had at least one letter, "A" through "J", next to it. At the end of the list, on the final page, he found an explanation for the letter code. And after he read the explanation, his heart sank into his shoes.

A .... Suspected of Arms Violations.
B .... Suspected of Narcotics Violations.
C .... Suspected of I.R.S. Violations.
D .... Suspected of Anti-Government Activities.
E .... Suspected of Supporting Anti-Government Activities.
F .... Suspected of Disloyalty.
G .... Released from Prison for Technical Reasons.
H .... Homosexual.
I .... Ex-Convicts and Probationers.
J .... Hoarding and Related Crimes.

James A. Clayton

"Might as well just arrest the whole damn country," Dobbins muttered. Only these people seldom arrested anyone. It was a catchall to catch all, and just about everyone was guilty of something.

He slipped the stapled SIS hit list into a file folder and carried it out to "E" Street. It was almost noon, but the usually-bustling streets of McCook seemed exceptionally empty.

"Morning, Lou."

"Bob."

"Looks like we have the entire town to ourselves."

"Everybody either moved out of town or went into hiding ... yesterday," Dobbins sighed.

Deputy Sheriff Robert (Bob) Lowell tightened his grip on the steering wheel until his knuckles turned white. His lips compressed into a tight, thin line and a low, rumbling growl escaped from his throat. He stared straight ahead, but saw nothing.

Dobbins had seen it once before, when Lowell's wife had died in childbirth. And when the doctor told him the baby had also died, Lowell had put his fist through a stucco wall before going to sit in his patrol car and stare sullenly into space.

"Don't panic on me."

"I won't," Lowell growled. "I didn't before. I won't again."

"Here, take this before they find out I have an extra copy."

"What is it?"

"The S.I.S. hit list for Western Nebraska. A list of names and dates, of when and where they'll strike next."

"The S.I.S.?" Lowell flipped his way through the file folder, growling softly. "What's their complaint? Local interference? .... Bartlett? .... Robbins?"

"Yesterday they got young Deputy Turner *and* Judge Carter."

"Bill Carter?"

Sheriff Louis Dobbins nodded grimly. "You'll find their names on the list. .... And you'll find their bodies in the morgue."

"Damn! The world has gone mad! It's been years since we gave the feds the runaround."

"They don't forgive. They don't forget. And they don't give up. *Ever.*"

"No wonder everybody left town."

Dobbins offered a half-smile of condolence.

"So what do I do with this list?" Lowell asked, holding up

the file folder.

"Take it to Stan Gorman. Have him get it to Ben Franklyn's militia group."

"That so-called patriot militia? They're not exactly local law enforcement."

"I know, Bob, but they're all I've got. Another week or two and there won't be any local law enforcement left. At least nothing we can count on."

"I thought you were still mad at him because of that Oklahoma City business a few years back."

"He was right ... and I was wrong," Dobbins shrugged. ".... Water under the bridge."

"Sure, but he's so unpredictable."

"Take a look at the last page." Lowell flipped to it.

"Suspected arms violations. Narcotics violations. Anti-government activities? Disloyalty? What the hell?"

"Look, Bob, these S.I.S. guys are worse than those Nazi Storm Troopers. And I have neither the manpower nor the firepower to stop them. Besides, Ben Franklyn owes us."

"What about the National Guard?"

"Most of them are over in Bosnia, or someplace. The highway patrol and state police have disappeared. And everyone else is out of town."

"Have you tried talking to Washington?"

"Of course. They put me on hold. Finally ended up with a recorded message, something about an independent command-and-control system ... otherwise known as bullshit."

"Yes, they're good at that," Lowell said. "Probably shoveling leftovers from the six o'clock news."

"Maybe. But you'd think that between closing the Job Service offices and losing their Social Security checks, people might have figured out something."

"They're only sheep, Lou. But we must protect them from the wolves." Bob Lowell hesitated, thoughtfully examining the steering wheel of his patrol car. "I remember that after my wife died, I thought those wolves would devour me, too. But I was wrong, Lou. .... I was wrong."

"No, you weren't wrong, Bob. Just a bit premature." He slapped the roof of the patrol car. "Have a nice day."

"My horoscope said I should take a long vacation."

Lowell backed his patrol car from the diagonal parking space and headed west. Past the *McCook Daily Gazette*, he turned south onto First Street West, heading downhill towards the highway. Some stores on "C" Street were open, but there were few customers. The presence of federal authorities did not help business. And the presence of two unmarked gray cars following him did not help his composure.

They would be monitoring his radio frequencies. He could not lead them to Stan Gorman's home. And the City of McCook was no place for a high-speed chase — especially if he was the one being chased.

He turned right onto "B" Street — Highways 6, 34, and 83. Past the Hinky-Dinky Supermarket and the closed AmFirst Bank, he turned left onto Federal, went under the railroad viaduct, turning right onto County Road 1535. So far, so peaceful; but the unmarked gray cars were getting closer and closer.

Turning south again, he squealed his tires on the asphalt and was doing ninety-five across the Republican River bridge. Beyond the bridge he floored his patrol car and flew off the asphalt onto the gravel, spitting stones and raising a cloud of gritty gray dust.

"Choke on this, you mothers!"

But they did not hear him, and they could not see him. They could only ram their accelerators into the floorboards and follow his cloud of gritty gray dust.

Let it be known that FBI agents are among the fastest and most reckless drivers in the nation, a fact attested by numerous automobile accidents. They cannot be stopped by traffic laws, but they are often stopped by the laws of physics.

In this case they were traveling at breakneck speeds over an unfamiliar gravel road. And they traveled all over the road, even to skidding almost sideways, in an attempt to catch the fleeing patrol car. Risking life and limb, they hurtled into the cloud of dust — and suddenly found themselves on the other side. The patrol car had made a sharp turn to the right, onto another gravel road.

The unmarked gray cars skidded to a halt and backed up. It was not a perfect turnaround, but at least they were headed in the right direction. On the other hand, they'd lost more than a mile to the speeding patrol car.

Deputy Bob Lowell skidded around two more intersections, first left and then right, leaving the unmarked FBI cars far behind. They probably saw him turn into Ben Franklyn's tree-lined drive, but he was committed. And so were they.

The patrol car slid to a halt near the two-story house at the rear of the tree-enclosed farmyard, and more-or-less in front of the old and apparently decrepit barn. One swift glance told him that several new items had been added to the ill-assorted collection gathered within the yard. Farm implements, hay bales, and stacks of lumber had been strategically positioned around the open farmyard. It looked innocent enough, but ....

Bob Lowell got out of his patrol car with a pump shotgun in one hand and the file folder in the other. Five militiamen, armed with rifles and shotguns, emerged from concealment behind bales of hay and stacks of lumber.

With their rifles and shotguns pointed at him, the five militiamen created a wide half-circle around the lone deputy. But his shotgun remained pointed at the sky.

"Ben! Ben Franklyn! It's Bob Lowell. — I need your help." Lisa came from the barn, smiling. The militiamen lowered their guns. And Benjamin Franklyn came from the farmhouse, laughing.

"You need my help? .... Sure you're not here to arrest me?"

The two unmarked FBI cars pulled into the driveway and parked side-by-side, blocking the entrance.

"Friends of yours?"

"It's no joke, Ben. We've saved your ass before. Several times. Now it's your turn." Lowell handed over the file folder and turned towards the two gray cars in the driveway. "Those feds have been following me all over the county, trying to get this file."

Ben Franklyn turned a few pages in the file, and curiosity turned into shock. "This is the current S.I.S. hit list for this area!"

"Yes, it is," Lowell said flatly. "And they'll kill to get it."

"Those bastards would kill all of us in an instant," Ben muttered, handing the file folder to Lisa. "You'd better hide this until we're ready to leave."

"Yeah, okay, but you keep an eye on 'em, huh?" Lisa cautioned. "Don't forget that stunt they pulled off up in Jordan."

"Jordan, Montana?" Lowell asked as Lisa left.

"Yes," Ben said. "Jordan, Montana ... where the F.B.I. used

trickery and deceit to kill freedom and take out their revenge on the so-called 'Freemen'.

".... Lisa's the best student I ever had. The daughter I never had."

At the far end of the driveway seven heavily-armed FBI agents carefully climbed from their gray cars to assess the situation.

"Careful," Lowell warned in a low voice. "Something's happening over there."

Tense and nervous, the seven FBI agents stayed close to their cars for reinforced self-protection. They were naked and vulnerable sitting at the end of the driveway, and they knew it. The situation was far less than ideal.

"Well, what do you think?" the agent-in-charge asked.

"Reminds me of Ruby Ridge."

"Ruby Ridge was a standoff. We can't afford to wait."

"Yeah. Okay. But we can't afford to attack either."

"Right. No choice," the SAC agreed. "I'll call for our backup."

The FBI man started to get back into his car, but stopped at the sound of Ben Franklyn shouting, "You are under arrest. Drop your guns and raise your hands."

Unfortunately two FBI agents, in a spirited self-defense, raised their weapons. It was a horrible, stupid, and tragic mistake. A fatal mistake.

At least fifteen automatic and semi-automatic rifles, and over a dozen shotguns, fired in unison. Unknown to the FBI agents, more militiamen were hidden in the trees on either side of them. And some of these militiamen had old scores to settle with the faceless federal men.

Bullets ripped into the agents and into their cars. Blood and gore spurted as they were jerked about and bounced off the unmarked vehicles in a macabre dance of death. One agent's head literally exploded as shells smashed his skull into pulp. Another died as bullets drilled their way under his bulletproof vest. Two more collapsed as their Kevlar vests shattered and shredded under the impacted of an uncountable number of blasts.

The unmarked FBI cars were smeared with blood and riddled with bullets. Their hoods and their trunks popped open. Their bulletproof safety glass shattered and crumpled. Chunks of side-paneling were gouged and ripped into jagged bits and pieces. And all eight tires were shredded and brutally deflated.

All seven FBI agents went down, and only one was barely alive. A bullet in the back of his head ended his pain and misery.

"I wonder if they would have been as kind?" Lowell asked, not really seeking an answer.

Two old John Deere tractors, with chains hooked around their drawbars, dragged the gray wreckage into the barn, while the militiamen removed the weapons and ammunition from the bodies and the shattered vehicles. (They also checked the satellite phones and computer uplinks, but these had been damaged beyond repair.) Bob Lowell, meanwhile, recovered two small black boxes, one from each trunk of the wrecked automobiles, just as Lisa drove up in an old and battered pickup truck.

"I got the pickup, but what do you want to do with it?"

"Put that one on the seat beside you," Lowell said, handing her a small black box. "I'll put the other one in back. Drive down the road about three miles and hide them in some tall weeds. But make sure you keep them apart. — Understood?"

She ran her long fingers through her short hair and shook her head. "Okay, but what are they?"

"G.P.S. satellite tracking," Ben explained as Bob Lowell walked to the rear of the pickup truck. "The F.B.I. doesn't trust its own people, let alone ordinary civilians. .... Now get going. We'll need the pickup back here."

Lisa slammed the pickup into first gear and drove away, leaving the young deputy and the old farmer in the dust. But neither man wanted to admit that civilization, as they knew it, was ending.

They watched, instead, as the militiamen dumped the bloodied bodies of the FBI agents into the wrecked remains of the gray government cars hidden within the barn. And they watched as the militiamen efficiently cleaned up the graveled entrance and the farmyard.

This one, they knew, would not go away.

"Well, that should buy us some time. Hopefully."

"Some," Lowell agreed, surveying the relatively pristine farmyard. "But I think you'd better make plans to move."

"Way ahead of you," Ben said, lighting a cigarette. "We'll be out of here in fifteen minutes. Well, almost. I want to leave a few surprises in the house and the barn ... just in case we have some unwelcome guests."

Bob Lowell nodded knowingly. "I guess this makes me a criminal, too. Murder in the first."

"I remember some stumble-bum of an attorney down in Arizona once told me that 'the Law' was morality. I suppose that means that you can buy morality for about two hundred dollars an hour. But if that's the case, it ain't worth it."

"No, you weren't buying morality," Lowell corrected. "You were buying freedom. And at that rate, the price was pretty cheap."

"Uh-huh. Well. At least they dropped the charges."

"Which were?"

"Felony possession of three milk carton cases."

"That's a crime?"

"In Arizona it is. — They had a gung-ho Attorney General who wanted to arrest everybody. Damn near succeeded, too."

"Sounds familiar." Lowell's eyes wandered to the now-clean and pristine driveway. "Like Lou always says: 'A cop without compassion is a tyrant'."

"It is a capital offense to kill a federal agent. But they can kill anyone, any time, for any reason ... and get away with it."

"Yeah, they're good at that," Lowell grumbled, letting his eyes roam across the farmyard.

"We did ... what had to be done."

"I'm worried about Lou. They came after me. They might go after him."

"You and Lou have always been close, haven't you?"

"Ever since my aunt died. He took me in, put me through high school and college ...."

"Maybe I was wrong," Ben admitted with an eloquent shrug. "Personally, I always thought Lou was a little stiff, especially after the Oklahoma City incident. — But maybe he had other things on his mind."

"Yeah, maybe," Lowell sighed. "Oh, I almost forgot — Lou wanted me to take that file folder to Stan Gorman, and let him deliver it to you. That was before the feds got on my ass."

"You're not making it any easier for me, son. We'll have to move both Lou and Stan, and their families, to ... someplace."

"Sorry about that."

"Let's just hope it's not too late." He glanced at his watch. "Len, can you spare the portable radio for a few minutes?"

"Yeah, sure," the militiaman said, setting the monstrous old 'boom box' on the hood of Lowell's patrol car. "Should be about news time."

"Hope we're not too late," Ben Franklyn muttered, adjusting the dials on the monster. Then, from the radio:

"Recapping the news to this hour," the newscaster began, "The President of the United States has requested time on all radio and television stations for a major public policy message. And while the White House has refused to discuss the nature of this policy address, they have steadfastly denied that it has anything to do with the plane crash which claimed the life of the Director of the Federal Bureau of Investigation, or with the strange and unexplained illness which has incapacitated the Chairman of the Federal Reserve Board. .... This just handed to me: Senator Nathanial Burdett, President Pro Tempore of the Senate, has just departed for Alaska on an unannounced fact-finding mission. .... What the hell is going on here, Brian?"

A burst of static wiped out the newscaster, who was replaced within a few seconds by a familiar commercial for a foreign automobile manufacturer. Ben Franklyn turned off the radio and signaled to Len.

"Now what?" Ben muttered, lighting another cigarette.

"I'm not sure," Lowell said, "but reading between the lines, I think we're in big trouble."

"I hate to say it, but I think you're right."

―――

The ancient lobby was now empty, as were the jail cells in back. Sheriff Louis Dobbins had instructed him to release all the prisoners and get them out of town as quickly and quietly as possible. They were, perhaps, the strangest set of instructions Dobbins had ever issued, but Senior Deputy Sheriff Tod Lawrence was becoming use to strange orders and directives.

"Sir, I released all the prisoners like you ordered. And I told them to get out of town. But ―"

"Good!" Dobbins snapped, cutting him off. "Make sure both your shotguns, and your pistol, are loaded and ready. And expect trouble."

"Sir?"

But Dobbins had already passed through the next door and into the hallway that passed his office.

There was a comfortable and familiar feeling about the old office, with its oaken desk and chair backed up against the tall double windows with their Venetian blinds. Opposite the desk a well-worn couch underlined the row of plate-glass windows that divided the office from the hallway, and stretched from the file cabinets against the west wall to the entrance door abutting the east wall. Except for the gun rack and a few commemorative plaques, the east wall was virtually barren.

He would miss this office, he thought, but he had no time for recollections. With a proficiency born of long practice, he loaded the pump shotgun and placed it on his desk. Then he heard the noise from the outer office.

"May I help you?" Then there was a crashing sound, as if someone was trying to break down the outer door.

"Hey! Hold it! That's restricted!"

Deputy Tod Lawrence was interrupted by the deafening double roar of two shotguns fired almost simultaneously. A short scream of agonizing pain provided an exclamation point.

Dobbins snapped the breech of the riot shotgun shut as six FBI agents smashed open the inner door and rushed down the hallway. In classical fashion, one of the FBI agents leaned back against the far wall and kicked open the office door.

Dobbins fired. The FBI agent was blown back out the door, his bulletproof vest punctured and shattered by the force of the blast.

Dobbins managed to fire twice more, cutting down a second FBI attacker before the others opened fire, shattering all the remaining plate-glass windows and ripping his office — and his body — to shreds.

"Bastards are using Shredders!" an agent shouted over the roar of automatic rifles and shotguns.

"But aren't Shredders illegal?" screamed another.

Then the rifle fire and shotgun blasts stopped. There was nothing left to shoot. But the silence made them feel exposed and vulnerable.

The four surviving federal agents were forced to step over the outstretched legs of the late Senior Deputy Sheriff Tod Lawrence.

New World Order

They were acting under orders, of course, but the uniformed body on the floor made that concept seem rather hollow and barren.

Two more federal agents were nervously waiting within the darkened lobby, ostensibly guarding the bloodied body of a dead FBI agent.

"Leave him," the agent-in-charge snapped. The lobby and outer office had been blasted apart. Shards of glass and splinters of wood covered the ornate marble floor. Plaster dust and broken furniture were scattered haphazardly around the room. The body, the blood smears, and the wreckage made all six FBI agents very nervous ... and rather ill.

They huddled together on the steps just outside the County Courthouse, terrified and blinded by the brilliant noonday sun. Searching through the glare for their unmarked gray sedans, they were unaware of the shadowy figure high above them.

Hidden behind the cornices around the roof of the four-story apartment building, Deputy Sheriff Ed Hudson took his time. He wanted to be sure of his targets. Dead sure.

Six shots rang out. Two agents bounced off the Courthouse and rolled across the sidewalk, splattering blood over the granite and the concrete. They died almost instantly, while the other four fired their pistols wildly in all directions, hoping to hit what they could not see.

But snipers must be patient. Ed Hudson slipped away undetected, letting the four federal agents blaze away at a target that was no longer there. Even inside the building, following a carefully chosen escape route, he could hear them shooting aimlessly at illusive shadows.

Eventually the shooting stopped. Four frightened federal agents, hot and sweaty and terrified, ducked into their unmarked gray automobiles and fled to the tune of squealing tires.

* * *

Chapter Eight

The President of the United States was uncomfortable, to say the least. The standard embellishments of the Presidency — the blue carpet with its gold presidential seal, the flags, the pictures, the paintings, the plaques, the papers, the potted plants, the lace curtains, the sofa, the set decorations, the Secret Service guards, the personal valet, the hair dresser, the make-up man, the maids, the cooks, the waiters, the doormen, the limosine with driver — were all gone. The White House was now an empty building where even the President of the United States had to get permission to pass through security checkpoints.

Years before Congress had, through an impeachment trial, stripped away the authority. Now European bankers had, through an alleged fiscal crisis, stripped away the dignity. And there wasn't much left of the Presidency.

Overwhelmed by depressive isolation, the President of the United States lit a Camel cigarette and contemplated the greenery beyond the second-story window. His vice-presidential nominee had been shipped to Wainwright, Alaska, along with several congressmen. His Secretary of State was wandering around Uzbekistan. His Attorney General had simply vanished. And he was about to commit political suicide.

He brushed aside the chilling thoughts and concentrated on the speech. It was not, of course, his speech. They had written it for him. And they had repeatedly assured him that once he declared Martial Law, he could rule the country through presidential proclamations.

That was, of course, a blatant lie. Once he declared Martial Law, FEMA would take charge of the government and the military ... and operate under the instructions of certain European bankers. But how do you tell the American people that European bankers now

New World Order

owned the United States of America?

With a confusing admixture of gobbledegook supplied by DCI Jacob Andrew Kent, the President had talked them out of videotaping his speech. A live speech, he had assured them, was essential for a peaceful transition.

Out of sheer cussedness he would see it through to the bitter end. He would deliver their speech with all the glib innocence he could muster. He would ask for a quiet and peaceful transition, knowing that the American people would never accept such a transparent dictatorship. Flying him into exile in Wainwright, Alaska, would be their final error.

Vowing revenge for their perfidy and their arrogance; he cleared his throat, hugged his wife, and began the long walk down the short hallway. After this, he thought, he would no longer take the easy way out. The price of expediency was too high.

The sign outside the sickly-green house read: *"Stan Gorman and family."* The family consisted of a maturing and rather tall wife named Sharon, a lazy and rather overweight fifteen-year-old son named Albert, a one-year-old black Labrador retriever named Misty, and a pure-white cat of questionable lineage named Cat.

A year before Stan Gorman had sold his convenience store and hid the profits in an offshore trust account. Now he was pushing fifty, his hair was turning gray, and he was planning to move his family out of Nebraska and out of the country within a year or two ... before the confiscatory taxing policies of the IRS caught up with him.

Located on Highway 83 about a mile south of the Republican River; the modest, nondescript, sickly-green, middle-classed, one-story house with attached garage was up for sale. The banks, however, refused to loan any money to anyone for anything, regardless of their so-called credit history. It was the Great Depression revisited, lacking only the soup kitchens and the stock market crash to make it really grim.

But farmers are an independent bunch, use to struggling through hard times. And Stanley Gorman was, in his heart-and-soul, a farmer. He lived with them. He worked with them. He suffered with them. He celebrated with them. But above all, he respected them.

Thus he had intrusted his home to a farmer and made plans to move. But with the coming of the SIS tactical raids, he had watched his dreams fall apart.

Sitting now in his overstuffed easy chair in the corner of the living room, staring at the threadbare carpet and the worn-out couch and the ancient television set, he considered the available alternatives.

Someplace in the middle of that contemplation his wife Sharon walked in and turned on the television. It was time for her "soap operas." And Stan began to regret giving up his satellite dish.

Some time later Albert lumbered in and plopped himself down on the worn-out couch in front of the wide double windows. Stan glanced at Albert, and his son shrugged. Stan raised an eyebrow.

"We need a new lawn mower."

Stan nodded. Their lawn mower was on its last leg. Or wheel. Even Albert's best efforts could not keep up with the parts that were breaking down.

"We need a new lawn mower," Stan agreed.

Then Sharon turned up the sound.

"Ladies and gentlemen, the President of the United States."

"Why do we have to watch this bullshit?" Albert grumbled.

"Well," Stan Gorman chuckled, "he might just be announcing the end of the world."

Albert shrugged again as the electronic reproduction of the President of the United States flickered into life on their forlorn television set. The picture was good, but the President looked bad.

"My fellow Americans," the President began, "please forgive me for interrupting your lives on this beautiful day. This matter is, however, so serious that I ask you to stop for a few moments and pray for the government of the United States and your elected representatives."

The television camera changed angles. The President still looked haggard and unshaven.

"As you know, ninety days ago I found it necessary to again veto a budget presented to me by the Congress, since it failed to provide the minimal aid I deemed necessary to protect the citizens of our great country. As a result, Congress forced me to close down a major portion of the federal government, including the National Parks, the Passport Offices, Social Security, the Veterans Administration,

Federal Job Services, Food Stamps, the Nuclear Regulatory Commission, the Environmental Protection Agency, the Federal Deposit Insurance Corporation, the General Services Administration, and many other agencies and bureaus servicing the citizens of our great country."

The President stopped then, and did something no other President had ever done on national television. He lit a cigarette ... and inhaled.

"It must be bad," Sharon said.

On the television screen the President exhaled, blowing smoke towards the camera ... and towards the viewers.

"I wonder what he's really trying to tell us?" Stan Gorman thought aloud.

"Maybe it's all smoke and mirrors," Albert offered.

"Because Congress repeatedly refused to give me an acceptable budget, or even an acceptable Continuing Resolution," the President continued, "the United States failed to meet a required payment on the National Debt Service. .... This shortfall was not acceptable to the World Bank. .... Nor was it acceptable to our creditors."

The President inhaled. A new camera angle flickered onto the screen. But no angle, no matter how unique, could conceal the stress and the strain. The President exhaled, blowing smoke towards the ceiling.

"I have, therefore, been ordered by the United Nations to declare that our country, the United States of America, is bankrupt and insolvent."

———

Although he was watching the convoy of cars and pickups in his rear view mirror, Deputy Robert Lowell's mind was on the President's depressing message of despair being transmitted through his patrol car's radio.

"In order to protect personal safety and maintain public order," the President said, "I am also declaring a State of Emergency to be enforced by Martial Law throughout this nation, in all fifty states, and in all our possessions. This Declaration of Martial Law will effectively suspend the Constitution of the United States, the Bill of Rights, and all subsequent amendments. .... All laws will be administered under the War Powers Act, the Uniform Commercial Code, the British Admiralty Act, and related codicils."

Stan Gorman was sitting on the edge of his easy chair, shaking his head and muttering, "Stupid," over and over again. Had everyone in Washington, D.C., gone stark raving mad?

The screen flickered again. At an oblique angle, just off to the left of the President's desk, a blue-helmeted United Nations' soldier, in full battle gear including a deadly M-16 automatic rifle, stood threateningly silent over an embattled and beleaguered President.

"To enforce Martial Law and to maintain public order, the Secretary-General of the United Nations will assume temporary command of all U.S. military forces. I understand that he plans to augment our present military forces with additional elements from NATO and other U.N. member nations. .... Please remember that these troops are here to serve and to protect you during this time of crisis."

Stan Gorman came off the edge of his easy chair and marched to the television set. For a moment Sharon wondered if he intended to turn it off or kick it into oblivion.

"Finally, I would ask that you be patient during this difficult time of trial and tribulation —"

"Fuck you, Mr. President."

And Stan Gorman switched off the television set.

"You were right, Dad," Albert chuckled. "He was announcing the end of the world."

"But there was nothing on the news ...." Sharon protested.

"They control the news!" Stan snapped. "All we heard were a few veiled references about a budget crisis."

"What about the army?" Albert asked.

But Stan was staring over Albert's head and out the front windows, lost in thought.

"I don't know," Stan murmured. "Let's ask Ben."

"Ben?" Sharon turned around on the couch. "What's he doing here?"

"Let's find out." And Stan opened the front door.

The long convoy of cars, pickups, vans, and miscellaneous vehicles, all escorted by Bob Lowell's patrol car, stopped the shoulder of Highway 83 to the south of Stan Gorman's sickly-green cottage. Ben Franklyn climbed from the patrol car's passenger seat and walked back to the second pickup in the long line, while Bob Lowell joined Stan on his front porch.

"Stan, I just delivered an S.I.S. hit list to Ben. The F.B.I. will be here shortly. It would be best if you and your family were ... elsewhere."

"Fuck the F.B.I.!" Stan snapped. "The President just announced that the country is bankrupt, and that the United Nations is taking over everything, including the army."

"We know, Stan. We heard it on the radio. We think that most of the bureaucrats and federal law enforcement agents are probably working for the same group that forced this country into bankruptcy."

"You'd better pack what you can," Ben added, joining them on the front porch. "We may have twenty minutes, but I want to be out of here by then."

"We're already packed," Stan said, leading them to the attached garage. "And I'll only need two minutes."

By then much of the long convoy had pulled around Lowell's patrol car and was headed north up Highway 83 at a modest pace, en route to an unknown location. For Sharon, it evoked memories of a televised news broadcast about the bloodshed in Bosnia, with endless convoys of refugees wandering about the countryside.

"What's happening, Ben? Are we really bankrupt?"

"Sharon, we've been bankrupt since 1938," Ben said with a sigh. "But facing threats from the Nazis and the Communists, the bankers didn't have the means nor the method to take over. Until now. Now they have NATO and the United Nations to enforce their quasi-legal swindle. And they're going to try to take us for everything we have."

"But how? How could this happen?"

Ben shrugged, shook his head, and lit a cigarette. "The Federal Reserve," he said. "They print our money, sell it to us, and charge us interest for using it in the first place."

"That sounds illegal."

"It is," Ben agreed. "The Constitution says that only Congress shall have the power to coin money, and determine the value thereof. .... It's a small technical detail that has been overlooked since 1913."

"Doesn't matter anymore," Stan Gorman said. "We saw a United Nations' soldier in full battle gear standing next to the Presi-

James A. Clayton

dent."

"With a rifle?"

"An M-16."

"He looked threatening," Sharon added.

"Interesting," Ben said. "Maybe he was a threat to the President. Maybe he was threatening the President."

"Bastard still caved-in," Stan snapped.

"Could be he was advising caution," Lowell said. "He could be trying to avoid another civil war."

"But it's all coming apart, isn't it?" Sharon asked.

"Yes," Ben sighed, "but maybe, with a little luck, we can put it all back together again."

"I wish I had your optimism."

"So do I," Ben said softly, helping her up into the cab of the pickup. "So do I."

The three-vehicle convoy — Bob Lowell's patrol car and two pickup trucks — headed straight north into McCook. The highway turned west on "B" Street, but they didn't. They drove north up the hill and up East Sixth, turning left on "E" Street. With a sinking feeling in the pit of his stomach, Lowell stopped in front of the remains of a burnt-out brick house.

"I have the strongest stomach," Ben said. "I'll take a look inside."

He went in through the missing front door. A few seconds later he came back to the curbside and vomited. Twice.

"They're all dead," he said, wiping his mouth with a tissue. "Adult female. Three kids. I think. Burnt and charred beyond recognition. Place looks like ... like its been fire-bombed."

"Dora? .... Was it Dora?"

Ben Franklyn shook his head and wiped his mouth with another tissue. "I couldn't tell."

"But Lou only had two kids."

Ben Franklyn shrugged. "Neighbor kid, maybe."

A sickly feeling engulfed Bob Lowell's stomach. These were his friends. His close friends. He'd lost count of the number of dinners he'd shared with them. He'd watched television with them, explained the intricacies of algebra to the kids, and cried with them when their goldfish died. But now he could not even take the time to bury them.

"What about Louis?"

"No sign of him," Ben said, climbing back into the patrol car, "but his office is only four blocks away."

The short, painful drive through empty, deserted streets seemed to take an eternity — an agonizing eternity. And the two overdressed corpses sprawled across the sidewalk near the south entrance to the Red Willow County Courthouse only raised additional questions.

Stan Gorman and Bob Lowell went inside this time, leaving Ben to watch the pickups and search the dead bodies. Five minutes later Stan returned with half-a-dozen riot shotguns, which he piled into the back seat of Lowell's patrol car. Without a word he went back inside the County Courthouse, still wearing the ugly look of a man who had seen too much.

Then it was Bob Lowell's turn to emerge with an armful of weapons and a black satchel. Ben held the car door open, but Lowell said nothing — not even a 'thank you'. He obviously had other things on his mind as he headed back into the gray-white building.

On the next trip Stan carried over twenty boxes of shotgun shells, while Lowell brought out more pump shotguns and four revolvers.

And on the final trip, both men returned with boxes of ammunition, which they stacked rather neatly in the back seat of Lowell's patrol car.

"They killed Sheriff Dobbins and a deputy named Lawrence," Stan said softly. "But they paid for it. Dobbins got two of them, and Lawrence took out a third."

"What about those two?" Lowell asked.

"Two shots apiece, through the head. High-angle. High-powered rifle," Ben said. "My guess, a sniper on the roof of that apartment building across the street."

"We should give him a medal," Stan said.

"At least," Lowell added. "Still, it's strange they left the bodies behind?"

"The bodies were still warm," Ben noted. "Guess their friends left in a hurry."

"A big hurry," Lowell said, wiping the tears from his eyes. "I wonder ...."

Bob Lowell took a crowbar from his trunk and popped the trunk of the Sheriff's patrol car.

"There was an unwritten rule, of sorts," Lowell said, carrying a cardboard file box from the Sheriff's trunk to his own.

"In case of an uncertain emergency, hide any vital evidence in the trunk."

Stan brought a second file box, which Ben helped him set down into the well of Lowell's trunk.

"Anything in there?" Ben asked.

"Won't know until I've had a chance to look at 'em," Lowell said. "But this is neither the time nor the place."

Bob Lowell slammed his trunk lid shut, while Ben took the pump shotgun and three boxes of shells from the open trunk of the Sheriff's patrol car. Lowell climbed into his patrol car.

"Ready?"

Ben repositioned the shotgun and slammed the passenger door shut. "Let's go."

"Yeah," Lowell said. "Let's get the hell outa here."

He threw the patrol car into gear and led the little convoy from the city of McCook.

———

The President of the United States was depressed, to say the least. He had violated the oath of office. He had failed to "preserve, protect, and defend the Constitution of the United States." And even if Jack Kent's carefully contrived message and subsequent deceptions worked perfectly, regaining the trust of the American people would be an almost impossible task.

This new array of imported "technical advisors" would be irritated by his final speech, but they would not be stopped by anything short of violence. There was no one left to defend the poor widow's child.

He wiped the tears from his wife's eyes and gently embraced her. After over thirty years, no words were needed. He followed her up the steps into the waiting helicopter, stopping at the door to turn and wave to the audience and the reporters. Only this time, no one was there.

* * *

Chapter Nine

Paul Bernard Latimer, Acting Director of the Federal Bureau of Investigation, sniffed haughtily and stood at attention beside his gray limosine, watching Air Force One rise above Andrews Air Force Base into a cloud-speckled sky.

"The office," Latimer said, climbing into the spacious rear compartment of the limosine.

His chauffeur snapped off a sharp salute and crisply slammed the limosine's rear door, isolating Acting Director from the vicissitudes of the savage and uncivilized world.

Paul Bernard Latimer had led a double life for most of his adult life. With the right connections he had vaulted into the upper echelons of political power within the Federal Bureau of Investigation in record time. Those connections were an accident of birth; he had been born into a banking family. And he had been carefully taught, almost from birth, about the virtues of a one-world-government.

'Government of the people, for the people, and by the people' had had its day in the sun and was headed the way of the Dodo. With DVD, color TV, cellular telephones, the Internet, plastic money, personal and laptop computers, and time now measured in nanoseconds; the world demanded a higher level of political efficiency. And he had no intention of letting a bunch of primitive peasants stand in the way. It was time for the educated and the elite to assume their rightful role as rulers of the world.

One world, one planet, one government, and one civilization designed and destined for perfection. Newspapers and televisions that said what you wanted them to say without circumlocution. Religions that taught only Humanism, rather than some vague and primitive monotheistic mythology. Men who did not smoke, drink, swear, or entertain prurient thoughts. Women who lived pure and virtuous lives of humble obedience to their spouses, washing and cleaning and cooking and tending to the needs of their children. And children who were obedient to their parents and respectful of their elders.

Acting Director Paul Latimer smiled at his own silly daydreams. Rabble were rabble and the elite were the elite. Only the rabble took up too much valuable space. His calm and authoritative leadership was needed to control the undisciplined peasants and maintain proper order.

———

Watching Air Force One climb into the cloud-speckled sky, Jacob Andrew Kent sank into a deep and dark depression. He had failed his president and his country.

Kent had planned a secret exchange at Denver International. That exchange would have diverted the President to a CIA safe house near Cut Bank, Montana; while thirty CIA operatives flew to Wainwright aboard Air Force One. The diversion would have severely damaged several of the New World Order's clandestine operations and put them on the defensive. Only now the exchange would never take place.

Latimer had inundated Denver International with FBI, BATF, DEA, and Interpol agents. He had temporarily arrested three CIA operatives, sending a clear and threatening message. The operation had been blown. An exchange at Denver International would endanger the life of the President, and perhaps several hundred innocent bystanders as well.

Lacking a viable alternative, Jack Kent had been forced to cancel the operation and somberly informed the President of his failure.

Still deeply depressed, he drove slowly back towards the Langley headquarters. Crossing the Woodrow Wilson Memorial Bridge he slowed even more while jotting down the license of the gray LeBaron sedan that kept appearing in his rear view mirror. Cruising slowly along the George Washington Parkway, he studied the LeBaron and its driver — what he could see of him, anyway — without success.

"Better a devil you know," he murmured, pulling up to the security booth.

"Sir?"

"There was a gray LeBaron sedan following me."

The security guard shrugged his shoulders. "Not anymore. .... Guess he knows where you live."

"Yes." But it was more a hiss than a word. "I'd better get another car."

Peter Gordon, his deputy director in Ops, tracked the gray LeBaron back to the FBI executive pool. He also reported another forty-three "layoffs."

Since the CIA did not fall under the aegis of the Civil Service Commission, Kent was more-or-less free to hire and fire as he saw fit. Presently, however, he spent as much time moving people around for their own personal safety as he did for security purposes. Knowing the jealousy of foreign intelligence units, Kent realized that the "layoff" disguise would not last very long. It would, however, buy him the time he needed to make other arrangements.

After two hours of "housekeeping," DCI Kent signed out an older model pool car and went for a long drive. Cruising the streets of Richmond, Virginia, he selected a telephone booth next to a coffee shop — seemingly at random — and placed his call.

"Operator, I'd like to make a 'bill-to' call overseas ... to Burgenstock, Switzerland."

―――

The *J. Edgar Hoover Building* is one of Washington's newer monuments to bureaucracy. Built on the site of the original FBI headquarters building, it is probably one of the more secure structures within the beltway. Its only weakness is — or was — the Director's private entrance. But that weakness was a privilege which Paul Bernard Latimer appreciated, if only for its practicality.

"Good afternoon, sir."

The Acting Director acknowledged his secretary with a special nod of recognition. In this town, a good secretary could make or break a man.

"Good afternoon, sir?"

Henshaw's masculine voice grated his nerves, but the little man was invaluable to Latimer. He generally shared Latimer's one-world views, which made him easier to talk to, a sounding board for the Acting Director's problems. But it was Henshaw's political savvy, knowing when to speak up and when to shut up, which had elevated him into the status of personal advisor.

"It's not," Latimer said. "Inside."

Henshaw nodded. The formality ended inside the Acting Director's office. Latimer closed the door and Henshaw lit a Marlboro cigarette.

"Don't you know those things can kill you!"

Henshaw laughed. "Careful, you'll end up believing your own propaganda."

"So? I know that look. What's wrong?"

"Everything. .... Remember that disarmament directive you issued last month?"

"The joint F.B.I. and A.T.F. policy thing? — Of course. .... You said there would be problems enforcing it."

"That, it would seem, was something of an understatement," Henshaw said, with a cough as an exclamation point. "At first, as anticipated, we suffered modest losses. Six agents in East Los Angeles. Two in Seattle. Three in Arizona. Nine in Texas. And so forth. .... Altogether, less than a hundred."

"So?"

"Resistance did not decrease, as you said it would. We have lost another thirty-seven agents in Greater Los Angeles alone. We also lost nineteen in San Diego, twenty-two in San Francisco, twenty-three in Seattle, and thirty-six in Denver. We've lost almost seven hundred agents nationwide. And another six hundred, or so, have resigned. We've even had a major riot down in Miami, Florida."

He took a final drag off his cigarette and crushed it out. "Fuck, I spend most of my time placating the press. But I'm running out of excuses."

"Recommendations?"

Henshaw lit another cigarette. "We have lost over six percent of our forces. Under such unstable conditions, I would recommend that we withdraw to Canada and regroup."

"Are you crazy?"

Henshaw took another long drag off his cigarette. He looked up at Paul Latimer with a cold, unwavering gaze and sadly shook his head.

"No," Latimer growled. "No way. At least, not yet. You can write the withdrawal instructions, just in case, but we won't be pulling out just yet. We can lose another twenty percent and still remain a viable organization."

The ringing telephone interrupted his thoughts.

"Latimer." He listened, he uttered a "thank you," and hung up the phone. "Let's take a walk."

Henshaw stubbed out his cigarette and followed Latimer from the office into the corridor. "We have cockroaches."

"Sir?"

"That was Packard over at the D.E.A. My office has acquired several bugs, apparently from the Central Intelligence Agency."

"Kent?"

The Acting Director nodded. "Strange man. Once he found out what was happening, he somehow managed to infiltrate their organization and join them."

"So whose side is he on?"

"His own, I guess," Latimer said with a shrug. "He was planning to isolate the President in Cut Bank, Montana; allegedly to thwart my plan to lose 'The Man' in Wainwright, Alaska."

"Which means?"

"That means someone else is involved. And that means that someone in Europe has doubts about my abilities. And that means that they don't trust me anymore."

Henshaw shrugged. "So? — Fuck Europe. Worry about saving you own ass."

The taxi was waiting when Packard of the Drug Enforcement Agency emerged from the shadows, briefcase in hand, and slid into the back seat.

"Dulles."

"My name is Pete Gordon," the cab driver said, half-turning in his seat.

"So what?"

The muzzle of a silenced revolver rose over the back of the seat and spoke softly.

They met shortly after sundown in an abandoned tool shop near the railroad station. Once inside, with the doors closed, they lit cigarettes and shined flashlights on each others' faces. It was security, of a sort.

"Gentlemen, we are at war with our own country. The F.B.I. and the B.A.T.F. are invading our homes at will and killing our people for the fun of it. According to certain confidential sources, tomorrow morning two S.I.S. units will invade McCook and raid the gun shop on 'B' Street. I suggest we empty the shop tonight, and give the S.I.S. a warm welcome tomorrow."

"You might need these, Ed."

Deputy Ed Hudson accepted the keys with a nod and a smile. "Thanks, Mr. Jennings. This will make things much easier."

"Better you folks than those federal bandits and imbeciles," Jennings said.

"It's your store. You want to lead the way?"

"Be my pleasure."

Hudson opened the door and followed Jennings into the pale moonlight. In the distance an empty freight train wailed a lonesome farewell to Nebraska.

"You realize this is an unlawful assembly," Hudson joked.

"Yeah," Jennings said. "And that used to be funny."

"They sort of take the fun out of things, don't they?"

"They sort of take the fun out of life," Jennings said, listening again to the distant wail of the departing train.

―――

Parking the gray LeBaron in his assigned space, Henshaw hesitated before climbing the two flights to his second floor apartment. Call it a feeling, but something about the atmosphere of the underground garage bothered him. Even after climbing the stairs and locking the front door behind him, he still felt engulfed by an uncertain sense of foreboding.

Henshaw lived in a section of Washington, D.C., that most informed people avoid. He could have afforded better, much better, but the seedy lifestyle appealed to his personality. Besides, he thought, he was saving a bundle on rent.

Beyond that, Latimer had approved expenditures to rent and renovate the apartment next door. It was now accessible only through a hidden door in Henshaw's closet. And it was filled with a plethora of gimmicks and gadgets, of ultra-high-tech computers and copy machines, of telephonic devices and DVD television sets.

Henshaw was watching a lesbian sex act on an X-rated channel from Belgium when the telephone rang three times — long enough for him to turn down the sound and zip up his pants.

"You are wanted at headquarters. Immediately."

Henshaw did not recognize the voice, but he recognized the

message. The caller-identification callback number was correct, and nobody else would have this number. Cursing softly, Henshaw turned off the television, strapped on his gun, and locked the security door.

Opening the front door, however, was a serious mistake. A flash of blinding white light, an explosive and thunderous roar, a ripping and agonizing pain, and a reddish haze hit him with the force of a runaway train — and with the same results.

The voice behind the blue bandanna said, "Clean it up and clear it out. You have thirty-two minutes."

———

Big signs had been painted on the papered-over windows, signs which read: *"Guns"* and *"Rifles"* and *"Shotguns"* and *"Pistols"* and *"Ammo."* The name of the gun shop and the name of the owner were covered by black paint. The windows and the glass double doors were covered by brown wrapping paper. And in spite of the bright sunlight, the concrete-block building was covered in gloom.

Two gray FBI cars, two brown SIS "SWAT" vans, and two tan BATF cars came to a screeching halt in the parking lot in front of the gun shop. Armed to the teeth and looking for trouble, six men emerged from each of the brown SIS vans and were joined by four-man squads from each of the federal cars. Twenty-eight men darted to the walls and pressed themselves against the cinder blocks of the gun shop, staying below the level of the windows, poised to attack.

The sign behind the glass double doors read: "Closed."

But these agents would not be taken in by such an obvious ruse. They smashed the glass doors with their rifle butts and ripped away the brown wrapping paper. And they found a very empty, deserted, and abandoned building. Inside they found four bare walls and some old wooden shelves. Carpeting had been ripped from the floor, exposing the dusty floorboards. The aged wooden shelving on the far wall was also covered with dust. And the room was filled with the odor of something that had died.

Special Agent Gregory Hanson summed it up in a single word: "Shit!"

Disgusted and depressed, they left the gun shop in groups of two and three, sullenly seeking fresh air and the security of their vehicles. But the last three agents permitted to leave the stench spent too much time near the entrance.

A dozen shots rang out. Two agents fell just outside the entrance. The third, badly wounded, tried to crawl to the cover of an SIS van. The other agents, with M-16 rifles at the ready, took cover wherever they could find it.

Then the empty building exploded with a deafening, shattering blast. Fragments of concrete cinder blocks ripped Kevlar body armor, flesh, and bones. Agents were thrown across the hoods of their cars. An SIS van tipped over, its side pitted and punctured by hundreds of concrete pellets. Shards of glass cut and ripped and slashed and punctured men and body armor and vehicles. Larger pieces of concrete and debris fell from the sky and rained across the parking lot. A chunk of concrete the size of a two-drawer filing cabinet destroyed the second FBI car — and the two agents hiding inside.

The second SIS van blew apart, enveloped in a fiery explosion that smeared bloodied bodies across the asphalt. At the same time, the flaming remains of the shattered roof returned in a firestorm of splintered wood, burning boards, and smoldering body parts.

Popping and crackling sounds came from the billowing dark clouds as cinder blocks cracked and crumbled amidst the flames. The cries and screams of dying men echoed along "B" street. And there was debris everywhere.

From out of the wreckage a bloodied agent unleashed his M-16, firing wildly across "B" Street. Then other guns returned the fire, and two dozen bullets tore him to shreds.

Smoke and dust drifted across the little parking lot and billowed into the sky. The stench of death, of bloodied and burnt bodies, strayed over the curb and across the street. And a lone FBI agent, his pants' leg torn and stained red with his blood, crawled from the debris.

Blood trickled down his face as he crawled to his knees and clawed his way up onto the trunk of the car. Four blurry figures slipped from the fog to encircle him. With a final act of defiance he flipped open his identification case.

"Hanson, F.B.I.," he croaked. "You are under arrest."

"Deputy Sheriff Edward Hudson, human being," a voice said. "Fuck you."

"I have a warrant," Hanson gasped.

"I have a rifle," Hudson replied.

And he shot Special Agent Gregory Hanson three times in

the head at close range, splattering brains and blood and fragments of his skull over the gray car.

"And this is a war," Hudson said softly.

Paul Bernard Latimer, Acting Director of the Federal Bureau of Investigation, read the Echo-Three report four times. Each reading increased his irritation. The raid on Echo-Three turned into a pointless embarrassment for him. The underground fortress was empty — very empty. It had, in fact, been "sanitized" by professionals.

Lost in his own paranoia, Latimer wondered if the Echo-Three report was somehow connected to Henshaw's failure to report. But after careful consideration, he dismissed the idea. It was simply too paranoid to consider.

Henshaw was not really required to report, *per se*. He could have overslept. He might be tailing a suspect. Or he may have departed for Canada. Maybe.

At noon Latimer sent a dozen agents to check on his wayward assistant. Thirty minutes later the agents reported that Henshaw's apartment had been vacated, and that all of the special equipment was missing. They also reported finding dried blood in the cracks between the floorboards and under the threshold of the hallway door. And Latimer knew that his assistant had not left the country voluntarily.

But a bunch of flag-waving FBI agents from Echo-Three might pose a direct threat to the United Nations' peacekeeping forces, and to himself as well. And if they were behind Henshaw's sudden demise ....

Considering an option he did not want to contemplate, the Acting Director wandered into his secretary's office to collect the daily statistics.

And the daily statistics were damning. There were three thousand five hundred and twenty-two resignations, one thousand eight hundred and eighty-nine agents killed in the line of duty, and over a thousand who had simply failed to report. He opened his pocket calculator and began punching buttons, but he knew the horrid answer before the LCD display flashed its gruesome facts. With his actual losses climbing over thirty percent, the Federal Bureau of Investigation was no longer a viable force.

"Think!" He pushed the speed-dial for the DEA.

"I'm sorry, but the number you have dialed has been disconnected. Please make sure you have the right number, and are dialing correctly."

He softly cursed the telephone. Then he tried several BATF lines — with equally horrific results.

After that, he considered calling his ex-wlfe. But after over two years of peace and quiet, her rancorous laughter would not give him any solace. And then his telephone rang.

"Latimer."

"Arkin, N.C.I.C., sir." Latimer groaned. "We're down across the board."

"What?"

"We're down. The entire N.C.I.C. system has crashed, sir." Arkin hesitated. "We've ... we've lost the entire data base."

"How could that happen?"

"Technically, it can't. We ... we suspect sabotage."

"Understood." Latimer hung up the phone and stared out the window.

At 3:15 p.m., Eastern Daylight Time, Acting Director Paul Bernard Latimer reluctantly issued Henshaw's pull-out orders. All field agents and office personnel were to make their own way to Edmonton, Alberta, Canada. There they would meet and regroup in a more civilized environment.

"Flag-wavers," he muttered, closing and locking the door to his office behind him.

The outer offices were empty. The hallways were empty. The entire building was empty. He would have to carry his own luggage — one briefcase and one suitcase.

Europe would understand that he could not enforce their laws without military support, he thought. But he knew that it was more a desperate hope. Those European powers did not care whether he lived or died.

He sighed, picked up his bags, and trudged down the long hallway to the elevator, wondering what Europe would say about this fiasco.

He turned the key and waited.

And then the security tape went blank.

They never found the briefcase nor the suitcase he was carrying on the security tape. They found his keys still in the elevator slot. They found his office door unlocked. And they found his body sprawled across his desk, bleeding all over his new carpet.

According to the Medical Examiner, Paul Bernard Latimer had been shot eight times — once in each kneecap, once in the groin, twice in the lower abdomen, once in each shoulder, and once through the left eye — before they slit his throat from ear to ear, leaving a gory mess in and on his plush carpet.

"Someone must have hated him a lot," the Medical Examiner said. But he was not a man given to understatement.

* * *

Chapter Ten

No doubt many Americans were surprised to find that just over one hundred thousand foreign troops — mostly from France, Germany, and England — were already concealed within the infrastructure of the United States' military machine. Others were undoubtably astonished to learn that the United Nations could fly four hundred thousand foreign soldiers into the United States within forty-eight hours. And even those allegedly in positions of authority were horrified to learn that over half-a-million troops had been parked off the East Coast, hidden in ships operating under the guise of a "training exercise."

No one had expected such meticulous planning, but then no one knew that General Heinrich Obermeyer had planned the invasion down to the last detail. In fact, few even knew of his existence ... or of his background.

Born in Stuttgart, Germany, in 1944, General Heinrich Obermeyer, Commander-in-Chief of the United Nations' Military Command, had lost his parents during the final days of World War Two. Had it not been for the terse note pinned to his threadbare jacket, he might have also lost his name.

For years he had been shuffled from orphanage-to-orphanage, lost and alone in the ashes and rubble of a defeated and divided West Germany. Later, out on his own, he had searched for relatives — brothers, sisters, aunts, uncles, cousins, or whatever. But even as he rose in rank and authority, his continued search continued to prove fruitless.

Indeed, for years the search was the only thing that kept him going. In 1955 the Federal Republic of Germany was established and re-armed. Less than six years later, on his seventeenth birthday, Obermeyer enlisted in the army. He rose quickly and steadily through the depleted ranks, valuing each promotion only for the additional authority it gave him. He had attained the rank of "general" before he stopped searching for his past and paid more attention to his military career.

The reunification of East and West Germany elevated General Obermeyer to an even loftier pinnacle of power and deceit. His moderate, non-political approach — so fashionable and proper — belied the dictatorial neo-Nazi dreams buried behind a facade of intellectual sophistication.

Both Germany and Japan had pledged never to allow their armies to be deployed beyond their national boundaries. But Germany, now a member of NATO, could transfer units to that command. And Japan, as a member of the United Nations, could transfer individuals and units to various "peacekeeping" forces and operations abroad.

Thus, while the two nations officially remained neutral, they could and did assign specific individuals and groups to certain foreign powers for miscellaneous and sundry duties.

With the beginnings of activities in Bosnia and elsewhere, the Secretary-General of the United Nations placed General Obermeyer within the NATO command staff with orders to prepare them for the forthcoming changes in command structure. In this Obermeyer was so successful that he was made command-in-chief of the entire operation.

Little did the Secretary-General suspect that Obermeyer was actually a well-trained version of Adolph Hitler, but without the mustache and the horrible hairdo. No one in the United Nations realized that their beloved Commander-in-Chief was seeking revenge for the misery he had suffered over fifty years earlier in the ruins of Nazi Germany.

In the later years of his ascent to power, General Heinrich Obermeyer had devised dozens of secret scenarios for the invasion and conquest of the United States of America. The scenarios had been object lessons in strategy and tactics, the hopes of a man obsessed. He did not want to bomb America into submission. He wanted to conquer and to rule "those stupid peasants" through intimidation and terror. And the bankers from Burgenstock had greatly simplified many of the strategic problems for him.

Obermeyer arrived unobtrusively in New York City near the end of Day Four, slipping quietly into the city on an almost-empty

James A. Clayton

night flight from London. His arrival was neither anticipated nor announced, but it soon created tremors within the million-plus United Nations' military force dominating the eastern seaboard.

With American soldiers and airmen notably absent, and with C5A Galaxy, C-141 Starlifter, and C-130E Hercules aircraft landing every five minutes at Dover and at Andrews Air Force Bases; the colonels and majors struggled desperately to hold their commands together and in check. But with troops and equipment scattered across the tarmac, and throughout the terminal buildings and aircraft hangars; organization suffered. And while there were no physical assaults, these tourists were obviously not welcomed under the spacious but gray skies.

But General Heinrich Obermeyer was very pleased.

The overcrowded prison population never bothered anyone who managed to escape the wrath of the politicians and bureaucrats. Operating on the principle: "out of sight, out of mind;" the long arm of pseudo-justice had buried over three million indigent adults behind brick walls and metal bars, effectively cutting them off from anything resembling humanity.

And under the guise of pseudo-justice, the bureaucrats locked up the guilty and the innocent side-by-side, leaving the horrendous expenses to the impoverished taxpayers.

The American pseudo-justice system only killed about two thousand felons, real or alleged, each year. This allowed the prison population to grow at an alarming rate. Obermeyer had solved this minor problem, however, before leaving Europe.

By the time he landed in the United States, his "Justice Squads" had eliminated most of the inmates on death row — and those serving "life" sentences — without noise or legalistic fanfare, simply by administering lethal injections *en masse*.

Working systematically, each seventy-man unit visited at least two maximum security prisons every day. They covered most of the major state and federal facilities, executing death row and "lifer" inmates with deadly efficiency. Objections from wardens, guards, or anyone else were quickly resolved by adding the objector's name to the termination list. And in those first four days Obermeyer's twelve "Justice Squads" murdered 316,802 inmates, wardens, guards, doctors, nurses, ministers, and sundry personnel.

On the fifth day, however, they hit a brick wall. Five squads were denied admittance to their respective institutions. Two units found only empty cells and abandoned guard stations in Lompoc, California, and Fort Huachuca, Arizona. The squad assigned to Huntsville, Texas, was isolated and confined in a corridor until a "relief task force" from the Houston garrison released them some twelve hours later. The unit assigned to the federal penitentiary near Atlanta, Georgia, lost twenty-three squad members and were forced to flee for their lives as guards and prisoners fired weapons and threw stones at them.

But they were lucky.

A "relief task force" was unable to locate the "Justice Squad" visiting the recently renovated and modernized Rahway State Prison in New Jersey. Except for the bodies of two drug dealers, Rahway was an abandoned monument to mankind's inhumanity.

―――

Obermeyer had anticipated minor resistance, not major defiance. He expected isolated incidents, not multiple engagements. He knew there would be moments of high tension, but not hours of stark terror and nightmarish brutality.

Between unpacking his gear and arresting congressmen, Obermeyer went over a dozen reports of major and minor hostility, seeking a pattern. In Houston an unruly mob had greeted a troop ship with jeers, catcalls, and rotten eggs. In Los Angeles a routine identity check erupted into a full-scale riot. In Denver an attempt to arrest the Governor of Colorado exploded into a fire fight between local police and UN peacekeeping forces. In Seattle a C-130 troop transport had crashed into a gasoline tanker truck parked on the runway. In Dallas over a thousand protesting civilians were shot and killed in order to quell a minor disturbance. And in Kansas City thirty-two United Nations' soldiers were found in a back alley with their throats slit.

Obermeyer did not find a pattern, but he did become rather ill. Their hostility knew no bounds. He would have to teach the American rabble a lesson in subservience.

―――

"The planes keep arriving, delivering men and trucks and men and armored personnel carriers and men and tanks and more men. These foreigners come with strange languages and even stranger customs. The Arabs can't stand cigarette smoke, carry little rugs, and bow to the east five times a day. The small Japanese contingent bows to everyone. The Turks want to slit your throat and the French want to kiss your cheek, or the back of your hand, or your ass. Or something."

Benjamin Ellsworth Franklyn chuckled as he read the message on the Internet. Somebody at Denver International was playing a dangerous game in sending this message. If he was ever caught spying on UN military operations ....

The old farmer signaled Lisa and headed for the pickup. Ten minutes later, far from the encampment and with Lisa behind the wheel, he flipped his cellular telephone open and called Mrs. Pratt.

Major Hermann Hoffman was a practical soldier — a soldier who followed orders without question and without conscience. Born in Dortmund, West Germany, in 1956, he had enlisted on his eighteenth birthday in 1974 and was transferred to NATO in 1989. Given time and a few hundred tanks, he might have been another Rommel.

Instead, he was given a command in NATO studying the American military structure and the integration techniques used in Europe and elsewhere. At Obermeyer's request, he had taken General Wilder "out of the picture" with frightening efficiency. Without question or conscience, he had simply followed orders.

Now he rode, rather uncomfortably, in the lead APC en route to North Platte, Nebraska, a small village set at the juncture of the North and South Platte rivers. He had studied the maps. He had read the backgrounders and briefing papers. But he was not happy with the assignment. North Platte was nothing in the middle of nowhere. And riding the APC along Highway 34, he wondered if anyone actually lived in this empty and desolate land.

He checked the map again and flicked the microphone switch.

"Command, this is Major Hoffman. We are in District Six, Sector Six-Nine, on Route Three-Four, approaching Intersection Six West, west of McCook, Nebraska, en route to North Platte. Requesting security status. Please advise. .... Over."

"Major Hoffman, this is Command," the radio squawked. "You are cleared to proceed. No opposition reported at this time. Copy?"

"This is Hoffman. I copy. .... Out."

"Command clear."

Hoffman turned off the ancient radio and studied the disgusted expression on the driver's face. "You disagree?"

Corporal Lingstrum, the APC driver, shook his head. "They have not had a spotter plane over this section in the past three hours. And the Americans have sabotaged their own satellite surveillance systems. — That report is not dependable."

"Understood," Hoffman said. "Advise our escorts. And proceed with caution."

Their escorts were two NYPD motorcycles liberated from a rather unfriendly New York City Police Department and driven in a rather reckless fashion by two FBI volunteers. Lingstrum did not trust them, however, and used his own map to check their route.

Behind the lead APC, twelve troop transport trucks carried three hundred United Nations' soldiers. Another APC brought up the rear. The armored personnel carriers were for Hoffman's command staff. The trucks held a small but vital section of his command.

He looked at the map again. There would be a left turn onto Highway 83, but the Americans had a fondness for wide highways. That turn, Hoffman thought, would not be a problem.

On the other hand, four convoys arriving simultaneously at *Lee Bird Airfield* might pose a problem in logistics. Burdened with obsolete equipment and inadequate support, only the dismal desolation of Western Nebraska offered him any hope of setting up a secure base of operations.

This area, he'd been told time and again, was a quiet rural backwater where nothing would or could happen. But looking out at the landscape through the thick windows of the APC, Hoffman was not as certain.

On the westside of McCook, where Highway 83 turns off towards North Platte, the burnt-out wreckage of an elderly car with four flat tires sat at an odd angle in the ditch just east of the tee-intersection. But this old car with four flat tires was no accident. From its darkened interior, two pairs of eyes watched the progress of the United Nations' military convoy as it turned left through a red light and the four-lane intersection, en route to North Platte.

"Mrs. Pratt was right," Kathy growled, sitting up in the front seat of the wreck. "Those lousy bureaucratic bastards in Washington sold us out to the United Nations and their mercenary peacekeeping army."

Deputy Ed Hudson rose from the back seat, checked the departing convoy, and lit a cigarette. "Which explains," he said, "why the B.A.T.F. and the F.B.I. were so rabid about gun control. .... It wasn't crime. It was revolution."

"Yeah. First Bosnia, now Nebraska." Kathy sighed and kicked open the passenger door. "I'd better tell Mrs. Pratt — and have her get the word out."

Rifle in hand, Hudson climbed out of the car while Kathy found her bicycle in the weeds and brought it up to the highway. He took a final couple of puffs, then buried his cigarette under the heel of his boot.

"Looks clear."

Kathy also looked, then she nodded. McCook was home to eight thousand people, yet the streets and highways were empty. There wasn't a moving vehicle in sight, creating an eerie feeling of complete isolation. An involuntary shiver passed through her body as she climbed on her bicycle.

With a quick wave she peddled away down the hill into town, while Hudson crossed the broad intersection towards the empty parking lot of the officially closed U-Save Supermarket.

―――

The city was lost in its own pollution. Trees struggled for life amidst the noxious fumes of cars and trucks and vans. People coughed and hacked and spit and choked and screamed and hollered and yelled and shouted and cursed and swore. Eyes watered and turned red. And the air pollution index read: "Good to Moderate."

It was a big city; filled with the noise, confusion, and chaos common to all overgrown slabs of concrete and steel. They said it had a heart, but it beat with the grinding of gears. They said it had a soul, but it had been buried within the grit and the grime. They said it was alive, but it was slowly being strangled by tourists wearing blue helmets.

They came. They saw. They threw up.

Within the smog and the haze, and hidden by the darkness of a damp alleyway, an all-metal door kept prying eyes and ears out, and admitted no one. Whatever was inside stayed inside. And whatever was outside suffered.

The lone United Nations' soldier marched back and forth past the metal door with tedious regularity. He was guarding the door, with no concern for what the door was guarding. He did not know and he was not interested. He was a tiny cog within a monstrous machine.

He stopped once to stare at the door, and the entire wall exploded outward; crushing him, burying him, and cremating him in the same instant.

From further away one could see the bottom of the building being blown outward while the upper levels sank into the ground. Soon everything was lost in a cloud of gritty, gray dust and buried under thunderheads of billowing, brownish smoke.

Five British *"Challenger"* tanks rumbled and rolled through the dust and the smoke, clanking and screeching and screaming their defiance. They rolled over chunks of concrete, reducing the stone to powdery particulates. They rolled over automobiles, reducing metal and fiberglass to scrap. They rolled over dead or almost-dead bodies, reducing flesh and bone to pulp.

Nothing could stop them.

Then, without any visible reason, the third tank exploded. It was not particularly spectacular; just a horrendous thud with flame and smoke ripping open the ports and spinning the monster machine crosswise. Underneath, the street gave way, dropping the tank a mere six inches as a spider-web of cracks and crevices fanned outward from the fallen beast.

And all the tanks stopped.

Through the dust and the smoke, and past the British *"Challenger"* tanks, a singular and lone civilian ran at breakneck speed down the street, chased by three angry United Nations' soldiers. Without breaking stride, he darted into an alley. Without breaking stride, the three soldiers followed him into the shadows.

A ground-shaking fireball of smoke and flame burst from the alley. The three United Nations' soldiers literally came flying from the alley, and rolled across the street. Their clothing was on fire. Their helmets were ripped off. They died with their boots on, and with just about everything else burnt off or blown away.

Moments later, bricks and concrete and metal and other pieces of the adjacent buildings came crashing down into the alleyway. —

James A. Clayton

But the unidentified civilian was never found.

There was something unsettling about the long lines of homeless people being crowded into the passenger coaches, boxcars, and cattle cars filling the railyard's multiple tracks. For the young soldier, the scene created a haunting sense of *deja vu* — a remembrance of something he'd seen on a flickering television screen.

His knowledge of the Second World War came from obscure and obtuse history books. Yet the vacant, vagrant eyes of the helpless refugees struck a sensitive chord in the youthful soldier from Gent, Belgium.

"This is not right."

His commanding officer — a Lieutenant Petersen from Bergen, Norway — offered a grunt and a shrug. "It's our job."

"It is not right," the young soldier said, riveting his eyes on Lt. Petersen's dour expression.

In that brief moment of careless indiscretion thousands of nameless, faceless, homeless victims surged forward. They knocked the young soldier down and took his M-16. They knocked Lt. Petersen down and took his pistol. They knocked dozens of other soldiers down and took their weapons. And suddenly the United Nations' troops were facing a massive and riotous mob of rabble and trash, intent on violence and anarchy.

With no alternative in sight, the soldiers opened fire, killing sixty or seventy homeless civilians before falling victims to the rioting mob.

In the chaos of the moment, thousands of vagrant rabble pored from Union Station, fighting and killing and dying. But even thousands more followed, mindlessly running into the streets in search of weapons. With savage brutality they attacked. They screamed. They fought. They yelled. They killed. They ran. And they died. .... To the last man, woman, and child; they fought and they died. And only a few classified videotapes and a few soldiers lived to tell the story.

Of the 23,052 vagrants selected to take the train ride to the gas chambers in Navajo County, Arizona; some 23,439 were killed in the Union Station massacre. And although they would not admit it, the United Nations' peacekeeping forces lost 2,825 soldiers dead, and another 750 seriously wounded, in the hostilities.

After reading the reports and studying the videotapes, General Obermeyer classified everything "Top Secret" and buried it in a file cabinet. Then he went to the bathroom and became violently ill.

* * *

Chapter Eleven

General Heinrich Obermeyer seldom smoked. It was simply a habit he had never acquired nor desired. But today was an exception.

Today he had a reason. He watched silently from the stage as the headquarters staff of the United Nations' Military Command filed into the opulent auditorium, filling it from front to back in a very orderly and proper manner. The higher ranking and more decorated officers entered first, and thus sat closer to the podium — and closer to his considerable wrath.

Located near the 39-story glass tower of the Secretariat, the auditorium was one of four designed as backup for "General Assembly" meetings, but seldom used for anything so noble.

Today this one would serve as General Obermeter's bully pulpit.

Although no one said anything, the headquarters staff knew it was trouble when Obermeyer marched to the lectern, bit off the end of his cigar, and spat the remains onto the floor. He also took a full minute lighting it, practically taunting them with his big cigar.

They did not smoke, of course, but they did listen to Obermeyer's cigar. Finally, almost reluctantly, he began to read his ill-prepared text.

"Gentlemen, I have read — no, that is not correct — I have scanned your reports. So tell me, are you soldiers or are you politicians?"

He blew a large cloud of cigar smoke over the front rows, letting it sink in.

"Set back. Inconvenience. A slight but anticipated delay. An unanticipated but slight delay These reports are worthless! I have been forced to rewrite everything!"

Obermeyer blew another cloud of smoke over them, and held

up a thick sheaf of papers to show them his labor of hate.

"Seattle. Rain stops all activities," Obermeyer read with a sneer. "San Francisco. Inhabitants ignore orders, five hundred shot without any results Los Angeles. Continuous riots since we arrived two weeks ago. Mobs cheer the public executions of local officials, then turn and attack our garrisons."

He puffed on his cigar and readjusted his papers.

"Las Vegas, Nevada. Entire city deserted?" He silently re-read it. "Phoenix, Arizona. Highly organized resistance. Governor and state legislators executed. Over a thousand troops killed. One garrison sacked. Hell!"

Obermeyer chomped on the cigar and blew the smoke down into the first rows. The message was clear.

"Salt Lake City, Utah. Passive resistance? — What's that? A whole state full of Ganhdis? — Denver. Two hundred dead. Another one hundred missing-in-action? Whatever that means."

He chomped down even harder on his cigar and blew more smoke at them.

"Houston, Texas. Your report reads that the city is secure with only small pockets of token resistance Those small pockets have killed over seven hundred of our best troops!"

He bit down on his cigar and puffed furiously.

"As far as I can tell, we only have safe havens in Boston, Washington, D.C., Atlanta, and Chicago. I am placing the rest of this country in your hands, gentlemen."

General Obermeyer composed himself as he crudely puffed on his cigar and wondered just how secure Chicago actually was. Then he looked down at the headquarters staff ... and wondered just how secure he was.

"We came here to preserve the peace," he concluded, "and we shall preserve the peace ... even if we have to kill every last son-of-a-bitch in this country to do it If we cannot teach these people to respect us, then we must teach them to fear us."

He blew several puffs of cigar smoke at the ceiling, sending yet another message. But the staff waited for the word.

"Dismissed."

———

Just as General Obermeyer was concluding his sarcastic diatribes, four of his best white United Nations' security police discovered an elderly black civilian rummaging through a trash bin in a nearby alley. Perhaps he was looking for food, but one solid stroke from an anodized police baton sent him spinning from the alleyway. Confused and terrified, the old man turned and ran across the across the United Nations Plaza. But flight offered no escape. Five more United Nations' soldiers and security officers cornered the frightened vagrant in front of the green glass walls of the Secretariat tower.

Trapped and isolated and surrounded by nine United Nations' security policemen, the old black man spun around, seeking a way out. The policemen offered him an idiotic grin. Then they lashed out with their anodized batons.

They rammed their batons deep into his gut. They slashed at his arms. They hacked at his legs. They broke his bones and fractured his skull. And for several ugly minutes they continued to beat him until he was unconscious.

After carefully considering the situation, the United Nations' soldiers dragged the battered and bleeding black man to a nearby squad car for transportation. By the time they reached the United Nations' Military Field Hospital, about thirty minutes later, their victim had expired. The United Nations' security police listed his demise as "death from natural causes."

———

The slipping and sliding stock markets had been kept afloat in a rather stagnant fashion by foreign investors. After the President's speech, however, they suspended trading and never reopened their doors. But since the stock markets were at the mercy of the all-powerful banks, they were granted a merciless death.

The banks themselves were technically open for business, but business was bad. Many depositors simply closed their accounts. Those depositors with outstanding loans withdrew whatever they could and left town. Safe deposit boxes were emptied. And all banking business ground to a stuttering halt.

It was not a run on the banks — it was a walk. During the preceding year individual and business accounts had stagnated, then slowly dwindled away. Insurance and investment accounts faded and disappeared. Demand deposit and savings accounts evaporated, and credit card accounts went unpaid.

It was a mess even the Federal Reserve could not paper-over. Within a week most of the ATM machines were robbed and vandalized until they were beyond repair. Several banks, both major and minor, went out of business. Others were forced, at least temporarily, to close their doors. And practically all of the remaining institutions had to curtail their hours and their services. It was, quite literally, no longer "a fun time" for the banking industry.

As the government collapsed around and beneath them, FEMA — the Federal Emergency Management Agency — stepped in with support and aid to direct the banking business nationwide. By then, of course, banking had no business ... and everything was coming apart.

Bank robbery descended from a federal crime to a worthless pastime. But the shooting of bankers and cashiers, according to some sources, became more popular than sex.

But crime was rampant throughout all major cities. With police departments fragmented and disorganized; mugging, rape, armed robbery, burglary, breaking-and-entering, drug rip-offs, and other miscellaneous felonies littered the landscape and the concrete.

In such matters the United Nations' peacekeeping forces did not discriminate. They killed both the criminals and the victims, and asked no questions.

———

The old reddish-brown edifice of the Wells Fargo on the northwest corner of San Pablo and University in Berkeley, California, had two entrances. One was on the east across from a Food-For-Less grocery store on San Pablo. The other was on the south side, facing the Payless Shoe Store on University. Both entrances had been padlocked prior to the President's speech. Both were now apparently open for business, complete with the official *"By Authority of FEMA ...."* sign. But unlike other banks, this one appeared to be busy.

Too busy.

It attracted the attention of the United Nations' San Francisco Garrison Command Center, and they telephoned FEMA. But FEMA had not approved the reopening of any Wells Fargo Bank, leaving the San Francisco garrison in a quandary. FEMA, they knew, was not always up-to-date with its records. And this busy bank was well-posted with official FEMA signs, according to Captain Abdul Hamid of the Turkish Brigade.

Four days later Hamid and his associates, accompanied by two FEMA employees, parked their two armored personnel carriers on University, entered the bank, and asked for the manager. Call it bad timing, but as they shook hands with the alleged manager, five men tried to rob the bank.

Captain Abdul Hamid had seen too many *"Dirty Harry"* movies. He pulled his gun and charged the bank robbers. Only the bank robbers shot first. Then the cashiers, the customers, and the bank manager produced automatic pistols and revolvers. And for the next few seconds the bank became a slaughterhouse.

The two FEMA employees and all fourteen "associates" of Abdul Hamid died in the murderous exchange of gunfire, along with two "cashiers" and a "bank robber." Hamid was hit three times, once in the shoulder and once in each knee. And with both kneecaps shot off, Captain Hamid passed out.

Twenty minutes later his APC stopped in front of the entrance to the United Nations' Berkeley Marina Garrison and dumped Hamid onto the asphalt like a sack of rotten potatoes. Someone fired a couple of shots into the air to attract the attention of the nearby security guards, and then the APC sped away down University and into obscurity.

Within an hour a security team had been dispatched to the Wells Fargo Bank, but the two-story brick building had been stripped bare, padlocked, and abandoned. The two FEMA employees, Hamid's fourteen "associates," and the two armored personnel carriers disappeared. Only rumors remained to befuddle and vex the investigating security team.

Five days and three debriefings later, Captain Abdul Hamid surrendered himself to the evils of alcohol. Drunk and disoriented, he steered his wheelchair off a dock and drowned in San Francisco Bay.

At the end of this long and unproductive day General Heinrich Obermeyer glared down the length of the over-polished mahogany conference table at his Tactical Planning Staff and growled. They would never find the launch codes for the remaining Intercontinental Ballistic Missiles. They would never find the equipment and access codes for the Space Satellite Surveillance Systems. They would never find former DCI Jacob Andrew Kent. But with luck, he thought, his tactical staff might be able to find and neutralize the new ruler of the United States of America ... whomever he was.

New World Order

With the President, the First Lady, and a large percentage of Congress imprisoned and isolated near Wainwright, Obermeyer was certain that someone had been selected by somebody to fill the vacuum. And that unknown someone gave him nightmares and daymares.

"If this person, whomever he is, can rally the rabble against us, we will have problems," the General observed. "It is too early to tell Burgenstock anything, but I must know who he is and where he is. .... And I must know now!"

Disorganized resistance was bad enough. Organized resistance could be a disaster. But a country without a ruler, without someone to tell the rabble what to do and when to do it, was beyond Herr Obermeyer's narrow-minded and intolerant philosophy.

———

Just beyond the concealed entrance to a small and shallow cave within a tree-filled ravine, hiding under a leafy umbrella of overhanging boughs within a hidden glade, Benjamin Ellsworth Franklin received a singular cellular telephone call which changed the course of history.

"Yes, Mrs. Pratt," he said, flipping his cellular telephone open. "Say again. .... Yes. Uh-huh. Well, of course I know where it is. ... They wanna what? ... You gotta be kidding? ... No, of course not. ... Yes, Mrs. Pratt. For that we will burn the midnight oil. — Thank you. Have a nice day."

Ben Franklin closed his cellular telephone and took a deep breath. "We have an appointment at midnight, gentlemen. At the National Guard Armory."

"You sure?" Lisa asked, not fully comprehending. "After all, that place is guarded."

"I'm sure," Ben said. "It's Haley and Goldfarb. And the North Platte commander is a German."

"*Sieg Heil!*"

"You got it," Ben said, pulling a map from his backpack. "I don't know if he's actually a neo-Nazi or not, but he is definitely German, right down to his well-developed accent."

———

The top half of each headlight was blackened with paint in the black-out-style of World War Two. The dark van was barely visible as it passed through the open main entrance into the parking lot of the National Guard Armory warehouse.

Security Guard Henry Goldfarb turned off the lights inside the guard shack while his partner, John Haley, closed the gate. Then they guided the dark van through the dimly-lit lot and around the corner to an oversized side entrance — a sliding door illuminated in a cone of light from somewhere overhead.

"Bob? — Bob Lowell?"

Robert Lowell and Ben Franklyn emerged from the van, stepped into the shadowy cone of light, and solemnly shook hands with the two security guards.

"John. — Hank."

"You gentlemen are acquainted?" asked Ben.

"Of course," Lowell said, with a sniff of laughter. "You might say we were in the same business."

"We still are," Haley noted before turning to Ben Franklyn. "Heard you're looking for weapons and ammunition."

Ben nodded uncertainly. "And what will it cost us?"

"The protection of your group," Goldfarb said.

"Membership in your organization," Haley added.

Ben Franklyn nodded with feigned indifference. He would have happily accepted both men with out any preconditions, but he needed those guns.

"We could use your help," he said, trying very hard not to appear too anxious.

But Haley wasn't finished. "Uh, Ben, Hank's last name is Goldfarb. He's Jewish. And in case you haven't noticed, I'm black."

"So what?" Ben asked, caught unprepared. "Look, I've known you, what? Ten years?"

"Yeah. You're right," Haley said, hanging his head. "Sorry, Ben."

"Forget it," Ben shrugged. "With all that divisive government propaganda bombarding us, most of us suffer from foot-in-mouth disease. .... Including 'yours truly'."

With a rather flamboyant gesture, Hank Goldfarb unlocked and opened the sliding door with a screeching noise that provided an exclamation point to end the conversation. Then, with a flick of his wrist, Haley turned on the overhead lights. A solid triangle of brilliance ten feet wide radiated from the metal building and onto the asphalt. And Goldfarb, Haley, Ben Franklyn, and Lowell walked

New World Order

into the light inside the warehouse.

For a full minute the four men stood in silent awe, trying to understand what they were seeing. Then, in the middle of the silence, Ben raised his arm and signaled Lisa. She gunned the van and drove into the brightly-lit interior of the cavernous National Guard Armory warehouse, into the ultimate expression of mankind's trust in the humanity of his fellow man.

Two 10-ton six-by military trucks, partially loaded with crates of rifles and ammunition, were parked in the narrow center aisle which divided the monstrous warehouse into two equal parts. Tall stacks of crates and rows of boxes packed with weapons, ammunitions, and explosives filled both ends of the oversized metal repository.

Lisa and six militiamen climbed from the van and gazed in wonderment at the accumulated stacks of death and destruction. The four men continued to remain still for a short eternity, still trying to comprehend the enormity of this stockpile of vain and cruel savagery.

"Oh, my God!" Lowell's whisper became an echo within the thin tin walls of the building.

"And don't you forget it!" Haley chided, his chuckle also echoing back and forth throughout this cavernous tin tombstone.

"I never even imagined," Ben whispered so softly that no echo reverberated. "It makes my collection look like the work of an idiotic amateur!"

"I heard about this place," Stan Gorman grumbled, climbing from the van. "I heard about it, but I didn't believe it. Not here. Not even Washington would be dumb enough to simply leave all this out here in a tin shack in the middle of nowhere."

"But they did," Goldfarb sighed, shaking his head.

Gorman shook his head. All of this had been in his own backyard, practically, and he had dismissed it as somebody's drunken dream. He shook his head again and went to help Ben, Lisa, and the six militiamen fill the waiting six-by military trucks.

"We'll need more trucks," Lowell said factually, ignoring the echo.

"We've got four more gassed-up and ready to roll," Haley said. "They're parked just outside in the shadows."

Lowell nodded with uninhibited admiration. The two security guards had obviously devoted a good deal of thought and planning to this operation.

"Wonder what they'll say when they find out this stuff is missing?"

"Not much," Goldfarb answered, helping Lowell load a case of M-16's onto the bed of a six-by.

"Over half of this stuff isn't even on inventory. .... Any inventory."

"Guess they don't know how to count," Lowell observed, heading back for another crate of rifles.

"We have some eight hundred Stinger missiles, seventeen hundred Claymores, twelve hundred M-16's, and over a ton of C-4," Haley said. "Uh, plus several thousand hand grenades, both frag and phosophorous."

"Not to mention over a million rounds of ammunition for the M-16's," Goldfarb said, picking up the litany. "Also two hundred mortars and twelve thousand mortar shells, rockets and rocket launchers, thirty-caliber machine guns, and — well, I think you get the idea."

"Yes, I think we get the idea," Lowell said, passing a crate of rifles on to Ben and Lisa. "But why here?"

"Most of this stuff is either obsolete or overstocked," Haley said, sliding a case of rifles down from the top. "We are essentially a munitions garbage dump."

"Well, I, for one, believe in ecology," Ben said, latching on to the case of rifles. "Let's clean up this dump."

Five minutes later the two 10-ton six-by military trucks pulled out, and two more trucks were backed into the warehouse. But they were no longer joking. The United Nations' Military Command had ordered a dusk-to-dawn curfew nationwide. According to some well-posted spotters, however, North Platte was still napping. Ben Franklyn crossed his fingers and loaded another crate of rifles onto the truck.

"Relax, Ben. North Platte is still sleeping. And we'll know if they wake up."

But Lowell's assurances provided little consolation for Ben Franklyn's worries. North Platte was seventy miles and an hour-and-a-half away. They would have plenty of warning ... if the spotters didn't fall asleep.

Then they heard the dreaded squelch of static, followed by a voice: "This is twenty-one. This is twenty-one. — I have traffic. I have traffic."

They moved quickly, loading the third and fourth trucks in three-quarters of an hour, while listening intently for static on the radio.

"This is nineteen. This is nineteen. They are headed westside. I repeat, westside."

"It's local," Ben sighed.

"For now," Lowell admonished. "They're staying local, in North Platte, for now."

"And God help the poor bastard they hit," Lisa murmurred, wiping her sweaty palms on her pant leg.

"Amen to that," Ben said. "How far are we?"

"About halfway, I'd guess," Lowell answered. "It's two-thirty now. — I figure we'll need another two hours."

"Four-thirty," Ben thought aloud. "That's cutting it close. — Damn close."

"At least the spotter planes don't fly at night," Lisa sighed.

"At least not west of the Mississippi," Lowell amended. "At least not for now."

"So thank heavens for safety and paranoia," Ben muttered, loading another crate of fragmentation grenades onto the truck.

Forty-five minutes later two more trucks left the National Guard Armory warehouse. Trucks five and six carried Stinger missiles, Law's rockets, and crates of hand grenades past the returning six-by military trucks waiting in the parking lot.

"Weather?" Ben asked.

"Fog," Haley answered with a glance out the open door.

"Good. That'll buy us some time."

"Sorry," Lowell said, "but I think we're gonna need another truck."

* * *

Chapter Twelve

It was a shock to the system that made the entire country shudder with horror. The people of the United States of America had taken their freedom for granted, and now it had been taken away from them.

Diplomats had created the United Nations as an instrument for worldwide peace. Bankers had turned it into an instrument for worldwide domination.

And like many of the bureaucrats in the Washington, D.C., the bankers of Burgenstock thought that the only way to keep the peace was through a rigid class system, that the only way to maintain order was to eliminate individual freedom. Only a few people living in the District of Columbia — people like DCI Jacob Andrew Kent — realized the dangers of such a skewered philosophy.

This skewered philosophy brought down the Roman Empire, gave birth to the French Revolution, destroyed the Nazis, tore apart the British Empire, annihilated the Soviet Union, and created anarchy in Indonesia. And now the bankers of Burgenstock wanted to impose their skewered philosophy on a global scale.

But like all bureaucrats everywhere, these UN-types could not see the forest for the trees. They could not connect the dots. They could not see the whole picture.

Jack Kent knew that he could not see the whole picture. But he also knew that hundreds — perhaps even thousands — of ordinary individuals were deliberately defying martial law by hoarding food and fuel, weapons and ammunition, money and valuables .... And under martial law, hoarding was a crime punishable by death. The foreign United Nations' peacekeeping forces would kill anyone they even suspected of "hoarding" ... just on general principles.

Just sitting in the empty basement of an empty building in the darkness of a dark room in the middle of a dark night was enough to get him killed. But DCI Jack Kent deliberately stayed at his post ... on general principles.

A sixty-ton tank rumbled past, shaking the building to its foundation, bringing concrete dust and grit down from the basement's ceiling. With his path faintly illuminated by the glow of streetlamps shining through dirty basement windows, Jack Kent looked in briefly on his gasoline generator, and was relieved to hear it quietly growling away in a vented storeroom.

And then the telephone rang.

"General?"

"Jack?"

"That's right, General."

"Can they be taken, Jack?"

"I think so. Remember Vietnam? They've locked themselves up in enclaves, in garrisons — just like we did."

"Go on, Jack."

"Well, this one isn't in the books, General."

"Never mind that!"

Jack Kent cleared his throat, lit a cigarette, and carefully considered his response.

"Lose the uniforms. Go in as civilians and mix it up from the inside out. Infiltrate their garrison and take them from inside."

"It's crazy, but what the hell have we got to lose. And who knows, it just might work. Anything else?"

"Yes, but you won't like it."

"Tell me anyway."

But Kent had to wait while another tank rumbled down the street, and another cloud of concrete dust drifted down from the ceiling, before he continued.

"Do you have the 'patriot militia' list?"

The General hesitated, "Yes."

"I would suggest that you integrate your command with them, or at least with some of their groups."

"Jack!"

"They won't take orders from you," he continued, "so you will have to follow their lead and back them up whenever you can ... perhaps even expand their operations when feasible."

"But they're outlaws!"

"They're guerrilla fighters," the DCI said. "And this is guerrilla warfare. They're independent bastards, but try to cooperate with them as much as possible. They're our last line of defense."

"Understood. I'll do what I can."

"Good luck, General."

"Thanks, Jack. I'll need it. And then some."

DCI Jack Kent hung up the phone and crushed out his cigarette. It did not matter whose side the General was on. He would either go along, or he would go alone. It was his choice.

———

"Sorry to interrupt, sir, but we have a situation," said Sergeant Farrell. "We have a report that the U.N. garrison in Denver has apparently sent a convoy down I-70 toward Goodland. Six troop trucks, two armored personnel carriers, and two low-boys carrying one tank each."

"That nut on the Internet?" the Lieutenant asked, buttoning his shirt.

"Yes, sir."

"About a hundred and fifty troops against our fifty-seven," Lieutenant Sanchez mused. "Not bad odds."

"Sir, Goodland has not been evacuated."

"Estimated time of arrival?"

"Two and a half hours, give or take."

"Okay, Sergeant, we're here and they're not. Evacuate the town and set your ambush sites."

"Yes, sir!"

Lt. Sanchez grinned. "We're a long way from Fort Riley, Sergeant. You'll have to make do."

"Of course, sir." But Sgt. Farrell needed no encouragement. Defending his native Kansas homestead required no special appeal. These were, after all, his friends and neighbors.

"I took an oath," Sanchez growled. "And I'm not going to be pushed around by some pointy-headed kraut!"

Sgt. Farrell shook his head and offered a lopsided grin.

———

The sun was rising through the fog as the dark blue van left the cavernous and empty National Guard Armory warehouse, heading into the clouds. Nine truckloads of weaponry had been carefully scattered throughout four counties in southwestern Nebraska. The van had been loaded three times and unloaded twice before Lisa parked it between the trees behind a 10-ton six-by truck on a dirt path in front of the tree-filled ravine.

But the weaponry it carried was not the subject of John Haley's immediate thoughts as he slid open the van's side door and leaped to the ground.

"My family comes first."

"Don't worry," Lisa said, trying to reassure. "We'll have your family in here by noon."

"In broad daylight?"

"It's the safest time," Lowell said. "Since the United Nations' Military Command has ordered a dusk-to-dawn curfew, a couple of pickups loaded with boxes and furniture traveling in broad daylight will attract less attention than a boy on a bicycle at sundown."

"Still sounds risky," Goldfarb said, picking up a case of hand grenades. "I heard that a convoy of over a hundred soldiers passed through McCook en route to North Platte a few days ago."

"Actually it was closer to a week ago, Ben said, "and there were four convoys. Two came through McCook. Two more took I-80. Over twelve hundred troops came in from Denver, and another twelve hundred from Omaha. Apparently the Midwest is a hotbed of patriot insurgency — a threat to their New World Order."

"You seem to be very well informed," Goldfarb noted as he turned to carry his case of hand grenades into the tree-filled gulch.

"Just don't ask how," Ben warned, looking up at the sky. "Some of my sources prefer to remain anonymous."

Overhead the clouds were moving in, darkening the land and threatening their tranquility.

———

The Battle of Goodland started when the convoy stopped. The pristine truckstop seemed to be filled with over a dozen big rigs, and with two men manning the pumps. But when the convoy stopped, the two men were gone.

They took the truckstop in standard military-fashion. Quietly and cautiously they fanned out from the six troop trucks and crawled under the restaurant's windows. They dived through doorways and ducked behind the counters. They invaded public bathrooms and took cover within a janitorial closet. But their stealthy tactics were for naught. No one was home.

With a reluctance born of suspicion, and with a curt nod from the lieutenant, Sergeant Obrenovic raised the whistle to his lips and blew the triple-blast of recall.

The soldiers stopped their advance. They hesitated, then cautiously retreated towards the six-by troop trucks. At first they inched their way back, seeking cover at every turn. But within three minutes they abandoned stealth for a casual stroll across the well-lit parking lot, lulled by the quiet tranquility of Goodland, Kansas.

Then a single shot rang out.

The first bullet drilled a hole in Sgt. Obrenovic's forehead and blew off his blue helmet. Then there were thousands of bullets flying everywhere. Blue helmets rolled across the asphalt as their owners were flung back and forth in a murderous cross-fire. Blood splattered the asphalt, the sidewalks, the buildings, and the trucks. Bodies of United Nations' soldiers were blasted across the parking lot, blown through the restaurant's plate-glass windows, and ripped to shreds around light stanchions.

For five terror-filled minutes fifty-seven deserter-soldiers from the Tenth Light Cavalry of Fort Riley, Kansas, fired again and again into the shredded remains of the blood-smeared United Nations' forces. Many may have been dead long before the shooting stopped, but no one wanted to take that chance. They continued firing until Sanchez called for a cease-fire, reducing the roar to an occasional explosion directed at a twitching body.

"Sergeant Farrell?"

He came from his ambush site among the semitrailer rigs. "We lost about a dozen, Lieutenant. Sorry, sir, but there are no prisoners."

"You did what you could," Sanchez said, blindly studying the asphalt at his feet. "I'll need a body count for ... the record."

"Yes, sir."

Neither man spoke of what was foremost in his mind. Killing and dying were parts of their job descriptions.

Major Hermann Hoffman called the small, insulated, tin shed near the *Lee Bird* terminal his home as well as his office, and with good reason: he lived there. He slept on a surplus couch alongside his desk. (It had been borrowed from a local 'used-furniture' store.) He hung his uniforms in a locker behind his desk. (It had been swiped from a local fire station.) And he ate his meals at his desk. (The food came from the unit's field kitchen, which had been set up inside the terminal. The desk had been liberated from a local 'office supply' store.)

The two-room tin shed east of the terminal and the two-story wooden barracks west of the terminal went up first. The construction of three additional hangars for yet-to-arrive aircraft and a six-hundred-ten-and-meter (two-thousand-foot) extension of runway 30R followed. But Hoffman's planned machine shop and weather station were repeatedly delayed by random acts of sabotage.

Sugar had been pored into the gas tanks of several six-by troop trucks. Stacks of corrugated tin, sheet metal, and a collection of power tools from a local hardware store had mysteriously disappeared. And over a hundred soldiers had become violently ill after eating tainted meat liberated from a local supermarket.

The people of North Platte had no intention of surrendering *Lee Bird Regional Airport* without a fight. They'd forced Major Hoffman into concentrating on checkpoints, fortifications, and protective counterstrike activities.

"Those meddlesome ingrates!" But his screams of anguish were meant only to relieve his own frustration. He would have happily sacrifice all his men and materiel for control of Section Sixty-Nine.

Hoffman flung the report aside, muttered under his breath in Low German, and lit a cigarette. The one thing the Americans do well, he thought, and their former President wanted it abolished! Trust the American politicians to louse things up! Those amateurish wimps never knew when to leave well-enough alone! Ignorant, self-serving imbeciles! But then his angry thoughts were interrupted by a knock on the door.

Captain Aritomo Yamaguchi offered a sharp salute. Hoffman disdainfully returned the salute and opened the identity case.

"Sullivan?"

"We found him last night —"

"Yes, I know," Hoffman cut in. "Single chair. And I want you beside the desk. .... Let us explore the dirt under the fingernails of this anti-American F.B.I. agent."

Aritomo Yamaguchi pushed the second chair into the corner opposite the door, while Hoffman turned around to study the gray clouds which were just visible through the plate-glass window behind and above his desk.

"It is overcast," Yamaguchi said, marching to stand alongside the battered desk. "I should stand here?"

Hoffman nodded. "Let them in."

Yamaguchi opened the door and resumed his post beside the scarred desk. Hoffman crushed out his cigarette and waited.

Sandwiched between the two burly blue helmets with "M.P." armbands, Sullivan looked miserable.

Hoffman waved him towards the chair. "Sit down. Sit down. .... Agent Sullivan of the Federal Bureau of Investigation?"

"You wanted to see me?" Sullivan asked.

Hoffman flipped the identity case across his desk.

Sullivan gave it a quick once-over and pocketed it within his stained and dusty suitcoat.

"You wrote a report on the Goodland massacre and filed it with the Lincoln F.B.I. field office. Correct?"

"I work out of the Lincoln office," Sullivan said.

"Yet you were on your way to Canada. —Why?"

Sullivan was silent for a long, suspense-filled moment as he considered the alternatives. To use the "secret-orders-from-Washington" defense, although true, would be pointless with these stereotypical soldiers.

Finally he said, "Because our infrastructure has been compromised. And because our attempts to neutralize illegal weapons ... failed."

"So you decided to escape to Canada?"

"Canada ... seems to be the best alternative."

Hoffman nodded complacently, knowing that Sullivan was lying.

"Yes, it probably is the best alternative." Pulling a concealed Lugar pistol from his desk drawer, Hoffman casually shot the F.B.I. agent between the eyes. "Unfortunately it is not available to you."

Sullivan's lifeless body slid from the chair and slowly crumpled to the floor. Major Hoffman stood up and leaned over his desk, examining the corpse as if it was an interesting insect he had just crushed under the heel of his boot.

"Rather messy," he complained, nodding to the two military policemen standing near the door.

Former DCI Jack Kent had never been formally removed from office. On the other hand, the Central Intelligence Agency no longer formally existed. He was the director of nothing.

Through a friend of a friend, however, he had created a small office in a small house nestled beside a small mountain lake near Hagerstown, Maryland. Through friends of friends in a certain telephone company, he had installed several hard-to-trace telephone lines, including two direct international connections.

Except for the hidden telephone lines, he was practically self-contained. His heavily-muffled gasoline generator had enough fuel for six years of continuous use, all carefully concealed within the surrounding woods. The lake — actually it was closer to a pond — supplied his water, while the walk-in freezer in the basement was well-stocked.

But he knew, even if they didn't, that the United Nations could not keep this charade going forever. Not even the European banks could dominate the freedom of all mankind, let alone the United States of America. .... Or could they?

Unlike other nations, the United States had rejected the "Divine Right of Kings" as a ruling concept. With multiple and diverse religions, conquest by religious domination was also impossible. But rule by economic fiat was another matter.

Few honest government employees had seen it coming, but for years they had willingly cooperated with the very forces which had now ordered the invasion of the United States in the name of "peace and order."

Jack Kent had seen it happening, but he had been far too late to stop the military invasion, let alone the financial subversion creating the situation in the first place. There was, however, something wrong with that equation.

"But of course!" It was barely a whisper.

The United Nations had moved too precipitously, *before* the bankers finished creating the degree of disorder and lawlessness needed in the United States to justify foreign intervention. And that lack of justification might unravel the entire mess.

"Be home," he commanded, punching the 011 numbers ... and the country-code for Belgium.

———

Obermeyer read the report twice. General Seminski scanned

it three times while smoking three Russian cigarettes. General Fawdi, who insisted his nameplate be engraved in Arabic as well as standardized English, had also insisted that the reports be written on paper rather than on the laptop computer screen. But only General Martin remained aloof and unmoved by the mysterious massacre of one hundred seventy-five troops at an isolated truck stop in the middle of nowhere.

"Goodland, Kansas." Obermeyer read the laptop screen with his fingertip. "Western part of the state. Near Colorado. On I-70. An unknown number of assailants with military ammunition. The bodies were stacked in the back of two troop transport trucks after being stripped of all weapons and identification. No trace of the other four trucks, the armored personnel carriers, or the two Russian T-80 tanks."

Fawdi flashed a look of pure anger as Seminski lit another foul-smelling cigarette. The Russian, Obermeyer noted, remained unperturbed.

"Anything on the computer hacker in Denver?" General Martin asked.

"We have searched over a hundred buildings, but all of them were empty." General Dupre sniffed haughtily at the mere thought of these rogue Americans evading his search plan. "He will make an error sooner or later, and then we will have him."

"Let us hope it is not too late," Obermeyer growled. "Complacency defeated Cornwallis. It could destroy us."

"Yes, this complacency will destroy us!" Fawdi said. "We need stronger contraband laws! And stronger enforcement! Stop the drugs, alcohol, cigarettes, coffee! Teach them the meaning of pain and suffering! Teach them to obey!"

"Trust an Arab to turn every battle into a *jihad*!" Obermeyer muttered. "Any other opinions?"

"From my reading of this report," General Martin said, "I would deduce that the attack was planned and executed by a detachment from the United States' Army. Probably deserters who refused to surrender."

"Are there many of them around?" Obermeyer asked.

"Several hundred groups, I should imagine," the Britisher said. "Perhaps ten to twenty thousand."

"Twenty thousand!" Obermeyer was obviously shaken.

"That is nothing!" Fawdi said. "We have ten million!"

"Fifteen," Obermeyer corrected. "And twenty million by the end of this month. But that much resistance could be ... very formidable. Have you communicated with their military officers about these ... rogue units?"

"I have," Martin said. "The situation, however, is quite beyond their control."

"We must have control of the military forces to have control of the country," Obermeyer said. "That is basic. .... They will obey, or they will die. Understood?"

General Martin kept a stiff upper lip, but his heart was stuck in his throat. "Yes, sir."

No wonder Air Commodore Harmon had 'gone missing.'

* * *

James A. Clayton

Chapter Thirteen

They came in low, lean, and mean: six Russian Panther attack helicopters in search of a target — any target. Their shadows darkened the sky as their rotor blades spun out a downdraft of death. Six ancient Pave Low III helicopters followed them across Colorado and into Nebraska. Like the Panthers before them, these Pave Lows were seeking something — someone — to kill.

Palisade, Nebraska — population 380, give or take — was not expecting any particular problems on that late Spring day, even when they heard the chopping whirr of the old Pave Low III as it dived to treetop height to look at the town. Palisade had nothing of intrinsic value to offer any invader, and it was too small to offer any opposition to anyone.

The little town had been selected almost at random as a test site, a place where twelve helicopters from Colorado would rendezvous with eight armored personnel carriers in a search-and-destroy practice mission.

Far below, the APC convoy turned north off Highway 6 and into Palisade. They bounced across the railroad tracks and fanned out down the side streets, parking crosswise to block the intersections. From each APC eight soldiers, each in full battle gear and wearing the familiar blue United Nations' helmet, quietly to their randomly selected targets — the houses on that particular street.

Divided into four-man squads, their assault techniques provided Palisade with a brutal introduction to international terrorism. The squad leader slammed on the door with the butt of his automatic rifle. The young man opening the door that Sunday afternoon wore a ragged tee-shirt and faded blue jeans. He was not expecting company.

"We are inspecting for contraband," the squad leader snapped.
"Fuck you!"

And the squad leader had the door slammed in his face.

"Peasant!" The squad leader stepped back and two soldiers hit the door with their shoulders, smashing it open.

"Who the hell do you think you are?"

"I give the orders here, peasant!"

Then the civilian's question was answered with gunfire. A woman screamed hysterically. All four squad members rushed into the little house. Sounds of breaking glass, crashing furniture, and ripping cloth mixed with the screams in a cacophonous melee.

Dressed only in bra, panties, and the ragged remains of a faded pink blouse, the screaming woman fled the little house, pursued by four sex-crazed soldiers. She managed to reach her neighbor's front lawn before the blue helmets dragged her to the ground and fell on her, laughing sadistically.

Up the street on the wide front porch of a two-story wood-frame house, another squad leader was less successful. There had been no response when he "knocked" on the door. And when his men slammed into it, they were rewarded with sore shoulders. With a nod from the squad leader, the fourth soldier slapped a small shape-charge onto the keyhole and stuck a timer-fuse detonator into it.

The small explosion blew the door apart.

"Hmm, I didn't think it was that powerful," the fourth soldier commented as he led the way into the house. Only then a shotgun blast blew him back out of the house, across the front porch, and onto the sidewalk.

The squad leader took one look at the bloody, shredded corpse and screamed his defiance. But the three soldiers froze when they saw the hand grenade roll over the threshold. They hesitated just long enough to die within the horrendous explosion which blew away the wide front porch and scorched the wood frame around the front doorway.

A squad searching the empty house across the street arrived just in time to find a yard filled with burnt and blasted bodies, and another empty house.

Back down the street the first squad pulled the young housewife to her feet. Surrounded by their lecherous, leering grins, she now knew why they had allowed her to live.

Flipping his blue helmet off and dropping his automatic rifle, the squad leader flashed a perverted grin of demonic lust and ripped away the remains of her blouse. Another soldier released the hooks of her bra. Hands slipped over her shoulders to intimately cup and fondle her breasts and nipples. Another hand slid across her stomach and into her panties, caressing her pudenda. Her bra slipped off her body. Lips nibbled and sucked on her neck and shoulders. Fingers roamed her flesh. Someone pulled off her panties. They pressed against her nude body. The squad leader's hands squeezed her buttocks. He unzipped his fly and pressed his exposed masculinity against her. A low moan escaped her lips.

With a leering grin, the squad leader took her down to the grass. And with his fellow squad members looking on, he raped her svelte body.

A single shot flung a squad member on top of the leader and his victim. A muffled shot raised the squad leader off his victim. A second muffled shot threw him off her nude body and tore a second hole in his chest. Blood soaked his shirt and splattered her exposed flesh.

A third shot from the dead squad leader's pistol blew the brains out of a helmetless young soldier. The fourth squad member hit the grassy front lawn at the same instant, drilled in the back by three angry .22-caliber slugs.

The young housewife screamed. She rose to her feet, naked and screaming, and shot three more UN soldiers running across the street towards her. She shot two other soldiers before the pistol clicked empty. Then a dozen automatic rifles blasted her nude body to bloody shreds, decapitating her in the process.

A single-story house on the west side of the street, opposite the decapitated body, suddenly exploded. Windows and doors were blown outward in a blast that shook the entire town and flung a flaming corpse into the street.

A Pave Low III helicopter wheeled over Palisade then, with its machine gunners firing randomly at anything that moved. Bullets kicked up turf, dirt, and gravel. Chips of asphalt and concrete were blasted from the streets and sidewalks. Windows were shattered and wooden buildings were tattooed. Eight civilians and seven UN soldiers were wounded by stray gunfire. Two civilians and three soldiers died in the hail of friendly machine gunfire.

Lumbering awkwardly, the Pave Low III and its backup wheeled away from the village towards the main highway.

New World Order

The blue helmets gathered their dead and wounded within the armored personnel carriers ... and left town.

Behind them, the bloodied and battered residents of Palisade tried to bring some semblance of order and sanity to a mess they could not comprehend.

The ancient, black sedan was fifty-years-old, yet it purred like a contented kitten. Its driver was not quite as old, but he loved the restoration. He had spent five years and thousands of dollars rebuilding the mechanical marvel now gliding sedately south-and-east over Highway 6 between Palisade and Culbertson. The slow-moving sedan provided an easy target, however, for the loud and obnoxious Pave Lows following it.

The soldiers manning the .30-caliber machine guns needed an easy target. Their shells pitted the highway, cut down two trees, demolished several shrubs, and clipped a lot of grass before killing the driver and turning the old sedan into scrap metal.

Their great victory was short lived. Seconds later the old Pave Low III disappeared within a bright flash and a shattering roar. It reappeared an instant later as hundreds of unidentifiable bits and pieces of scrap metal falling from a fireball in the sky.

Down below, among the trees, Bob Lowell felt a mild surge of pleasure in the flaming destruction of the old MH-53J Pave Low. Destroying one helicopter was only a symbolic victory, but at least it was a victory.

"Word on the Internet is that there have been massive desertions throughout the military," Ben Franklyn said, examining an oil stain on his military camouflage outfit.

"Massive desertions?" Lisa shook her head. "A bunch of generals without an army?"

"Something like that," Ben said. "Hell, little squad-and-platoon-sized groups have been deserting left-and-right ever since the President quit. But the Goodland ambush apparently frightened the powers-that-be. So the U.N. high command issued an order: '*obey-or-die*' ... and over half the army went A.W.O.L. over night."

"Are they serious?" Lowell asked, searching for a clear field-of-fire.

"Of course they're serious," Ben said as he set up another Stinger site. "They think that after a nationwide campaign of terror and violence we're all gonna roll over and play good doggie."

"Why don't we roll over and bite 'em in the ass."

"Very poetic, Lisa," the old farmer sighed, "but I don't think they'll appreciate it."

"They're coming," Stan Gorman warned, dropping to one knee and lofting the Stinger onto his shoulder.

Six Panther attack helicopters came over the rolling hills in a staggered and disorganized formation, looking for revenge. They found four Stinger missiles looking for a heat source.

Four Panthers disappeared within bursting fireballs and thunderous explosions. A fifth arced away into a green hillside and a fiery crash. The surviving Panther ducked behind a hill and left in a hurry.

"Five for four," Ben noted, trying hard not to gloat. "Five for four."

"The others got away," Lisa observed.

"We were lucky," Stan Gorman added. "We just happened to be in the right place at the right time with the right equipment."

Bob Lowell set his launcher back into its box at the rear of the innocent-looking sports van.

"And your opinion?"

He looked at Ben and shrugged, "They used to say that flying was the safest way to travel. .... But then they use to say a lot of things, didn't they?"

Ben and Lisa nodded, but their nods had nothing to do with flying. It was not a job they liked, but it was a job that had to be done.

It was the fifth "safe-house" they had visited in as many weeks. Isolated in the middle of the Harz Mountains of Germany, the less-than-impressive farmstead was protected by hills and trees and a rutted, muddy path which barely qualified as a road. Beyond that, however, its remote solitude had the virtue of not attracting unwanted attention.

For Air Commodore Sir George Wesley Harmon of the Royal Air Force, the farmhouse and its basement apartment offered almost everything he could want — food, shelter, and a communications system that plugged directly into a handy space satellite.

For Lieutenant Victor (NMN) McVey of the United States

Marine Corps, it was a damp little foxhole in a big mud puddle covered with soggy debris. He felt trapped, imprisoned, and alone within the dingy darkness.

Now wearing workmen's clothing, they bore little resemblance to the two neat and proud military officers who once strolled the corridors of NATO. McVey sported a full beard and chemically-stained teeth. Harmon opted for a mustache and eyeglasses, with special shoes designed to make him walk with a limp. Neither man could be mistaken for a military officer.

Except for the location of certain "safe-houses," McVey knew little about the European underground beyond its existence. He was careful not to discuss anything, no matter how insignificant, with their guides and other "travel agents." And he wisely chose not to bother Air Commodore Harmon with unnecessary inquiries about their hosts.

(During a rather mundane weekend the Air Commodore did confess to putting in some time with MI-7 and with the U.S. Central Intelligence Agency. He also reluctantly admitted to knowing something about the European underground, which apparently had been born during the Second World War, grew up during the 'Cold War,' and still maintained loose and vague connections with certain groups and individuals. Harmon's reticence suggested, however, that he knew a good deal more.)

The farmstead appeared to be just another stopover in an endless journey to nowhere ... until the fourth day. The arrival of the unimpressive itinerant electrician, although irritating, did not seem too unusual — until he took Harmon and McVey aside for a few moments and a quiet chat.

"It has been checked and confirmed, sir. General Wilder has been delivered to the High Security Section of the United Nations Military Prison near Mannheim."

"I was not aware that they had such facilities over here," Harmon whispered tersely.

"Their existence is not ... general knowledge," the electrician candidly admitted. "Most of their prisons and concentration camps are in the United States. Something their banker friends acquired on-the-side, so to speak. — Mannheim, however, is a renovation of an old castle used by the Nazi S.S. for ... various things."

"Torture chambers?" McVey asked.

The electrician hesitated. "Among other things. They used it mostly for ... special political prisoners. Beyond that, I do not know."

"Hell, you weren't even born then," McVey snapped. "None of us were."

"Checked and confirmed?" Harmon asked.

"Checked and confirmed," the electrician said. "There are maps in my toolcase. I will leave them with you, but you will wait for me. Otherwise their alarm system will ... alert others. Understood?"

But McVey wasn't satisfied. ""You're not even German, are you?"

"Of course not, old boy," the electrician laughed. "Even the Germans know that!"

He handed them a packet of maps, drawings, and notes from his toolcase. Then, toolcase in hand, he climbed into the van and slammed the door.

"And, uh, if I were you, sir, I would not spend too much time outdoors during the daylight hours," the electrician added, "just to be safe."

"Quite right," Harmon acknowledged.

With the van's tires spitting gravel, the electrician drove from the farmyard and vanished someplace beyond the barn.

'Torture,' Wilder concluded, 'was probably a lost art.'

He did not, of course, say it. There was no point in telling his tormentor that he almost enjoyed these sessions. Even standing in a puddle of water and being attached to a six-volt car battery was beginning to provide a certain amount of pleasure, almost sexual in nature, to Wilder's psyche.

Of his surroundings he knew practically nothing. He had been brought to this place in a completely-enclosed van from another cell in another prison. But his previous incarceration had been in a fairly well-lit institution. This prison offered no such benign errors. It was a dungeon of wet brick walls and damp rock walls, with rough concrete passages and low-voltage lighting within its dark and dismal tunnels.

He had arrived in the darkness of a cold, wet morning and had been thrown bodily into a cold, empty cell. Later an unshaven man wearing a guard's uniform brought him breakfast — a hot cereal which was cold and a cup of lukewarm tea.

After an eternity of trying to sleep on an unpadded metal cot in a cold and damp cell, he'd been awakened by two toughs in blue berets. They'd dragged him from his cell and through a long corridor, then down a flight of rough concrete stairs to another long corridor that ended at a thick, wooden door.

Beyond the thick wooden door he met his tormentor, a pimply-faced youth in need of a shave, a haircut, and a bath. His tormentor did not speak any English, only German, and apparently not very well.

(Wilder, himself, spoke English, French, and German with a fair amount of fluency. His captors were not as well-educated nor as polite. They'd never heard of the Geneva Convention.)

The first time they'd just roughed him up a bit — a few well-aimed punches and a few incomprehensible questions. The second time they tried a needle filled with an unidentifiable liquid which made things a bit fuzzy, and made General Wilder rather ill. The third, fourth, and fifth visits — in as many days — brought variations of the old shock treatment. These ruffians, however, lacked inventiveness.

On the sixth visit beyond the wooden door, the tormentor brought a translator, and strapped Wilder to a wooden chair.

"Name?"

"Donald Thornton Wilder. General, United States Army. Serial number five-two-seven ... four-two-seven ... oh-one-six."

"You are a smart ass," the translator said without any inflection. Wilder said nothing.

But then the tormentor said something to the translator.

"He wants to know who else belongs to your underground organization," the translator said. "He wants names and addresses and recognition codes Now!"

"The Geneva Convention —"

"To hell with that!" the translator interrupted. "Geneva can screw itself! .... Now, who else, General?"

"Go fuck yourself," said Wilder.

For a moment the translator stood silently over the General, looking down at the old man with a contempt which defied all translations. Then the translator hit the General. He hit hard, tipping the man and the chair over.

The dull lightbulb flickered into existence as consciousness filtered back into Wilder's foggy mind. Dangling from the ceiling on threadbare wires, the lightbulb seemed almost threatening.

"You hit harder than he does," Wilder said.

"Yes, but he enjoys it."

"And you don't?"

The translator studied the splintered remains of the wooden chair with disdain. The tip of the bullwhip effortlessly sliced through the prisoner's frayed shirt. Wilder cried out. His tormentor laughed. The translator shook his head.

"Like I say, he enjoys it."

The tormentor cracked the whip again, slicing another ragged cut through the shirt's thin cotton and Wilder's pale flesh. And when he did not draw blood, he at least raised red welts. He flogged Wilder mercilessly, laughing as he turned the General's gray prison garb into bloody-red rags.

"Names!" the translator shouted. "Addresses! .... Codes!"

Wilder rolled back and forth across the stone floor, smearing his blood over its wet surface as he tried to avoid the lash. But the tormentor just laughed and lashed out again and again until he had stripped the old man naked.

Stark naked and covered with blood-smeared red welts, Wilder lay face down on the cold stone floor, shivering but only semiconscious. Irritated, the tormentor grabbed Wilder's wrist and yanked the old man to his feet. The tormentor smiled. Then he hit Wilder in the stomach.

"I teach meaning of freedom," the tormentor snorted in heavily-accented English. He leaned forward, expelling his fetid breath into the old man's battered face. "I teach meaning of freedom."

His tormentor snorted again as he jabbed the electric cattle prod into Wilder's bloodied stomach and thumbed the switch. The old man cried out as the electrical charge tore through his body like a thousand red-hot needles puncturing his flesh.

"I teach freedom." And the tormentor again thumbed the switch.

Wilder screamed.

"He really does enjoy it," the translator said.

Wilder moaned.

"Maybe we try little lower." The tormentor brought the electric cattle prod up between the old man's blood-smeared legs and pressed the switch.

The hysterical screams echoed throughout the room. They could even be heard, rather faintly, in the stone corridor beyond the wooden door.

But no one was listening.

* * *

James A. Clayton

Chapter Fourteen

Violence may be the last resort of the incompetent, but it is also the ultimate resort of the allegedly competent as well. As far back as mankind can recall, nations have warred against nations and tribes have warred against tribes.

The New World Order solution of a singular one-world government proposed to eliminate violence through a dictatorship of the elite. It was a new singer, but the same old song. "Law and order" would eliminate violence ... and crush individual freedom. But no person who has ever known some degree of freedom would willingly surrender it for the "betterment of mankind" — or any other philosophical gibberish.

The Rothchilds and other European banking families grew rich exploiting violence. And as their fortunes grew, their manipulative powers grew. But to use that power efficiently, they were forced to establish intricate methods and mechanisms within their own banking systems to control the external forces seeking their money and their power.

Soon the presidents, general managers, and other officers of the banks found themselves spending more and more time winding their way through the labyrinthine twists and turns of European power politics. In what must have been something close to utter and total desperation, the banks took an attorney or two from each of their various legal departments and set them up as a separate unit to handle such complicated matters.

But as they say, give a lawyer an inch and he'll take your wallet — and anything else he can steal. These lawyers soon became a law unto themselves, establishing yet another sub-group to handle international situations. This sub-group, composed of the best and the brightest in their profession, quickly learned how to suborn and undermine both the bankers and the politicians. Thus, they were ultimately able to gain total control of the entire banking system's subsidiary operations for their own personal use.

The Chairman gazed through the plate-glass picture window at the green hills and rugged mountains, and wondered about Banker Six — 'the young one.' Naming the group "*Law Merchants*" did show a certain flair, a certain classical touch; but such a name had to be confined, to remain within the group.

The elderly Chairman uttered a heavy sigh. This third floor lounge was too soft and too posh for his own appreciation. There was, he had to admit, some irony in this. He had designed the lounge area, including the fireplace and the side rooms for television viewing, billiards, and other games. He had even suggested placement of the windows and the color scheme for the padded sofas. But he had been very young and optimistic in those days.

Like 'the young one,' The Chairman had once possessed a certain flair, a certain classical touch. He remembered spending days, even weeks, designing the command-and-control center hidden under "*The Sacred Blood of Jesus*" Roman Catholic Church in Brussels, and decided to support 'the young one.' The name "*Law Merchants*" would not become general public knowledge until it would be far, far too late for anyone to object to anything.

But The Chairman could not waste time on memories. He had anticipated some discontent as the American peasants were guided into a more structured and protected life-style. He had not anticipated general insurrection. He had expected to finance a resettlement. He had ended up paying for a war.

And he found it irritating.

The old C-130 Hercules transport finished its bank-and-turn towards its final approach, and glided down to the end of the primary runway 30R at *Lee Bird Field*, just east of North Platte, Nebraska. With tires screeching, the pilot brought the old four-engine turboprop down to an almost-textbook landing, and rolled almost lethargically passed the two blue-helmeted officers walking alongside the ptarmic runway.

"That makes thirty-five hundred, Major," Yamaguchi said, watching the C-130 roll by. "That is seven hundred over our assigned complement."

"So I've been told," Hoffman growled. "But yesterday they

shot down six of our helicopters. — Six helicopters, Captain." Do you understand?"

He waited to see if it sank in, but Yamaguchi's expression did not change. He observed, but he did not react. Did the Captain understand?

"Six helicopters," Hoffman continued, "and that is organized resistance. Some sort of secret underground group or organization, perhaps."

"I understand a secret underground. But organized?"

"Do not underestimate them, Captain Yamaguchi. These Americans can be quite clever."

"I graduated from the University of Southern California, Major. I know these Americans. They may be clever, but they are not civilized."

"Then we must teach them some manners, Captain."

Yamaguchi remained silent for a quarter of a kilometer or more. They reached the parking aprons for the three A-10 Warthogs before he spoke again.

"These Americans lack self-discipline," Yamaguchi said. "They live in a disorganized dreamworld. They confuse freedom, independence, and individualism with responsibility, power, and authority. Eventually they will destroy themselves."

"They must learn obedience to law and order," Hoffman said rhetorically. "They must learn to be respectful and obedient to their superiors."

"The only thing you can teach them is how to die, but I doubt that they will ever learn to do that correctly."

A dozen shots rang out across the airfield, echoing back-and-forth throughout the cantonment.

"The three saboteurs, the spy with the cellular telephone, and the old man hoarding coffee," Yamaguchi said without inflection. "Violating the law is a popular American pastime."

"Stupid peasants!" Hoffman shook his head and shrugged his shoulders. At least he did not have to pay for the ammunition.

It was a cool Tuesday morning, but the streets of McCook were unusually quiet and empty. These were not usual times for southwestern Nebraska. The murderous attack on the village of Palisade had shaken them. More than half the town was now in permanent exile. Most of the remaining residents now lived in basements, either their own or their neighbors, and spent most of their time preparing for the inevitable attack.

Thus on that cool Tuesday morning most of the town knew within minutes when the six heavily-armed soldiers parked their stolen station wagon in the city lot at the corner of "D" and First Street East. Many eyes followed them down Norris Avenue past the boarded-up frontage of Sehnert's Dutch Oven Bakery & Coffee Shoppe and through the red light on "C" Street.

(The six German-speaking UN soldiers apparently thought that Schnert's, like many businesses in McCook, had permanently closed its doors and gone out-of-business. They were wrong. The front had been carefully boarded-up and the plate-glass windows removed, but the mayor and city council still met there every weekday morning. Patrons were now forced to enter through the kitchen, but they obviously didn't mind this minor inconvenience. A cup of coffee at Sehnert's was worth a good deal more.)

The soldiers saw no one, and did not know they were being watched. They spoke in German, not realizing that McCook was quite proud of its German-American heritage. They were not drunk — at least not yet — but they often paused during their ambling walk to drink from a hip-flask or light a cigarette.

Across "C" Street and still headed downhill on Norris, they slowly became aware of the empty feeling along the town's main street. Passing the boarded-over frontage of the McCook National Bank, all six came to a stumbling halt.

"This does not feel right," Lieutenant Frederick said quite clearly in passable English. "This town is too empty, too quiet. They have boards over everything, but there has been no looting. Why?"

"Perhaps there is nothing worth stealing," one of the troopers said just before he guzzled his hip-flask dry.

The others, however, said nothing. When Frederick spoke in English, they kept quiet and listened carefully.

Frederick unstrapped his M-16 and aimed it across the street, randomly waving the gun back-and-forth in search of a target.

"Yes," he sighed, "perhaps they have nothing worth taking."

His gunbarrel wavered between the "closed" sign in the window of the A & M Drug Store and the boarded-up front of Modern

Cleaners for at least another minute, but nothing moved. The streets were empty, and only an occasional gust of wind disturbed the silence. Electric tension traveled from their commander through the soldiers like a live current, leaving them looking nervously at the emptiness.

Tension oozed from Lt. Frederick's blond Teutonic form. A tremor of adrenaline-withdrawal rippled through his muscular frame and quivered to death within him. He had to be wrong, but he didn't feel right about that.

With nothing to shoot, he found himself ambling aimlessly down Norris and through the red light on "B" Street. But "B" Street was actually a major thoroughfare for McCook, in spite of its label. The four-lane street was also three federal highways. And combining four routes into one meant that "B" Street was never "empty" — at least, not until now.

That vacated look bothered Lt. Frederick. Had the town been abandoned by all of its inhabitants? For Lt. Frederick, such a thought seemed unthinkable. Norris Avenue leveled out south of "B" Street, but the inlaid-brick main street managed just over one more block, past "A" Street, before abruptly ending in a cul-de-sac at the railroad tracks. On the west side of Norris and just south of "B" Street, plywood panels now covered the front of Eakes' Office Plus. The paneling appeared to be brand-new, and that made Lt. Frederick very nervous.

Where did they get the plywood?

He was still wondering about the plywood paneling when he smashed his way through the front door of the Looking Glass Lounge. Had he concentrated more on the problems at hand, he might have seen the bartender disappear through the back door. But his first concern was booze, not bartenders.

War is Hell, especially when you don't know who you're fighting. And when you don't know if you are fighting, it's even worse. They were to "maintain order" in the area, whatever that meant. For Lt. Frederick it meant stopping looters, checking identification papers, searching for contraband, and occasionally getting drunk. And after his walk through downtown McCook, only the "getting drunk" seemed to apply.

Then he realized that there were ice cubes in his drink. And he remembered that the traffic lights were also working. But why should this town still have electricity?

"Sergeant!"

"Sir?"

"This village has electricity, Sergeant," Frederick slurred, trying to maintain some semblance of military decorum.

"Yes, sir."

"Why does this village still have electricity, Sergeant?"

"General Order Twenty-Seven, sir."

The Lieutenant flipped open his pocket notebook and read General Order Twenty-Seven twice. He finished his drink in two swallows and marched out the front door.

"So this is supposed to be a safe area?" he slurred under his breath, again wondering about the plywood paneling.

The Sergeant and the four privates followed Lt. Frederick into the noonday sunshine, perhaps wondering if they were as drunk as he looked. The Lieutenant swayed back and forth, his eyes roaming the intersection of "A" and Norris, and to the old brick railroad station beyond.

"This is safe area?" Frederick asked again, his words blurred by booze.

The Sergeant shrugged, a gesture of helplessness to an impossible question. Like the Lieutenant, he could only assume — he could only hope — that command intelligence was correct in their assessment.

"War is Hell. So what are we doing over here?"

Sergeant Kohl offered a half-smile of commiseration. "It's our job."

Then a little old man with a white cane and thinning white hair hobble around the corner from "A" Street onto Norris, interrupting their philosophical discussion.

"What are you doing here, little old man?"

But the little octogenarian could only shrug and cock his head to one side in an attempt to understand the Lieutenant's question, an attempt complicated by the Lieutenant's poor and inebriated English.

"What is your name?" Kohl asked.

There was a moment of silence as the feeble, elderly man considered the question.

"Your name?" Frederick shouted.

"Simon," the old man finally croaked in a small, frog-like

James A. Clayton

voice. "Yes. .... Simon."

"*Juden,*" the Lieutenant muttered under his alcoholic breath.

"Your identity papers," Sgt. Kohl commanded. But the feeble old man could only look up through his wire-rimmed bifocals and offer a shrug of incomprehensible confusion.

"Your identification papers, sir," the Sergeant repeated. But the old man obviously did not understand.

"Your identification papers ... now!" Frederick shouted. But the octogenarian could not understand them.

Kohl shoved the old man back against the wall. "Your papers!"

The old man feebly raised his white cane to fend off the attackers. Kohl brushed off the white cane and backhanded the octogenarian. "Your papers!"

Kohl pushed the old man into the circle of young privates, who shoved him back-and-forth like a soccer ball. Then all four brawny soldiers took turns knocking him down to the sidewalk and yanking him back up onto his feet. They practiced pounding his battered body with butt-strokes from their heavier artillery until even that soon became too tiresome for the blue-helmeted "supermen." Still discontented, they finally resorted to kicking him with their steel-toed combat boots.

The young woman screamed.

She had been concentrating on pushing the baby carriage across "A" Street when she saw the blue-helmets kicking the old man to death. Stunned to disbelief, she'd screamed. Her one, shrill, agonizing cry had reverberated along Norris Avenue.

They answered her scream with gunfire, ripping her clothing and her flesh into bloody rags. The baby cried once. The solders slammed fresh magazines into their HK11A1 machine guns and shredded the baby carriage, the baby blankets, the baby's clothing, and the baby.

Within a few seconds they had blasted the mother, the baby, and the baby carriage into singed and shredded bits of flesh and bone and blood-smeared rags. Like some footnote of history, only the lower frame of the carriage had survived somewhat intact to mark the hideous spot.

"It was ... a baby," Lt. Frederick callously growled.

Sgt. Kohl shrugged.

The privates checked their weapons.

Then the six blue-helmets swaggered around the corner and headed west on "A" Street, letting the bloody memories of their victims fade away.

Thirty minutes later the six UN soldiers were swaggering across the mostly-empty parking lot between the Best Western Chief Motel and the Country Kitchen Restaurant, headed generally in the direction of the restaurant's entrance.

The Country Kitchen had been designed with the motel as its primary focus, with its entrance facing the parking lot and the motel. Many had been welcomed through this entrance, but the six blue-helmets were not among them. As they drunkenly swaggered in, the Hostess hustled four patrons out ... and kept on going. The soldiers, however, were too drunk to notice that they were now alone.

They wandered aimlessly from the lobby through the double doors into the first section of the restaurant's main dining room — an area plastered with "No Smoking" signs. Frederick selected two adjoining booths next to the windows overlooking "B" Street, removed his blue-striped helmet, sat down, and lit a cigarette. At the second booth, two of the privates followed his lead, lighting their own cigarettes.

The Sergeant came last, reluctantly removing his helmet and setting it on a nearby table next to his MP5K submachine gun. He also spent over a full minute examining the eight-inch-square, slatted window panes making up the four-foot-square windows above each booth. Then, reluctantly, he too sat down.

"I do not like this place," he said. "It is too open, too airy, too bright."

"And too empty," Frederick added.

The Lieutenant was almost right. Seconds later a waitress, followed by two waiters, pushed a serving cart from the rear section of the dining room into the center of the "No Smoking" section.

"We want some service here, *fraulien*," the Sergeant commanded.

"With pleasure, *you swine!*"

The waitress pulled two .45-caliber semiautomatics from the serving cart. The waiters produced a matching pair of Uzis. And all were pointed at the six UN soldiers.

It was not the kind of service Kohl had in mind.

The waitress and the waiters were excruciatingly methodical. Working from the outside to the inside and from the inside to the outside, they blasted the six UN soldiers and the two booths and the two tables and the wall ... and eighty-four panes of glass.

One private, intent on escape, was blown through the slatted window panes and onto the sidewalk. Lunging for his MP5K, Sgt. Kohl had been cut to ribbons in mid-stride, adding reddish-black splotches of blood and gore to the light brown carpet beneath his body. Further back, the body of another private had also stained the restaurant's carpet.

The waitress pulled two more forty-fives from under a white linen cloth on the serving cart. The waiters came up with two more Uzis. More gunfire echoed through the restaurant.

The pale white decor was splattered red with blood. Clouds of bench padding floated from the ceiling like overgrown snowflakes. And gunfire chewed even more bloody holes in the already-dead bodies littering the dining room.

Lt. Frederick's mutilated corpse was sprawled across the tattered booth bench, while his brains were splattered on the wall and over the punctured table. The other two privates now sat perfectly still, staring into space as their greenish uniforms turned a revolting red.

"Messy Very messy," one waiter observed.

"So what do we do with 'em now?" the second waiter asked.

"That's already been arranged," the waitress said, slamming another clip into one of her forty-fives. "Meanwhile, let's dump these bodies out in the parking lot."

The two waiters were carrying the last body from the sidewalk on "B" Street to the motel parking lot when the two militiamen arrived and began stacking the corpses in the bed of their pickup truck. The restaurant manager, meanwhile, taped a handwritten to the inside of the glass-door entrance.

"Closed for Repairs"

Rachel, the waitress, emerged from the Country Kitchen, read the sign, and grinned. Now wearing a simple but attractive skirt-and-blouse outfit, she no longer looked like a waitress. (She had, in fact, been the secretary in the sheriff's office prior to her too-brief marriage to a wanna-be farmer. But the wanna-be had more money than brains. He'd piled his sports car into a tree and she'd leased the six hundred forty acres to a neighbor.) Watching the waiters and the militiamen cover the six battered bodies with a canvas tarpaulin, she carefully considered the careless mistake she had made several years before when she had resigned from the sheriff's office. But then Bob Lowell arrived in his repainted patrol car, and she had no time to think.

"Rachel."

"Bob."

"You called?"

"Good timing."

"You got 'em?"

"All six."

He breathed a sigh of relief and stepped from the patrol car. "We have their stolen station wagon."

"Hmm, so what did you do to your car?"

"My car? .... Oh, yeah. Took off the light bar and gave it a new coat of paint."

"Dark green is not much of an improvement," she said, raising a corner of the tarp to let him see the bodies. "On the other hand ..."

"You realize," he said, "that this will not improve the tourist trade."

"Depends upon what tourists you're trading with."

He opened the passenger door of his repainted patrol car and waited for her to climb in.

"Yeah," he growled. "Service with a smile."

And he slammed the car door shut.

* * *

James A. Clayton

Chapter Fifteen

As the philosopher said: "The trouble with the rat race is that even if you win, you're still a rat."

Premier Li Peng of the People's Republic of China was a tough old "hard-liner" whose iron-fisted rule persistently prevailed in an era dominated by "moderates." His stomach growled and his joints ached, but he refused to surrender to the infirmities. He was one of the last of the "iron men" — in an age given over to hedonistic pursuits. He had provided a restraining balance of fortitude and support against the seductive quicksand of "the soft life."

But in recent months he had been under constant pressure from Iran, Iraq, Syria, Libya, France, Germany, Italy, and others to send a military contingent to the United States of America to assist their "peacekeeping" efforts. His first response — that China already maintained a five-thousand-man brigade near Vancouver, British Columbia, and had recently added two more five-thousand-man defensive brigades to supplement their first contingent — impressed no one in Europe or Asia. These brigades were not under NATO or UN control. Other nations had committed a large percentage of their military forces to the effort, while China's combined forces barely amounted to tokenism. And the potential possibility of Chinese involvement, alone, would assure an easy victory.

But Li Peng was not so certain. He had listened to the pro and con and noncommittal arguments bandied about the State Council without resolution, knowing that it was really a decision for the generals. With paranoidal cynicism and doubts running rampant, the Chinese generals rejected the European pronouncements and platitudes. Through their own sources they knew the Americans would resist any intrusions. Sending five or ten million troops to the United States would not lead to an easy victory, but might result in a bitter defeat.

Even worse, a few million Chinese troops fighting in the United States could lead to a civil war within the People's Republic of China — a war which no one could win, but which might result in their own untimely demise.

But beyond all of this, Premier Li Peng and the Chinese generals knew that the only victory the Europeans would ever realize could only be a Pyrrhic victory — a war that no one would ever really win.

And for China, the price was too high.

China's neutrality did offer some hope to the beleaguered patriot militia, leaving the disparaging words to be uttered by General Obermeyer's command staff. This neutrality, however, was a double-edged sword. It could easily reinforce European resolve. It could also make the patriot militia overconfident. And at two o'clock in the morning, it could be the start of an unpleasant headache.

General Heinrich Obermeyer awoke with a ringing noise in his ears. He bolted upright. He stared into the darkness. The ringing noise continued. He turned on the lights. He closed his eyes, blotting out the glare. The ringing noise continued. He cautiously re-opened his eyes. And finally he identified the ringing noise. It was the telephone.

"Obermeyer."

"Major General Kerensky, Western Command Garrison at Los Angeles, sir."

"Kerensky, it is two o'clock in the morning here in New York City. I am — were — was sound asleep. .... Now, how important is this?"

"Sir, we have lost San Bernadino Garrison, including most of their arsenal."

For a long time only static interrupted the silence.

"How long ago?"

"We estimate two hours," Kerensky said. "They probably eliminated communications first. Relief units arrived two hours later, and reported that the garrison is ... is now completely empty. All they found were some bloodstains ... and a few blue helmets."

Obermeyer took a deep breath but said nothing. He let Kerensky listen to his heavy breathing. He let Kerensky listen to his rumbling stomach. He let Kerensky wait.

James A. Clayton

"How many? .... How many men?"

"Three thousand two hundred," Kerensky said.

"Then I suggest you shoot three hundred and twenty thousand civilians," Obermeyer casually remarked. "That should teach them a lesson."

And after a long moment of silence, Obermeyer hung up the red telephone.

The old and dilapidated-looking "factory" buildings had been hidden among the pinon pines near Milepost 10 on State Route 377 between Heber and Holbrook in Navajo County, Arizona, for over two decades. Whether this factory ever actually produced anything was a matter of conjecture. Only a few cement slabs, a couple of reddish-brown brick buildings, and some seemingly-pointless walls originally marked the spot.

Perhaps, as its metal double doors suggest, it had once been an ancient glass foundry. A dozen semitrailer trucks and three hundred soldiers had converted it, however, into something that resembled a health spa. Only a few of its builders knew it was actually a modernized version of an efficient extermination camp — a death camp.

Residents of Holbrook, Heber, Overgaard, Aripine, Pinedale, Clay Springs, Snowflake, and Taylor were told that it was a special government hospital built to handle a new epidemic, variously described as: a strain of *Eboli, Hanta* virus, *E. Coli, Kawaski* disease, et.al. At first it sounded horrible, especially since the "medical technicians" suggested that the disease may have been brought in from the Middle East by several soldiers, and that it had created a traumatic response in Europe. The local residents were assured, however, that this illness could be prevented by a single injection, or that it could be cured by a series of injections and a simple chemical shower treatment.

The "medical technicians" were, of course, lying about everything. There was no disease. There was no epidemic. Their own medical experience was very limited. And whether the technicians elected to administer an injection or order a chemical shower treatment, the ultimate results were always very lethal for the patients.

By providing local bus service, the United Nations Military Command successfully depopulated the southern half of Navajo County — including Show Low, Lakeside, Pinetop, Silver Creek,

Shumway, Woodruff, Joseph City, and Winslow — in just under three days. And with the local residents silenced, they were free to reopen the railroad line through Holbrook — and to "cure" over two million Americans in less than seven weeks, just in Navajo County alone.

Nationwide, in just seven weeks, the United Nations Military Command managed to exterminate 37,376,900 Americans. And the cure really was worse than the disease.

But their cover stories indiscriminately proliferated across the countryside like Internet addresses at a computer convention. The disease they cured soon became an incurable disease. The incurable Middle Eastern disease actually came from Russia, Mexico, South America, or Australia. It had allegedly been transported to the United States by UN soldiers, Olympic athletes, tourists, missionaries, sacks of grain, killer bees, or Unidentified Flying Objects. And the incurable epidemic soon became a terrorist plot hatched by drug dealers, the patriot militia, the Israelis, and/or the Vatican against the benevolent Humanism of the United Nations Military Command.

By then, of course, no one believed their outrageous lies. No one accepted their assistance. No one believed their televised propaganda. No one accepted their advice. No one believed their hypocritical friendship. And no one accepted their malevolent kindness. On the other hand, no one laughed either.

Oh, what a tangled web they did weave, yet only themselves did they deceive.

―――

"Your identification papers, please," the Sergeant commanded with pretentious etiquette.

Backed-up by thirty-two well-armed troopers, Sergeant Abdullah ibn Hussein confidently strolled along San Antonio's crowded but disarmingly peaceful River Walk in broad daylight, dispensing justice and checking identification papers. He had already incarcerated over a hundred people today — people who offered him only a Texas driver's license. This businesswoman, to judge from her suit and her shoulder-strap purse, probably carried a passport or other federal identification for his examination.

But instead of a passport, she carried a .32-caliber Taurus revolver. She put one soft-nosed slug through his right eye at pointblank range, flinging Sergeant Abdullah ibn Hussein's uniformed corpse into the narrow waterway.

James A. Clayton

The thirty-two-man backup unit was not as fortunate. Between the walkway crowd and the people poring from the shops, the backup soldiers were trapped and outnumbered. Angry Texans armed with large Bowie knives, small ball bearing saps, and studded brass knuckles sliced and diced and battered the backup troops into a bloody, gory mess. And within minutes San Antonio's River Walk was empty, with only a few bloodstains to mark the event.

"I am Captain Wilheim Schlegel, United Nations Military Command — Los Angeles." His badly-accented English was further marred by his heel-clicking salute. "I must examine your identity papers, *mein herr.*"

Schlegel's disdain extended far beyond this little, haggard-looking, emaciated old man standing on the southwest corner of Fifth and Spring Streets in downtown Los Angeles. That such a filthy, unshaven *creature* should even be allowed to walk the streets of this or any other city was almost beyond Schlegel's comprehension. But then he had never met a wino.

Backed by a seventy-man team under his second-in-command, Lt. Jean-Luc Valois, this first patrol through central Los Angeles was fast becoming a nightmare for the arrogant German aristocrat.

"Your papers, *mein herr!*"

But the filthy old man could only shrug. Another night in the detox tank meant nothing to him. Being flat broke again, the thought of a lukewarm shower and some clean clothes appealed to his booze-befuddled mind. By then, of course, Capt. Schlegel had pulled his Mauser and was squeezing the trigger.

With sullen contempt Schlegel watched the sodden old man bounce against the brick wall and collapse onto the sidewalk. The bluish-gray gunsmoke still swirled through the foggy air long after the emaciated old man died.

"Leave him," Schlegel commanded, returning the monstrous Mauser to its holster. "Let them pick up their own trash."

He haughtily sniffed the foggy night air, marched across Fifth, and turned left towards Broadway. With Lt. Valois and his men following, Schlegel crept into the dark heart of the City of Angels.

"Fifth and Broadway," Valois whispered tersely. "Where your predecessor was killed."

"I am aware of that, Lieutenant," Schlegel growled softly. ""How am I doing ... otherwise."

It took Valois a few seconds to interpret the question. Then he nodded. "Acceptable. The men understand your cautious approach ... and shooting the wino. But there is a fine line between being brave and being foolish."

"Is it always so dark?"

"We have restored electrical power," Valois chuckled, "but not the burnt-out light bulbs."

Only the light bulbs on Broadway had not burnt-out — they had been blown away by high-powered rifles. And with the gases of the street lamps dispersed into the foggy night, only a few sparking hot wires and the glow of interior lights from a handful of stray buildings made note of the darkened thoroughfare.

Even the signal lights had been extinguished, Valois noted with some apprehension. He glanced up and down Broadway. All the signal lights were out. He held up his hand, silently halting the advancing columns. With a flick of his wrist, he sent them up against the wall. Then, without a word, he quietly hauled his night-vision goggles from his pack and took another look. But the night-vision goggles revealed nothing unusual. The feeling, however, would not go away. Valois took yet another look, but again saw nothing.

"Lieutenant?" Schlegel's whisper was answered with silence.

With a curt wave, Valois signaled the radioman forward.

"Lieutenant Valois, Ops Two-One," he whispered, pressing the two-way radio tightly against his ear. "Fifth and Broadway. Los Angeles. —Full alert!"

"Lieutenant?" Schlegel's whisper was now filled with its own anxiety.

Valois handed the night-vision goggles to his superior.

Schlegel looked. "I see nothing."

"Nothing at all?"

"Nothing at all."

"Exactly."

If looks could kill, Valois would have died then and there.

"You just called a full alert, Lieutenant," Schlegel rasped. "Explain yourself."

"We saw *absolutely* nothing," Valois hissed.

It took Schlegel several seconds. "There should have been

somebody. A bum. A wino. A night watchman. .... Somebody."

"Not even a cat or a dog," whispered Valois, unstrapping his AR-18.

Schlegel nodded. "On Broadway?"

"Or right here, if we do not move in a minute or two," Valois said, lighting a cigarette.

"The cigarette," Schlegel hissed.

"I know," Valois said. "Sergeant, I want everybody to light up a cigarette and mill about — uh, walk around. Make them think we are taking a break."

The Sergeant nodded and began moving quietly among the men. Glowing cigarettes and flaming lighters wandered and roamed across Fifth and Broadway in a casual and seemingly haphazard manner. Valois waited a full minute before beginning his walk, quietly assigning positions and cover.

One-by-one the glowing cigarettes were crushed into the darkness. Seventy soldiers vanished into pre-selected positions. Twenty armored personnel carriers rolled down Broadway from Temple Street. Twelve 6-by troop trucks moved up from Pico Boulevard. And fifteen old but modified Russian T-72 tanks clanked and growled their way up Fifth Street.

Two tanks turned north onto Broadway. A radio signal was sent. Flares were ignited. Spotlights and floodlights were turned on. In an instant the streets of downtown Los Angeles were bathed in hellish brilliance.

In that same instant a teenager sprinted from the shadows of Main Street onto the rear of the last T-72. He flung two hand grenades through an open hatch and leaped to the street. A muffled explosion gutted the tank. Several 120-millimeter shells and the gas tank followed with a thunderous blast that ripped the old tank apart. Flaming scraps of twisted metal, like deadly shrapnel, sprayed outward in a circle of fiery horror.

The unknown teenager, burnt and bleeding and badly wounded, crawled across the sidewalk and through the shattered front door of an abandoned building. There, within its lonely darkness, he collapsed and died.

But he had given the signal ....

Within seconds Fifth Street became a charnel house of flaming phosphorus and high-explosive (HEAT) grenades, of burning tanks and roasted bodies. In the midst of this madness a civilian darted across Broadway, flung a satchel charge under the second T-72, and sprinted towards the nearest doorway. The satchel charge blew up the tank. A machine gun cut down the man. The T-72 flipped over, crushing its turret and splitting its armor-plated shell. The man fell forward, his bulletproof vest shredded and punctured by a fusillade of machine-gun fire.

An M-16A2 combined with an M-203 grenade launcher makes a very nasty weapon. Mounted underneath, the 40-millimeter "bloop tube" — nicknamed after the unique sound it makes when fired — can deliver a wide range of specialized destruction, as the blue-helmeted tourists soon discovered.

Staying inside an armored personnel carrier meant certain death, but leaving it was not a popular option either. Staying in the street was suicidal. Running into a building often meant running into a booby trap. And the alleyways were just as deadly.

Still, to their dubious credit, the one hundred sixty soldiers from the armored personnel carriers did kill a few civilians before being blasted to pieces.

On the other hand, the three hundred soldiers riding the troop trucks wisely disembarked before the column crossed Sixth Street. Several of the drivers and their helpers also managed to escape the rain of hand grenades. But while trucks disappeared within the fiery explosions ripping up Broadway, and while several UN soldiers were wounded by flying shrapnel, about two hundred seventy-five survived long enough to completely destroy two buildings and kill several hundred civilian rebels.

By then, however, garrison troopers began arriving on foot and in buses. They were blown to bits by booby traps, bombed with hand grenades, and shot in the street — but they kept coming. And they slowly retook downtown Los Angeles — room-by-room, floor-by-floor, building-by-building, and block-by-block. Several were killed by "friendly fire." More stumbled across trip-wires, while others were lured into ambush traps. They fought door-to-door and room-to-room. They shot and were shot. They killed and were killed.

By sunrise, downtown Los Angeles — or at least what was left of it — was held some one hundred eighty-three surviving United Nations soldiers. Three minor high-rise buildings had been leveled. All the buildings between Fourth and Sixth Streets, and from Spring

Street to Hill Street, had been gutted. Every door and window had been smashed and shattered. Every wall had been punctured by bullets or blackened by fire bombs. Blood and gore covered the ruins like drying paint casually splattered with seeming indifference over a pothole-pitted highway.

"Losses?" Schlegel asked, staring at his shattered field radio.

Lt. Valois stared at his empty AR-18 through burnt-out eyes, studying the rifle as if it were an alien device he could not comprehend.

"Lieutenant Valois?...."

"You should be in hospital," Valois said.

Schlegel shook his head. He had a bullet in his right arm and a few pieces of shrapnel in his right leg. His wounds might require a few hours at a first-aid station, not several days in some germ-infected hospital.

"Losses?"

Valois caught his breath. "Fifteen tanks, twenty-three armored personnel carriers, fifteen troop transport trucks, four buses, and about two thousand troops — plus or minus three hundred."

"Civilians?"

"We estimate their losses at about ninety-five hundred," he lied, knowing the actual number to be about half as many.

Schlegel nodded, "It sounds correct."

"Even at five-to-one," Valois said, "we would still lose."

General Heinrich Obermeyer watched in silent anger as his headquarters staff filed into the auditorium in a very orderly manner. As usual, the higher ranking and more decorated officers entered first, marching in military quick-time. No one said anything, but they knew this discourse meant trouble — the auditorium was less than half full.

The higher ranking officers had already nervously noted the absence of far-too-many of their aides and assistants. They knew the value of their missing aides, and the meaning of the absence. They watched Obermeyer light a large cigar, confirming their worst fears. .... They were losing the war.

Obermeyer puffed crudely on his overgrown cigar and waited until his officers were seated before stepping to the podium. He took a full minute to examine their terrified faces before setting down his cigar.

"Gentlemen," he began, "something has gone horribly wrong. We have lost thousands of troops in Seattle, San Francisco, and Los Angeles. We have lost contact with many of our garrisons and outposts in Utah, Idaho, Oregon, Montana, North and South Dakota, Wyoming, New Mexico, and Oklahoma."

He took a couple of extra puffs on the cigar. They read his angry smoke-signal and took a deep breath of fear.

"We do not yet have access to their nuclear missile nor their satellite tracking systems. Their Central Intelligence Agency has been less than cooperative. The Director and most of his staff have ... gone missing, as the British say."

He took another puff off his cigar. "Their Department of Defense — what is left of it — has been very difficult. Even hostile. It would seem that some of the commanding officers have not understood the message."

He tapped the cigar in an ashtray hidden behind the podium and re-read his notes on the laptop screen.

"Gentlemen," he continued, "yesterday I dismissed two hundred and fifty-five junior grade staff officers who were less than enthusiastic about our mission. .... They will not be missed."

He again puffed on his cigar, deliberately daring them to say something. They had not, however, attained their rank through frivolity. Enveloped in a grayish cloud of smoke, several officers refused even to blink.

"This is not a game, gentlemen," Obermeyer growled. "I will not tolerate any further inefficiency or inattentiveness. Nor will I accept excuses. We will, we must, secure the peace and establish authoritative control within the next ninety days. We must establish law and order throughout this land by then. —Is that understood?"

The silence was deafening.

"That is all. .... Dismissed."

* * *

Chapter Sixteen

Edward Eugene Robinson, formerly of the Bureau of Alcohol, Tobacco, and Firearms, cast his line into the center of the pond with an agility which belied his advanced years. Retired, but now frozen out of his pension, he did not ask about the secretive trip to this quiet glade. He would not ask why his youngest son had urged him to put on the blindfold and take a ride into the countryside with one Peter Gordon. At the end of the ride, he had removed the blindfold, climbed from the BMW, and shaken hands with Jacob Andrew Kent.

"You sure there are fish in this pond?"

"That's what they tell me," Kent said, casting his own line.

"Well, okay, but you didn't bring me all the way out here to go fishin'?"

"Of course not," Kent answered. "You were an Assistant Director in the A.T.F. when I was a junior grade over in Europe."

"Hardly a recommendation," the older man grunted. "I've been out-of-the-loop for years. — Besides, all we did was to make glorious mistakes."

"So I've heard," said Kent, playing out more line. "Tell me, have you ever heard of man named Avery Lucas?"

"Avery Lucas?" Robinson hesitated, lost in thought. "Yeah, F.B.I. field agent. Worked out of Chicago. Met him once. Slimy son-of-a-bitch."

"Trustworthy?"

"Well, you can shake hands with him, but be sure to count your fingers afterwards."

"Bad?"

"Very. .... Arrested in Nebraska on murder one. Killed a deputy sheriff. Released on orders from Latimer shortly before the President's last speech."

"But you retired long before that. You were ... out-of-the-loop."

"I had friends in low places."

"Maybe I should talk to them."

"They're dead now."

"Oh. — I am sorry," Kent said. "Is there anything else I should know?"

Robinson shrugged. "Hmmm. Lucas had a partner. I think his name was, uh, Larson. —Yes. Larson."

"Oh, yes, Mr. Larson. .... Unfortunately he had a falling out with Lucas. Fell out of a rowboat on Chesapeake Bay."

"Hmmm, gives a whole new meaning to the expression: 'wet work'."

"Now there is an old expression."

"Mind if I ask why you want to know about Lucas?"

Kent smiled. "I don't mind, but I won't tell you. Sometimes it's better not to know."

"I see ...."

"I think you got a bite."

Robinson pulled up sharply, setting the hook.

"Yes, I see," he said, reeling-in his catch.

Fifteen and a half miles south of McCook, Nebraska, just across the state line and Beaver Creek, an unmarked blacktop road will guide the unwary traveler into the green darkness of Cedar Bluffs, Kansas. A small village with a long history, the twelve residents of Cedar Bluffs now shared a dark secret with Lt. Luis Sanchez and his men.

After using three troop trucks as a misleading graveyard marker, Sanchez had taken the three remaining troop trucks, the two APCs, and the two tank-carrying low-boy flatbed trucks up Highway 83 to Oberlin, Kansas. But Oberlin provided neither rest nor relaxation for anyone. The historical town was almost deserted, and the surviving residents didn't trust these military tourists. Without electricity and low on rations of any kind, both the town of Oberlin and Lt. Sanchez could do little more than hide within the tree-lined streets and wait for the United Nations to attack. With only a few shotguns and rifles, Oberlin had to trust in their spotters and their Internet connections. But posting guards and monitoring the Internet

was not the Lieutenant's idea of engaging superior enemy forces.
"You know this part of the country?"
Sgt. Farrell shook his head. "Too far north."
"McCook, Nebraska. Twenty-eight miles. .... Opinion?"
"It's bigger."
"Gene ...." Sanchez struggled to hold back the laughter. "Sergeant Eugene Allen Farrell ...."
"Only been there once," Farrell said. "About three years ago, as best I can remember. And at night, to boot. — We took some old munitions and stuff to a storage depot, part of their National Guard Armory, I guess."
"Worth going after?"
"Might be," Farrell said thoughtfully. "They had a lot of stuff up there."
"Security?"
"They had a civilian armed guard, probably with the Reserve. Even if he's still there, I don't see that it will be a problem." But then Sgt. Farrell raised his right index finger. "Crossing the state line, however, might be."
"Huh? .... Come again?"
"We've always taken it for granted that we could travel anywhere in this country without any restrictions."
"But the U.N. just might put up roadblocks at the state lines?"
"Exactly."
Wiping the perspiration from his brow, Lt. Sanchez pulled out his map collection and went to work. Sgt. Farrell went for a walk.
Farrell had spent most of that week cultivating a friendship of sorts with gas station owner Tom McDermott, a crusty and cantankerous curmudgeon who ran the truck stop at the intersection of Highways 36 and 83. Yet surprisingly, McDermott actually seemed pleased with their desertion from Fort Riley. He apparently had little respect for the higher ranks.
"Those political generals sold us out!" he stormed. "We shoulda shot all of 'em to begin with! Instead, them U.N. fellas did it for us. And that's about the only good thing they've done so far!"
"They shot some good guys too."
"I suppose some of 'em must be okay," McDermott admitted. "But frankly, Gene, I never met one that was worth a damn."

Sgt. Farrell smiled, knowing that the old curmudgeon would never acknowledge the worth of any high ranking officer. On the other hand, Eugene Farrell was only a sergeant.

"So, have they set up any roadblocks around here?"

"Oh, they got a dandy up north on Highway 83, just across the state line at the end of Highway 89," McDermott said. "Two rattletrap Humvees to block the road and a chemical toilet down in the ditch. .... Then they got another one over on Highway 25 somewhere between Atwood and Trenton. I hear that they also have a third one on Highway 283, where it crosses Highway 89 between Beaver City and Hendley, but that's too far away to be sure."

"And that's it?"

Tom McDermott shrugged. "They run a roving checkpoint along State 117 every so often, but I don't think they even know about the backroads we use. Of course, they're gravel roads. If you're pulling any weight ...."

"About seventy tons. — Each."

"Seventy tons?"

"A couple of Russian T-80 tanks."

"With an automatic loading 125-millimeter cannon, laser range finder, and night-vision equipment?"

"Among other things," Farrell said.

"Where'd you find that?"

"Goodland."

"Goodland? .... Goodland!"

With a flick of his head he motioned Farrell to follow him to the graveled parking lot. "You and your men were at Goodland?"

"Uh-huh."

McDermott nervously lit a cigarette. "Swore I was gonna give these up."

"Uh-huh. .... So how come you know so much about the T-80?"

"Twenty-five years ago I was a mechanic at Fort Bragg. So I've tried to keep up."

Farrell nodded thoughtfully. "We'll need some diesel fuel ... and a guide to get past the roadblocks."

"The diesel fuel is free for you and your friends," Tom McDermott said with a touch of awe in his voice. "I'm sure you will ... put it to good use."

James A. Clayton

"And the guide?"

"That's a bit more complicated, but I think we can figure something out."

Tom McDermott, the cantankerous curmudgeon, guided their convoy to Cedar Bluffs for two more weeks of rest and recuperation within the forest of trees and underbrush that dominated the village. Located about a mile west of Highway 83 and well-hidden by its own private forest, Cedar Bluffs had kept its privacy by pulling down the four road signs that announced its presence.

Most of the morning had been cool and cloudy, threatening rain. (Without the National Weather Service, however, any prediction could only be a matter of guesswork.) By noon it had started to drizzle. Then, with a nod from one of the elder residents, Mrs. Peabody led Lt. Sanchez and Sgt. Farrell down an ill-marked path to an old, dilapidated, wood-and-brick building hidden among the trees near the grain elevators, the railroad siding, and Beaver Creek.

"You know, we don't get many tourists out here," Mrs. Peabody said, slowly opening the ancient door.

"Camouflage tarpaulin?" Sanchez asked, more than slightly puzzled.

"About a hundred and twenty rolls of it," the elderly lady said, readjusting her wire-rimmed glasses. "We have a friend who occasionally drops-by with ... some useful things. You know, electric generators, gasoline, food ... things like that, you know."

"Mind if we use a few of these?" Sgt. Farrell asked.

Mrs. Peabody chuckled. "That's what they're for, young man."

"Your friend, does he have a name?"

"Ben Franklyn."

Lt. Sanchez tried to keep a straight face. He tried very hard. But he failed, finally surrendering to laughter.

"But that is his name!" Mrs. Peabody sputtered. "He owns a large farm up in Nebraska."

Lt. Sanchez shook his head, then looked over his shoulder at the drizzling rain. "Round up the men, Sergeant, and I'll show you how to build the world's largest tent."

"Uh, yes, sir."

"And Gene ... don't get wet."

Sgt. Eugene Allen Farrell looked up at the ceiling and breathed

New World Order

a sigh of disbelief. Then, with a shake of his head, he stepped into the drizzling rain.

For the next two weeks the Lieutenant and the Sergeant became civilians, taking to the backroads of southwestern Nebraska in a variety of decrepit-looking automobiles and pickup trucks to map-out their future moves to nowhere.

Fortunately it was not as complicated as they had contemplated. After two weeks of rest, relaxation, and more than substantial sustenance, it took less than two cautious hours of inching forward over the now dried-out graveled roads of Decatur County, Kansas, to reach the border. And it took only a few minutes to guide their two low-boy flatbeds and the heavy payloads through the shallow "S-bend" marking the state line.

"Welcome to Nebraska," announced Mrs. Peabody as they slid through the muddy intersection into Red Willow County.

About a mile north of the state line and four miles east of Federal Highway 83 on State Route 89, only unassorted clumps of trees and the ruins of a dilapidated church now identified the unincorporated village of Marion. Often omitted from commercial maps of the state, its name was occasionally misspelled in sundry publications — such as the local telephone directory.

Once a thriving town with a long and checkered history, Marion died in bits and pieces after the Great Depression. The decaying ruins of a few defunct businesses and old houses defined its demise. The aged two-story brick school building became a vacant lot. And most of the surviving residents had moved away or passed away. By the time Sanchez arrived, only seven elderly adults lived within its undefined boundaries.

Sanchez's column had followed the rough graveled road through a tight left turn and an equally sharp right turn past the abandoned Fish Farm — a double row of old evergreen trees standing on embankments around two artificial, rectangular mud puddles. Beyond the mud puddles, the little white house was now showing its age with chipped and flaking paint, cracked and broken windows, and a badly-sagging roof. To the east an open field refused to offer any protection for the three neglected houses on the west side of the road. And beyond them, next to the railroad tracks, a singular barn-like garage, large enough to hold a couple of six-by troop trucks, was

filled with one rusted and inoperable RV trailer.
   North of the Union Pacific and Burlington's single tracks and abandoned siding, and east of the main road, a large and modern tin shed garage stood proudly behind a plethora of rusted and ruined farm equipment from another time and another era. The shed, Sanchez was told, had originally been built by a farmer as a garage for his pickup and his tractor. Local residents could not, or would not, say whether that farmer had died or moved elsewhere. They did agree, however, to allow Sanchez and his men use of the shed, and a certain tree-covered lane, to hide their trucks and APCs.
   On the other hand, as Mrs. Peabody put it, "These folks have been burnt too many times to trust anyone very much."
   "Except Ben Franklyn?"
   Mrs. Peabody smiled. "He's not government-issued."

   The First Boardmember gazed in awe at the grandeur of the rolling green hills and jagged mountain peaks framed by the plate-glass windows of the luxurious third floor executive lounge. The incredibly beautiful landscaped views surrounding Burgenstock, Switzerland, had made the real estate agents very wealthy. The white marble mausoleum hiding above the city, however, had been acquired by default. For The Chairman, it was merely an elaborate office. For the First and Second Boardmen, it was a comfortable room with a spectacular vista. And for the others among them, it was home.
   "This view makes it all worthwhile," the First Boardman said.
   "This particular view?" The Chairman asked, joining him at the window.
   "Especially this view," the First Boardman affirmed, turning to watch the Second Boardman join them. "It makes things ... much easier."
   "Solving all of the world's problems is never easy."
   The Chairman actually smiled. "If not us, who would? That is why our predecessors chose us. That is why we can only permit ourselves a mistress, rather than a wife and children. That is why this is ... a full-time job."
   The Chairman took a deep breath and gazed out the window, seeing nothing.
   "There is trouble in America," the First Boardman said with

icy certainty.

"Obermeyer?"

"No, the American illusion of freedom," The Chairman said. "They believe the people rule the government. The idea of the government ruling the people is apparently abhorrent to them."

"A dangerous ideology — letting common, ordinary people rule themselves," the First Boardman noted. "They will destroy their own economy. .... And ours as well."

"It is a question of whether we can maintain control over these savages," The Chairman said. "If the Chinese sent ten million soldiers to the United States and put them under the command of General Obermeyer, we would not have to worry about maintaining control."

Boardman Two twitched under The Chairman's angry glare. "The People's Republic of China will not send any more men," he snapped. "They're too afraid of an internal revolt."

"Do we have enough soldiers over there?" the First Boardman asked. "Can we maintain control without the Chinese?"

"Twenty million well-trained, professional soldiers against three hundred and fifty million rebellious .... peasants? .... It is much too soon to say," The Chairman reluctantly admitted. "We acted much too quickly. I admit that. —I must send a coded message to Obermeyer. I must have him alert our central western asset — uh — Major Hoffman. We can, perhaps, still salvage this ... action."

―――

The *McCook Daily Gazette* began life as a weekly newspaper in 1911, but owner-publisher Harry D. Strunk soon elevated its status to that of a daily newspaper and moved it to the four-hundred block of Main Street, which would later be renamed: George Norris Avenue. As a civic leader, Harry Strunk pioneered water conservation and flood control throughout Southwestern Nebraska. Thus, there is a *Harry D. Strunk Lake* in southeastern Frontier County and a *Harry D. Strunk Roadside Rest Area* on Highways 6 and 34 about a mile east of McCook. And it was at this rest area on a windy hilltop that Lt. Luis Sanchez first met Ben Franklyn.

Neither Lt. Sanchez nor any of the six men in his squad were impressed by the gray-haired farmer driving an ordinary-looking but slightly banged-about Jeep Cherokee Sport 4x4 alongside their APC. They were, however, quite efficient in quickly folding their maps, and casually readying their weapons for any unexpected threat.

"Welcome to Nebraska," said the gray-haired farmer, opening the Cherokee's door. "I'm Ben Franklyn."

"Ben Franklyn? .... Ben Franklyn?" Sanchez questioned, putting on a display of alleged ignorance. "I've heard of you, I believe. One of those patriot militia groups, right?"

"One of 'em," Ben admitted. "And you are Lieutenant Luis Sanchez, formerly with the Tenth Light Cavalry out of Fort Riley, Kansas. And currently absent without leave. — A.W.O.L."

"Yeah," Sanchez muttered. "Well, actually, I guess now we're all deserters."

"It all depends on your point-of-view," said Ben. "As I see it, you deserted the army, not the country. I heard about what you did down in Goodland. —Thanks."

"We were lucky."

"Of course you were," the grizzled old farmer agreed with total disbelief. "So what now?"

Sanchez hesitated uncertainly. "Well, we were thinking of going to Canada."

"A good idea on paper, maybe. But unfortunately the Canadians have already sold out to the blue helmets without even so much as a twitch."

"Another great idea shot to hell," Sanchez grumbled. "But I suppose I should have known. Those Canadians never really could understand freedom. They bowed to the Queen, now they're bowing to the U.N. .... So what's the U.N. doing?"

"They've set up a base near Edmonton to execute fleeing F.B.I. and B.A.T.F. agents. About fifteen hundred of them. .... So far."

"So if we were to visit their sorry little country ...."

"Uh-huh. — Sorry about that," Ben said, gazing skyward. "By the way, hiding out here in the open isn't such a great idea either. They don't have access to our satellite surveillance system yet, but ground-positioning locators are widely available ... and very cheap."

"We used their black boxes for target practice several weeks ago," Sanchez said, shaking his head. "Anyway, they're using old French-made three-oh-sevens. We figure that if a spotter plane should see us, they'll write off the lack-of-signal as a malfunction. .... And if they don't, well, then they're in for big trouble."

Ben Franklyn smiled, remembering when he had been young

and cocky. But those "good-old-days" were now far behind, in the distant past, never to be seen again. Dealing with current problems presented a much greater challenge.

"Ah! The good ol' days!"

"Huh?"

"Never mind. .... Look, I got a place down the road that would be a lot safer than out here. — And it's big enough to hide you and your men and both T-80 tanks."

"You know about them?"

Ben Franklyn shrugged. "Oberlin, Cedar Bluffs, and Marion. Your progress has been noted. But the North Platte Garrison operates their inspection grids with geometric precision and timetable accuracy. They'll be checking out Marion in four or five days. — And you should be someplace else."

"They're that predictable?"

"I wish they were," Ben Franklyn sighed. "I wish they were."

"Meaning?"

"Every so often they change their pattern. Sometimes they catch us off guard."

"Countermeasures?"

"Hit and run."

Lt. Sanchez studied the concrete sidewalk, but found no answers in the cement or in the scenery. Ben Franklyn did not look like an altruistic individual, and his offer seemed too good to be true. On the other hand, any alternative course could easily be filled with even greater hazards. And this just might offer a viable solution. Maybe.

Sanchez took a deep breath. "Saddle up, gentlemen. Let's take a look at ... his place."

Major Hermann Hoffman usually began his day by reading the "dailies," the unclassified garrison reports. And he was, as usual, soon depressed by the highly-censored reading material.

Major General Kerensky of the United Nations Western Command had again been the first to file the bad news. His report, as always, read like an obituary column in a major newspaper.

The body of Major Jacques Daudet had been found by a patrol in Vasquez Rocks County Park near Agua Dulce, California. One Captain R. Lefevre had been found floating facedown in San Francisco Bay. The body of a Captain Wilheim Schlegel had been pulled from the Merced River near Newman, California. A few miles away the body of Schlegel's second-in-command, one Lieutenant Jean-Luc Valois, had been discovered in a canal adjacent to South Mercy Springs Road near Los Banos. Lieutenant Aleksei Ostrovsky of St. Petersburg, Russia, had been stabbed to death in a pedestrian tunnel under Wilshire Boulevard in Los Angeles. One Sergeant Muammar al Suhel had been found beaten to death in a public lavatory in a pedestrian tunnel at the west end of the civic plaza adjacent to the Los Angeles County Courthouse. One Sergeant Nkomo was found sprawled across the fifty-yard line of the Los Angeles Olympic Coliseum. The emaciated body of a Sergeant Jacques Soubirous had been discovered floating in a canal in Venice, California.

".... Et cetera."

He scanned through the rest of Kerensky's "report" with little hope and less enthusiasm, only to be rewarded by the epitome of pessimism in his concluding remarks. By then, of course, he did not feel like reading Major General Karageorge's United Nations Central Command epistle from Chicago, which was nothing more than a reprint with different names and locations.

Captain Aritomo Yamaguchi's sharp rapping diverted Hoffman's attention and opened his office door.

"Sir."

"Captain?"

"The lieutenants have arrived, sir."

Hoffman offered a grunt and a nod as the sixteen lieutenants crowded into his now too-small office, and came to attention in front of his battered desk. Flipping through their reports, he wondered if they thought Obermeyer was handing out medals for creative report-writing.

"Gentlemen ...."

All sixteen lieutenants snapped to stiff attention with a sharp salute.

"At ease." He flipped through their reports again, making them wait. "Empty houses? Too many roads? Too many escape routes?"

"Yes, sir." They answered in unison.

"They seem to know your every move. They hide out until you leave, then return to their empty houses. —Correct?"

"Yes, sir," snapped Lt. Ahriman, who was senior among them.

"I suspect so, sir."

"Well, the next time you find an empty house, Lieutenant Ahriman, you blow it up! — Understand? You blow it straight to hell!"

"Yes, sir!"

"Perhaps a little 'scorched-earth' policy will teach them a lesson. Perhaps they will think twice about running away." He gave them a brief salute. "Dismissed."

Sixteen lieutenants snapped to attention, saluted in unison, turned on their heels, and filed from his office. He waited for fifteen full seconds after the last man had closed the door before lighting a cigarette and blowing smoke across the room.

* * *

Chapter Seventeen

They could have started as far north as Valentine or even Crookston. They could have started as far east as Ansely or even Holdrege. They could have started as far west as Ogallala or even Big Springs. But they chose, instead, to start just forty-five miles away in the little town of Curtis.

But why Curtis?

Because it was there.

Just over seven miles off Highway 83 in Frantier County, Nebraska; Curtis had only a few new houses, and all of them were allegedly empty. Those new but empty houses were a good place to start, thought Lt. Ahriman. And when he again found that those new houses were still empty, he blew them up.

Imperial was almost a typical small Nebraska town, complete with grain elevators and tree-lined potholes. They boasted about their all-volunteer fire department, but were mostly silent about the new mayor and her boyfriend. And most of them were out of town when Lt. Malinovsky and his men arrived. But Lt. Malinovsky was not one to be bothered by small technical problems. He selected six empty houses at random, and fire-bombed them into ashes.

Lt. Foscolo selected Gothenburg. He liked its name. Set on the intersection of State Route 47 and Highway 30, with Interstate 80 and the Platte River running alongside, Gothenburg should have been an excellent choice. Foscolo and his men apparently burned or blew up some twenty-three homes before they "went missing." Three days later a search-and-destroy squad from the Grand Island Garrison found most of them floating down the Platte River. Each man — including Lt. Foscolo — had been repeatedly shot and/or stabbed to death by person or persons unknown.

Avoiding or preventing these random strikes was logistically impossible. But Benjamin Ellsworth Franklyn would not accept such an idea. Hit-or-miss randomization was not a strategically viable plan.

"There *must* be a plan," he repeatedly insisted, studying the maps as if they were the enemy. "Those military-types wouldn't go to the toilet without a battle plan!"

He wandered hopelessly through word and name combinations, geographic and physiographic patterns, time and distance relationships, population and ethnic formulations, resources and productivity evaluations, parapsychological and astrological variations, and other possibilities without finding an answer ... or even a clue. It took Lisa, the always-anonymous tomboy, to unravel the devious European mind-set. Her solution, much to Ben Franklyn's embarrassment, was utter simplicity.

"Empty houses!" she blurted.

"Come again?"

"Empty houses. — They're going back to the towns where they found a large number of empty houses."

"And blowing them up," Franklyn concluded.

"Following their original patrol patterns," Lisa added. "But they're hitting only towns that have suspicious-looking, empty houses."

"Which means? ...."

"Ogallala and McCook. Today or tomorrow."

———

Lt. Mohammed al-Ghazzali hated Western Nebraska. All the grass, trees, and shrubbery created a too-green nightmare for a man born to sand and rocks. The humidity intimidated his desert-dry heart. All the booze and cigarettes offended his pure Islamic spirit. The polluted air filled his lungs with poisonous pollens from a dozen different plants. And the Western women went around practically naked.

He stepped from the APC and unleashed a torrent of invective insults in Arabic against this quagmire of infidels called McCook.

Since no one else under his command spoke Arabic, the literal interpretation of his invective remained unknown. The message, however, was quite clear to those who heard him. And they responded with alacrity.

Standing at the intersection of George Norris Avenue and Elizabeth Lane, with beads of sweat trickling down his neck and underneath his shirt collar, Lt. al-Ghazzali spat at someone's green lawn and pointed at his first target. The long-and-low, blue-and-white, single-story, ranch-style house with a double-glazed picture window was the ultimate model of innocence. It was also "number one" on his hit list.

The slightly higher, gray-and-white, split-level neighbor looked a little older but equally innocent. Lt. al-Ghazzali listed it as "number two" for destruction.

The mid-sized and older, two-story, off-white house was the third home on the north side of Elizabeth Lane. It was also the third house on Lt. al-Ghazzali's list, a footnote to his Islamic ferocity.

With a nod, the three search squads smashed into their respective target homes and found them mostly empty. The third search squad did find an old and battered console television, which under closer examination turned out to be an old and battered console television. Its innocence, however, afforded no protection to the ancient black-and-white monster console.

The third search squad dragged it from the two-story house and threw it onto the front lawn, just to be on the safe side of Simtex. The third search squad checked the two-story, off-white house thoroughly. With the open and unobstructed pastureland to the north, and an extra one-hundred-plus troops guarding the perimeter, nothing would disturb their operations.

A second nod sent three sapper squads into the selected houses. Guarded by the eight-man search squads, the six-man sapper squads needed only two minutes to plant their lethal plastic hardware. And protected by the perimeter guards and the search squad, nothing could disturb their operations.

Nothing, that is, except the thunderous explosion that blasted the two-story frame structure into a hellish fireball of instant death and destruction, annihilating the house and the six sappers and the eight-man search squad. Two perimeter guards standing in front of the house were also instantaneously incinerated, and their fiery remains were blasted across the street.

Seconds later, amidst the turmoil of the first explosion, another blast blew out the windows and doors of the split-level second house, scattering flaming debris and flaming bodies over the front yard.

Fourteen soldiers stumbled from the first house, ran into the street, and were ripped apart in a hailstorm of bullets. Sappers and searchers were cut into bloody ribbons, splattering their blood and their guts across the lawns and the pavement.

A satchel charge from some shrubbery on the south side of Elizabeth Lane slid under an APC. A brave but foolish soldier also slid under the vehicle ... just before the satchel charge exploded. The APC disintegrated as it cartwheeled end-over-end into the driveway of the blasted and burning split-level house. The soldier simply vanished.

A patriot militiaman tumbled from the roof of a house on the south side of Elizabeth Lane. Another fell through a window of a house on Norris Avenue. And the blue-and-white, ranch-style home exploded into a million flaming scraps of wood and glass.

Simultaneously, another satchel charge was hurled under the sole surviving APC. Within a firestorm of falling flaming debris, Lt. Mohammed al-Ghazzali leaped from the APC and staggered down Norris towards the troop trucks.

He had covered twenty or thirty feet before the satchel charge exploded, knocking him to the asphalt. The armored personnel carrier blew up ... and up ... and up. Flaming bits and pieces flew here and there and everywhere as it flipped over and over and over. The incinerated APC came apart in mid-air and fell to the earth as a collection of charred scrap metal.

Stunned and somewhat disoriented, Lt. al-Ghazzali rose unsteadily to his feet, wobbling slightly. Three perimeter guards ran to his aid. A dozen shots rang out. The three soldiers fell to the asphalt, dying.

More shots rang out. Al-Ghazzali's left arm suddenly was a bloody stump ending at his elbow. And before raw shock wiped out all his pain, a few extra shots chopped off his right leg at the knee.

He fell down again. A dozen soldiers risked death to come to his aid. Thirty or more rifle shots echoed across McCook. A dozen soldiers died.

Looking at the blood-covered bone-and-sinew stump that had once been his right leg, Lt. Mohammed al-Ghazzali knew that he had been badly hurt by someone. Perhaps he heard the running footsteps. Perhaps he heard the echoing gunshots. Perhaps he heard the screams of the dying. But he did not react until he saw the gray-haired old man. Then he blinked.

James A. Clayton

"Hi, my name is Ben Franklyn," the gray-haired one said. "And this here young fella is Deputy Sheriff Bob Lowell."

"Infidel."

"Al Grizzly?" Ben asked, trying to read the nametag.

"Al Grizzly, you are under arrest," Bob Lowell began. "You have the right to remain silent. If you give up the right to remain silent, anything ...."

"Never mind, Bob." Ben Franklyn held out a restraining hand and shook his head. "This tourist will remain silent ... forever."

The graveled road heading south from Stockville provided a rough washboard for the four ancient armored personnel carriers, and offered no compensation to the four 6-by troop trucks that followed.

Riding uncomfortably in the first APC, Lt. Blavatsky was hot, tired, and irritated. The stuffy inside was a sauna without the steam, and the rattling growl of the engine was fighting a losing battle with the bumpy, bouncing ride. And being assigned to Indianola, rather than McCook, put him in a very foul mood. He didn't like playing second fiddle to anyone.

Putting Corporal Tanaka behind the wheel of his APC had been the final insult. She may have been the best driver in the entire Japanese army, but Captain Yamaguchi had included her as a personal effrontery.

Her presence added a sense of foreboding to his foul mood, and a greater resentment to his surly disposition. Her presence turned his short, rough trip into a long, rough journey. He was certain that her silent, seemingly subservient attitude masked a smug forbearance of pseudo-intellectual arrogance. Her ultra-formal, prim-and-proper, scrape-and-bow personality was totally repugnant to his plebeian lifestyle.

"Watch the road, Corporal!"

"Yes, sir."

But she was, of course, watching the road. And her overly-subservient response transformed Blavatsky's command authority into a hollow shell of petty vanity.

Located ten miles east of McCook and fourteen miles north of Danbury on Highways 6 and 34; Indianola, Nebraska, belonged to

New World Order

another time and another age. Here ultramodern technology ran headlong into the classical era of Midwestern moralistic refinement, creating a crazy quilt pattern where a modern library in an old building faced an old-fashioned restaurant-and-tavern with a wide-screen DVD satellite television system.

Just up the street at 201 North Fourth, the Bank of Indianola, like its relatives and associates, had been closed and padlocked. It remained unique, however, in that several unidentified individuals first removed both sets of double plate-glass doors to the vestibule and to the lobby, and then stripped the building to its bare walls. Now the Bank of Indianola was a hollow shell — a ghost of its former greatness.

Across the street at 202 North Fourth, the Indianola Post Office (69034) had also been stripped bare, losing not only both its single glass doors to its lobby and customer-service section, but also its plate-glass picture window.

A couple of doors north of the post office, Mom & Pop's Grocery Store was also empty. In this case, however, the small-town version of a city supermarket had simply moved its stock to a new location ... outside of town.

The United Nations Military Command's invasion had forced many changes on this small and supposedly-insignificant town which once boasted a population of almost eight hundred. The city-supported computer center on the Highways 6 and 34, for example, was apparently replaced by an appliance store selling refrigerators and stoves. Only the computer center was still there, hidden behind a false rear wall and a few appliances on loan from Lord's Hardware & Furniture to aid in the elaborate deception. A complicated, interfacing, high-tech communications system had been added to the center, the connection to a disconnected world.

Lord's, itself, had undergone several alterations, including some extreme decentralization. The entire computer and communications system had been duplicated behind a false wall at the rear of their main store, just across the highway and half-a-block east of the new "appliance store." If the United Nations' troops did find one, they had reasoned, a second communications center might pass unnoticed. —Maybe.

With grim determination they met behind the false back wall of the Rocket Inn, the old-fashioned restaurant across the street from the storefront public library. An unidentified rural spotter near Stockville reported that Lt. Igor Blavatsky's convoy was less than thirty minutes away and definitely headed for Indianola. With grim determination twenty men toasted each other with steaming cups of coffee and frosty cans of soda pop. Then they picked up their rifles and shotguns, and marched out the back door.

———

Neither Lt. Igor Blavatsky nor anyone else in the convoy noticed the abandoned farmstead on the hilltop to their left. They'd seen too many abandoned barns and abandoned farmhouses throughout Western Nebraska. They'd also seen too many rough graveled roads. The much-appreciated transition onto smooth blacktop was followed by a sharp left and then a sharp right turn, which sent them plunging downhill into Indianola.

"Slow down!" Blavatsky barked.

Without changing her expression or revealing her personal amusement, Corporal Tanaka tapped lightly on the brakes, slowing the monster to a pitiful ten kilometers per hour (about six miles per hour), until it slowly crawled down Indianola's tree-lined Fourth Street to the painful accompaniment of grinding gears.

"Turn right!" Blavatsky snapped. But Tanaka waited until she reached the next intersection before turning off Fourth Street.

"Stop at the next intersection," Blavatsky growled, perhaps personally irritated by the notably-missing street signs.

Without asking, she brought the heavy APC to a halt *within* the next intersection ... and let Lt. Igor Blavatsky take a long and studied look at the middle of middle America.

"Why should they want such trash?" he asked aloud, denying his own covetous jealousy of this bucolic township.

No one answered his rhetoric.

Then, after a few moments of careful study, he said, "Outside."

Corporal Tanaka said nothing, but breathed a sigh of relief once Blavatsky and his sergeants had climbed from the overgrown tin can. Blavatsky's overbearing egocentricity made her nauseous, while his self-righteous self-importance amused her. Yamaguchi had put her behind the wheel as his own personal spy. Both of them realized, however, that Blavatsky would never make any deliberate or massive error. This trip would serve, instead, as her apprenticeship.

New World Order

Three rapid-fire explosions turned her daydreaming reverie into confetti. They were neither large nor loud blasts, but they did blow out the windows and doors of the first three houses on Fifth north of "D" Street. Smoke enveloped the three homes in a hellish black-and-white cloud. The sounds of creaking boards grew to a cacophony of crashing walls and falling roofs. Then, flickering through the billowing smoke, flames fluttered and flittered upward, crackling and spitting and hissing and finally roaring into an all-consuming conflagration. And the three former houses became three blazing bonfires, darkening the blue sky on a bright and sunny day.

Corporal Tanaka climbed from the APC and lit a cigarette. Emotionlessly she watched Blavatsky send his search teams into the first three houses on Fifth south of "D" Street. But the casual approach demonstrated by the search squads bothered the young woman. It wasn't just casual, it was careless.

Popping noises? Firecrackers in Indianola?

No, they were shots fired in the third house. A UN soldier, the front of his camo-shirt stained red with his blood, staggered from the front door and flipped over the wrought-iron railing. He landed flat on his back, almost lost in the small but untended front lawn. His body twitched for a moment or two before a low groan of pain and anguish announced his demise.

And when the other seven members of the search squad failed to emerge, the third house was quickly surrounded and isolated by the perimeter guards. Lt. Blavatsky's casual complacency vanished in an instant, replaced by a cold and hard efficiency which frightened even the imperturbable Corporal Tanaka. With an icy edge clipped to his words, he sent in the two other search squads.

"All seven," the Sergeant reported, trying to keep his quavering voice under control. "Two assailants, both armed with old repeating rifles. Both dead."

"Four-to-one," Blavatsky muttered under his breath.

"Sir?"

"Never mind!"

She offered him a cigarette and he said, "Thank you."

He took several long drags, letting his thoughts follow the curling smoke skyward. This could only be another no-win situation, he reluctantly admitted. The United States had its Vietnam. The Soviet Union had its Afghanistan. And now the United Nations had its North America.

Blavatsky blew another cloud of smoke skyward before he ordered them to stack the eight bodies in one of the APCs. "Leave the other two in the street," he ordered. "Perhaps they will get the message."

"Just another in a long series of lies?" she asked.

He nodded, and watched the perimeter guards carry the bodies of the two assailants into the middle of the intersection.

"Line them up neatly," he commanded. "And be reverent about it. —In their own way, they too were soldiers."

The perimeter guards may have eyed him warily, but they obeyed his orders exactly, even to offering a salute to the fallen assailants.

"Policy!" Blavatsky spat. "The politicians think this will cause fear. It will only cause more anger."

"Perhaps we should withdraw," Tanaka suggested, testing him.

"If we don't kill them over here, they will kill us over there."

"We are here as peacekeepers," Tanaka reminded him. "After their President declared bankruptcy, law and order broke down."

Blavatsky shook his head. "Their police were just as mean and vicious and cruel as ours ... so we killed them too. Law and order? — No, this is about money and politics."

The explosions and flames which destroyed the last three houses seemed almost subdued. The party was over, the festivities were history — a bitter remembrance of lost illusions. Blavatsky ground the butt of his third cigarette into the asphalt and signaled his sergeants.

"It's over, Corporal," he said, watching the flames die away. "It's all over. .... Let's go home."

* * *

Chapter Eighteen

"Kent?"

The Sixth Boardman — 'the young one' — nodded affirmatively. "He was the first. Naturally I have checked with Major General Kerensky and General Martin. They ... confirmed ... everything."

The Chairman wiped the sweat from his forehead, glanced at the linen handkerchief, and then flung the slightly soiled piece of cloth into a nearby wastebasket. He had made mistakes before, but this one was bad.

"It is my fault," The Chairman sighed. "I permitted him to order the executions. He seemed ... as reluctant as I was, but his reasoning seemed to be objective. — 'Just to maintain order, just to eliminate the troublemakers and the riffraff,' he said."

'The young one' again nodded, understanding The Chairman's dilemma.

"Obermeyer is a very good liar." The Chairman smiled, then frowned.

"Too good. Thirty-five million Americans marched into gas chambers, or otherwise executed. Another three-point-five million killed in .... fighting his soldiers. .... And he is worried about losing four hundred and fifty thousand troops?"

"Kent puts our losses at about four million," Boardman Six said. "He estimates American military losses at eight million."

"And which one is correct?" The Chairman asked.

"Neither," the young one said without hesitation. "The correct figure, I suspect, is somewhere in-between. Truth is usually one of the first casualties of war."

The Chairman was silent, lost in thought, for several minutes. "It is a complex problem. We are riding a tiger. We may encounter some difficulties if we attempt to dismount."

"But Obermeyer ... is going his own way, is he not?"

James A. Clayton

The Chairman nodded.

"Yet you do not think we should ... eliminate him?"

"That is not as easy as ... getting a haircut," The Chairman said. "He has many friends. Political and military friends who might regard his sudden removal as a personal threat. And the Secretary-General of NATO certainly would not risk his own career on something like this."

"Besides, Obermeyer has started this. If he cannot complete it correctly, it will be his problem. And as long as we are not involved ...."

The Sixth Boardman groaned with melodramatic indifference, shaking his head. "Nonintervention?"

"Well ... nothing overt," The Chairman purred.

———

Former DCI Jacob Andrew Kent was a long way from Langley. But placing an international telephone call to Switzerland required a great deal of discretion ... and a large dose of caution. Through various dubious connections he had obtained a comfortable Messerschmidt MG 650 Sports Coupe with valid United Nations' plates and auto-transponder, which gave him an open and safe route to Atlanta, Georgia. Another questionable source had provided electronic keys and codes to a certain telephone company relay-and-switching office housing the international trunk lines of a former television news network.

"So far, so good," he muttered, quietly closing the car door.

By now Burgenstock had checked with its other sources and confirmed his report. They would not, of course, be able to take direct action against General Obermeyer and his cohorts. On the other hand, his report would force them to take some sort of indirect action. It did not matter that Obermeyer ordered the genocidal massacre of forty-five million Americans. Such a destabilization would present too many random options to the Burgenstock group, including the threat of Obermeyer directing his murderous wrath against his own employers. And that distrust could eventually destroy the conspiracy.

Jack Kent slammed the irritatingly-fragile sports coupe onto Interstate 85, racing northward at a frighteningly-obscene speed. Just over two hours later near Gastonia, North Carolina, he stopped for a UN military checkpoint. One look at the United Nations' license

New World Order

plates, however, and they waved him through. The computerized license log checked off one Colonel Juan Quiroga, a staff officer who was now sipping sewage at the bottom of the Hudson River. But Jack Kent didn't hang around to illuminate their curiosity.

Just north of Charlotte he reached under dashboard and found the specially-installed and slightly illegal transponder toggle switch. He permitted a half-grin of satisfaction to flicker across his face as he turned off the auto-transponder and the vehicle's GPS idenifier.

"This one's for you, General," he muttered, turning north up I-77. Within seconds he was back up to ninety miles per hour and passing Lake Norman. He was well ahead of schedule, but he had been pushing it. At Elkin he turned off onto Highway 21, heading north at a more sedate speed.

At a little after eleven a.m. he was rumbling through the deserted ghost of Independence, Virginia. He was still ahead of schedule.

A forty-five minute rest within the verdant wilderness of the Mt. Rogers National Recreation Area didn't help very much. He was still ahead of schedule as he slowly growled through Wytheville and back onto Interstate 77. A quick but thorough look eastward confirmed his hunch — the UN had established a "rolling checkpoint" over the nine miles of roadway shared by I-81 and I-77.

On a map it looked like a promising bottleneck, but this was not the Capital Beltway. In reality neither interstate carried enough traffic to justify such an obscenity. Only the UN-NATO alliance apparently was not aware of that small but strategic fact. And Jack Kent was not inclined to correct their error.

He stepped on the accelerator, speeding northward at over a hundred miles per hour around Bland, Virginia, but slowing to a mere eighty as he crossed into West Virginia near Bluefield.

The West Virginia Turnpike — Interstate 77 — was no longer a toll road. Like all other toll roads, its tollbooths had been vandalized into extinction while its tollgates and toll collectors simply disappeared. The toll roads were now free, and that particular method of double-billing and bilking the general public had gone the way of the *Dodo*, vanquished in bloodshed.

North of the border I-77 became rather busy. Between Atlanta, Georgia, and Bluefield, West Virginia — a distance of about four hundred miles — he had counted some eighteen vehicles. Be-

James A. Clayton

tween Bluefield and the I-64 interchange — a distance of about forty-three miles — he counted at least sixty private vehicles. After that, he stopped counting.

Skirting Charleston, he headed east on Interstate 79. Thirty minutes later he turned onto the newly-repaved State Route 16 to Arnoldsburg. But someplace between the interstate and the village, Jack Kent took a graveled backroad into the trees. He drove slowly now, searching for landmarks among the trees. He turned, finally, into a rutted lane leading to an overgrown driveway. Still hiding his covert course under the leaves and limbs of a thousand trees, he guided the new Messerschmidt MG 650 Sports Coupe across the implement-cluttered farmyard and into an ancient, dilapidated barn.

"You're early."
"So are you."
"I'm Bill."
"Jack."

The bland voice came from the darkness and shook hands.
"Costa Rica, wasn't it?"
"Uh-huh," Bill nodded. "I was running the school when you pushed the panic button."
"Too late," Jack Kent muttered. "Far too late."
"Hell! The President pulled you in from Europe too late."
"Yeah." But for Jack Kent, it would always be his own personal failure. "Got anything for me?"
"Thought you'd never ask." Reaching into a stack of hay bales, he produced a manila envelope. "Your new identity. You are a farmer from Pennsylvania named Robert Christopher. Should be good for about thirty days."
"Hopefully I won't need it that long."
"You also get the multi-colored pickup parked over there."

It took a few moments to separate the truck from the shadows that occupied a dark corner of the barn. "That old rust bucket?"
"Uh-huh. That rust bucket. A rusted old body set on a new frame, with new suspension and a brand-new engine. Looks like a wreck, purrs like a virgin," Bill said. "On loan from the C.I.A."
"Funny."
"Don't knock it," Bill said. "Pete was very emphatic about the pickup and everything."
"Pete? —Pete Gordon?"

"Of course. He's been working with various militia groups in Virginia and North Carolina, trying to separate the good guys from the bad guys, you might say."

"Any luck?"

Bill nodded. "He's turned quite a few infiltrators."

"What about defectors?"

"More than we can handle," Bill laughed. "Pete insists we treat them ... as friends. But there are too many for our little group, so he lets the local militia handle logistics — keeping them separated, sheltered, and well-fed."

Jack Kent smiled. "Better him than me. — He's got the head for it."

"You charge blindly ahead, while he covers your backside?"

"That sounds like Pete all right."

Bill glanced at his wristwatch. "Speaking of Pete ... time to wake him up."

"He's here?"

Bill pointed at the pickup. "Up and at 'em."

"Pete?"

He sat up in the front seat of the ancient-looking quad-cab, an outline of shape and shadow. He yawned, and then climbed out of the "rust bucket" to shake hands.

"You're early."

"This time," the former DCI murmured, lighting a cigarette.

"And where did you get that scar?"

"Shaving."

"You're a lousy liar."

"Yes," Jack Kent growled, "and I'm almost getting use to telling the truth."

"Uh-huh. But Atlanta's still a long way to go just to make a phone call."

"It was a long-distance phone call."

"Funny." But there was no humor in Pete Gordon's somber tones. "Disinformation? .... Or the truth?"

"Under the circumstances, the truth is deadlier."

"Obermeyer's been lying?"

"Of course," the former DCI said. "What else could he do? — Hell, his own subordinates were lying to him."

The man called Bill shook his head. "Vietnam all over again.

—Lie, and make it sound good."

Both Pete and Jack nodded in unison.

"Obermeyer's been lying from the beginning," Kent said. "Those boys from Bavaria probably went on the official records, but never understood the man. They gave him the power and he used it."

"And tonight we take the power away from them," Pete said, glancing at his wristwatch.

"Huh?"

"Tell him, Bill."

"Tell me what?"

"You sure?"

"I'm sure," Pete said. Noticing Bill's hesitation, Jack Kent dusted off an old wooden stool and patiently perched on it. Trying to look casual and unperturbed, he proffered a pack of Marlboro cigarettes to ease the conspicuous tension.

"The Federal Reserve Bank in New York City holds the gold reserves of several major foreign countries," Bill started, pausing only long enough to light the offered cigarette. "It also holds a portion of our own gold reserve, although most is now held in Denver ... and elsewhere."

Bill took a drag off his cigarette to cover his uncertainty. "In just under six hours several large groups driving several large trucks will be making several large withdrawals from several selected Federal Reserve Banks throughout the country. You want the details?"

"No," Jack Kent snapped. "The less I know about it, the better. — Hell, wish I thought of it!"

"You did," Pete Gordon laughed. "Remember the 'alternative measures' study you wanted us to run through the computer?"

"Vaguely. You came up with something like a hundred and twenty different scenarios, as I recall."

"And you wouldn't look at any of them."

"As I recall," the former DCI mused, "things got a little busy just about then."

"Uh-huh, but we've been hiding the printouts here in the woods since *they* took over. And when I came across that little idea ...."

"Just be careful. After all, these jokers rely more on the G.N.P. than they do on gold."

"After tonight," Pete Gordon said, "they won't be getting

much of either."

The bone-cracking blow to his left cheek splintered the wooden chair under him. Suddenly set free of the binding ropes and wires, he hit the wet, abrasive, concrete floor with a sickening "splat" of blood and water — his crimson blood and their filthy water. A few drops of spittle dripped into the pool of blood and water within a shallow depression in the uneven concrete. A groan of agonizing pain escaped his cracked lips.

Every bone, ligament, tendon, muscle, and nerve-ending in his bruised and battered body sent messages of torturous pain and anguish to a benumbed brain. A size 12 brogue then crushed the bones of his right hand, but only evoked a whimpering moan from the shredded remains of General Donald Thornton Wilder.

"Maybe you would like to talk?" the translator asked. "Talk? — Yes?"

The tormentor laughed. Still laughing sadistically, he kicked the emaciated prisoner in the ribs. He took a deep breath of damp air and mumbled an unintelligible something to the translator.

The translator shook his head. "No, not today, Gregor. .... Perhaps you will wait for tomorrow? —Yes?"

By then, however, nothing made any sense to General Wilder. He was lost in a fog-shrouded mist, floating euphorically through a gauzy gossamer dream of a place that did not exist. And then he slammed into something similar to reality.

Wooden door. Stone steps. Dark cell. Damp walls. Metal cot. Blinking "gestapo" light. Slime and mildew. And endless pain. United or segmented, the Mannheim prison block delineated his world and his universe.

Technically, Wilder was alive. —Technically. Denied medical treatment, tortured with infinite caution to prolong his suffering, fed a minimal diet of food scraps, and surviving in a twilight world that was neither day nor night; he existed in a perpetual purgatory, suffering a damnation beyond understanding. He was somewhere, with pain and misery as his companions, and that was all he knew.

The "gestapo" light blinked off, plunging the cell into darkness. Trying to ignore the pain, Wilder closed his eyes in search of sleep — in search of oblivion. Muffled shouts and screams went unnoticed. Distant firecrackers did not move him. Crashing noises did not disturb him. And the bright light streaming in from the hallway was only a minor irritant.

"Jeez! — Looks like someone did a number on him!"

"A rather nasty mess, that."

There was something about those voices, especially the second one, with its thick stiff-upper-lip British accent. It was something from the distant past. But thinking about it hurt too much.

The two men took his arms and dragged him into the brightly-lit hallway. He closed his eyes against the brilliant flashes of light, but could not silence the roaring cannonade echoing and reverberating along the corridor.

Gunfire? —But who was shooting at whom?

"Can you walk, sir?"

It sounded like the first voice, but to whom was it speaking?

"Can you walk, Don?"

The British person?

"General Wilder?"

It took a moment to put it all together. —General Donald Thornton Wilder! He stumbled, but they caught him.

"Donald?" The Britisher again.

"Help me," he croaked, half-opening his eyes. "Can't see much. .... Not much strength."

"We have you," the British accent said.

"Where am I?"

"United Nations Military Prison near Mannheim, Germany," the younger one said. "I'm Lieutenant Victor McVey, United States Marine Corps. And I believe you know my associate, Air Commodore George Wesley Harmon of the British Royal Air Force."

"Ah, Harmon, of course," Wilder croaked. "I think I am out-of-uniform."

"So are we," McVey said.

The uniformed body of a prison guard propped open the metal door at the end of the corridor. Oddly enough, the guard seemed to be sitting in a small pool of red paint. And his blank stare at the rock wall remained fixed against his pallid complexion, even as they passed through into the guards' station.

Unshaven men wearing camouflage fatigues and carrying M-16s or AK-47s watched over the guards' station and pointed escaping prisoners through an open pair of double doors into a wide, friendly-looking, tiled hallway. With a nod from Air Commodore Harmon, the unshaven soldiers led the way down the wide corridor and into the small lobby. — A small lobby littered with uniformed prison guard bodies, Wilder observed.

"Your uniform is probably in there," Harmon said, pointing to a darkened room apparently filled with shelving units. "Sorry, but we cannot spare the time to find it."

"Probably wouldn't fit anyway," Wilder said, taking another bite of the candy bar McVey had given him. "Let's get the hell out of here."

Staggering with some degree of efficiency, Wilder lurched forward through the open doors into the dark and moonless night, towards a freedom he could barely remember.

The cool night proved almost intoxicating. The exhaust fumes of the five dark delivery vans concealed their own perfume-like essence, bringing a lopsided and painful grin to Wilder's bruised and unshaven face. Even the stench of his soiled and torn rags was now at least tolerable.

"Fresh air."

Harmon and McVey smiled.

Two plain-looking, nondescript, unshaven, undercover operatives opened the double rear doors of the middle van and nodded.

"Up we go," Harmon commanded, lifting Wilder's bashed and battered body into the high, blockish vehicle.

There was almost enough room inside to allow him to travel standing up. Such an idea, however, held little appeal for his weakened and trembling legs. Lt. McVey carefully lowered the former prisoner to the white-and-bright, heavily-padded, single mattress while Air Commodore Harmon closed and locked the double rear doors.

"We have a rather well-stocked hamper here," Harmon said, opening a large picnic basket. "Sandwich? Hard-boiled egg? Fish and chips? Fruit juice? Tea?"

General Wilder took a deep breath and groaned as the dark, boxlike delivery van pulled away from the building, following the four other vans towards the unhinged front gates.

"Were there other prisoners?"

"About fifty or sixty," Harmon said. "Most were in better shape. We will take as many as possible, if only to create confusion."

Wilder took a bite of the ham sandwich and chewed. It hurt his teeth and it hurt his jaw, but it tasted ....

"Of course, we can only take a few out in these vans," Harmon continued. "That's why we also brought the bus."

With a good deal of effort and assistance from McVey, Wilder sat up long enough to see the fifty-four-passenger commercial bus waiting near the remains of the front gate.

"But how did you manage all this?"

"My dear boy, this war is not very popular over here, either."

"I see," Wilder said. "Interesting. — It would seem you thought of everything."

"I hope so," the Air Commodore replied. "I sincerely hope so."

"Hmm. 'Tres Estrellas del Norte,'" McVey read. "I suspect that they were not designed for this side of the Atlantic."

"Mexico?"

"Quite so," Harmon said. "Brand-new and fresh from the production line. We volunteered to take it, uh, for a test drive."

"Rather obvious," McVey noted, pushing another pillow under General Wilder's head.

"Not nowadays," Harmon chuckled as they pulled out and away from the prison grounds. "Not nowadays."

* * *

Chapter Nineteen

One man can change the world. One man can change the future. One man can change history. One man can change ... everything. And Craig Starr was such a man.

His father had been a lawyer. His mother had been an heiress. And as an only child, he had been spoiled rotten. Having savored the bittersweet wealth accumulated by his parents, he had driven his BMW to Wall Street and donned the mantle of an aristocratic internationalist.

Craig Starr had built his life around lying, cheating, stealing, and suborning. These 'patriot militiamen' wanted only to preserve a *status quo* created on a piece of parchment over two hundred years ago. Obedience to the New World Order was far more important, especially since it would preserve his wealth and his foreign investments.

Thus, shortly after sundown, he scurried across town to report the planned bank robbery. Since he was supposed to be hiding in a doorway on Nassau Street, no one would discover his dastardly defection. And since he brought them his little MP5K submachine gun as a gift, he felt certain they would listen and believe him. —He was almost right.

Colonel Pepin and Captain D'Annunzio had listened, They had examined the submachine gun. And they had him escorted to the cafeteria for dinner. But they didn't trust him.

"It must be a trap," D'Annunzio insisted.

"Agreed."

"I disagree."

Both men leaped to their feet, snapped to attention, and saluted the new arrival. General Martin waved them off.

"There is no time for that," he said. "I've been watching that blighter on the telly. He is trying to protect his overseas investments.

Cunning sod! —Not that it will do him any good."

"Sir?"

"His overseas assets have been frozen," General Martin muttered. "But if they steal that gold ...."

It took less than fifteen minutes to draw up a plan of action, and just over fifteen minutes to implement it. But as General Martin told Colonel Pepin, "Be prepared for surprises. Starr was told only what they chose to tell him."

Colonel Pepin nodded, saluted, and headed for his assigned position. General Martin worried and wondered and climbed into the back of his armored limosine. But the night was still young.

Ten minutes later, while the Simmons Building was being blown up in the Bronx, General Martin was halfway across town, raiding an allegedly-empty building near the Holland Tunnel.

Manhattan is a small, overcrowded nightmare amidst a larger, overcrowded nightmare. Built on two rocks divided by a swamp called Central Park, this man-made labyrinthine maze of streets and alleyways works overtime to confuse and befuddle residents and tourists alike. One solitary building could hide a small army. This allegedly-empty building, however, hid even more.

Screaming and shouting, over two hundred United Nations' troops rushed the singular building, only to be greeted by exploding shrapnel that ripped the front and rear lobbies apart. With over fifty soldiers dead and another one hundred seriously wounded, their backup and relief units displayed a good deal more caution in invading this dark domain.

A second building exploded, this time in Hackensack, New Jersey. To his credit, General Martin realized that these feints were intended only to distract him. He also knew that his time was limited. Within the next thirty minutes the rebels might rob the Federal Reserve Bank, blow up city hall, or release VX nerve gas in the subway system. And it was his job to stop them.

Ambulances arrived and departed with sirens wailing, evacuating the wounded and the dying from the chaos and the carnage. On the building's seventh floor, a small but powerful blast scattered shards of shattered glass across the street. An anonymous soldier screamed. A dull thud made the building shake. Soldiers emerged carrying their wounded. The stench of death permeated the night air.

"Major Bocklin, isn't it?"

"Yes, sir."

"Any idea what we are up against?"

"Booby traps, sir. — But no rebels."

"A trap?"

"Yes, sir."

"Damn!"

General Martin stormed into the back seat and began pushing buttons on his car-phone. "Colonel Pepin?"

"This is Captain D'Annunzio," came the response, mixed with irreverent static and stuttering gunfire. "Colonel Pepin and Captain ... Captain Koller are dead. Now under attack at Nassau and Wall. Estimate —"

Static replaced words, and General Martin's anger was replaced by a sinking sensation in the pit of his stomach. This was *the attack* — the one he'd hoped would never come.

"Recall your men, Major. We are needed elsewhere."

But the recall took over five precious minutes. Traveling slightly over a mile and redeploying along Nassau between Fulton Street and Exchange Place took more valuable time. And time was their worst enemy.

By the time they arrived, Captain D'Annunzio was dead, punctured by twenty or thirty bullets and bleeding all over the street. Across the street three 6-by troop trucks, their tires shredded and their windows smashed, smoldered under the flickering streetlights. The New York Stock Exchange was surrounded by dead and dying soldiers. Nassau Street had been repaved with the blood and the bodies of soldiers and rebels locked in fatal hand-to-hand combat. And in front of Federal Hall National Memorial, someone was flying an illegal United States' flag — upside down.

"Bloody Hell!"

Staring at the gruesome carnage, with his British stoicism at the breaking point, General Martin tightened his grip on the armrests until his knuckles turned white — and his mind went blank. Quivering muscle spasms rippled through his arms and legs, fighting to control his body. His stomach heaved.

"Sir? .... Are you ill, sir?"

He turned to look out the limosine window. "After seeing this ...."

"Yes, sir."

"Get a body count and clean this mess up," General Martin commanded nervously. "Keep the men busy."

"Yes, sir."

Major Bochlin offered an obligatory salute and took command of the nervous troopers, calming them with a few terse words of reassurance, and sending them down Nassau and Liberty Streets to count and collect the bodies of their fallen comrades. It was not a decent task for a well-trained soldier. It was not appreciated by the ill-trained soldiers either. But it was, unfortunately, a part of their job.

"Reverse, Paul."

"Sir?"

"Back up into the intersection."

"Yes, sir."

General Martin sat in stone-faced silence in the back seat, studying the slaughter on Nassau Street. Something was bothering him. Something made him uneasy. Something about the gravedigger detail and the flickering streetlamps disturbed him. He picked up the car-phone and pushed three buttons.

"This is General Martin," he said. "I want ten light tanks, twenty armored personnel carriers, and a thousand soldiers around Nassau and Wall Streets as soon as possible. — Oh, yes. I also want three spotter helicopters over Lower Manhattan, and sooner than possible."

"Yes, sir!" The answer snapped and crackled and popped before surrendering to static.

Lost within an intricate maze of deep and dark thoughts, it took the General a minute or two before the beeping told him to hang up the telephone.

"Paul, find Major Bochlin. Tell him that I want to see him as soon as possible. And Paul, tell him to stay off the radio."

"Yes, sir!" his driver snapped, opening the car door.

A brilliant white flash of light and a thunderous explosion scrambled everything upside down and inside out. The heavily-armored, black, command car flipped end-over-end, crushing its trunk and landing on its roof to the sickening crunch of crumpled metalloids being ground into the pavement. Exploding grenades and blazing gunfire flamed into hellfire, lighting General Martin's tumbling flight down to the ceiling of the bashed-about command car — and into the blackness beyond.

It had taken two men — one to throw the satchel charge and one to provide cover fire. The perimeter guards responded quickly, but they just weren't fast enough. And the explosion had exceeded all expectations, annihilating both friend and foe.

Nassau Street vanished in a firestorm of phosphorous and fragmentation grenades. High-tension wires snapped in front of the permanently-closed Federal Hall National Memorial, slashing a fiery electric arc across a dozen soldiers and instantly incinerating anything within its deadly glow. Rifle shells and shotgun blasts obliterated John, Liberty, and Wall Streets. A gas main exploded in front of the now-defunct New York Stock Exchange, erupting like a volcano and splattering the area with molten asphalt. Crossfire raked the path of three militiamen running across Broadway near Trinity Church, transforming them into ghoulish red puppets spastically dancing to a macabre rhythm of machine guns and tracer bullets.

Within seconds Lower Manhattan became a war zone. Within seconds every street and alley between Fulton and Battery Park became a killing ground. Within seconds Nassau and Liberty Streets became a "no-man's-land" of instant death. And then, within seconds, the shooting stopped.

For several long and terror-filled minutes, silence ruled Lower Manhattan. The roaring flames of the burning gas main dwindled to a hissing jets of blue radiance. The crackling of the high-tension wires slid down into an irritating buzz. The cooing of pigeons, the gurgling of water pipes, and the soft hiss of steam flowed into the emptiness.

A low moan of pain or a deeper groan of agony occasionally escaped from the darkness of the errant shadows, only to be lost in the intense silence. Now and then a distant noise invaded the tension. And grinding sounds randomly irritated this nervous realm. But the silence dominated.

Then an ill-trained private with an overdeveloped sense of bravado darted recklessly into the intersection of Nassau and Liberty Streets, headed for the overturned command car and its injured passenger. But a single shot brought the private to full-attention ... and to a sudden, terminal ending. He stood at attention and crumpled into death.

Over a hundred automatic rifles and machine guns scarred

the masonry around the second-story window. They pitted the bricks with bullets and pulverized any remaining glass fragments into powder, but whether they shot anyone was strictly a matter of conjecture.

Five old British *"Centurion"* Main Battle Tanks rumbled across the Brooklyn Bridge. Ten armored personnel carriers roared through the Brooklyn-Battery Tunnel. They met and merged at the intersection of Nassau and Wall Streets ... in front of the late but unlamented New York Stock Exchange.

A hundred UN soldiers, mostly non-coms, stepped from the transient shadows of Liberty Street to rip open the wreckage of the armored command car and carry the injured General Martin to the relative safety of a nearby APC. At the same time, while still being treated for — and tortured by — multiple bullet and shrapnel wounds, Major Bochlin ordered his men into the battle-scarred buildings on an unlimited, unrestricted, and uninhibited search-and-destroy mission.

By then, of course, the shooting had stopped and the silence had returned to the battered and blasted "Financial District" of Lower Manhattan. Only the pitted remains of forty or fifty buildings and a thousand bloodied corpses were left to provide an *ad hoc* momument to mankind's inhuman brutality.

Jacob Andrew Kent reluctantly lit an illegally imported Savoy cigarette and tried to return his attention to a local map, only to find his thoughts wandering back to the bloody carnage of Lower Manhattan.

It was more a diversion than a thought, but he noted, in passing, that the Savoy was 'weaker' than his usual Marlboro.

"We should never have come down so hard on the tobacco companies," he thought aloud, drawing on the cigarette. "They only wanted to make a buck, same as everyone else."

"They became too powerful," Pete Gordon muttered, "a threat to authority."

Jack Kent shrugged. "Yeah. —'Authority' sucks!"

Pete Gordon smiled. "Yeah."

The former DCI let his attention wander back to the map of Manhattan littering his table. He let his mind roam, computing time and distance. But he could find no fault in Pete's plan.

"Damn!"

"New York?" Gordon asked.

"Yeah."

"Musta been a leak ... which means it was my fault."

"Why yours?" Kent demanded. "Anyone of a hundred different things could have gone wrong. An innocent inquiry from some civilian. An out-of-place spotter plane who saw something suspicious. A rumor based on little or nothing. And anyone could have tipped off the U.N. military."

"Denver, Dallas, and San Francisco went okay," Gordon continued unabashed. "Only New York City was blown. —It was my command. And my fault."

"Nuts! They're killing a million people every day. You came up with a plan to hit 'em where it hurts most. In war, Pete, you have to expect some losses ... but at least you've got the right idea. — Hell, three-out-of-four ain't bad."

"Jack!"

"Yes, I know. It hurts. .... Sorry, but it's part of the job. And to tell you the truth, I didn't like it much either."

"But somebody must do it?"

"Something like that. What was it Ben Franklin said: 'We must hang together, or most certainly we shall all hang separately'?"

"Nowadays they're much more efficient," Gordon grumbled. "Gas. Electricity. Lethal injection. Firing squads."

"Just what America needs — more death camps."

"Yes, but they've got only a few locations in a few isolated areas around the country."

Jack Kent took a final draw before he crushed his Savoy into the ashtray. "Now that is something to think about."

The illusion of "the Rule of *Law*" — the great hoax foisted upon the people of America by a frightened and inept government — had evaporated in the mists of military dictatorship, leaving only anarchy. Contracts could only be enforced at gunpoint, and the concept of values was debatable. Respect for private property, however, managed to survive with only minor changes or variations. Only arbitrary military interventions created an exception to rules based in mutual propriety, but no amount of militaristic force could ever find any real respect in violence. And perhaps for that reason alone, business at Milepost 10 on State Route 377 between Heber and

James A. Clayton

Holbrook, Arizona, had drastically declined.

With rare tongue-in-cheek military humor, the anonymous extermination camp had now officially been named: *"The Western Regional Reformative Rehabilitation and Recuperation Center of Arizona."* But its commandant and three-hundred-man garrison now had little to do.

The hundreds of thousands they had once processed dwindled to a few hundred. Within a few days they had emptied the one-hundred-thousand-plus overflow concentration camp near Cottonwood, Arizona, and the military units established at Deer Valley and Fort Huachuca. And they had "cured" all their patients.

But now people had learned where to hide and when to run, and few surrendered without a bitter and bloody fight. Casualties "in the field" climbed to alarming heights. Resistance had moved from possible to probable to inevitable. And any idea of a peaceful takeover died stillborn.

Struggling against reality, Brevet Major Fritz Schlieffen — affectionately known as "Uncle Fritz" by his men — had repeatedly called Major General Kerensky for information, inspiration, and advice. As camp commandant, Fritz feared actual combat. As an accomplished child molester, he feared the inactivity of routine military life. And as a too-young military officer, he feared being abandoned in the middle of nowhere by his own men.

Born in what was then the Soviet-dominated German Democratic Republic (East Germany), Fritz Schlieffen grew up within the brutality of a dying dictatorship. He had just learned the rules of survival inside that dictatorship when it dissolved into an allegedly "true democracy." The food, clothing, and shelter provided by the dictatorship's "make-work" job vanished, abandoned to individual freedom and "true democracy."

Without a job and without any money, he soon shaved his head and joined a local neo-Nazi faction in a village near Friedland. His particular skinhead group was no more violent than any other, but it was a favorite target for the new "federal police." He'd accumulated almost a year behind bars before a Captain Hermann Hoffman suggested that he might be better off serving his time in the military, rather than in prison. And after basic training, a certain Major General Heinrich Obermeyer had transferred Corporal Fritz Schlieffen to an unnamed special training unit for "former neo-Nazi hooligans"

New World Order

— where he learned more effective methods of murder and mayhem. But now he was here — and here was not a nice place to be. With only a couple hundred "patients" per day, his men spent most of their time playing soccer and watching old X-rated videotapes. His selection of female companions, ages eleven through sixteen, had been severely limited — and they didn't scream in terror anymore.

Being commandant of an extermination camp offered certain advantages, especially to someone who'd spent his entire life as a member of the disadvantaged class. Society had given the Uncle Fritz an intimate working knowledge of insecurity. He had been born with it. He had grown up with it. It was a part of him. But now he found a unique escape mechanism for his social insecurity.

Edging towards a manic-depressive psychosis, Schlieffen's military training and his current assignment kept him from total collapse. Understanding the problem, Kerensky sent a courier to deliver "a highly-classified statistical report" ... and to check on the Brevet Major's mental health. The report, however, did not have the desired effect.

The final page of the report concluded with the:

"Statistical Totals To-Date: (Week 12)

Location	**Patients**
Heber, Arizona	3,232,201
Forsyth, Montana	3,098,990
Midland, Texas	3,017,498
Arock, Oregon	2,908,602
Kane, Pennsylvania	2,795,204
Rome, Pennsylvania	2,775,880
Greenwood, New York	2,683,000
Southfield, Massachusetts	2,670,345
Richville, New York	2,590,379
Sardis, Kentucky	2,562,884
Pine, Georgia	2,487,123
Eureka, Kansas	2,396,680
Winona, Mississippi	2,388,564
Hugo, Oklahoma	2,202,785
Enos, Indiana	2,178,300
Table Grove, Illinois	2,162,647

James A. Clayton

Verdi, Minnesota	2,000,062
Opaldale, Colorado	1,821,493
Fallon, Nevada	1,569,135
National City, California	1,395,633
Barstow, California	1,173,900
Copeland, Florida	<u>967,025</u>
Total	**51,078,330**

Schlieffen, however, was not impressed by Kerensky's lavish praise. They were, he calculated, about twenty-four million short of their intended goal. And the idea of twenty-four million radical riffraff running rampant throughout the open countryside terrified him.

"Or if you look at it another way," he muttered in Low German, "it could be an interesting challenge!"

He filled his glass with more of an obnoxious brew called tequila, and emptied it in three ferocious gulps. Only the high White Mountains of Arizona do not mix well with cheap booze in the middle of a hot Summer day. By the time Uncle Fritz had staggered from his desk to the outside door of his three-room office, his body was drenched in sweat and his stomach was twisted into a Gordian knot.

With a voice more resembling a frog than a German, he croaked for his driver.

"Sir?"

"'*Red Hands*'," he croaked, climbing into the passenger seat, "but take it easy. I feel like ...."

"You look like it, too," his driver quietly murmured, starting the ancient jeep.

"*The Red Hands*," as they are locally known, were originally within a cave-like overhang alongside Black Canyon Creek. Here a large tribal family of "*Ancient Ones*," erroneously referred to as the Anasazi, lived over a millennium ago. Except for a few fragmented boulders, the cave and the overhang are gone now, leaving only the group's glyptic pictographs of mountains and sky, and fourteen red-colored handprints, on a cliff above the ledge which marks the site of their ancient home.

Over the years the creek had cut a deeper channel from Chevelon Creek to Black Canyon Lake, gouging a wide cliff-lined groove through the pine forests above the Mogollon Rim. Through

New World Order

the icy winters and humid summers, the walls of the cave fractured and split into a collection of large rocks and boulders that slipped off the ledge and into the waters of Black Canyon Creek. Much of the overhang also came crashing down into the streambed, building a new creekbank some eight-to-ten feet below the ledge.

By the time "civilization" reached the Mogollon Rim, the creek had cut an even deeper groove along an even narrower channel through the high tablelands. Riders of the Hashknife Outfit chased cattle along the creek and under the rock-wall cliff. The stagecoach from Gallup, New Mexico, to Phoenix and Prescott, Arizona, passed within fifty yards of the site. The ancient Model A's and Model T's set their narrow trends over this route. But whether anyone ever visited the *Red Hands* can only be a point of speculation.

With the gradual arrival of smoother and more accessible routes, this "road" was ultimately absorbed and then virtually abandoned by Navajo County. Sections of the "road" were often reduced to a narrow lane wandering across local ranchland, while the quarter section of mesa behind the *Red Hands'* site became an isolated and neglected bit of the Sitgreaves National Forest.

But Brevet Major Fritz Schlieffen professed no great interest in their history or even their existence. It was simply a "nice" place to go, someplace where one could be alone and isolated. And with all the cattle slaughtered and the local population "cured," the fencing gates across this rutted and dusty roadway had been cast aside, leaving the lane open to the ancient jeep and its perverted passenger.

"Uncle Fritz" endured the bumpy ten mile ride from the highway to Black Canyon with stoic indifference. The steeply-inclined, shallow S-bend curving down into the canyon had been sliced with little gullies from not-too-recent rains, turning it into an old washboard that would strain even the most professional of drivers.

Schlieffen ordered his driver to park the old jeep at the bottom and accompany him, on foot, across the almost-dry creek. On the far side he offered his driver a Gaulois cigarette, and also lit one for himself.

They walked side-by-side up the roadway climbing out of the canyon, smoking and occasionally talking about something. Halfway up the climb, where the incline becomes less precipitous, with the mesa rising to their right and a tree-lined gulch falling away to their left, the two men crushed their cigarettes into the dust. Then they were promptly shot and killed by a sniper carrying a high-powered rifle.

On the following day a search team from their camp found their bodies. Their killer was never found. And the *Red Hands* would never speak.

* * *

Chapter Twenty

Security is an odd disease, a cancerous illness fed by fame, money, authority, and responsibility. It exists only as a feeling, an illusion of safety in a world full of duplicity. Insecurity is, sadly enough, the only real security in this blighted and befuddled world, the only real safety within the illusion.

Yet in a moment of careless indiscretion, both Lisa and Rachel claimed to feel safer with Bob Lowell guarding the camp. Confusing sex with security hardly qualified as an original sin, but Ben Franklyn chuckled all the way to the bashed-about quad-cab pickup.

"So what are you chuckling about?"

"Why, Bobby, didn't you know? —At heart, I'm just a dirty old man!"

"You? Ben Franklyn? — You're saying you had a prurient thought?"

"Several," Ben Franklyn murmured, opening the quad-cab's front passenger door. "You know, in my day I've seen the F.B.I. and the B.A.T.F. turn from enforcing the law to breaking the law, and then hiding behind their badges. I've seen cops use the RICO statutes as a license to steal. I've seen our rights whittled away until anything you say or do might be subject to legalistic persecution. — And justice be damned!"

"Prurient thoughts," Lowell agreed, sliding into the quad-cab's rear compartment. "Prurient thoughts."

With a wisdom born of inexperience, Ben claimed the center seat next to Lisa. She was the daughter he'd never had, and she often referred to him as "the father she'd never known." It was not a comfortable relationship, but a cohesive bond embracing respect and affection that went beyond a father and daughter kinship.

Ben Franklyn had never been married. And although he had lost his virginity long before Vietnam, memories of that faraway land had destroyed any latent sexual desires, leaving only an emotionally burnt-out shell and a deep-seated hatred of technocratic "civilization" in their wake. Time and a grim, grime-besmeared kid named Lisa had given him hope. And that, he hoped, was enough to give her some kind of a future.

Lost in his own musings, Ben barely acknowledged Haley and Goldfarb as they climbed into the rear seat next to Lowell. And his greeting to Stan Gorman consisted of a single but undefinable grunt.

"Let's get this show on the road," the old farmer finally muttered. "Hopefully we'll get there before I reach senility."

"Bad night?" Lisa asked, guiding the old quad-cab onto the blacktop.

"Bad Internet," Ben grumbled. "Apparently they lost a nasty battle in New York City. Got burned pretty bad. —Guess those Easterners never learned how to fight."

"What about the roadblocks?" she asked, pulling onto Highway 83.

"Mrs. Pratt says the one at eighty-three and 'J' has been eliminated," Ben advised. "That leaves only the one out by Culbertson and that one on the Interstate."

"A rather expensive project," Lowell noted. "They've lost what? —An even dozen, so far?"

"Nineteen, so far," Stan corrected. "Don't forget Kearney and Holdrege."

"Oh, yeah. Almost forgot them!"

"Take the next left," Ben commanded.

With a puzzled look to cover her confusion, Lisa turned onto the graveled road. "Indianola?"

Ben nodded. "They wanna see the rural sights of Nebraska, right? —So let's give 'em something to see."

Lowell shook his head. "Ben, you're getting mean."

Across the railroad tracks and south of Indianola, where Fourth Street becomes a paved county road curving over the Republican River bridge, three 6-by troop transport trucks carrying eighty UN soldiers and two T-72 tanks carrying death and destruction rolled placidly southward in search of new targets to terrorize.

South of the river the road curves east towards the Bartley

Diversion Dam. The convoy, however, had chosen another route, turning right and grinding its way up the hill above the wetland forest of trees and underbrush filling the river valley. After a sharp left and an equally sharp right turn over the blacktopped roadway, they topped the hill totally oblivious to the eyes and ears recording their progress.

Life has its ups and downs, and so does the road to Danbury. After a brief pause to examine a farmyard covered with combines, cornpickers, plows, and tractors; the convoy continued south onto the graveled section of roadway. Tank treads tore the hardened surface apart, while truck engines and soldiers growled in protest as they bumped and bounced their way southward behind the tracked vehicles.

Like most roads in the Midwest, tin-plated drainage culverts have been tunneled under the graveled section of roadway between Indianola and Danbury. Packed with shaped-charges and plugged at both ends, these culverts can be converted into rather large pipe bombs. And this explains, more-or-less, what happened to the first T-72 tank.

The tank and the road disappeared within a thunderous, ground-shaking, fiery blast. Dirt and flame and gravel and metal were thrown into the air. With its guts ripped open and its fuel tank ruptured, the T-72 flipped over in the air and blew apart above its companion. Shrapnel-like slivers of metal ripped into the shell of the second T-72 and pierced the troop truck behind it. An instant later a few tons of metal — the remains of the first T-72 — fell onto the second, setting off yet another series of violent explosions.

The first 6-by troop truck, already ripped by metal fragments, was flung into the ditch just as its gas tank exploded. The blast ignited its canvas tarpaulin and the bodies of the dead soldiers caught within the hellish fireball.

Several secondary explosions later, UN troops leaped from the second and third transport trucks into a downpour of hand grenades. Death came in forty minor but telling blasts that sliced and diced flesh and bone and cloth and metal, splattering blood and gore across the roadway and into the ditches. A few shots rang out, announcing the death of another battered and burnt "peacekeeper" beyond medical assistance, and probably beyond caring.

And then came the silence, occasionally interrupted by the

crackling and popping of flickering flames. Billowing black clouds of smoke curled upward from the unrecognizable wreckage of scorched and twisted metal. A football-shaped crater cut across the road and marked the beginning of the carnage. Charred, burnt, and mangled corpses scattered across the landscape announced its ending.

Within the silence twenty-two men and women rose from the tall grass and underbrush. There were no cheers of victory, no chit-chat about the blood and gore, and no speeches about some vague "historical prospective." Unprotected by trees or buildings, they knew they were exposed to the inevitable overflight.

"That smoke is bound to attract attention," Lisa noted.

Ben Franklyn took a long, deep breath. "So let's get the hell out of here! — Now!"

Lieutenant Zelle came from Groningen in the northern part of the Netherlands. His ancient, dual-engined, Cessna 310B spotter plane came from a farmer in central Kansas.

"This is Zelle in one-oh-seven, to North Platte Base. Have spotted large volume of ground smoke in Sector Six-Nine, Sub-Sector Oh-Three-Four at coordinates ...."

The final message of Lt. Zelle abruptly ended with a loud, undefined noise. Remnants of the old Cessna were found in a field near Buffalo Creek four days later. The remains of Lieutenant Zelle were never found.

Major General Kerensky of the United Nations Western Command (Los Angeles) felt better now. Twelve hundred houses and businesses in South-Central Los Angeles had been leveled with fire and high explosives. Much of Hollywood Boulevard between Vine Street and Highland had been ransacked and gutted. Two blocks of Rodeo Drive just off Wilshire had been shredded and brutalized by a dozen T-72 (Russian) and M-60 (British) tanks. The historic Beverly Hills Hotel had been razed, reducing the bucolic landmark to ashes. And his troopers, bloodied and beaten by countless riots and insurrections, had killed over four hundred thousand rebels.

"That should teach them a lesson in proper humility," he muttered, gazing through the bulletproof plate-glass windows of his palatial office on the eighth floor of the Los Angeles County Hall of

Administration at 500 West Temple Street in smog-shrouded downtown Los Angeles. Then he noticed the five men working on the roof of the Los Angeles County Courthouse, a scant quarter-of-a-block south of his bulletproof plate-glass windows. The identical-looking, grayish-white buildings were separated by a politically-correct and very neutral plaza dedicated to horticultural apathy and architectural indifference. But the five men atop the courthouse building displayed no appreciation for politics, horticulture, or architecture. They obviously were only interested in quickly assembling some exotic technical equipment.

But what were they assembling?

And where were the rooftop guards?

A second later he pulled the building-wide emergency fire alarm just outside his office door. After a mad dash down an almost-empty hallway, he paused only long enough to trip another emergency fire alarm next to the stairwell exit. And then he was bounding down the stairs, taking two or three steps at a time, in unreasoned panic.

Bulletproof plate-glass windows notwithstanding, the first 106-millimeter shell hit his ornate office as he hit the seventh floor landing. The blast blew the office walls, ceiling, and floor into small, fiery fragments. It also flung him down the stairway to the sixth floor landing.

Pain told him that a couple of ribs had probably been cracked, but he could not afford the luxury of stopping to examine his injuries. Two more shells slammed into his eighth floor office complex before he landed, rather shakily, on the fifth floor.

More explosions followed his panicky flight down the stairs. Staff workers, shocked and dazed, stumbled into the stairwell to impede his flight. None, however, offered any aid or assistance. Fear — sheer terror — claimed all their attention. Someone had declared an undeclared war.

The Broadway entrance lobby on the first floor was filled with billowing black smoke, flickering reddish flames, and hysterically-screaming people. He saw staff workers vanish into the smoke-filled darkness. He heard their cries of pain and anguish mingle with the explosions and the alarm bells. He knew this exit was no longer available. And he knew the basement exit, through the underground parking garage, was his only remaining chance.

By the time he reached the bottom, his legs were aching and his stomach was growling. He struggled against the pain and the muscular tension, clumsily flinging his body through the open doorway into the basement's marble-lined main corridor. Smoke created a grayish haze, while the sprinkler system created a tropical rainstorm. Turning to his right, he splashed past the double doors of the waterlogged cafeteria to the side hallway in the center of the building. Soaking wet and miserable, he turned to his left and marched down the side hallway and into the underground parking garage.

Silence!

The underground parking garage was very empty ... and very quiet. Only the distant, dull thud of a random explosion invaded this dank mausoleum. And only the cold, moist air belonged down here.

There were, as best he could recall, six other entrances — two street ramps to his left, two automobile tunnels to his right, and the double doors of courthouse's first floor side hallway straight ahead.

The street ramps curved up and into the open on Broadway. The automobile tunnels went under Hill Street into The Dorothy Chandler Pavilion underground parking garage. The courthouse hallway could not even be considered.

He hesitated for a moment at the escalator cubicle. It was a way out. Its exit, however, was a kiosk in the middle of the plaza near the glass doors of the second floor lobby. He took one look and immediately dismissed it.

Major General Kerensky marched decisively towards the nearest automobile tunnel. Seconds later he discovered that his escape route had suddenly been blocked by a mob of ill-clothed and grimy peasants. Then he saw another mob emerging from the second automobile tunnel.

Spinning around, he spotted two other ragtag hordes running down the curved ramps at the far end of the parking garage. Other bums and low-lifes oozed through the double doors from the courthouse, and from the Hall of Administration. A few more even stepped from the escalator room. And Kerensky knew then that he would not escape.

"There he is! — There he is!"

But the mob already knew that.

"Major General Kerensky?"

Kerensky's icy-cold stare dissected the filthy, unshaven creature without compassion.

"Who wants to know?"

"Major General Kerensky, you are under arrest ... for crimes against humanity."

Defiant to the end, Kerensky sneered, "Fuck you!"

The filthy, unshaven man hit the neat, fastidious general once in the stomach. Kerensky doubled over in pain. The unshaven man stepped back. And then the mob closed in.

Someone slapped him alongside his head. He straightened up. A fist struck his groin. He doubled up. A boot slammed into his face. He fell backward. Someone caught him ... and threw him into the screaming crowd of peasants. They hit him with fists and bricks and clubs and tire irons. He went down. They kicked and stomped and hit his battered body until his mind slid into unconsciousness.

They hesitated for a moment, glaring down at the mangled body sprawled across the concrete. A muscle spasm offered a minuscule twitch. The mob kicked and pummeled his unconscious form. One woman, screaming hysterically, ripped at his face, her razor-sharp fingernails gouging bloody scars across his pallid complexion. Another drove a spiked heel into his back.

And eventually he died. But the mob continued to stomp and kick and stamp and walk over the smashed and bloodied pile of torn and tattered rags which allegedly contained the flesh and broken bones of the late Major General Kerensky.

Even from six or seven miles away they could hear the thunderous explosions shatter the silence of a foggy Monday morning in Red Willow County, Nebraska.

"Sounds like Sanchez started early," Ben murmured, watching the two armored personnel carriers maneuver along the rarely-used country lane.

"This road," Lowell pointed out, "doesn't go anywhere."

"But they don't know that. .... Amazing what you can do with a small hand-mirror, a piece of string, and a flashlight."

"Like what?"

And Ben Franklyn pushed the button, blowing the two armored personnel carriers into the sky and end-over-end with a ground-shaking blast that could be heard several miles away.

"Like that," Ben Franklyn said.

Bob Lowell took a deep breath of cordite-laced air and shook his head. "Like that."

Haley and Goldfarb, being younger and quicker, went first. With a nod from Lowell, they ran from the trees to the wreckage for a quick but not-too-subtle look inside the rolling morgues.

"Enough to wake the dead," Stan Gorman observed. "Or bury them."

Still covering the two point men, Lowell and Franklyn stepped from the woods and marched together towards the burnt-out wreckage. Feeling alone and out-of-place, Stan Gorman followed, ready to ... do something.

But no one emerged from either APC.

Rising from her bed of moist earth and matted leaves, Lisa calmly walked from her blind within the grove of trees to the shattered wreckage. Ben, she felt, was being too overly-protective, and had again left her on the sideline.

"About time you showed up."

"I wasn't sure you wanted me here at all," she snapped.

"I can understand that," Ben said, "but we needed you to provide cover fire, to back us up ... just in case something went wrong."

"So did anything go wrong?"

"Take a look ...."

But one look at the twisted and burnt wreckage told her that there would be no survivors emerging from this charred and blackened vision of Hell.

"I don't think they're gonna like this," she said, examining the burn marks and bloodstains.

Ben studied the wreckage, then turned to Bob Lowell. "Maybe you should give 'em a ticket for littering."

Stan Gorman offered, "Illegal parking."

Haley suggested, "Busted taillight."

Lowell shrugged his shoulders and folded his arms. "How about ... creating a public nuisance."

Lisa smiled and sauntered back towards the grove of trees and the hidden quad-cab pickup.

Men were such children.

* * *

New World Order

Chapter Twenty-One

Lebanon was a town reborn from the ashes of invasion and rebuilt in sheer desperation. The grain elevators were still on the north side of State Route 89, next to the railroad and Beaver Creek, with the town to the south. But now its village park, and the two dilapidated saloons facing each other across Main Street, were no longer its major attractions.

Lebanon had now given birth to three new but rather ugly buildings — a two-story brick monstrosity posing as a furniture store, a single-story concrete block wanna-be library, and a combination structure that actually was a restaurant. These buildings were actually, and voluntarily, built by the town to help house the growing number of refugees traveling the so-called "underground railway" across the country. And this particular Tuesday morning proved to be no exception.

At about ten o'clock five cars, three pickups, and an old Jeep Cherokee turned onto Lebanon's only main street and parked in front of the "restaurant." These particular new American refugees came from Omaha and Lincoln. Each had his (or her) own tale of brutality and terror. Each had seen their home or business destroyed by some local "UN military mission." Each had lost at least one family member to the nightmarish depravity of the foreign militarists' elitist dictatorship. And each one had been victimized by those foreign tyrants.

But these twenty-three refugees were no longer alone. The population of this little village had swollen from less than seventy to more than two hundred in less than four months. And the fleeing victims were breathing new life into the dying village.

None of the new refugees realized, however, that their large nine-vehicle convoy had finally caught the attention of a high-flying spotter plane. No one in Lebanon knew that the spotter had radioedin their route, and eventually their destination, to the communications center at *Lee Bird Field*. And no one reported the UN military convoy on State Route 47.

An APC and a 6-by troop transport pulled across Route 89 and came to a skidding halt, blocking off the north end of Main Street. Seconds later another 6-by troop truck and another APC had blocked the intersection next to the village park.

The new refugees had been too busy shaking hands and sipping welcomed cups of hot coffee to notice the arrival of the United Nations' soldiers ... until it was too late. A few alert individuals had managed to slip inside the "restaurant" or the tavern or the "library." But far too many were too far away to do anything more than wait.

The United Nations' troops didn't make them wait very long. Within seconds the soldiers had leaped from their trucks and formed assault squads at both ends of the block.

Then they stopped, freezing into a *tableau vivant* as an overly-decorated Russian lieutenant with a thick mustache stepped haughtily from the APC. He was followed by a petite and demure-looking Japanese sergeant, and an even smaller male sergeant who could only be described as nondescript.

"I am Lieutenant Igor Blavatsky of the United Nations Cental Command," the mustached man shouted. "And this is Sergeant Tanaka," the woman stepped forward, "and Sergeant Yost."

The little man with the bland face was too tall to qualify as a dwarf, but he was shorter than Sergeant Tanaka. His stance and his expression, however, defied anyone to say anything either friendly or derogatory about him.

The petite woman, on the other hand, had a totally blank expression, a face devoid of any emotion. She could have been a ceramic china doll, a fragile imitation of a human being.

But the haughty Lieutenant Blavatsky rose above them. He did not even attempt to conceal his contempt for the rabble gathered on Main Street. Instead, he stepped forward, treading incautiously to the edge of the riffraff.

"Under the Articles of Martial Law," he continued, "this is an unlawful assembly. You are all under arrest. .... Lie down — on the ground — with your hands clasped over your head. .... Now!"

But no one moved. Blavatsky pulled his Luger automatic, threatening those refugees nearest him. His soldiers, meanwhile,

New World Order

moved into the crowd to check identification and separate refugees from residents.

"Face down on the ground *now!*" he screamed. He grabbed the nearest refugee woman, yanking her forward. "Down on the ground now, you peasant bitch!"

She raked her hand across his cheek, gouging four bloody scars into the side of his face.

"Fuck you, asshole!"

Blavatsky shot her in the face at pointblank range.

The screams of the mob merged with the screams of the soldiers. A trooper slammed his rifle butt down into the crowd, only to disappear with it into the ocean of angry rabble.

Blavatsky fired his pistol into the air. Twice.

"I am in command here! I give the orders here!" he shouted. "You will —"

Another refugee, a woman with a noticeable limp, suddenly broke free of restraining troopers and slammed a concealed steak knife into Blavatsky's exposed chest. She stabbed him three times in rapid succession, giving the knife an extra twist on the third try.

Sinking to his knees, Blavatsky shot the woman twice. Dying, she stabbed him again. Tanaka fired a three-round burst from her MP5K submachine gun, and blew off the woman's head. Bloodied and dying, Blavatsky fired his pistol one last time, killing an unidentified man.

By then, of course, the United Nations' soldiers were firing indiscriminately into the crowd, shooting whomever came within their sights. Within the melee, however, many of their shots went wild and wide, going into the sky or into the asphalt. Soldiers were hit by bricks, or tire irons, or fists, or knives, or whatever-was-available. Some were even shot by their own rifles.

With the sudden riotous eruption just a few feet away, the troops guarding the south intersection immediately found themselves under fire from rooftops, through broken windows, and from partially-opened storefront doors. They scattered, leaving their dead and dying in the street. Some ducked behind the APC. A few ducked inside the armored personnel carrier. Some ran into the riotous melee. A few took cover behind the 6-by troop truck. And a couple of soldiers even tried, unsuccessfully, to duck into a nearby building.

A few United Nations' soldiers managed to unleash hand grenades, blasting storefronts open and flinging civilian bodies into Main Street. Others were not quite as agile. Their grenades exploded in their hands or under their feet, killing both soldiers and civilians alike. But no words could ever really describe the bloody carnage on Main Street. No words could ever really describe the brutal bestiality of the hand-to-hand battle. No words could ever describe the violence of a dozen grenades blasting the APC apart. No words could ever describe the gruesome slaughter that followed. And no amount of words would ever adequately describe the battered dead bodies and fragmented debris strewn across the street.

With guns blazing, armed townspeople and refugees charged from the "restaurant" and the "library." Mostly freed from the riotous mob, the surviving soldiers returned the gunfire. A grenade exploded. A few more shots were fired. And somewhere a casualty moaned in agony.

The wind whistled through a flue pipe. Leaves gently rustled in the trees. And Lebanon surrendered to silence.

Sergeant Tanaka, Sergeant Yost, and three privates survived to stand guard over sixty-one deceased soldiers and an estimated two hundred dead civilians. Five unarmed civilians faced them and impending death with as much courage as they could find within an essentially hopeless set of circumstances.

"You will now lie down on the ground with your hands clasped over your head," commanded Tanaka.

"Why don't you just shoot us and get it over with, you bloody butcher!"

For a moment she was taken aback. "I gave you an order."

"We don't take orders from you, bitch!" a woman refugee snapped. "Go to Hell!"

Sgt. Tanaka sighed. Sgt. Yost raised his MP5K.

"Enough is enough. You're under arrest. —Drop your guns and raise your hands." He emerged from the tavern, riot shotgun in hand and Police Positive on his hip.

"Who are you?" Tanaka demanded.

"Hudson. Deputy Sheriff. Red Willow County."

Then Sgt. Yost pulled the trigger, blasting two refugees into bloody shreds. He might have done more damage, but Hudson blew him away with a single blast from the riot shotgun.

From the darkness of a "restaurant" window, Kathy Smith

fired Hudson's high-powered rifle again and again, drilling ugly holes into the three privates. But Sgt. Tanaka managed to shoot and kill two local residents, and wound Deputy Hudson, before he could turn the riot shotgun on her petite form ... and pull the trigger.

He sat down on the curb and closed his eyes, not wanting to look at the mess beyond the battle-scarred automobiles. There were times when it all seemed so hopeless, and this was one of those times.

"I'm hit," he said.

"But you'll live," Kathy answered. "Sorry about that."

Hudson smiled. "It only hurts when I laugh."

"So don't laugh."

"Then don't tell jokes."

"Surrounded by over two hundred and fifty dead bodies, and you're worried about me telling jokes?"

He coughed, spitting gray-white phlegm onto the asphalt.

"Looks like it glanced off a rib before leaving," she said, examining his wound. "You lost some blood, and it probably hurts like hell, but you'll survive."

"Anybody else?"

"Local resident caught one in the shoulder. He's in the bar now, fortifying himself with an eighty-six proof painkiller," she said, helping him to his feet. "Maybe half-a-dozen left standing, most with minor cuts and bruises. — And then there's Jim."

"Jim?"

He was in the middle of Main Street. His aged body was propped up against a couple of corpses. And he was spitting pinkish blood.

"Jim," the old man coughed. "My name is Jim."

"Can you help us, Jim?" He looked up at her, trying to focus. "I'm not a doctor," he finally said, struggling to climb to his feet to examine the bloody slaughter surrounding him. "I think our doctor is lying over there ... dead."

Hudson had to look twice. "Doctor Barry ... isn't it?"

The old man coughed again. "Use to be up in Indianola, wasn't it?"

"Cambridge," Kathy corrected, wiping the sweat from his elderly brow. "Furnas County."

"Before ... the invasion," Jim added.

Hudson nodded. "We gotta find someplace to hide."

James A. Clayton

"Library basement," Jim gasped, spitting up more frothy, pinkish blood. "If you give a hand ... I'll show you."

Kathy nodded, knowing the aged man was breathing his last.

"The Internet was up again for about two hours this morning before they started jamming the relays," Ben Franklyn said, "but it was just the usual stuff."

"The usual stuff?" Lisa asked, steering the dark blue van onto State Route 89 and eastward out of Marion.

"Riots in Denver. Brutal fighting in Los Angeles. The President, Congress, and about thirty state governors imprisoned in Alaska. —You know, the usual."

"The usual," Bob Lowell sighed.

"Actually, it's been heading this way for a long, long time," Ben said sullenly. "It's just that most people didn't know about it. Or didn't want to know about it."

"By the end of the last decade," Lisa added, "the United Nations had established some forty-three operational cantonments or staging areas throughout the country, including National City and Alameda in California, Deer Valley and Higley in Arizona, and someplace near Pueblo, Colorado ... among others."

"And all right under our noses," Stan sighed.

"Yeah," Ben growled, "right under our noses."

Gazing at the peaceful countryside flashing past outside the van, Lowell caught a glimmering of Ben Franklyn's paranoid reality. This peace and beauty could easily lull you into complacency. But then he felt a tingling sensation in his fingertips.

"Wait a second, Lisa. —Pull in here."

"Lebanon?" Ben asked. "Nothing ever happens in Lebanon."

Lowell shook his head. "Call it a feeling ...."

But then they saw the APC blocking the intersection.

Bob Lowell went in first, his M-16A2 at the ready. But one look on the far side of the APC told him more than he wanted to know. And his single wave brought the others.

"Welcome to Hell." Ben Franklyn's soft whisper was almost a prayer.

The entire block was covered with bodies and with blood. The bodies of soldiers and civilians, of men and women, of youngsters and elders were mixed and tangled and mangled together in pools of drying blood. Some were stacked two or three high. Some had been bludgeoned to death. Some had been shot. Some had been garroted. Some had been stabbed. And some had apparently fallen victim to hand grenades, and been blasted into unrecognizable bits and pieces.

"Oh, my God." And for Lisa, it was a prayer.

The Rheinhold Chalet was almost hidden within the Black Forest near Freiburg, Germany. Designed by an architect from San Francisco, California, who had spent almost a year in the area selecting the site and making the preliminary drawings; the Rheinhold Chalet blended stone and natural woods with rustic beauty, offset by triple-thick plate-glass walls offering incredible vistas of rolling hills covered in dark-green pine forests.

Owned through a dummy corporation by a rich anglophile businessman from Hamburg. The virtually self-contained chalet took its identity from the German translation of the *Rhine*, and its anonymity from the secretive and remote location. Even Air Commodore Harmon did not know exactly where he was.

Relaxing within the warm depths of an overstuffed easy chair, General Donald Wilder sank into the panoramic view of green pine trees. No longer looking like a patchwork quilt of gauze and bandages, and with most of his bruises slowly fading away, he did not even care where he was. The sling holding his right arm was, however, a constant reminder of the pain and the agony he had endured.

"Now?" Harmon asked.

Wilder glanced at the wall clock and made a quick calculation. "It's a little after nine a.m. in Washington, D.C."

Harmon nodded and extracted a dozen or more sheets of paper from a manila envelope. He selected one and gave it to the American. He also offered a weak smile of acknowledgment, but it was a wasted effort.

"These are very expensive telephone numbers," Harmon said. "It took M.I.-Seven over a week and several thousand Euro-dollars in research, only to have an anonymous agent walk into our consulate in Zurich with this envelope ... addressed to me at an old 'dead-drop' postbox!"

"Rather audacious," Wilder teasingly noted.

Harmon was not amused. "The address is one I shared with a certain C.I.A. agent."

"Jack?"

Air Commodore George Wesley Harmon reluctantly acknowledged the association with a curt nod. "You knew?"

"I know now, not that it would do anybody much good."

"Yanks!"

"Yup," Wilder chided, rising painfully from the easy chair and taking a few agonizing steps towards the telephone. "So, did your people check these numbers?"

"Officially, these numbers don't exist. It would seem that our Jacob Andrew Kent has found a way to activate a nonexistent telephone exchange!"

"Yes, only Jack could do something like that," General Wilder agreed, grinning broadly. "Hell, I recommended him to the President. .... Said he was a man who got things done and kept his mouth shut."

"That President," Harmon said, "has been imprisoned and held incommunicado at a detention camp in Wainwright, Alaska, for several months now."

"So you've told me," Wilder sighed. "But then a lot of things happened while I was ... away."

"Forget it."

"Like hell I will! Those bastards did a lot of damage to me, both physically and psychologically, in that Mannheim hellhole. And I'm not about to take orders from some two-bit bureaucrat from FEMA, even if he is strutting around carrying the wash-and-wear title of Acting President!"

"Of course not," Harmon said, lighting an English Oval cigarette. "I doubt, however, that this so-called 'Acting President' is even aware of your existence. — I have been told, in fact, that this bloody blighter needs instructions just to visit the loo."

"Almost ten o'clock there," Wilder noted, settling into the couch near the telephone. "You're certain this line is secure?"

"It is the best that money can buy, and you bloody Yanks paid for it. —Direct uplink to somebody's communication satellite, then directly back to someplace in America, and all untouched by human hands."

With a solemn nod, Wilder raised the receiver to his ear and punched-out the sixteen-digit telephone code. By then, however, he was bathed in sweat and breathing hoarsely. Harmon brought him a glass of water while the telephone relay clicked its way into outer space.

"Hello, Jack? —Don Wilder. .... General Donald Thornton Wilder, NATO Liaisons, Alpha-Tango-Three. .... No, still alive and kicking, more-or-less."

He took a deep breath and three small sips of water. "Yes, that was George Harmon, all right, but he's now an Air Commodore. .... Yes, I know. I heard about it. But I'm not taking orders from the Bilderberg Group, nor their servile toadies! .... No, don't even ask where I'm at. I'm not certain, and I wouldn't say, even if I was. — But I do need a favor, Jack. .... That's right, it's time to be heroic."

He took several more sips while listening to Jack Kent's familiar voice, then set the almost-empty glass on the floor.

"Okay, listen up. We have some associates in Washington who have been working rather diligently for the opposition. And they are hurting us. .... Well, I want you to pay them a little visit — and re-arrange their furniture."

He picked up the glass and emptied it completely.

"Right. Now, here's the shopping list ...."

———

Exhausted and sweating, the doctor shook his head, pocketed his stethoscope, and pulled the sheet up and over the man's pallid face.

"I'm sorry," he said. "I just don't have the equipment necessary to ...."

He looked up to find Ed Hudson, Bob, Ben, Kathy, Lisa, and the others folding their hands and bowing their heads in a silent prayer for an elderly man they barely knew.

"I couldn't find ... any identification on him," the doctor continued. "We need a name on the gravemarker."

"Jim," Kathy said. "His name was Jim."

Silently the doctor nodded, then he followed the others up the stairs into the lengthening shadows along Main Street.

"Over two hundred unarmed civilians massacred," Stan Gorman said, "and Lebanon is just one little town."

"They fought," Hudson reminded him. "With knives. With bricks. With their bare hands. —But they fought."

James A. Clayton

" '*The battle is not to the strong alone; it is to the vigilant, the active, the brave*'," Ben quoted.

"Patrick Henry," said Lowell.

Ben nodded, "He knew."

"And Jim?" Lisa asked.

"He was vigilant and brave," Ben Franklyn offered. "Oh, foolish, perhaps, but vigilant ... and brave."

* * *

Chapter Twenty-Two

"Kansas - Nebraska Border
Inspection Station
All Vehicles Must Stop"

Sandbag bunkers backed by two armored personnel carriers created a formidable barrier along Highway 83, the broad north-south corridor between McCook, Nebraska, and Oberlin, Kansas. Set just south of the tee-junction where the westward-bound State Route 89 comes to an abrupt end atop an exposed, empty, and rather lonely hill in the well-cultivated middle of nowhere; this outpost was a beautiful example of the futility of martial law in the Midwest.

No one used Highway 83. Long-haul truckers now guided their big rigs over selected backroads across state lines and around strategically-positioned checkpoints. Local residents went out of their way, assiduously avoiding this too-infamous Highway 83 eyesore.

Illuminated at night by mercury-vapor lamps, this deadly "Inspection Station," surrounded by an unobstructed 360-degree killing field, was innocently notable as the epitome of tyrannical martial law. The position was untouchable and unapproachable.

But then the lights went out. At about three a.m. the mercury-vapor lamps, set atop fifty-foot poles, dimmed briefly. Five minutes later all eight lamps flickered out, leaving the intersection and the area in darkness.

They started both APCs and turned on their lights, providing a dim and shadowy glow. The glow was just bright enough, however, to help them prime a portable emergency generator that had been gathering dust in a nearby ditch.

The generator sputtered and groaned and growled to a choking and raucous hum. But then the mercury-vapor lamps flickered and brightened back to life on their own, without explanation. Once again the killing fields were bathed in a warm and deceptive glow, a glow which made the intersection look ... almost friendly.

Their steady glow lasted for about thirty-five minutes, long enough for the UN soldiers to regain their trust and reliance in the lamps. Then, shortly before four o'clock in the morning, the lights again flickered and dimmed.

Once again, after approximately ten minutes of darkness, the generator sputtered and hummed and cranked-out electricity. Two well-trained and highly paid "technical experts" wired the generator to the junction box.

It took only twenty minutes to restore electrical power to the mercury-vapor lamps, but when the lights came back on, only four UN soldiers — including the two "technical experts" — were still manning their posts around the emergency generator. And they were very much alone. The twelve other members of their unit, including their commanding officer, had quietly vanished into the darkness.

"Drop your weapons and raise your hands."

The grim and foreboding masculine voice thundered from the nearest APC bunker, threatening an instant and dire response. The four remaining UN soldiers dropped their weapons and clasped their hands over their helmets, surrendering to an invisible enemy.

There were at least thirty militiamen (including five or six women), dressed mostly in camouflage fatigues. Moving with intimidating efficiency, they had the four soldiers stripped to their underwear and tied up in an APC within ten minutes. Now the selected militiamen wore United Nations' uniforms. Each wore a helmet with a blue stripe encircling its domed crown. And each militiaman carried a NATO rifle.

An hour and a half later the sixteen selected militiamen took on an appropriate "end-of-watch" stance, seemingly half-asleep at their posts, as the school bus from North Platte arrived.

Traveling eighty-seven miles — one hundred forty kilometers — to the checkpoint every day in a bouncing school bus had taken its toll on the men. They considered it a punishment posting. For those chosen to man the checkpoint, it offered positive proof that Hoffman hated their guts.

(Hoffman, of course, was unaware of their anger. To him, the permanent roadblock was merely another checkpoint, another colored pinhead on his area map.)

Having been rudely awakened at three o'clock in the morning by an irritated sergeant-major, the relief unit was not prepared for a second rude awakening. And by the time they awoke, the militiamen were escorting the driver and his backup to the back of the bus at gunpoint. Other militiamen then relieved them of their weapons, their helmets, their shirts, and their shoes before introducing them to the sixteen prisoners they were supposed to relieve.

"Consider yourselves lucky," Ben Franklyn told them. "You will probably come out of this mess alive. Definitely older and hopefully wiser, but most of all — alive."

With a nod from Bob Lowell, the school bus took the thirty-four prisoners, four armed guards, and new designated driver southward to the newly-built jail in Oberlin, Kansas.

"Opinion?" Ben Franklyn asked, watching the school bus navigate the checkpoint barriers and pull away.

Stan Gorman shrugged, "Let's hope they don't come back."

Linda Kelton, secretary to the Assistant Director of the Federal Emergency Management Agency, zealously guarded her own personal and private domain within the posh government building at 500 "C" Street Southwest, where she worked and virtually lived. Her boss permitted her to use a couch in the office, and the private bath and shower, in exchange for certain after-hours sexual favors which both women candidly enjoyed.

On the other hand, she did not appreciate the telephone repairmen ruining her morning by wandering throughout the building in search of ... something. The time they spent examining her automated switchboard unit further aggravated an already intolerable search under her desk for some transient signal line ... or something. And although the repairmen were long-gone by ten-thirty, their aggravating politeness lingered to ruin her day.

"Fortunately," she muttered to no one in particular, "it is a very slow day."

And then the telephone rang. —Twice.

"FEMA Regional. Miss Kelton speaking."

"Hello, Linda. This is Jack."

"Jack? .... Jack who?"

"Jack, the telephone repairman," the telephonic voice said. "Sorry for the inconvenience. I just wanted to check the signal clarity."

Three 'clicks' ... and Linda Kelton's desk blew up. The fiery blast engulfed the woman and the room, instantly incinerating everything and everybody.

Like a string of exploding firecrackers, rapid-fire blasts ripped apart every room on every floor of the building. Every window was blown from its frame. Every door was torn asunder. Walls cracked. Ceilings buckled. The screams of the injured and the dying were lost within the thunderous, reverberating blasts. A firestorm flashed and flared throughout every level and within every cubicle. And all their furniture was re-arranged.

From within the "Signal Corps" telephone van parked near the corner of Fourth and "C" Streets (Southwest), Jacob Andrew Kent ejected and pocketed the audio tape, lit a Marlboro Gold, and studied the black smoke billowing from the slowly collapsing ruins of FEMA headquarters. Actually it didn't look so bad. All the doors and windows had been blown, and all its structural integrity had been lost, but collateral damage had been kept to a minimum.

"There probably were some innocent people in that building."

It didn't take a second look to understand Pete Gordon's fears. But Jack Kent took a long drag from the Marlboro before he formulated his answer.

"Probably," he said. "The innocent often end up paying for the work of the wicked."

"Now that is grim."

———

Although illegally parked about two hundred feet apart along Tenth Street Northwest between Constitution and Pennsylvania Avenues alongside the Department of Justice, the three customized Dodge Ram IV vans failed to attract any attention.

The first van was repainted a bright red. The second was painted a pure white. And the third van was a deep blue. All three were customized with matched sliding doors behind the driver's and passenger's seats. All displayed United States' military license plates. And they were the only vehicles on Tenth Street Northwest.

But apparently no one working across the street within the gray granite mausoleum of the Internal Revenue Service headquarters noticed the the intrusive interlopers. Around ten-thirty the low rumbling of distant thunder echoed across *"The Mall"* to let the fifteen sweaty occupants of the Ram IV vans know the fate of FEMA. Responding to the message, the passenger-side sliding doors opened in unison. An instant later, again in unison, the driver-side doors slid open. A singular, pregnant second of high tension ended in the violent roar of seventy-two small but deadly missiles launched through the open doors of the three Ram IV vans.

The headquarters of the Internal Revenue Service simply disappeared within the overlapping, thunderous, multiple explosions. The east side of the building — all six hundred fifty feet from Constitution Avenue to Pennsylvania Avenue — was blasted inward in a horrendous firestorm of smoke and flame and powdery concrete.

Without support, the upper floors came crashing downward into the fiery ruins, crushing all that was beneath them. The militiamen, meanwhile, quickly reloaded the rocket launchers ... and were preparing to fire a second salvo of death and destruction.

Roiling clouds of smoke and dust rose within the ruins. Fragmented shards of shattered glass windows tinkled down from the battered west wall of the Justice Department's abandoned headquarters building. The red Ram IV pulled away from its curbside location, parking crosswise in the street to aim the rocket launcher towards a more worthwhile target. By then, of course, both the white and blue vans were ready to create more havoc in the neighborhood.

The white van fired twenty-four rockets into the clouds of smoke and dust and debris. Twenty-four ground-shaking blasts combined to smash and rip through the ruins, dumping bricks and rubble and miscellaneous debris onto Twelfth Street Northwest.

Two seconds later, amidst the ground-shaking explosions and the crushing structural collapse, another twenty-four rockets were launched into the smoke-shrouded wreckage. Like an echo, they blasted through the smoke and dust and rubble to destroy the remaining front tier of offices facing Constitution Avenue, and dropping the upper floors down to a pulverizing conclusion.

About a minute later the red van's second salvo flamed into the billowing dust clouds, adding their violent blasts to the secondary explosions and raging fires within the smoke-shrouded rubble. Sheets of flame and bits of concrete burst beyond the roiling and swirling clouds of smoke and dust, pitting and scorching anything and everything within range.

It was, however, an exercise in futility. The building had already been leveled, reduced to chunks of concrete, bits and pieces of wood, slivers of metal, and burning debris. Pounded and pulverized beyond recognition, even the remaining rubble seemed to be disintegrating.

"Now this is the way," the militiaman said, "that I want to remember the Infernal Revenue Service."

Beyond the van's sliding door, engulfed in roiling clouds of smoke and dust, shattered chunks of concrete mixed into an accumulated and almost-homogeneous mass of undefinable debris.

"To the last of the bloodsuckers," muttered another militiaman. "May they rest in bits and pieces."

Having re-arranged the IRS furniture, the militiamen slammed the sliding doors shut and drove away through billowing gray clouds of dust and smoke.

———

As usual, Bill had used too much Simtex and C-4. On the other hand, he could always argue that "too much" was far better than "too little."

With the help of at least two dozen other militiamen, he had spent the night scurrying through the dark shadows across Virginia Avenue Northwest from the Department of the Interior and, through the catacombs of ancient and deteriorating storm drain system, into the sub-basements of the headquarters of the Federal Reserve Board. Once inside, he and a select squad of co-conspirators had planted some twenty-seven listening devices ("bugs") at various points throughout both buildings. Then, under his guidance, they wired twelve shaped-charges, over two hundred and forty pounds of high explosives, mostly C-4, to a precise timing mechanism.

Although architecturally dissimilar, the two buildings facing each other across "C" Street Northwest are united in their contempt for "the average, hard-working individual." Listening to Von Hagen's rambling monologue on the devaluation of the "almighty dollar," however, was nauseating. Disgusted, Bill yanked off the earphones and took a deep breath. Von Hagen's speech went far beyond contempt.

Bill glanced at his wristwatch, took another deep breath, and repositioned the earphones. Silence dominated the blue-and-white van, interrupted only by Von Hagen's continuing diatribe against the

New World Order

"inept FEMA administration" and the "American cowboy mentality."

".... Today, however, gentlemen, we need not consider the American cowboy mentality of the so-called 'patriot militia'. Today, gentlemen, I wish to finalize our discussions on the redistribution of wealth within the United States —"

Both the ancient H-shaped building on the south side of the street and the block-like cube on the north disappeared in billowing clouds of dust. A deep, rumbling noise accompanied the growing clouds of dust and smoke and debris into a chaotic, cacophonous melee of sights, sounds, and vibrations. The blue-and-white van quivered and quaked as the roiling clouds fired spikes of smoke and debris skyward.

Secondary explosions flashed and burst throughout the blasted ruins, sending debris-laden fireballs upward over the shattered rubble of the Federal Reserve. Of the buildings, however, nothing remained. Shrouded in smoke and dust, they had been reduced to two small heaps of smashed and fragmented bricks and concrete, crushed within the aftermath of total destruction.

"So that's what you meant about 're-arranging their furniture'," the driver said, smiling.

With a nod from Bill, the driver threw the van's grumbling engine into gear and guided the bulky beast onto Twentieth Street Northwest, heading out of the city.

"This is a horrible disaster!" the Secretary-General said. "They have destroyed at least three or four of their most historic and important buildings."

"Yes," Obermeyer sighed, gazing through the porthole at the smouldering ruins passing beneath the helicopter. "And they have also murdered thousands, including the employees of FEMA."

In earlier days jets would have been dispatched from Andrews to intercept the low-flying helicopter buzzing the nation's capitol. Nowadays they flew almost unnoticed (and virtually unchallenged) past the tinted-and-bulletproofed windows of government office buildings.

"Why?" the Secretary-General demanded.

"Why not?" Obermeyer muttered. "This so-called patriot militia bunch are nothing more than a few criminals trying to disrupt

James A. Clayton

our ... restoration of their society." The Secretary-General nodded in agreement. The Secretary-General knew Obermeyer was lying. But the Secretary-General did not object. He wanted to go on living.

They met around an elongated, dark hardwood, conference table set within a luxuriously-appointed boardroom on the twenty-first floor of the fragile glass tower known as the United Nations' Secretariat Building. This elegant table was divided by a row of four steaming-hot coffee carafes and surrounded by fourteen high-backed, swivel-and-rock, executive chairs. Thirteen executive chairs commanded space at the table, a lap-top computer, three ballpoint pens, a 6x9 notepad, a half-filled styrofoam cup of coffee, a glassine ashtray, and an oversized nameplate. The empty fourteenth chair was a footnote to the polished-hardwood table.

They were thirteen overly-decorated generals wearing thirteen different dress uniforms representing thirteen different countries in various shades of blue, gray, brown, and tan. They were seeking their own nameplates and their own seats within the opulent grandeur of light-blue pastel walls and ivory-shaded deep-pile carpets reflected and illuminated by the plate-glass picture window just beyond the head of the conference table. They were milling about, seeking a commonality to Obermeyer's all-inclusive demand for their attendance and their attention.

It was difficult, however, to read General Heinrich Obermeyer's expression from the plate-glass window's reflection. He had his back to them, apparently studying jagged New York City skyline for answers to unasked questions.

"Be seated." But General Obermeyer did not turn away from the plate-glass window. He waited until the others were seated, and somewhat relaxed, before he turned and took his seat at the head of the conference table.

General Martin, the battered Britisher, sat to his left. With his arm in both a cast and a sling, and with his head wrapped in gauze bandages; General Martin belonged to the walking wounded. His mere presence frightened Obermeyer.

"You should be in hospital."

General Martin offered Obermeyer a curt nod, but said nothing.

New World Order

General Fawdi sat across the table from General Martin, and even further away socially. The Afgan, who insisted his nameplate be inscribed in Arabic as well as English, was openly hostile and contemptuous of all the "Western" infidels roaming the streets of America. He complemented General Martin's silence with an unbroken stream of incomprehensible, and almost-inaudible, Arabic invective.

For General Dupre, the Frenchman seated next to the battered Britisher, Fawdi's monotonic mutterings were an intolerable embarrassment. His aristocratic arrogance could not admit to the sly and savage weasel concealed within his pretentious uniform.

Sitting across the dark table from the haughty General Dupre, a depressed and dour General Seminski stoically accepted (and ignored) the Afgan's grumbling. Neither Fawdi's mumbled invective nor Obermeyer's textbook 'divide-and-conquer' philosophy could ever compare with the 'double-barreled' threat he faced at home. Not only was he the pseudo-commander-in-chief of the dwindling Russian army, he also was the principal director of the reformed Moscow mafia, which had evolved into a semi-autonomous, quasi-official, legalistic enforcement group. That volatile position, accidentally acquired during the so-called "Soviet meltdown," made Seminski one of the most beloved and one of the most hated men within the sphere of Russian influence — a less than enviable situation.

Obermeyer turned away from the Russian's icy stare, ostensibly taking time to light another smelly cigar while he contemplated the Spanish representative.

General Rodriguez of Spain was seated next to the haughty General Dupre. Although outwardly smiling, he obviously felt out-of-place. ('He would rather be somewhere else,' Obermeyer thought, 'wherever that might be.')

Obermeyer finished lighting his cigar and took a puff while studying General Hoiaas of Norway, who was seated further down the dark table, just beyond Seminski. The Norwegian General refused to look up from his laptop, presenting only the top of his head for Obermeyer's cursory examination.

The German commander-in-chief set his cigar in the glass ashtray, cleared his throat, and smiled. It was not a good sign.

"Gentlemen," he began, "we are in trouble. Deep trouble. West of their Mississippi River only four of our garrisons are fully operational — Omaha, Des Moines, North Platte, and Leavenworth."

Obermeyer took several puffs off his smelly cigar before he spoke again.

"Three generals and an admiral agreed to help us," he continued, "to turn their commands over to us. ... All four are dead. And their commands have simply disappeared."

He blew a cloud of grayish cigar smoke down the length of the dark conference table, watching them pull back and away from the cloud of smoke. The representatives of Iraq and Saudi Arabia were blatantly offended, while the generals from Poland and Finland appeared unperturbed. Andolini, the Italian general, turned and stared daggers at Obermeyer; but General Abdul Mosef, Algeria's representative, maintained a look of stoic indifference.

Obermeyer waited one full, tense, and irritating minute before starting again.

"Earlier today I spoke with the Secretary-General," he said, keeping his voice soft and mild. "Since we have been unable to gain access to the American gold in Denver, Fort Knox, and elsewhere; Russia, Poland, France, Great Britain, and several other nations have refused to send us more soldiers. .... It has become just too expensive."

He blew another cloud of gray cigar smoke upward towards the ceiling, letting them feel the icy chill of his anger in a new and frightening form. Like an electric charge, the icy chill shocked their passivity, demanding their attention.

"And finally," Obermeyer hissed, "to add insult to injury, just over six hours ago a group of terrorists blew up the headquarters of the Internal Revenue Service, the Federal Emergency Management Agency, and the Federal Reserve Corporation — all in Washington, D.C."

Obermeyer stopped for a deep breath of smoke-filled air.

"I propose, therefore, to regain control of these territories with the soldiers currently under our command and available to us. To do this, we must act swiftly and forcefully, and without mercy. .... If we do not eliminate these terrorists — these patriot militia — they just might eliminate us."

General Heinrich Obermeyer eased his way down into his chair and took a few more puffs from the cigar before crushing it into oblivion. "Comments, gentlemen?"

New World Order

Haughty General Dupre filled the silence by lighting a mentholated Gaulois cigarette and blowing blue smoke into the gray smoke. And General Fawdi granted both infidels a look of total disgust.

"Bah! You are too timid, General Obermeyer!" Fawdi exploded. "We must punish these heathen American infidels! We must teach them the wrath of Allah!"

Dupre shook his head. "General Fawdi, we have suffered over four million casualties."

"General Dupre, we still have sixteen million soldiers at our command."

"Fourteen million five hundred thousand," Obermeyer said coldly. "And over half of them are new recruits. .... They leave much to be desired."

"I do not like to say it," General Martin interjected, "but I'm afraid that these American patriots do truly have us by the 'short-and-curlies'."

But that was not what they wanted to hear.

* * *

Chapter Twenty-Three

They had changed the nameplate on the door from a dour "*Major Hoffman*" to a dour "*Colonel Hoffman*" just a few minutes before Yamaguchi entered.

"Congratulations. You are now Major Yamaguchi."

"Yes, sir. — Thank you, sir."

"Do not be too grateful, Major," Hoffman sneered, handing the Oriental a sheaf of papers. "This promotion is not for what you have accomplished. It is intended to insure your loyalty."

"Is that why you were promoted?"

"Of course!" Hoffman snapped, trying to hide his own depression. "We're trapped here, and apparently things are not going well back east. —Rumor is that terrorists simultaneously destroyed three large government buildings in Washington, D.C."

"Three? —At once?"

"And we have lost twenty-one battle tanks, thirty-seven personnel carriers, forty-nine troop trucks, thirty-five helicopters, and ... over nine hundred combat soldiers."

Hoffman rose from behind his battered and scarred desk, and glanced briefly through the plate-glass window. Beyond the ten-thousand-foot long Runway 30R, and just above the distant treeline, the sun was rising into an overcast sky.

"This place depresses me," Hoffman said, opening his office door. "Let's walk."

Originally Runway 30R had been one hundred fifty feet wide and eight thousand feet long. This, however, wasn't quite long enough for the German commander. Hoffman had added another two thousand feet to its length, while moving the Middle Marker Beacon a mere six hundred feet — almost to the edge of the wooded area marking the airport's southeastern boundary.

But while Hoffman had worried about the length of Runway

30R, Yamaguchi had been concerned with the security of *Lee Bird Field*. He had ordered the building of over fifty bunkers and machine-gun pillboxes throughout the airport, including several places just beyond the "Object Free" strip alongside 30R. He had established checkpoints at the airport's entrance and along Highway 30. And he'd set up a series of roving patrols around the field and into the woods.

Hoffman, however, was not satisfied.

"Your 'roving patrols' are taking too many troops out of the field," he complained. "If we are to subdue these animals, we must strike directly at their bases ... wherever they are."

Yamaguchi looked up from the sandbagged bunker just in time to see the C-17 on final approach.

"We have very little choice," the Oriental said, watching the C-17 descend. "Who knows what these stupid American pigs will try next. They might even —"

The C-17's wheels touched the tarmac, and the huge transport plane exploded in a monstrous fireball, sending bits and pieces and chunks of metal, shredded sections of wings and flaming parts of engines, down the runway and across the landscape. The cockpit and part of the fuselage skidded from the fireball to the dissonance of screeching metal, rolled and flipped over, smashing and bursting apart.

Hoffman and Yamaguchi dived behind the bunker's sandbag barricade as burning pieces and scraps of C-17 fell around them. Scraps of sheet metal, pieces of burning padding and insulation, bits of wiring, and unidentified parts of shattered equipment flew and fell onto and alongside 30R. Wreckage and smoldering body parts mixed with flickering flames and rumbling secondary explosions into a chaotic maelstrom of destruction.

More explosions echoed across *Lee Bird Field*. Black smoke bubbled and billowed into the overcast sky. Alert sirens, fire sirens, and crash sirens united in a shrill, wailing, shrieking cacophony of nerve-shattering vibrations. Two partially-filled troop transport trucks, an ambulance, and a fire truck raced from Taxiway "B" onto 30R towards the crash site.

With a singular roar half-a-dozen missile contrails swiftly shot up from the trees, arced over the racing troop trucks, and crashed downward into a nest of F-18 Hornets and ancient A-10 Warthogs.

Propelled by thunderous, blinding explosions of flame and fury, an F-18 flipped over into two other Hornets. Their ground-shaking, metal-shattering blast ignited a fourth F-18 into this cataclysmic firestorm. Within this fiery holocaust three Warthogs also exploded, destroying an adjacent T-hangar in the process and sending an old fuel tanker truck onto an equally-old C-130. And everything seemed to blow up all over again, blasting flaming debris and shattered bodies across the aircraft aprons and taxiways.

A modest portion of the Terminal Building was blown to bits by a second flight of missiles, while the third flight headed for the blasted and burning aircraft apron, intent on destroying everything south of Taxiway "B" and the Terminal Building.

As the second and third flights of missiles exploded beyond the west end of 30R, the partially-filled troop trucks came to a screeching halt near the runway's east end. The fire engine also skidded to a stop, and the firemen-soldiers immediately attacked the flaming cockpit-and-fuselage debris. The ambulance halted just a few feet further on, but apparently it was enough. The unseen rocket or missile blew the ambulance apart, shattering it beyond recognition.

"Where are they?" Hoffman screamed, climbing from the bunker. "Where are they?"

Another explosion flipped the first troop transport over on its side, gouging a large and jagged hole in the tarmac while the troop truck crushed three or four ill-prepared UN soldiers under its twisted wreckage. A secondary explosion, even louder and more violent, ripped open the punctured gas tank and tore the twisted wreckage asunder.

Hoffman watched in ashen-faced horror as slivers of sheet metal shredded yet another UN soldier into six or seven unequal and bloody pieces of ripped flesh and splintered bone.

More explosions. Gunfire. Rockets and missiles streaking to deliver death and destruction. UN troops advancing against a line of trees and random death.

An old Russian T-72 tank growled at top speed, racing east alongside Taxiway "C" towards the trees and its own destruction. In an instant six missiles struck the lumbering behemoth. Bursting fireballs engulfed the beast and tore up the turf. The T-72 simply disappeared within the multiple blasts, leaving only black smoke and flaming wreckage to mark its passage.

A few more minor explosions, a few more rifle shots, and they — whoever they were — gone. Now only flickering flames, roiling grayish-black smoke, and the anguished cries of wounded soldiers shrouded the remains of *Lee Bird Field*.

"Major Yamaguchi, I want you to take charge of this personally. I want you to find out who did this. And I want them dead. — Is that clear?"

"*Hai!* I mean — yes, sir!"

Major Aritomo Yamaguchi snapped off a crisp salute, turned about sharply, and marched away. Hoffman spent several precious minutes watching Yamaguchi rally the men around him and lead them into the wooded area south and east of the base.

"This could be a problem," he muttered aloud, studying the smoldering wreckage surrounding him.

Leaving their light-blue backup van in the garage at Lake Maloney; Ben Franklyn and Bob Lowell had crammed themselves, twelve militiamen, and Lisa into the gray-green step van along with several hundred pounds of equipment and headed down the hill, without headlights, into the Platte River Valley. At four in the morning only a few flickering fires and an occasional distant explosion betrayed the ruins of North Platte, Nebraska.

But another flickering bonfire, surreptitiously set on Highway 83, provided Lisa and the overcrowded step van with an illuminating beacon to guide them through the cool, moonlit darkness onto State Farm Road. A second bonfire guided them northward to the 179 interchange and Interstate 80.

Like neighboring North Platte, the town of Maxwell had been burnt and blasted into oblivion. Located just north of Exit 190, the UN invaders had chosen this village to test-fire their weapons — with horrendous results. And the town of Maxwell had ceased to exist.

But Highway 30, minus its road signs and partially blocked by bomb craters and fragmented debris, was still open to westbound traffic ... and to the burnt-out farmhouse marking the narrow lane into the wooded area east of 30R.

Deer and elk had made motion sensors impractical. Evading trip-wires had been more of a game, lacking only the challenge of a worthwhile opponent. But the roving patrol presented a unique and formidable obstacle requiring stealth and cunning and a good deal of luck.

But "luck" is a fickle creature. Within five minutes they had brought down the C-17 transport, destroyed the F-18 Hornets and A-10 Warthogs, and had blown the T-72 tank apart. And in the midst of this messy melee, two militiamen had paid the ultimate price. Their textbook approach and precision assault had been ruined, however, by a rather disorganized and ignominious withdrawal.

According to the plan; Jennings, Rowland, and two other militiamen would provide cover-fire while Lisa, Dwight MacPherson, Andy Gottlieb, and Larry Lainson made a strategic retreat towards the step van. This left Bob Lowell, John Haley, Hank Goldfarb, and Ben Franklyn free to arm the Claymores and arrange a few other booby traps within the equipment they would leave behind.

According to the plan.

But Len Duggan caught a couple of stray slugs, forcing Rowland and Hatcher to half-drag and half-carry him into the woods beyond 30R, with Lowell and Haley taking their place.

Two more troop trucks arrived at the end of 30R just as Franklyn and Goldfarb finished planting the Claymores. The two militiamen grabbed their rifles and disappeared into the trees and underbrush.

"The odds are fifteen-to-one against us," Franklyn whispered.

"Sounds about even," Lowell countered, dropping three more pesky UN soldiers who insisted on wandering beyond the clouds of billowing black smoke.

But Ben Franklyn was persistent. "Let's get the hell outa here!"

"If you insist," Lowell sighed, picking off two more wanderers.

Later they might say that it was "not quite a rout," but that would be later. Simply put, they ran. Occasionally they would stop to fire a shot or two, slowing the pursuing UN troops; but mostly they ran through the trees and underbrush, ignoring the scratching thorns and leaping over the trip-wires.

Behind them, the sounds of exploding booby traps promised at least some minor measure of relief, but hardly enough to assure their escape. Yamaguchi had spread his troops outward in a broad, concave curve designed to encircle the fleeing militia. But would it work?

There was no time to even think about it. Through a thicket of older trees and saplings, they watched a roving patrol attack the empty step van. Their ride home was about to be eliminated from their planned escape.

Call it desperation. Call it heroic. Call it suicide. Call it ... their only chance.

Slipping and sliding down the hillside, Uzi in hand, a badly-wounded Len Duggan charged into the roving patrol, firing as he fell among them. Rowland, Hatcher, and Gottlieb slid into action immediately behind the wounded militiaman, firing into the confused and disorganized roving patrol with maddening intensity and savage disregard for their own safety.

Franklyn and the others followed them down the hill, but it was too late. All eight members of the roving patrol were dead, annihilated in a wild fusillade of automatic gunfire that had ripped them to shreds and punctured the body of the gray-green step van.

The lopsided victory was not, however, without cost. Len Duggan had collected two more bullet wounds, while the militiaman named Hatcher had collocated a small plot of ground on the wrong side of the grass.

Miraculously, neither Rowland nor Gottlieb had been touched within the maelstrom of gunfire, although both were badly shaken by the violence of their singular experience.

"Adrenaline letdown," Lowell said after a one-second diagnosis. "Let's get 'em into the van before they really get the shakes."

A minute later they were all in the van, and Ben Franklyn closed the backdoors. By then Larry Lainson, who'd been a veterinarian before the invasion, had Gottlieb and Rowland wrapped in blankets and was working, as best he could, on Len Duggan's punctured and ravaged body. Jennings, Haley, Goldfarb, and Lowell occupied the middle of the step van, oozing tension as if it were a precious commodity; while MacPherson guarded the sliding door at the front.

"Son-of-a-bitch!" Lisa swore, grinding the gears and racing the engine. "Sure you couldn't find a narrower lane to turn around in?"

"Sorry," Ben Franklyn said with a mischievous smile, "I'm afraid this is as small as they come."

"Son-of-a-bitch!" she snapped again, fighting to keep the dinosaur between the fence posts.

"You remember the route?" Ben asked, bending to take a better look at the burnt-out farmstead.

"Yeah, of course," Lisa growled, turning left onto the highway, "but I still think it's crazy."

"Of course it's crazy!" Ben Franklyn said. "That's what I'm counting on."

But heading westward on Highway 30, directly into a United Nations' checkpoint, held little appeal for Lisa. Groaning with frustration, she started downshifting ... and praying.

Glancing over his shoulder, Franklyn watched as Jennings, Haley, and Goldfarb took up positions at the back, while Lowell and Lainson moved the battered body of Len Duggan towards the front of the step van. Gottlieb and Rowland, although obviously badly shaken, had managed to crawl towards the front also, dragging their blankets with them.

Franklyn turned to look through the windshield, and then grabbed his old M-16. "Get ready!"

Lisa stopped the gray-green step van and Ben Franklyn gave a curt nod. MacPherson slid the door open and flipped two grenades under the nearest armored personnel carrier. Ben Franklyn opened up with his M-16 an instant later, while Lowell fired an Uzi through the open driver's window. Then Lisa gunned the engine, and the step van shot forward like a frightened rabbit, laying rubber as it rocketed from the checkpoint.

Jennings and Goldfarb were now lying shoulder-to-shoulder, firing their matching M-16s through the open rear door of the rocketing step van at rapidly dwindling targets.

Both grenades exploded simultaneously, blasting the APC into the air and end-over-end, turning their transportation into scrap metal and slicing the legs off a nearby UN soldier.

Seconds later they passed the second checkpoint just east of the East Bypass at a mere eighty miles per hour, catching the checkpoint guards off-guard and smashing the sawhorse barricades into kindling wood. Jennings, Haley, and Goldfarb sent six hand grenades tumbling out the open rear door, followed by bullets from Lainson's M-16.

"That should hold 'em for a while," the ex-veterinarian said, setting his M-16 aside while Haley angrily slammed the rear door shut.

"For a while," Jennings agreed, listening to the distant roar of exploding hand grenades.

"God bless America," Ben Franklyn sighed. "Or at least what's left of her."

To which Lowell added an, "Amen."

But then the van suddenly and inexplicably slowed to a crawl.

"Bob, I think you'd better take the wheel."

"Lisa?"

"I think I've been shot," she said. And then she tumbled from the driver's seat into Ben Franklyn's waiting arms.

"Fool kid!" the old farmer muttered as Lowell climbed into the high-chair-like seat and turned off Highway 30.

"Give me a hand with her, Dwight." And then, *"Dwight!"*

Dwight MacPherson was lying face down on the floor of the gray-green step van. Three splotches of blood stained the back of his gray-green camouflage shirt, and his corpse moved in rhythm to the rocking of the step van.

"Damn!" But Ben Franklyn could not raise his voice above a whisper.

"He's dead," Lainson said flatly, almost coldly. "Sorry."

"How about Len?" Franklyn asked, lowering Lisa to the blanket on the floor of the van.

"It's only a matter of time," Lainson admitted. "Hell, I'm only a horse doctor. .... And he needs a miracle."

"And what about her?"

Lainson shrugged. "Ask me later."

Lowell swung the cumbersome dinosaur off Fourth Street — (Highway 30) — onto Dewey, and past the shattered shell of the Lincoln County Courthouse. The engine groaned in protest and steam hissed from the bullet-punctured radiator as he guided the damaged step van around the burnt-out cars and scattered debris strewn across the cracked and chipped asphalt. Hissing and pinging and clanking and groaning, the shattered and shuddering engine dragged the metal monster over the South Platte River and up the hill.

"Will we make it?"

Lowell shrugged. "Pray, Ben. — Pray."

Gravel crunched under the wheels of the step van as Lowell pulled off the pavement. Whiffs of dead fish drift through the van as the former Red Willow County Deputy Sheriff brought the lumber-

ing, quaking, groaning dinosaur to a halt.
"Welcome to Lake Maloney," he said softly.

* * *

Chapter Twenty-Four

"Goose Island. — Fast."

The old man nodded, watching the others load the stretcher carrying Lisa into the skiff. "The fishing shack?"

Now it was Ben's turn to nod. "The fishing shack. — And I want you to take Lainson also."

"Lainson?" the old man asked. "Lainson? —The vet?"

"The vet," Ben admitted with a heavy sigh. "He's all we've got right now, but I want him with her."

Again the old man nodded, and waited for Lainson to sit down in the boat before touching the electric starter. Watching the little rowboat churning from the dock into the man-made lake, Benjamin Ellsworth Franklyn offered a silent prayer for his best student, and wondered — for perhaps the millionth time — about his own self-worth in leading thousands of friends and neighbors against the mercenary cutthroats imported from Europe. But once you've mounted the tiger ....

"I guess they'll remember us in North Platte," Bob Lowell said, watching them close the garage doors on the bashed-about step van.

"Without a doubt," Ben Franklyn agreed, checking his ancient pocket watch.

"We're behind schedule?"

"By almost five minutes," the old farmer muttered, heading for the light-blue van.

"Then let's get the hell out of here."

They were already loaded and waiting when Ben Franklyn slid into the passenger seat with an alacrity which belied his age. Behind him, Haley and Goldfarb had closed both sliding side doors and were examining the Stinger missile setup. Further back, Gottlieb and Rowland were loading six old XM-18 hand-held, recoilless, grenade-launchers, while Jennings checked out the double gunports in the van's armor-plated rear wall.

"Ready?" Lowell asked, sliding into the driver's seat.

Ben Franklyn adjusted the earpiece and plugged it into the radio receiver. Then, with a nod, he said, "Hit it."

With its tires spitting gravel, the light-blue van lurched forward, and raced up the hill to Highway 83.

"Last report says they're ten minutes away."

But Lowell could see two armored personnel carriers climbing side-by-side over a hillock a few hundred yards to his left.

"How many minutes?"

Ben took one look, shook his head, and muttered, "Oh, shit!"

Lowell slammed his foot into the accelerator, making the tires squeal onto Highway 83 and leaving black streaks to mark his passage.

Rowland and Gottlieb were forced to wait until Lowell could straighten out the van's erratic fishtailing course before unleashing their lethal barrage of XM-18 mortar-grenades upon the charging armored personnel carriers. Within a very small fraction of a second both carriers vanished within a firestorm of multiple explosions, their shattered remains flung aside, ripped and smashed and instantly incinerated in one brief and terror-filled moment.

Another salvo of death and destruction followed, shredding apart a pair of troop transport trucks skidding to their doom behind the first firestorm. Flaming bodies and flaming tarpaulin and fragmented slivers of glowing-hot metal flew through a cacophonous blast of flame and smoke and thunder.

The outraged engine screamed aloud as they flew over the hilltop at eighty miles per hour, leaving the burning wreckage and their pursuers far behind.

"We could have destroyed all of 'em," Rowland protested as the van bounced over the hill.

"Only until they start to shoot back," Ben Franklyn chuckled.

"My thoughts exactly!" Lowell added, stepping down on the gas, making the engine scream even louder.

"Easy," Ben cautioned. "We don't want to lose them."

"As if we could!" Lowell muttered, easing off on the gas.

"Bad news," Ben Franklyn growled, pressing against his

earpiece. "U.N. forces apparently stole a couple of 'Whiskey Cobras' from a base near Omaha and are heading our way. E.T.A. is twelve-to-fifteen minutes."

Lowell's mind raced ahead of the van across the treeless prairie. "Maywood?"

"We'll be lucky if we make it to Wellfleet," Ben snapped.

"Mostly open between here and there," Lowell returned.

"We've got company," Haley cut in, sliding the right side door open.

"Too early," Ben muttered.

"Two Hueys behind us," Haley continued, "one left, one right, and closing fast."

"But they're not gunships?" Ben said.

"And this is not a coordinated attack," Lowell noted.

"Not in the least," Ben added with a grumpy sigh.

Goldfarb opened the side door behind the driver's seat and Lowell slammed on the brakes. Haley fired a Stinger missile as the Huey on the right slid into view. And the waistgunner managed to punch four thirty-caliber in the roof of the van just before the Stinger blew the chopper apart.

The blast also sheared off the first Huey's rotor, sending it spinning over the van in a deadly arc that curved back into the second helicopter's cockpit. In an instant the spinning rotor slashed its way into the second Huey, turning it into an airborne fireball. And as the flaming debris of the first helicopter hit the ground, the second chopper blew apart in the sky.

"Two for the price of one!" Haley shouted triumphantly as the wreckage of second Huey fell into an open and empty pasture.

"Well, don't break your arm patting yourself on the back," Lowell growled, throwing the van into gear.

"One Cobra down," Franklyn reported. "Apparent engine problems. And the second Cobra has been delayed two or three minutes."

"Whoopie." Lowell's voice was dead.

"Don't sound so enthusiastic about it!" Ben Franklyn boomed. "Two minutes is two minutes."

Lowell took a deep breath. "I'm going to try for Maywood."

Sprawled along State Route 23 just east of Highway 83, the village of Maywood was more a collection of houses scattered among the trees than a town centered around a business district. The tree-lined pathways and lanes could, however, provide the cover that Lowell was seeking, if he could reach Maywood before the AH-1W "Whiskey Cobra" could find him.

Lowell estimated that the AH-1W was about nine minutes away. He estimated that Maywood was about fourteen miles away. Then he stepped on the gas and pushed the speedometer needle up to the one-hundred-mile-per-hour mark.

"Do you fly here often?" Ben Franklyn asked, eyeing the speedometer.

"Only on holidays."

"Today isn't a holiday."

"Not yet," Lowell chirped, tightening his grip on the wheel and tightening his concentration on the road. "Not yet, but ... maybe ... someday ...."

Ben Franklyn took a deep breath and tightened his grip on the hand-hold.

Eight minutes later Bob Lowell slammed on the brakes and slid the van through a precarious left-hand turn into the trees of Maywood. Another turn, to his right, parked the van in a dirt lane under a bonnet of leaves and limbs.

Within seconds Goldfarb, Gottlieb, Jennings, and Rowland had dived from the van into the surrounding trees and underbrush, just as the AH-1W came a hovering halt above the intersection of the two highways. Then, with foolish and daring bravado, Rowland ran out into the middle of Route 23.

It is thought that he fired five or six rounds from his XM-18. It is believed that the first mortar-grenade blasted the tail section away, hurling the "Whiskey Cobra" into the pavement. The armored gunship apparently managed to fire its twenty-millimeter cannon twice before two or three more mortar-grenades shredded its shattered wreckage into a million splintered shards of plexiglass and metal. It is known, however, that the two twenty-millimeter shells from the Cobra eliminated Mr. Rowland in a single instant. Only a small crater in the asphalt, a few splotches of blood, and a few scraps of singed cloth survived the brief but hideous fireball that swallowed his ashen remains.

"Convoy approaching Wellfleet," Franklyn reported as the three survivors climbed into the light-blue van.

But the survivors said nothing.

Lowell backed carefully out from the covered lane, and steered wide of the smoking crater. A smaller secondary blast announced the final demise of the Cobra's wreckage, which he also assiduously avoided.

But once back on Highway 83, and well-beyond the battleground, Lowell hit the accelerator with alarming force.

At a sedate eighty miles-per-hour, it took about twenty-five minutes to reach McCook. Turning south off West "B" Street at Federal Way, Lowell dawdled along County Road 1535, slowing to a five-mile-per-hour crawl across the Republican River.

"First convoy now in ... U-Save parking lot."

"Spotter planes?"

Benjamin Ellsworth Franklyn released a discontented sigh and shook his head. "Not yet. Bob. .... Not yet."

Thick woods and forests conceal and cover two-and-a-half miles of the south bank of the Republican River from County Road 1535 to Highway 83. Stretching southward for about a mile from the river, this heavily forested area a natural hunting ground for deer, raccoon, fox, rabbit, and other wildlife. But now it had become the hunting grounds for Ben Franklyn's patriot militia.

They'd spent over six weeks, altogether, transforming this pristine forest into a lethal trap. They'd planted pillboxes, booby traps, and land mines. They'd built bunkers, dugouts, and other covered shelters. And they'd established redoubts and fall-back positions, anticipating this day and this attack.

Lowell turned left off the asphalt paving of County Road 1535, and onto a muddy farm lane squeezed between the forest and a barren field. The muddy lane didn't go anywhere. Along with the field, it dead-ended a few hundred yards east of the turnoff at a southern extension of the wooded area.

After deliberately slipping and sliding over a hundred yards, or more, of muddied and rutted farm lane, Lowell edged the light-blue van onto the barren field, parking it diagonally just off the muddied path.

"Spotter planes?" he again asked.

"Finally!" Ben Franklyn sighed. ".... In about two minutes."

"Haley. Goldfarb. Gottlieb. —Take the weapons," Lowell

commanded, climbing from the driver's seat. "Jennings, you're with Ben and me. — We're gonna turn this van into a bomb."

"We've got company," Albert said, adjusting his earphones. "Spotter plane, half-a-dozen choppers, troop trucks, armored personnel carriers, tanks .... You name it, they've got it."

If Stan Gorman was distraught, he hid it well. "This isn't a game, Albert. They're using real guns ... and real bullets."

"Like Mom said, if we're gonna die, at least we'll be with our friends and neighbors."

"Comforting thought," Stan Gorman muttered, loading the old M-16. "This had better work."

"It will," Albert assured his father. "Like Ben said, 'they're just not that good'."

"Well, you remember what I told you and keep your head down. —Okay?"

"Okay, Dad. Okay."

But understanding his son's psyche, Stan Gorman left the ammo bunker with a grimly-depressing sense of foreboding, a sense of impending doom.

The Spotter plane was first. Hit by a ground-to-air missile, the old Cessa 310B blew apart in the sky and fell into the trees east of Highway 83.

The two AH-1 Cobras, flying at treetop height, ran into a blizzard of Stinger and old Redeye missiles ... and never made it south of the Republican River.

The two Hueys came in from the west, however, sliding towards the barren and empty field. Even before the first Huey touched-down, the shock troops were leaping from the chopper. They went down in pairs and went up in pieces.

The first Huey's skids touched the ground, and the entire chopper was ripped to shreds in a rapid-fire series of violent explosions that scattered plexiglass and metal and parts of human bodies across the barren minefield.

The second Huey tried to stay airborne, but it was too late. With bits and pieces of the first Huey smearing and scratching the plexiglass windshield, and detonating mines throughout the area; the second could not reverse its rotor in time to avoid the thunderous explosions which blew it apart.

While land mine detonations blasted the barren field and the arriving helicopters asunder, three armored personnel carriers and six troop transport trucks slid wildly down the muddy farm lane to the supposed-wreckage of the light-blue van ... and straight into trouble. The first two personnel carriers slid to a stop, disgorging a dozen blue-helmeted UN soldiers and halting the entire convoy. An instant later the light-blue van, the blue-helmeted soldiers, and the first two personnel carriers vanished within a blinding flash of light and a horrendous roar. The third personnel carrier flipped end over end, landing on its roof, as a monstrous fireball consumed everything in front of it within clouds of roiling black smoke and spikes of incendiary horror.

Moments later more land mines detonated under the fragmented debris falling from above, while hundreds of blue-helmeted United Nations' troopers leaped from the trucks in a desperate scramble for protection from the spray of machine-gunfire coming from within the forest. And then the invaders started shooting back.

The air was suddenly filled with whizzing bullets and exploding grenades, with the chatter of machine guns and the thumping of mortars, with gunfire and explosions echoing and reverberating throughout the Republican River Valley, with the screams of the wounded and the moans of the dying, until the chaos of battle annihilated any semblance of sanity.

Trees splintered and fell to their doom. Trucks tipped over and were blown to bits. Saplings were reduced to pulpwood, and shrubs were turned into mulch.

———

A second convoy had turned south at East Sixth and "B" Street, following Highway 83 over the railroad bridge and past the eastern entrance to Barnett Park, to the tree-lined southern bank of the Republican River. Led by three Apache helicopters, the second convoy apparently completed the classic military pincers movement without opposition.

Unfortunately one of the Apaches decided to peel-off and waste some of its ordnance on a tank predominantly parked on a concrete slab at the west end of the park. The ancient M-1A3 tank was, however, essentially a statue — the relic of an earlier war — without fuel or usable weapons. After blowing up the statuesque tank and destroying an adjacent picnic pavilion, the Apache wheeled back towards its formation, only to have its flight rudely interrupted by a ground-to-air missile.

Seeing the first Apache explode in mid-air, the two surviving helicopters turned to attack their assailants. (Since their only "radar-lock" detection came from the missile being fired at them, much of their electronic gear was virtually useless.) Together, the two Apache helicopters managed to destroy six or seven trees before being blown into scrap metal.

Meanwhile, the second convoy had encountered a slight problem. South of the river, Highway 83 is neatly sandwiched between two wooded areas, and is set on an exposed embankment four to five feet above the ordinary ground level. The convoy's commander, one Lieutenant Arif, had unwittingly led them into this deadly trap.

Heading up the convoy, Arif's armored personnel carrier was inevitably the first target of the patriots. Hit simultaneously by missiles from both the left and the right, the first personnel carrier disappeared a thunderous blast, flipping about and returning to the pavement later as a dozen or so pieces of burnt and twisted metal.

The strung-out second convoy came to a stuttering, staggering stop, and a hundred machine guns ripped it apart. Blue-helmeted United Nations' soldiers leaped from the 6-by troop transport trucks, and died on their way to the pavement. Hundreds of hand grenades flew through the air, blasting the trucks and their cargo into a long and grim line of flaming destruction down the center of Highway 83.

The last three trucks in the second convoy, however, survived long enough to allow their troops to leap to the bridge, run to the embankment, slide into the ditch, and duck into the trees and shrubbery on the west side of the road. Most of them made it.

Another troop truck and an armored personnel carrier at the front of the column also survived long enough to unleash their dogs of war into the carnage. Though a whim of circumstance, these troops chose the forested area east of the highway, blasting their way through the barbed wire fence into bushes and underbrush surrounding half-hidden pools of brackish water.

County Road 1535 was lined with burning trucks and exploding gas tanks, with dark smoke and detonating ammunition. Through this gruesome nightmare, six men — six blue-helmeted

United Nations' soldiers — darted across the south end of the bridge and into the trees. And they continued to run through the forest. They fired their semi-automatic rifles. They threw grenades. They ran swiftly. And they died.

But before they died, they killed a lot of patriot militiamen, and punched gaping holes in the patriots' first line of defense. More UN troops plunged through those holes, fighting desperately for every inch of ground and every bit of cover. The order of the day was attack ... and they did.

Stuck in the mud east of Highway 83, the blue-helmeted UN troops were out of options. With deadly precision they advanced on the forested area. They used hand grenades to topple trees. They used expert sharpshooting to eliminate snipers.

Yet, in spite of their cautious approach, they suffered horrendous casualties. By the time the last sniper fell from his perch to the matted leaves on the ground below, only three blue-helmeted soldiers were still alive on the east side of the highway. But the three survivors were in no mood to celebrate anything.

Three exhausted and bedraggled UN soldiers staggered from the trees and clawed their way up the grassy embankment. With little concern for their own safety, they plodded across the highway and slid down the western embankment. Mindlessly, they staggered forth into the woods.

Then, within sight of their blue-helmeted comrades, one of the three stumbled across a trip-wire, triggering the explosive detonation of two Claymores. In an instant the three were ripped, sliced, and blasted into bloody shreds.

Approximately ninety UN soldiers survived the mad dash from the last three troop transports into the trees west of Highway 83. Driven by sheer desperation, their wild shooting had brought down four patriot snipers in as many seconds.

Stunned by their frightening assault, the ferocious and deadly counterattack quickly became a hand-to-hand bloodbath, with many patriots falling victim to "friendly fire" from their own comrades. The loss of three comrades to a couple of Claymore mines was, to their way of thinking, inconsequential. For them, the few moments of peace granted by a retreating enemy was far more important.

The twin A-10 Warthogs came screaming out of the clouds in a death-defying dive designed to terrify. As instructed, both Warthogs unleashed three salvos of missiles across the center of the wooded area before pulling back into a neck-snapping climb towards the clouds.

But even the fireballs of death and destruction blowing apart the center of the forested area below could not stop the four Stinger missiles and the two Redeyes from chasing the Warthogs skyward. At an altitude of perhaps a thousand feet, or so, all six missiles caught up with the two A-10 Warthogs. Both twin-engine jets disappeared in an instant within a hellish fireball explosion.

* * *

Chapter Twenty-Five

The moans and cries of the injured and the dying fatally distracted many of the patriot militiamen, allowing the 'first-convoy' UN soldiers to deeply penetrate the forested area at several points, creating chaos and confusion along the way. On the other hand, the blue-helmeted troops paid a horrible price in advancing upon the militiamen.

In the southwest corner of the wooded area, near where the muddy farm lane rose to County Road 1535, two sandbag-reinforced bunkers, each with a 30-caliber machine gun, guarded the intersection and each other. Manned by men of the Tenth Light Cavalry and commanded by Sgt. Eugene Farrell, these bunkers were a major stronghold in their defenses. In their brief lifetime they had not only guarded the intersection, but they had spelled death in bloody letters for the incautious UN soldier. Only now they were spending more time and firepower protecting their own flanks. And they were running out of ammunition.

"Pull back!" Farrell shouted over the din of gunfire and explosions. "Pull back! — Regroup at 'C' for Charlie."

It was not a retreat, it was an advance to the rear. They came from the bunkers shooting at anything and everything and nothing. With grenades exploding around them and bullets flying everywhere, they ran for the cover of the trees.

But before Farrell could climb from the bunker, a Private Sloan caught a bullet in his chest and fell, knocking the Sergeant back into the sandbagged hole. An instant later a hand grenade exploded somewhere near the rim of the bunker, killing Private Sloan and shattering Farrell's helmet.

With blood trickling down the side of his face, Sergeant Eugene Allen Farrell rose through the smoke and fire of battle, and yanked the 30-caliber from its tripod. He squeezed the trigger, and the 30-caliber spit death in lethal doses across the charging hordes of blue-helmeted troops. He climbed from the bunker and marched forward, firing as he went, mowing down the UN invaders like weeds in an open field, slicing them to ribbons with a cadence that was all his own.

Time was suspended in disbelief. Now firing the 30-caliber from the hip, Sgt. Farrell marched across the fallen ranks of UN soldiers. He chopped down two trees with the 30-caliber, killing three more UN soldiers in the process, until he ran out of ammunition.

Flinging the 30-caliber aside, he threw three hand grenades and picked up an Uzi. The grenades exploded, and he sprayed the trees with the Uzi, but there was no response from anyone.

With sagging, empty shoulders he turned back towards the bunkers. He'd taken a few halting steps before the blue-helmeted UN soldier popped out from behind a large tree and shot him five times in the back. Sgt. Farrell stiffened and fell dead.

The blue-helmeted UN soldier had about one second to gloat over his victim before being ripped to shreds by over a dozen bullets and two hand grenades. Needless to say, there wasn't much left of him.

Jennings was beside himself with grief and horror as he knelt over the bullet-riddled and burnt flesh of Andrew Gottlieb.

"I'll kill 'em all," he swore, picking up both M-16s and crawling to the western edge of the muddy depression.

Looking just over the lip of the hollow and around the big tree, Jennings could see the blue-helmeted UN troops ducking and darting from tree to tree; seeking cover, seeking shelter, seeking a hiding place — wherever that might be. Jennings, however, felt no such restraint. He wanted to kill them, and nothing else mattered.

Blind with fury, he launched himself from the muddy depression, screaming obscenities as he raced forward, firing both automatic rifles simultaneously at the blue-helmeted invaders.

"Die! You bastards! —Die!" he screamed, plopping down at the base of a medium-sized tree.

Leaning back against the trunk of the tree, Jennings raised his automatic rifle and fired five times into the trees. One UN soldier fell to the ground dead, or dying.

He flipped a hand grenade over his shoulder, and was rewarded by the dying screams of another blue-helmet.

Nicked on the right shoulder by a flying chunk of shrapnel, Jennings twisted about to make certain he threw the next hand grenade a lot farther. He did, and three blue-helmets went flying through the air.

By then, however, whistling bullets were chipping the bark off the bole of his little tree. He grabbed the second rifle, rolled in the opposite direction away from the tree, and came up firing at a dozen exposed targets. Only this time, he had help.

Jennings fired five more times, emptying his rifle into the blue-helmets. All twelve UN soldiers fell. Then, rising from the underbrush and shrubbery, seven or eight angry patriot militiamen screamed in defiance and charged the sheltered UN troops.

Covered with blood and sweat and a soggy uniform, Jennings grabbed the other M-16 and staggered to his feet. He fired twice, took two steps forward, and disappeared inside an exploding hand grenade.

It was, however, too little and too late for the embattled United Nations' troops. With eight angry militiamen bearing down upon them, all they could expect was death.

With Kevin and the other militiaman already dead, Rachel felt alone and abandoned within the empty sandbag bunker guarding the end of the muddy farm lane where the trees and underbrush marched southward to create the eastern end of the barren mine field. But with the major UN thrust pounding its way through the woods to the north and west of her bunker, guarding that particular position was almost an exercise in academic futility. She was guarding against nothing.

Kevin and the militiaman had risen from the bunker and revealed their position to a distant marksman. Rachel had seen him, and killed him with a single shot. But the blue-helmeted forces of the United Nations had chosen another route, and she now stood guard over an empty and desolate landscape.

As Ben Franklyn had once suggested, the United Nations' Military Command's over-reliance on hi-tech solutions could be used against them.

She picked up the satellite radio-telephone and ran northeast to the southeast corner of the "bombed-out" area, where the Wart-

hogs had unleashed their ordnance and burnt-away the underbrush.
"What the hell are you doing here?"
"Letting our U.N. friends know where we are," she said, pressing the transponder-locator button. "Or at least, where they think we might be."
Bob Lowell smiled. "Why you sneaky little bitch!"
"Get your men outa here, Bob," she snapped, setting the satellite radio-telephone within the cleft of a small tree. "Our friends in blue helmets now have a new target."
"Rachel, I could kiss you!"
"Later," she murmured hopefully. "Later."
Two minutes later she was back in the bunker, tucking the nine-millimeter parabellum into her backpack and loading a new clip into her M-16 rifle. She was double-checking the mounting for the mini-gun when the two blue-helmeted soldiers oozed from the forest. After thirty seconds both men marched confidently towards the trees at the end of the muddy lane.
Rachel shot both of them twice, and then turned her attention back to the multiple-barreled mini-gun. She swiveled the mini-gun around to the north towards the semi-open forest, concentrating all her energies and attention upon the United Nations' upcoming attacks.
Rustling leaves interrupted Rachel's concentration. She spun around, her brown eyes flashing, seeking the interloper.
"Greetings, *Mademoiselle!*"
The ugly Frenchman cast aside his blue helmet and leaped from the sandbagged rim of the bunker, slamming into her like a runaway freight train. He fell on her like a lion in heat, ripping away her camouflage shirt. Lost within a lust-filled frenzy of lascivious desire, he yanked off her bra off and unsnapped her slacks.
He froze, awed by the magnificence of her bounteous bosom.
"Like my tits?" she asked, purring softly.
He nodded dumbly, unable to express his enthrallment.
She pulled the nine-millimeter from her pack and blew the back of his head off, splattering parts of his skull and most of his brains against the far wall of the bunker.
"Nice." The militiaman dropped into the bunker as she pushed the Frenchman's body away. "Carl, the carpenter."

"Rachel, the waitress."

"Sorry, but I couldn't get a clear shot."

"I could," she said, smiling.

"We've got company."

"Now?" she asked.

"Now," he said.

She spun around, saw the blue-helmet, and fired three times.

The blue helmet went one way and the dead soldier's body went another, falling backwards with three puncture wounds in its chest.

"There's one good European," the carpenter growled.

More UN soldiers emerged from the trees, running and shooting and screaming and dying. They came to kill, and stayed to die. From behind a dozen different trees militiamen opened fire, slicing the blue-helmeted UN troops apart in a fusillade of gunfire.

Rachel angrily emptied her pistol into the onrushing melee of blue-helmeted mercenaries, then turned to triggering the multi-barreled mini-gun's lethal barrage. She cut down trees and saplings and blue-helmeted soldiers. She pulverized shrubbery, hacked through underbrush, and shredded UN troops. And then she mulched anything that remained.

Carl caught a bullet in the shoulder and was thrown from the bunker. Rachel, meanwhile, had emptied the mini-gun and picked up her M-16. But then a hand grenade bounced over the lip of the bunker and blasted everything into small bits and pieces — including a waitress named Rachel.

Tom McDermott, who owned a gas station in Oberlin, Kansas, had been trapped behind enemy lines, bypassed by hundreds of UN soldiers intent on covering ground and pushing forward. Between twenty-five to thirty of the blue-helmeted mercenaries, however, now just covered some ground, the bloodied victims of a Tom McDermott ambush.

Buried under a carpet of damp leaves within a thicket of small trees and bushes at the edge of the Republican River, Tom McDermott had almost casually killed any blue-helmeted UN soldier who came too close to his protective concealment. Armed with two M-16 automatic rifles and well-hidden within the foliage, he did not count his victims. They were blue-helmeted United Nations' soldiers intent upon conquest, upon stealing his country and enslaving him in perpetual servitude; like the blue-helmeted UN troops that had butchered his wife and his daughter. But now, for Tom McDermott, the blue-helmets were only targets on a rifle range.

For McDermott, the blue-helmets were simply target practice — until one of them caught a bullet in his side and turned mean. Spinning around, the blue-helmeted soldiers pulled a seven-inch Marine Commando knife and smashed through the bushes surrounding McDermott's lair. Five bullets drilled bloody holes in the soldier's chest as he plunged the long knife into McDermott's shoulder.

Exposed, McDermott flung himself behind one of the larger trees and resumed target practice, while the UN troops chopped the underbrush and saplings into twigs and debris with submachine guns and hand grenades. Lying prone within his sheltered thicket of trees and underbrush, McDermott calmly fired round after round into the nearby woods, occasionally picking off an unwary soldier. Bullet burns scarred his legs and tore at the back of his shirt. Stinging shrapnel seared his flesh and burnt holes in his clothes. But nothing could deter his methodical and deadly gunfire.

Then someone else entered the fray. To the right of and just behind the blue-helmeted UN troops, towards the southeast, and well-hidden behind a couple of rotting logs; murderous gunfire erupted, trapping the soldiers within a deadly crossfire. Some soldiers froze in place and died. Some soldiers moved and died. Others, who apparently couldn't make up their mind, simply died.

Call it a lucky shot. It clipped the bark at the base of the tree, punctured the right orb, and blew out McDermott's brains. The body rolled over once. A dozen shots into the corpse confirmed McDermott's death. The surviving UN blue helmets could now devote their attention to the new kid on their block — whoever it was.

The new kid on their block proved to be a deadly shot. At least fifty bodies now littered the immediate area, a grim testimony to the newcomer's abilities.

Replacements reluctantly reinforced the attacking blue-helmets, realizing only too well that this battle was not going as planned. Their greeting was a moment of carelessness ... and four dead "replacement" troopers.

Under the shelter of cover-fire and exploding grenades, the attackers dashed and darted forward, diving behind trees and bushes in search of a safe sanctuary. Some made it. Some didn't. Some were wounded. And some were killed.

"Hang on, Mom! — I'm coming!" It sounded like a child. Carrying a 30-caliber machine gun, fifteen-year-old Albert Gorman stepped from the underbrush near McDermott's fortress and ripped into the blue-helmeted soldiers with a 30-caliber ribbon of death. Saplings, shrubbery, and soldiers were clipped and shredded within a few horror-filled seconds.

And as the soldiers died; a beautiful, six-foot-tall, willowy blond rose from behind the rotting logs and calmly fired her M-16 into their midst.

More shots rang out as Stanley Gorman marched in through the trees to the southwest. It was almost too much, as more blue-helmeted UN soldiers fell under the withering crossfire.

Albert threw down the empty 30-caliber, then reached behind a tree for a Law's Rocket. Moments later seven soldiers, several shrubs, and a young oak tree disappeared within an earth-shaking blast.

Sharon shot three more blue-helmets before the fourth put a bullet in her shoulder, knocking her back onto the wet leaves. But while Sharon was busy trying to patch the bullet wound, the blue-helmeted soldiers were busy gunning down her son.

Shooting and screaming, Stan Gorman charged into the battle with no regard for his own safety or vulnerability. His charging, shooting, rush from the dark trees to the southwest killed five more professional UN blue-helmets and sent many diving for cover.

Then Sharon rose from the leaves and fired twice, only to be knocked over by three hand-thrown hand grenades. The thunderous triple explosion was instantly fatal, both to her and to a grenade-thrower standing too close to the destruction.

Three more blue-helmeted UN soldiers fell into the fallen wet leaves covering the muddy ground, the victims of Stan Gorman's insane charge into their midst. But his insane charge abruptly ended when a badly wounded UN blue-helmet suddenly rose from the leaves and tackled the older man. One UN soldier fell on the M-16, while two others fell on Stan Gorman. The wounded man rolled over onto the wet leaves, looked up at the overcast sky, gasped once, and died.

They were all over Stan Gorman then, punching and kicking and stabbing at his battered body. His helmet fell off, and they kicked his head as if it were a football.

But Stan Gorman apparently felt nothing.

"Wait. Wait. Wait. — Drag him over there behind those bushes," the lieutenant ordered. "There is a good stump over there, and I wish to be comfortable when I interrogate this prisoner."

Then, as his men dragged Stan Gorman into the bushes, the lieutenant took a quick look around the local wooded area. "You four, stand guard out here."

With a nod and a smile, the lieutenant turned and headed into the bushes, while the four privates searched for a comfortable place to sit.

"So you will tell me, how many people you have here in the woods?"

"Oh, about thirty or forty thousand, I guess."

The sharp crack of a backhand slap shot from behind the bushes.

"Do not lie to me, Mister Patriotic Militiaman!"

"Hey, you ever see four hand grenades all go off at once?"

"Stop him!" the lieutenant screamed.

The deafening fireball blast ripped up the bushes and toppled two trees. It rained leaves and twigs and splinters. Scraps of burning cloth and pieces of burnt leather fluttered from the treetops. Two shattered helmets and three battered helmets dropped into the clearing.

One of the soldiers had apparently failed to loosen the chin strap on his helmet. The charred remains of his head were still encased within the helmet's metal dome. And he died with his boots on.

Some time later: "Now what?"

The most-senior private shrugged, "We wait for reinforcements."

"And if they do not come? .... If we lost?"

"Then ... we surrender."

Major Aritomo Yamaguchi dismounted from the APC and slapped his swagger stick against his knee-high leather leggings. It did not, he concluded, look good. The convoy had blocked off the south end of the bridge over the Republican River and cluttered County Road 1535 with burnt-out wreckage.

"I suppose that is one way to stop them from escaping," he muttered disapprovingly as he lead his ten-man retinue across the bridge and up the embankment, and into the woods.

It was not exactly a clearing, but it clearly was a battleground. The open space just inside the forested area was littered with equipment and weapons and bodies and parts of bodies. Some of the bodies were his, he noted, and some were theirs. Smoke still rose from smoldering ashes, but nothing else moved within the haze-filled graveyard.

"It must have been a horrible battle," Yamaguchi murmured, leading his eight-man retinue down a footpath and deeper into the forest.

Horrible indeed! There were discarded weapons and brutalized bodies on both sides of the footpath. And on three separate occasions Yamaguchi had to step over dead bodies — two of his men and one of their men — as he lead his six-man retinue even deeper into the woods.

Another clearing. And more bodies. Waves of deep, dark depression swept over his short frame. They were mostly his men, and they obviously died in agony.

The survivors, he reasoned, must have joined up with the Highway 83 convoy. But what a horrible price they'd paid! Most of their communications equipment had obviously been lost in the fighting, and now only their satellite radio-telephone signal remained to guide him and his four-man retinue through the wooded area.

But Yamaguchi never looked back. Hoffman would be unhappy with their dreadful losses, but he would see the necessity of the sacrifice. On the other hand, Yamaguchi had not expected that a bunch of farmers could cause so much carnage.

"These are, after all, just a bunch of hick farmers!" he said aloud, leading his two-man retinue down the forested footpath.

Yamaguchi stepped daintily over the body blocking the path into the next clearing, noting in passing that the corpse was smiling. He had two bullet holes in his chest, yet he was smiling. Yamaguchi shook his head in awe. At least this one didn't look like a farmer.

"His name was Henry Goldfarb. — He was Jewish."

Which meant absolutely nothing to Major Aritomo Yamaguchi.

"And I'm Bob Lowell, Deputy Sheriff, Red Willow County,

Nebraska."

Which also meant absolutely nothing.

"Bow!" Yamaguchi hissed, bowing deeply. "You must bow!"

"I don't bow to nobody!" Lowell said.

"But you *must* bow," Yamaguchi murmured, straightening up. "We are the victors."

"No," Lowell said, shaking his head. "You lost."

"To a bunch of fuckin' American farmers?" the Japanese-American blurted. "*No way!*"

In the momentary silence that followed, Yamaguchi could only stare in anger, while Lowell smiled and shook his head. Then slowly, one by one, the militiamen stepped into the clearing.

Still looking like an old farmer, Ben Franklyn came first. Then John Haley, his arm in a sling, stepped into the open, followed by Kathy and many others, until the militia practically filled the clearing.

Yamaguchi turned to his ten-man retinue, only to find that the ten were all patriot militiamen. His disbelieving eyes flashed wildly in all directions, seeking escape.

"Not what you planned on, huh?" Lowell asked.

"The finest fighting force ever assembled ... and we lost to a bunch of farmers — from Nebraska!"

Yamaguchi pulled a shiny, chrome-plated, automatic pistol. Lowell grabbed his wrist and twisted his arm. A right to the groin was followed by a right to the jaw, and Yamaguchi lost the gun and fell on his backside.

"You lost. — Again," Lowell said, yanking Yamaguchi to his feet.

"*Ah! So desu ka!*" grumbled Yamaguchi, pulling his Marine Commando from its sheath.

"Drop it!" Lowell commanded, stepping back.

"Fuck you, country bumpkin!"

And then Ben Franklyn shot the Japanese-American twice in the chest. .... It was enough.

"Now what?" John Haley asked.

"I think we should let his escorts ... view the body," Lowell said.

Benjamin Franklyn nodded his concurrence.

It took a few minutes to arrange, but marching the ten-man

retinue past Yamaguchi's body did have an effect — of sorts. Obviously they did not particularly care about Yamaguchi, but worried that one of them might be next.

Lowell drove their nervousness towards the edge of panic by ordering them to sit on widely-separated chairs around the body of Major Aritomo Yamaguchi, then carefully (and slowly) studying each member of the retinue. Finally, after several nervous minutes, Lowell selected a soft-skin-bureaucrat-type with bifocal glasses, a thick mustache, and a thicker waistline.

"Lieutenant?"

"Lieutenant Blumenbach," the man said with a German accent that rivaled his girth. "Serial number —"

"Okay," Lowell cut in. "Tell me. — Where is Colonel Hoffman?"

"The Geneva Convention specifically forbids —"

"The Geneva Convention is for prisoners-of-war."

"I am prisoner-of-war. Yes?"

"No," Lowell smiled. "You're an illegal alien."

"Illegal alien? ... What does that mean?"

"That means that if you don't tell me what I want to know, I can beat the shit out of you."

Lieutenant Blumenbach looked ill.

Lowell stepped back, and Ben took his place, moving even closer to Blumenbach. The old farmer smiled warmly, resting a fatherly hand on the German's shoulder.

"You have to understand that *Joe* here —" He waved his hand towards Bob Lowell. "Well, Joe here sometimes gets carried away. ... You understand?"

Blumenbach blanched. "Yes. — Yes. — Yes."

"Now, tell me," Ben purred. "Where is Colonel Hoffman?"

Again Blumenbach blanched, and looked ill.

* * *

James A. Clayton

Chapter Twenty-Six

"Switzerland
45 km"

The two unshaven intelligence operatives — the driver and his assistant — offered a grunt of begrudging acknowledgment as McVey dropped the divider curtain separating the driver's seat from the gray van's isolated rear passenger compartment. The young Marine lieutenant, now unshaven and rather unkempt, flopped into a captain's chair behind the curtain and began re-checking his specially-modified semi-automatic riot shotgun.

"We're about twenty-seven miles from the border."

"Relax," the Britisher murmured in a totally disinterested monotone. "Our ... 'friends and associates' have been planning this exercise for quite some time. I can assure you that they have allowed for every possible contingency."

McVey shook his head. "Whatever happened to the rule of law?"

"They only believe in the golden rule," Harmon snapped, his voice laced with bitterness. "He who controls the gold makes the rules."

"Still, I find it hard to believe," Wilder said. "The idea of a few bankers or a few lawyers controlling the world —"

"Control the banks and you control the world," Harmon growled. "It's just that simple."

"And they control the United Nations?" General Wilder persisted.

"Governments," Harmon explained, "are not run by elected officials. Oh, the elected officials give the orders, all right; but only with the advice of venial bureaucrats. Those orders are issued to other less-than-honourable bureaucrats, who interpret the orders as they see fit."

"You mean —" But Harmon silenced McVey with a wave of his hand.

"The bankers of Burgenstock control those bureaucrats, and those bureaucrats manipulate the governments," the Britisher continued, "and those governments manipulate the United Nations ... and the media ... and a few powerful religious leaders."

Air Commodore Harmon expelled a discontented sigh. "And that's all it takes to run the world."

McVey shook his head again. "And just when I thought I knew it all ...."

———

"When?"

"At approximately one o'clock, this morning."

"Rikers Island?"

Colonel Schuster, Obermeyer's principal aide-de-camp, nodded vigorously as he pushed the button to the Seventeenth Floor. "Yes, sir. We were holding approximately twelve hundred New York City policemen and about seven hundred other law enforcement personnel on Rikers prior to their transfer to Attica or Elmira."

"Any idea who released them?" Obermeyer asked.

"No, sir," Schuster said, "but we suspect —"

"Of course you do!" Obermeyer cut in sharply. "Anything on the bombing of the I.M.F. headquarters in Washington?"

"No, sir, but —"

"Spare me," Obermeyer sighed. "We have suffered at least seven million casualties. And according to field reports, the enemy has suffered over eighty million casualties. — And over half the people on your 'list-of-suspects' are already dead and buried!"

He eased himself into his luxurious, black, high-backed executive chair and rolled it up to his luxurious, black, overly-wide executive desk. Dismissing Schuster with a half-hearted nod of acknowledgement, he opened one of the desk's many drawers and found a small wire-recorder. Recorder in hand, he rose from his desk, only to turn and stare vacuously out the window ... and into the fog bank hanging over the East River.

Then, with a sadness born of despair, Obermeyer's fingers found the tiny switch on the little wire-recorder and flicked it on. He spoke softly but clearly into the built-in microphone, calmly announcing his own demise.

"*My dear Chancellor:*" (he began.) "*I have made a grievous and fatal error for which no amount of apology would suffice. I have always considered these Americans to be decadent and slothful — always choosing the expedient solution, and always avoiding any personal sacrifice.*

"*.... I was wrong.*"

He switched the wire-recorder off, and studied the roiling fog-clouds rise and fall above Roosevelt Island. After a few precious moments of contemplative introspection, he turned the recorder back on and resumed his soliloquy.

"*To date, however, almost a third of their population has willingly sacrificed to kill five million professional soldiers. At this rate, no victory is possible.*

"*Whether they kill me in a week or two over here, or in a month or two overseas, is of little consequence. They will kill me, and I will be remembered in history as the greatest mass murderer in the world, eclipsing even the infamy of Hitler and Stalin.*"

Obermeyer switched off the recorder and lit a cigar. Outside, the fog-clouds were slowly dissipating above the East River.

"*I cannot, in good conscience, blame anyone but myself,*" he continued, turning the recorder back on. "*As Supreme Commander of the United Nations' Expeditionary Forces, the decisions were mine, and I shall live and die with them — and by them. I had hoped to shock these Americans into an immediate surrender. Instead, they have destroyed me, and everything I hoped to accomplish.*

"*At this time I see no alternative but to completely withdraw ... and sue for peace. After one hundred million casualties, enough is enough.*"

He paused. "*Sincerely, General Heinrich Obermeyer, Supreme Commander, United Nations' Expeditionary Forces.*"

He flicked off the recorder, tapped his cigar into the glass ashtray dominating his desk, and pushed a button on his telephone-intercom. "Send up an international courier."

"*High-tech weapons have little value against a bunch of peasants armed with torches. We are going to lose, and lose badly.*"

The Sixth Boardman — 'the young one' — had always been the most optimistic of the group, but this dark and dismal seven-page report was pessimism warmed-over. On the other hand, Boardman Six was their resident "expert" on the United States of America. And if he was worried ....

The Chairman added his initials at the end of the report and handed it back. "Obermeyer?"

"The Americans will not be bullied," the Sixth Boardman said. "Obermeyer came on too strong."

"So, tell Kent to take care of him."

"Kent?" Boardman Six breathlessly rose from the plush cushions of the easy chair. "Jacob — Andrew — Kent? — The Director of Cental Intelligence?"

"He is ... not one of yours?"

"No, sir, he is not."

The Chairman's face turned beet-red. *"Then how in the hell did he know my private Burgenstock telephone number?"*

'The young one' took a step backwards. "I ... I don't know. It should not be ...."

"How?" The Chairman growled.

"'The Blood Church'!"

"What? — Explain!"

"Kent was in charge of European Ops when you expanded our communications center under *'The Sacred Blood of Jesus'* church in Brussels, and we knew that three of the construction workers were actually employed by the American C.I.A."

"So? — They were completely isolated from any important information. They could not —"

"What if there was a fourth man? — Someone who got through our security checks?"

"God!" The Chairman growled, "Kent must know everything!"

"I assumed he was your private, backdoor contact," the Sixth Boardman said.

"Hardly," The Chairman sighed. "Still, I might be able to use him ... and save ourselves in the process."

"How can we do that?"

"Get command-and-control on the telephone," The Chairman said. "I need a secure and direct line to our friend Jack Kent."

Boardman Six picked up the table telephone and punched three digits. Then, "No, I'm trying to call Brussels."

'The young one' listened. The Chairman watched. And the luxuriously-plush lounge was buried in gloom.

"When?" Boardman Six looked grim. "Thank you."

"Well?"

Boardman Six slowly hung up the telephone. "That was our local exchange. .... There was an accident in Brussels. *'The Sacred Blood of Jesus' Roman Catholic Church* has apparently suffered severe structural damage when several substrata either compressed or collapsed, sinking the church and much of the surrounding real estate."

"Command-and-control?"

Boardman Six shrugged helplessly. "Buried. .... Crushed."

The Chairman sighed and wiped the sweat from his brow.

A distant explosion rumbled ominously through the marble mausoleum, shaking the building from foundation to roof. A single photograph of Baron Rothschild was flung from the wall onto the thick carpet.

"What was that?"

"Something to get our attention," The Chairman murmured.

Seconds later three mean-looking men hidden behind camouflage gear emerged from the stairwell kiosk, gliding quietly into the luxurious lounge.

"Who are you?" The Chairman demanded.

The man in the middle spoke. "General Donald Wilder, United States Army, at your service."

After that, Wilder let his automatic rifle speak for him.

General Heinrich Obermeyer closed the door and strolled confidently across the conference room to the plate-glass view of the Manhattan skyline. He calmly lit a panatela cigar while studying the gray essence of the Chrysler Building. The performance was merely a front, but it was all he had left.

"We've lost contact with North Platte, Omaha, Des Moines, and Chicago," Obermeyer sighed, staring through the overcast at Chrysler's gray essence. "What's left?"

"The East Coast," Seminski said, not looking at anything. "With a strong base of operations here, we can re-conquer the lost territories beyond the Mississippi River within a few weeks, at the most."

New World Order

Obermeyer shook his head and waved Seminski towards his seat at the table. Like Fawdi, Andolini, Dupre, and the rest; Seminski had his own ideas about conquest. Obermeyer again shook his head and took his seat at the head of the table.

He glanced at the security camera tucked away in a dark corner of the ceiling, and again considered whether such an intrusion was necessary. But again he did nothing. For Obermeyer, the security camera was just another insignificant irritant.

He cleared his throat. "You have noted, no doubt, that General Martin is missing. — We believe he has been kidnapped by rebel elements, and is currently being held right here in New York City."

General Obermeyer angrily crushed the panatela into an ashtray. "This afternoon I learned that twenty-thousand of our soldiers — *our soldiers* — have deserted. .... *Deserted!* — No NATO or United Nations' peacekeeping mission has ever had a single desertion ... until now."

Obermeyer lit another panatela and rose from his chair. "General Seminski suggests that, with a strong base of operations here in the East, we can somehow re-conquer the western territories. — Idiot!"

Obermeyer angrily spun away from the conference table and glared at his own reflection in the plate-glass window.

"What else can go wrong?" he asked.

A tiny white cloud suddenly flashed into existence, surrounding a metallic dot that seemed to grow larger and larger.

The security camera's image was a brilliant white flash, and then the camera blinked out of existence.

A pinhole flash of light and a tiny cloud of smoke in the middle of the United Nations Secretariat Building's glass wall seemed insignificant, until it was followed in rapid succession by a dozen more, and then a hundred more. The pinpoints of light and little clouds of smoke drew a ragged, jagged line diagonally across the glass-walled front of the building. The cracking and rattling of exploding firecrackers accompanied the flashes of light and the puffs of smoke around the glass-walled building.

And then slowly, very slowly, the upper floors began to sink. Girders twisted and shrieked. Welds fractured and cracked. Glass broke and splintered. Desks and chairs and tables and file cabinets and computers and people fell with the upper stories of the building, or were crushed within its lower floors.

Plaster and glass and steel girders crashed downward in a shrieking, screeching, cacophonous roar that echoed throughout the narrow canyons of Manhatten. The cacophony seemed to last forever as the building crumpled and crunched and crushed its way downward, until it was a twenty-foot-high pile of twisted steel girders, rubble, and debris buried within a cloud of dust.

"What a mess. What a mess." Jacob Andrew Kent lit a Marlboro before turning his back on the cloud of dust.

"Do you realize what you've done?" General Martin demanded. "The hope of the free world —"

"Died in a declaration of bankruptcy," Kent concluded with chilling finality. "Consider yourself lucky. If it weren't for a request from Air Commodore Harmon, you'd be a part of that pile of junk over there."

"What a mess! What a mess!" the old man muttered, eyeing the wreckage of the demolished building.

"Did you find them?" Kent asked.

Edward Eugene Robinson shook his head. "Avery escaped. He is probably out west somewhere."

"Uh-huh. Well, what about General Martin's friend? This Craig Starr?"

"Oh, yes. Too bad about him," Robinson said. "He had an accident this morning. Cut himself shaving. .... With an electric razor."

General Martin tried to look horrified. Jack Kent tried to smile. And Edward Robinson tried to look innocent. They all failed.

"It's been a very busy day," Kent said. "I still have to put General Martin on a flight to Heathrow ... and meet a flight from Wainwright, Alaska."

———

Colonel Hermann Hoffman angrily punched one set of telephone buttons after another, but no one responded to the incessant beeping of the intercom-telephone. Over an hour earlier, his secretary and his aide-de-camp had gone to lunch in the main terminal building, leaving his office empty.

"Zayed? .... Answer the phone, Zayed!" But no one answered

Colonel Hoffman's call.

He tried again. "Fong? .... Answer me, Fong!"

"Sorry, Colonel. I'm afraid your people are all tied up."

Hoffman's office door swung open, and Bob Lowell sauntered in. "Robert Lowell, Red Willow County Sheriff's Office."

Dressed in camouflage battle gear, Lowell did not look like a deputy sheriff. And the old man who introduced himself as "Ben Franklyn, Nebraska farmer," left Hoffman speechless.

"Colonel Hermann Hoffman, you're under arrest ... for crimes against humanity."

Hoffman sniffed haughtily, answering Lowell's charges with a sneer of derision. "Why do you foolish people persist? .... Do you actually believe you can win against the whole world?"

Bob Lowell pointedly pointed over Hoffman's shoulder, and the Colonel turned to find himself staring down the muzzle of the biggest gun he'd ever seen — the 125-mm gun mounted on a Russian T-80 tank. Aimed through the rear window, the cannon virtually dominated his office ... and his life.

"That's Lieutenant Luis Sanchez of the Tenth Light Cavalry, out of Fort Riley, Kansas," Lowell said. "A few months ago he and his men picked up a couple of Russian T-80 tanks down in Goodland. Today he and about ten of his men picked up every soldier that Yamaguchi left behind. — About a hundred of them, I guess."

"And Yamaguchi?"

"Well, we hauled in about fifty or sixty survivors," Lowell drawled, "but he wasn't among 'em."

"And the wounded men, you are taking them to hospital?" Hoffman asked.

Lowell nodded. "You didn't leave us with much, but there's a medical clinic in McCook."

Hoffman nodded as Bob Lowell disarmed him. "An officer's first duty is to his men."

"We're not that fussy," Lowell said, tying Hoffman's wrist in front. "We look out for everybody."

"You have never known freedom, have you, Colonel?" Ben asked, offering the German soldier a cigarette.

Perhaps Hoffman wondered if the old man had all his marbles, but he accepted the cigarette from Ben Franklyn and the light from Bob Lowell.

"Have you ever known freedom, Colonel?" Ben asked again, lighting his own cigarette.

But Hoffman only shrugged. This disturbingly-odd courtesy from a bunch of savage peasants upset him. But he would never let them know ....

"Well, we've had a little taste of it," Ben continued, "but people like you keep trying to take it away. .... You've infiltrated our government, our banks, our schools, our churches, our police departments, our newspapers, our television, and our way of life. — And it almost worked."

The old farmer took the Colonel's arm and guided him from the office.

"But, uh, well, you see, we are not about to accept your slavery," the old farmer continued, "no matter how you disguise it."

"Slavery?" Hoffman sounded incredulous.

"Call it what you will. — Call it a zip code. — Call it a social security number. — Call it welfare. — Call it the RICO statutes. — Call it NATO, the United Nations, GATT, the Federal Reserve. — Call it the New World Order. — It's still slavery."

Hoffman stepped off the 'porch' and onto his cast-off cigarette butt. "You cannot have a society without laws."

"Nor can you have a society strangled by those laws," Ben Franklyn countered. "And in your case, Colonel, you cannot have it either way. .... We're going to take back what you took away — a very real and lasting freedom."

Hoffman shook his head and sneered. "You will find that your freedom is only an illusion."

"Once upon a time it was real — very real," Lowell said. ".... And we can make it very real once again."

"I wish you luck."

"Thank you," Ben said, helping the German into the back of the van.

Lowell slammed the sliding door shut, tapped on the side of the van, and stepped back. The battered van pulled away, turning out onto the driveway towards Highway 30.

Three people — an old farmer, a young girl, and a not-so-young peace officer — stood silently in front of the battered terminal building at *Lee Bird Field,* watching the van turn onto the highway and speed away towards downtown North Platte.

266

New World Order

"So, did we win?" Kathy asked.

Bob Lowell shrugged, and Ben shook his head.

"No, Kathy," Ben finally said. "No one won this one. There will always be people like Hoffman around. .... People who have never known freedom. .... People who cannot understand what it means to be free."

"Odd," Lowell said. "I found this in Hoffman's office."

"A bumper sticker?"

"Take a look." And he handed the thin strip of cardboard to the aging farmer.

"The Constitution of the United States of America —
Void Where Prohibited By Law"

* * *

James A. Clayton

Epilogue

The President of the United States, the First Lady, and the Vice-Presidential nominee returned from Wainwright to a mess — to a land of destruction and desolation. Best estimates placed the death toll at sixty-five million United States' citizens, two million illegal immigrants, and nine million foreign soldiers. Financial losses were estimated to be between three to six trillion dollars. The President insisted that "the European bankers should pay for their folly."

The withdrawal of just over ten million United Nations' "peacekeepers" was not a well-organized effort. It forced most of the soldiers to sneak away by boat or plane in the middle of the night. Disarmed and disoriented, many also slipped into Canada, and were promptly shipped to Belguim. Others fled to Mexico, and were never heard from again. Quite a few simply disappeared. And over nine hundred officers, including Major General Petrovic Karageorge and Colonel Heinrich Hoffman, were held for trial on various "warcrimes" charges.

Meanwhile an angry and frustrated President of the United States spent much of his time rejecting formal apologies, ousting foreign diplomats, and firing the more high-ranking military officers. (Seventeen faced courts-martial; three committed suicide.) In his spare time he reorganized and restructured Executive Department. But he refused to share the guilt of his personal failure.

"Do you think they'll ever forgive me?"

"Can you forgive yourself?"

"No."

"We couldn't crash the entire worldwide system," Jack Kent said, lighting a cigarette. "That would have alerted them."

"So you opted for this, uh, selective numeric transposition thing?"

Kent nodded. "And it worked great until somebody blew up

the communications center under '*The Blood Church*' in Brussels."

"So what are you saying, Jack?"

"I am suggesting, Mr. President, that you tell the American people the truth. The whole truth. .... And then get the hell out of the way."

"Do you think for one minute that they'll understand?"

"Never underestimate the American people," Jack Kent said, grinning broadly. "Tell Congress to take off the handcuffs and let the people run this country. — Then get out of their way."

"I'll give it a try," the President sighed, "but Congress will never agree to it."

And he was almost right. The surviving Congressmen soon scrapped their political and philosophical differences to repeal volumes of archaic or totalitarian laws and edicts, often dismantling whole bureaus or agencies in the process. They repealed the RICO statutes and transferred illegal narcotics to the Health Department. They repealed Section Four of the Fourteenth Amendment, Section One of the Sixteenth Amendment, and the illegal Federal Reserve Act of 1913. Ultimately they even dismantled the BATF enforcement units and placed harsh restrictions on the battered remains of the Federal Bureau of Investigation.

And after the smoke had clear, they devoted most of their time and energy evaluating the strength of the dollar.

But envious eyes watched the surviving politicians slice and dice their way through the surrounding bureaucratic mountains into the chaos of liberty. They would never understand freedom nor politics; but the Chinese generals were well-acquainted with opportunity. They had used it to capture, enslave, and destroy Taiwan. Now, with the West torn asunder, they could embraced it with open arms ... and closed minds.

Li Peng, the Premier of the People's Republic of China, was a tough old "hard-liner" whose iron-fisted rule persistently prevailed in era dominated by "moderates." He was, he felt, the last of the "iron men." His stomach growled and his joints ached, but he refused to surrender to the infirmities of old age.

In an age given over to hedonistic pursuits and "moderation," he provided a restraining balance of fortitude and support against the seductive quicksand of the "soft life." He was the backbone of the People's Republic, sustaining and upholding the two-thousand, nine-hundred and seventy-eight deputies of the National People's Congress that re-elected him every five years. And as the Premier, he was also the head of the State Council. But he was not a dictator. China was simply too large a country for a singular ruler.

"General Wu. General Chan. Gentlemen. — Report."

"As expected," General Wu began, "the Americans won the war. To do so, however, they were forced to sacrifice almost one-fifth of their population, and suffered considerable damage to their infrastructure, their economy, and their self-esteem. Likewise, they have completely destroyed the United Nations, the North Atlantic Treaty Organization, the General Agreement on Tariffs and Trade, as well as numerous other treaties and agreements. They have, in fact, completely isolated themselves from the rest of the world, insofar as that it is possible for them to do so.

"— General Chan."

Like Wu, General Chan wore baggy, unpressed, battle fatigues. And like General Wu, only the red star on his cloth cap denoted his rank. But while General Chan was obviously several years older and three inches taller than General Wu, in every other way they were equals.

"Comrades," Chan began humbly, "the American military is in total disarray. Many of their highest-ranking officers went over to the other side before a single shot was fired. Others have been dismissed because they remained neutral after civilians had engaged the enemy.

"Any existing command structure apparently vanished shortly after the Europeans arrived. Numerous platoon-and-company-size units operated independently throughout the country, usually in conjunction with civilian groups. These groups, however, have suffered extensive losses, and should no longer be able to offer any significant opposition."

General Chan stepped back smartly.

Li Peng had one question: "When?"

"Within the next thirty days," Wu said, stepping forward. "The six hundred ships of our *Cosco* fleet can move fifteen to twenty million soldiers to the West Coast of the United States within thirty to forty-five days. Once established, we can then move approximately five-hundred-million settlers there within about a year."

"Then it can be done?" Li Peng asked.

New World Order

"Yes, we can do it," General Wu said.

Li Peng glanced around the table, measuring the reactions of the State Council members. Their backing was essential for the initiative he had envisioned.

He fixed his eyes on the middle-distance across the room and mentally reviewed the highlights of the plan one more time. He cleared his throat and spoke softly.

"Then do it," he said.

Any imbalance in power or in wealth, whether real or not, will eventually lead to conflict. And that imbalance need not be a matter of actual difference, but only a matter of perception.

Violence, however, lacks conclusive contemplation. Wielding a baton yields no victory. Force will never achieve a balance of power. And no balance of power will ever create either peace or freedom. That requires a strength which comes from within the individual, and from within the society of man.

* * *

ORDER FORM

To order more copies of *NEW WORLD ORDER*, send $19.95 plus $3.50 shipping to:

      Betoi Publishing
      5804 W. Vista #355
      Glendale AZ 85301